RUSSIAN
Short Stories

SENATE

Russian Short Stories

Previously published as part of *The Masterpiece Library of Short Stories, Volume XIII, Russian, Etc. / American,* issued by Allied Newspapers Ltd., in association with The Educational Book Company Ltd, London.

This edition published in 1995 by Senate, an imprint of Studio Editions Ltd, Princess House, 50 Eastcastle Street, London W1N 7AP, England

ISBN 1 85958 116 1
Printed and bound in Guernsey by
The Guernsey Press Co. Ltd

Contents

CONTENTS

EUGENE N. CHIRIKOV
B. 1864

FAUST

WHEN Ivan Mikhailovich awoke one morning, the whole household was already long up, and from the distance came the ringing voices of the children, the rattling of the breakfast dishes, the commanding voice of Maria Petrovna, his mother-in-law, and from the drawing-room the chirping of the canary, which sounded to his ears like a policeman's whistle. He did not feel like getting up ; he felt like lying a bit longer, too lazy to dress ; therefore he smoked a few cigarettes before getting up strength for the ordeal.

He usually rose dissatisfied and out of sorts, because he did not much fancy the rules of life by which one had to hurry with ablutions, toilet, breakfast, and then go to the bank.

" Go and see if papa has wakened yet ! " he heard his wife say, and a moment afterwards a round little head was thrust through the doorway, and a child's treble chimed in :

" Papa ! Are you up ? "

" I am, I am ! " Ivan Mikhailovich replied, ill-pleased, and angrily washed his face, gurgling, sputtering, and groaning.

At the breakfast table he sat sulky and preoccupied, as if wholly taken up with some very important thoughts, and did not deign to pay the least attention to any one. His wife, casually glancing up at him, thought : " He must have lost at cards at the club last night, and does not know now where to get the money to pay up."

At ten, Ivan Mikhailovich went to the bank, from which he returned at four, tired, hungry, and out of sorts. Sitting down to the table, he tucked his napkin under his chin, and ate with a loud smacking of the lips ; after he had filled himself he invariably grew good-natured, and said : " Well, now we shall take a little nap," and went into his study, in which were displayed a bearskin, a pair of reindeer antlers, and a rifle from which he had never fired a shot. There he coughed and growled for a long time, and afterward snored so loudly that the children feared to approach too near the door of the study, and when the nurse wished to stop a fight or a quarrel between them she would say : " There—the bear is asleep in papa's room—I will let the bear out after you ! ''

Ivan Mikhailovich was usually awakened about eight in the evening, when he would once more grow angry and shout : " Yes, yes, I hear," immediately falling asleep again. Afterward he came out of the study puffy and heavy-eyed, looking indeed very much like a bear, and began to shout in a husky voice :

" I would like to know why I was not wakened in time ? ''

" You were, and you replied, ' I hear ! ' ''

" I did ! Well, what of it ? A person is not supposed to be responsible for what he says when half asleep. Is the samovar ready ? ''

Then he went into the dining-room, and sat down to the tea-table with his paper—and again with the appearance of a man whose thoughts are wholly occupied with very serious and important matters. His wife, Xenia Pavlovna, poured out the tea, and he could hardly see her face from behind the samovar. Maria Petrovna sat at the other end of the table, in her hand a child's stocking, which she was for ever darning.

They were generally silent, only rarely exchanging laconic questions and answers : " More tea ? ''—" Please."—" Again there is no lemon ? ''—" Why, it is lying before your very nose ! ''

After tea Ivan Mikhailovich went to his club, where he played cards, after which he had his supper there, and coming home about two in the morning, found his wife already sleeping. Only Maria Petrovna was still up, and she usually met him in *déshabillé*, with an old wrap thrown over her shoulders, her hair in disorder, and with sighs. Ivan Mikhailovich understood but too well the hidden meaning of these sighs : they expressed silent reproaches and indirect disapproval of his conduct. Therefore, while taking off his snow-boots, Ivan Mikhailovich said : " Please spare me your sighs ! ''

Xenia Pavlovna never reproached her husband. She had long ago become accustomed both to Ivan Mikhailovich's snoring and to his being away. Only Maria Petrovna could not become resigned to it.

" What kind of a husband is he ! All you see of him is his dressing-gown on the peg," she said.

" Oh, don't say that, mother. All husbands are like that," remarked Xenia Pavlovna, but her face became sad and clouded, and at last a sort of concentrated musing settled upon it. Walking up and down the drawing-room in the twilight, she would keep thinking about something or other, and sing in a low, sweet voice : " Beyond the distant horizon there is a happy land."

Then she shook her head with a jerk and went into the nursery.

Here she played dolls with the children, romped about with them, and told them fairy-tales about Sister Alenushka and Brother Ivanushka.

The older boy was very like his father, before the latter got into the habit of snoring and spitting and appearing before Xenia Pavlovna in his shirt sleeves. Gazing at this boy of hers, Xenia Pavlovna was carried away into the past, and the dreams of her far-away youth, dimmed and partly obscured by time, drove out of her heart the feelings of emptiness, oppressive ennui, and dissatisfaction.

" Mama ! Mamochka ! Now tell us about Baba Yaga ! Good ?"

" Well, very good. Once there was a Baba Yaga, with a bony leg——"

" Did she snore ? " asked the little girl, and her blue eyes opened wide, resting with fear and expectation on her mother's face. Xenia Pavlovna broke out in a hearty laugh, caught her girlie in her arms, and, kissing her, forgot everything else in the world.

About twice a month they were at home to visitors. All their guests were sedate, respectable, and dull ; people whose whole life ran smoothly, monotonously, without a hitch, through the same deep rut ; they were all very tiresome, and loved to tell the same things over and over, and behave and act as if by long-established rule. First they sat in the drawing-room and spoke of their homes and of the weather ; and while Xenia Pavlovna entertained them with conversation, her mother set the tea things, and while she filled the dishes with preserves she looked apprehensively into the jars and muttered : " It's lasting so well that fresh fruit is not even to be thought of. The Lord grant it lasts till Easter." And putting the sugar from the large paper bag into the cut-glass sugar-bowl, she thought aloud : " Twenty pounds, indeed ! Why, even forty would not suffice ! "

" Please come and have some tea ! " she said invitingly, with an amiable, pleasant smile on her face. In the dining-room, where tea was served, they all took their places in a staid and dignified manner, making fun of those who were unlucky enough to get places at the table corners, telling them that they would not marry for seven years ; and playing with their teaspoons, they said : " Thank you ! " and, " If you will be so kind ! " And then they once more returned to the talk about their apartments, the high price of provisions, and the ailments of the little ones. Tea finished, they repaired to the drawing-room, in which the little card-tables had already been placed, and provided with candles, cards, and chalk ; everybody became livelier, and the oppressive frame of mind, under which people always labour when they are called upon to do something they had not come to do, was dispelled.

The ladies and gentlemen sat down at the tables, quarrelled, disputed, reproached one another, and broke out simultaneously into peals of merriment ; in the main, they all seemed now the most happy people in the world. They were so much engrossed with their play that they were like lunatics, who could hardly understand if an outsider, there by some chance, not playing cards, and therefore suffering with ennui, spoke to them about some outside matter.

Xenia Pavlovna did not play : she and her mother were wholly taken up with the preparations for supper, while the guests were occupied with the whist-tables. She and Maria Petrovna quarrelled a little on such occasions, but always managed to hide their differences from their guests.

When supper was announced all the guests sprang from their seats, pushed back their chairs, and laughingly went to the table. Only two of the most enthusiastic would remain in their places, and continue to wrangle and to gesticulate over the knave of spades, seeming not to care whether they had their supper or not, if only they could prove to each other the truth of their own assertions. The master of the house would put his arm about the waist of each and carry them off.

"Well, let us have a tiny one !" Ivan Mikhailovich generally began. A few " tiny " ones were drunk without any well-wishing, then they drank the health of Xenia Pavlovna and the other ladies present. Their faces reddened, their eyes became languishing, and from across the table was continually heard : " Please pass the caviare this way, Peter Vasilievich ! " or " Please send those delicious herrings our way, Nicolai Gregorievich ! "

Puns, jests and anecdotes were incessantly exchanged, some of them very stale and told for the fiftieth time at that very table. On these occasions Ivan Mikhailovich never failed to recount with evident pride that he and Xenia had married for love. " Ours was a love match. I can almost say that I abducted Xenia Pavlovna."

" Is that so ? "

" Yes, just so ! I remember it as if it happened to-day. I nearly committed suicide ! Yes ! We had an appointment in the garden (a luxurious garden it was ! They very foolishly sold both the house and garden !). Well, so I stand there in the old arbour, stand and wait. And my heart is beating so loudly that it seems to me that a train must be passing somewhere—tock-tock-tock ! " Here Ivan Mikhailovich began to tell in detail how it all happened, and Xenia Pavlovna listened to his narrative from where she sat, slightly blushing, with half-closed eyes, and a little shiver. " At last she arrived in a carriage ! "

"Came on foot, not in a carriage!" Xenia Pavlovna unexpectedly corrected him, because every stroke, every detail of these far-away recollections was inexpressibly dear to her.

"Well, in a carriage or on foot. What material difference does it make!" angrily remarked Ivan Mikhailovich, greatly displeased at being interrupted, and continued his story, totally ignoring the corrections as well as Xenia Pavlovna herself, as if this Xenia Pavlovna and that other one, about whom he was tell his guests, had nothing whatsoever in common.

After supper they once more drank tea, yawned, covering the mouth with the hand, or with the napkin, and breathed hard, looking at their watches, and exchanging glances with their wives. "Yes, it is about time!" replied the wives, and the guests began to take their leave, the women kissed good-bye, the men looked for their snow-boots and hats, and again joked.

After the guests had gone, leaving behind them tobacco smoke, glasses half-full of undrunk tea, and the scraps of the supper, the house suddenly subsided into quiet and peace, and Xenia Pavlovna sank into a chair, and remained motionless in a silent antipathy to her surroundings. She rested from the idle talk, noise, amiable smiles, and entertaining, and felt as if she were just recovering from a serious illness or had had to go through some severe penance. The mother, passing through the drawing-room, quickly threw open the ventilators, and remarked : "Just like a barrack," pulling out of the flower-pots the cigarette-ends which had been stuck into the earth by the smokers, and, waxing angry : "I purposely placed two ash-trays on each card-table, but no! they must go and stick their cigarette-ends into the flower-pots!" Then she began to set the house to rights and clear the tables ; and all this she did with irritation. Ivan Mikhailovich threw off his coat, opened his vest, and, walking through the rooms, yawned, opening his mouth wide and displaying his teeth. Then he went into the bedroom, undressed, and stretched himself comfortably on the soft mattress of the splendid, wide bed.

"Can't you leave off putting the things in order till morning! Lord, how cleanliness has suddenly taken hold of them!" he shouted through the whole house, and listened : "Well, now even the children have revolted!"

From the nursery came the crying of the children and the soothing voice of his wife. Well, now he knew that the racket would go on for a long time—she would not get away from them very soon. And turning to the wall, he pulled the coverlet higher.

Once or twice during the month they went visiting. And there the same story was repeated : conversations about the health of the little ones, the houses, servants, the green tables, cigarette smoke, disputes about the knave of spades, and a supper with vodka, cheap wine, caviare, pickled herrings, and the indispensable cutlets and green peas. And after they left, here, too, no doubt, was an opening of ventilators, and a perfect enjoyment of the ensuing quiet and peace.

And so their life went on from day to day, monotonous and tiresome, like a rainy evening, when everything is wet, grey, and cloudy—an oppressive, colourless life. " We live just as if we were turning over the pages of a cookery book. One day only differs from another in so far as that yesterday we had rice soup and cutlets for dinner, and to-day cabbage soup and cutlets," sometimes thought Xenia Pavlovna, and a kind of despair suddenly took possession of all her being, and it seemed to her that she must decide on something, do something. But what should she do ? And in reply to this a sad smile appeared on her lips—gentle and helpless—and her eyes filled with unbidden tears.

Then she would get a fit of the blues. Everything suddenly began to bore her ; she did not care to see any one, nor talk to any one ; it seemed to her that people spoke not of what they thought, nor of what interested them, but were, on the contrary, doing their best to hide their real thoughts ; that they laughed at things not because they thought them laughable, but simply from politeness and wishing to appear amiable. And that all of them were only pretending to be good and clever, while in reality they were trivial, stupid, and unbearably tiresome.

She sat down at the window, resting her head on her hand, and looked out upon the street, where the tiresome, hateful day was dying away in a grey twilight. She remembered her youth, when life had seemed so great, with immeasurable horizons enveloped in an alluring, dove-coloured mist, so interesting in its endless variations, so enigmatic and incomprehensible ; when it seemed that the most important and wished-for thing was still before her, when her maiden heart stood still with fear and curiosity before the unknown future, when her heart was filled with a vague alarm in the expectation of a great happiness, perhaps the happiness of a triumphant love. And here it is—real life. The horizon ends with the grocer's shop across the street and is enveloped in the poetry of the cookery book. All of then live from day to day, are bored, gossip, speak of their dwellings, servants, occupations, play cards, bear children, and complain—the husbands about their wives and the wives about their husbands. And there is no triumphant love anywhere—but only triumphant triviality, rascality, and ennui. All that was interesting in life was already a thing of the past, it had all happened long before ; then she had been supremely happy, and that happiness—which is given to one only once in life—passed away imperceptibly, and would nevermore return.

It grew darker ; on the streets appeared timidly blinking yellow lights. The bells rang for vespers, and this ringing of the church-bells awakened in her soul something vague and a little frightening : a sad longing for something which had gone for ever ; or was it that it reproached the soul soiled by life ? " Evening bells, evening bells ! " Xenia whispered with a deep sigh.

Suddenly in the dim drawing-room appeared a whitish figure : it was Ivan Mikhailovich, who came out of his study without a vest. He stretched, yawned, let out an " O-go-go-go ! " and remarked : " I dined well and enjoyed a splendid snooze. What are you dreaming about ? "

" Oh, just this. I was thinking what a tiresome affair it is to live in this world ! "

" How is that ! After you have had three children you all at once begin to find life tiresome ? "

" Oh, how commonplace and trivial this is ! "

" Well, you are again in the dumps ! " Ivan Mikhailovich spoke angrily and turned away. Xenia Pavlovna broke into a laugh, then this laugh became intermixed with crying, and ended in hysterics.

" Oh ! The devil is loose ! " muttered Ivan Mikhailovich, and rang for the maid, whom he ordered to fetch some water. " Cold, from the tap."

His mother-in-law, rushing into the room, cried : " What is the matter ? What have you done to her ? " The whites of her eyes glittered in the dark, and her whole demeanour expressed a thirst for revenge and complete redress. " What have you done to her ? "

" I have done absolutely nothing to her ! And I do not know, absolutely do not know, why she started all this humbug ! She is simply an unbalanced woman, your daughter is, absolutely unbalanced ! "

" You have offended her ? "

" Neither by word nor intention ! I came into the drawing-room and found her moaning at the window ; all at once, without provocation, she began to laugh, then to cry," said Ivan Mikhailovich, shrugging his shoulders and gesticulating ; but Maria Petrovna, whom Ivan Mikhailovich, in moments of exasperation, sometimes called " the old witch," did not believe him, and insistently demanded an explanation : " Don't you tell me that. Where did you get it that she is unbalanced ? We never had any one of an unbalanced mind in our family—every one was healthy and sane. What have you been doing to her ? "

" All right, then ! All right, if they were all sane and normal !

I am glad to hear it ! " said Ivan Mikhailovich angrily, and speedily left the house. He went to the club, where he played cards, playing high from pure spite, and losing also from pure spitefulness. In the meantime Maria Petrovna paced the room with a pained expression on her face, unable to understand what had passed between the two. Several times she approached Xenia Pavlovna, and began :

" Why is all this quarrelling going on in the house lately ? What is the reason for it ? Have you found out anything wrong about him, or what ? "

" I have found out nothing ! "

" Has he offended you in any way ? "

" No, no. What makes you think so ? "

" You do wrong to hide it from me. It will leak out somehow, do not fear. I shall find out everything, my lady ! " Then she suddenly changed her tone and approached the matter from a different side :

" He is jealous. You should not provoke him.'

" Oh, please don't ! He is simply stupid, that is all ! " Xenia Pavlovna interrupted her, laughing through her tears, and Maria Petrovna grew angry.

" If a wife speaks like that about her husband, no good will ever come of it ! " And she began to defend her son-in-law with all her might, and in the end it appeared, according to her own words, that a better man than Ivan Mikhailovich could not be found the world over. " Just look at others, little mother ! Take, for instance, the husband of Kapitolina Ivanovna ! And it is nothing to her, my lady. She does not complain ; she suffers in silence, and would not even think of dubbing her husband ' stupid,' as you are doing. Of course, what we have we are careless of ; and once we lose it, we cry ! "

Nevertheless, she could get no explanation of what had occurred, and could only take refuge in guesswork and surmise.

She did not go to sleep until the return of her son-in-law, and sitting in the drawing-room on the sofa, she continually pondered over what now most interested her, letting escape from time to time an exclamation.

And Ivan Mikhailovich, after he had supped and taken an extra glass or two, came home and announced himself by a ring so angry and imperious that it sounded noisily through the quiet rooms, and frightened Maria Petrovna. " He must be drunk," she thought, and opening the door, she did not even sigh as usual, but spoke lovingly, " There is some supper left for you in the dining-room."

Ivan Mikhailovich did not reply. He passed through the rooms with protesting step, banged the doors, coughed loudly, and, in general, gave one to understand that he was his own master. And still more to emphasise his independence, he did not go to sleep in the superb double bed with its silver ornaments, but lay down on the sofa in his study under the reindeer antlers and the rifle from which he had never fired a shot.

" Here, at least take a pillow ! " came Maria Petrovna's meek voice from the other side of the door, and the white corner of a pillow was thrust through the slightly open door of the study. Her son-in-law did not reply. " It is uncomfortable to lie that way, your neck will hurt you."

" Don't you trouble yourself about my neck ! " came from the bear's den.

But Maria Petrovna threw the pillow on an easy chair, and the door closed. Ivan Mikhailovich was a man who prided himself on the strength of his character, and therefore did not take the pillow, but supported his head with his fist, and puffed while he thought of the oppressive disagreeableness of married life.

The dog Norma evidently took the part of the husband, for whenever the couple quarrelled and occupied different bedrooms, the dog would not stay with the wife.

Opening the door of the study with her paw, she approached the sofa, placed her black muzzle on Ivan Mikhailovich's breast, and gazed at him with eyes that wished to say : " What hags they are, all of them ! They even do not know how to appreciate a man like you ! " Ivan Mikhailovich felt a silent gratitude toward Norma, and patted her with his hand, pulling lovingly at her long ears. But the door of the study again opened slightly, and from the other side came the whisper of Maria Petrovna : " Norma ! Norma ! " But Norma did not go. Ivan Mikhailovich held her by the collar and patted her with redoubled energy. " She will let in fleas," again came the low voice. " Norma ! Norma ! "

Ivan Mikhailovich sprang from the sofa, closing the door tightly, and the melodious sound of the lock ended the diplomatic overtures of his mother-in-law.

" Sleeps with the dog. A fine thing that ! " said the grumbling voice behind the door, and all became quiet.

These were scenes with dramatic elements and effects in them. But there were other scenes of the ordinary sort, without the dramatic effects, scenes which were repeated regularly in the same form and in the very same expressions.

These scenes always took place on the twentieth of the month, when Ivan Mikhailovich received his salary, and the large number of small creditors had to be paid. Somehow there was never sufficient money to settle all the bills, and each time Ivan Mikhailovich thought that the money ought to be enough to cover all

expenses, and railed at the womenfolk who dreamed so much about
the emancipation of women, while they did not even know how to
regulate their own household. "Emancipation!" he grumbled,
taking the money from his pocket-book and throwing it on the
table.

"But what has emancipation to do with this?"

"They go and teach you the devil-knows-what—all kinds of
geography, algebra, trigonometry, but you do not know how to
make both ends meet—emancipation!"

"And you should go a little less to the club, Ivan Mikhailovich,
then probably the income would cover the expenditure!" replied
Maria Petrovna bitingly.

"And where, pray, can I get it for you? I am not coining
money. I suppose you know I am not a counterfeiter?"

And all three started to upbraid and reproach each other, and
for a moment they became submerged in such trivialities and
unpleasantness that they were afterward thoroughly ashamed of
themselves. After every twentieth of the month there remained
in the soul of Xenia Pavlovna a kind of soot; and this greasy soot
dimmed her eyes, made her apathetic and slow, and it seemed as
if she had all at once become old, ill-looking, and disheartened.
This young and very charming woman looked at such times like
a beautiful bouquet of flowers that had withered and been thrown
out of the window. So they lived day after day, months and
years, and when an acquaintance asked, "How are you getting
along?" they invariably replied: "Very well, thank you!"

It sometimes became necessary to refresh themselves after this
kind of life—to depart, at least for a day, from the beaten track—
and so Ivan Mikhailovich went on a short spree two or three times
a year. "One must overhaul himself thoroughly from time to
time; it is not only useful, but necessary," he usually said on the
next day after such an exploit.

The only thing that ever brightened Xenia Pavlovna's life a
little was going to the theatre. This happened so seldom, however,
that she looked upon such rarely occurring occasions in the light
of important events. Ivan Mikhailovich did not like to go to the
theatre, and when Xenia Pavlovna said, "We ought to go to the
theatre and refresh ourselves a little," Ivan Mikhailovich was sure
to remember how, ten years before, when they visited St. Petersburg on their honeymoon, they had been to the opera and the
drama, and would reply: "After seeing Figner and Mme. Savina,
it is not worth while, my dear, to go to see such small fry, and it
only spoils an impression for us!"

But whenever *Faust* was presented on the stage of the local
theatre, no pleadings were necessary: Ivan Mikhailovich never

failed to take seats in the third row of the orchestra for himself
and Xenia Pavlovna.

"To-day we go to see *Faust*," he said in an angry tone on
returning from the bank, carelessly throwing two coloured tickets
upon the table.

"*Faust!*" joyfully exclaimed Xenia Pavlovna, and her face
became radiant with joy.

Gay and exalted with the pleasure that awaited her, Xenia
Pavlovna usually began to get ready very early. And while she
was dressing and combing her hair, Ivan Mikhailovich stood close
by to see that it was all done properly, because when he appeared
with his wife in society he liked everything to be " just so," and
was pleased to have every one think, as they saw her pass on his
arm, "A charming woman that ! Really charming ! " Therefore
he was a very stern critic, and while she dressed he continually
vexed her by his remarks : " Your coiffure is too small ! You have
the face of a Marguerite, and you dress your hair to make you
look like a Jewess ! "

" It is not true ! "

" A curious thing, really : women understand less than any one
else what is becoming to them and they care least of all to win the
admiration of their husbands ! "

Xenia Pavlovna also wished to look well ; but she did not trust
overmuch to the good taste of Ivan Mikhailovich, and at the same
time distrusted herself too ; and the upshot of it all was that they
invariably quarrelled, and left the house sulking and displeased
with each other. Deeply aggravated and disheartened, they went
to the theatre without any pleasurable anticipation, as if some
one were driving them thither. First they walked arm in arm,
feeling angry with each other, and longing to pull their arms away
and walk apart ; then Ivan Mikhailovich called a cabman in an
angry voice that seemed to hate all the cabbies in the world.
Having helped his wife into the vehicle, he sat down by her side
and placed his arm around her waist. The whole way they never
exchanged a word, but Ivan Mikhailovich gave vent to his irritation
in a shower of abuse directed at the poor cabby : " Careful there !
Don't you see the hollows, you stupid ! "—" To the right,
you dolt ! "

The orchestra played the overture from *Faust*. Ivan Mikhailovich
and his wife walked arm in arm through the long, carpeted aisle
between two long rows of orchestra stalls toward their seats. Ivan
Mikhailovich felt as if all eyes were directed toward him, and he
tried to walk with greater dignity, with his head proudly thrown
back and his rounded paunch thrown forward. Xenia Pavlovna
walked with downcast eyes and a face which looked rigidly cold

and offended, as if she had been sentenced to die and were walking toward the gallows. The electric lights went out ; the curtain rose upon a sea looking very much like a sky and a sky very much like a sea, with some sort of fantastic ruins and tropical vegetation. The traditional Faust, in his brown dressing-gown, night-cap, and long, grey beard, sang in his metallic tenor voice, smoothing his beard with his hand :

"Accursed be human science, human prayer, human faith ! "

At first Xenia Pavlovna was not much affected by either the music or the singing. She looked more than she listened. When the red Mephistopheles appeared and sang that everything was well with him, and that he had plenty of money, Xenia Pavlovna remembered that it would soon be the twentieth and that they owed the butcher for two months. "Emancipation ! " she seemed to hear Ivan Mikhailovich exclaiming, and when she stopped thinking of the butcher and emancipation, Faust had already thrown off his dressing-gown and beard, and had changed from a decrepit old man into a handsome, strong youth, and this unexpectedness called forth the first smile upon her lips.

"To me returned lovely youth ! " victoriously sang Faust, approaching the footlights and raising his hand, and Xenia Pavlovna began to think how old she was and how old Ivan Mikhailovich was ; that their youth had already passed, and would nevermore return. Xenia Pavlovna sighed and stealthily glanced at Ivan Mikhailovich's face. He sat deep in his chair, with head bent to one side and his hands locked over his paunch, and in his well-groomed face, with its waxed and twisted moustaches, there was so much self-sufficiency and native sleekness that Xenia Pavlovna hurriedly turned away.

During the first *entr'acte* they went into the lobby of the theatre, she leaning on his arm, and he feeling uneasy the whole time at the thought that his wife's hair was badly dressed, and that her face was not alight with the joy and rapture of the other women, who, with their sparkling eyes and rustling skirts, laughed and talked incessantly in their ringing, happy voices.

After walking a little up and down the spacious lobby, engrossed in their own thoughts, the pair returned to their seats. Under the cascades of electric light, the stalls dazzled the eyes with the beautiful dresses of the ladies, and buzzed like a beehive from the multitude of noises, motions, and rustling ; but this talk, glitter, and dazzle seemed to Xenia Pavlovna distant and strange, and the walls of people, the boxes resembling rich bouquets of flowers, awakened in her a feeling of loneliness and remoteness. She sat with her hands lying listlessly on her lap and with downcast eyes ; she did not wish to be disturbed in her present brooding mood, and feared that some acquaintance might approach them and ask how they were, or that Ivan Mikhailovich might suddenly begin to compare the singers with those they had once heard.

When the lights went out and the curtain rose again she felt a great relief, and it suddenly seemed to her that she was once more in her maiden bower and had locked the door on the outside world. Gazing at the scene before her, she was gradually carried away into the realm of sound and melody, and wholly surrendered herself to the vague, disturbing emotions that had arisen in her soul under the influence of music and song. The rancour and vexation she had felt toward her husband gradually subsided ; the memory of the harsh wrangles, petty disputes, all the tiresome prosiness of her daily life, vanished, and an exquisite calm and tranquillity took possession of her soul, brightening and clearing up everything within her. In the third act the soul of Xenia Pavlovna flew away from her native town, and she forgot herself and everybody else, and wholly surrendered herself to the power of music and song, to the moonlit night, the silvery shimmer of the stars, and the contemplation of a happy love, which waxed stronger and stronger, seemingly measureless and all-powerful, but at the same time full of a sadness and pensiveness as quiet and gentle as this moonlit night itself, and as this exquisite young girl before her, with her thick, long braid of golden hair, who, with the sincerity and straightforwardness of a child, was kneeling before her handsome, youthful lover, pleading with him for mercy. Here she stands flooded by the radiant moonlight, trembling with fear and happiness, her head resting on the shoulder of the handsome youth. Here she sings at the wide-open window, telling the stars, the quiet night, and the slumbering old garden, that seems to have been enchanted by dreams of love, of her happiness ; and her song, pure and sacred like a prayer, soars upward to the starry, blue heavens.

How very dear and near this is to people who have lived through the phantom of happiness. She, Xenia Pavlovna, had once been just such a sweet girl, with a thick, golden braid hanging down her back ; she had been just as happy and free of care, and sang just as sweetly to the stars and the silent garden flooded with the mysterious, sad moonlight, and she also, just as this maiden, had trembled with fear and pleaded with the man she loved for mercy.

" Ha ! ha ! ha ! ha ! " rolled the thundering laugh of Mephistopheles—such pitiless, powerful, and provoking laughter ; and the chord, which echoed in Xenia Pavlovna's heart with inexpressible tenderness and sadness, broke and grew silent, leaving room only for this laughter, oppressive and revolting in its triumphant triviality and truth. And reality suddenly broke into the realm of dreams and fancies. Xenia Pavlovna lowered her eyes, compressed her lips, and a smile passed over her face, the strange smile of a person who has been caught unawares.

"He laughs first-rate!" remarked Ivan Mikhailovich in an earnest voice, slightly moving in his chair.

Xenia Pavlovna looked at her husband and sighed sorrowfully. She had already resigned herself to Ivan Mikhailovich, to his pompous solemnity, and his hands crossed over his paunch. Those hands no longer awakened her ire. Once this very same man who now sat by her side was *her* Faust, and with him was closely bound up her love-drama. Even if it had been a mirage, a mistake, it was the mistake of her whole life, a mistake which would never be repeated—like youth itself.

The curtain came down. The noise of applause, like a rainstorm, and the wild roar of the over-enthusiastic gallery filled the theatre from top to bottom. The curtain rose once more on the sea and the ruins, and Faust, Marguerite, and Mephistopheles appeared holding each other's hands, bowing and smiling to the public ; and Xenia Pavlovna felt as if she had been suddenly awakened from a sleep full of tender, delicious dreams, vague and enchanting, but already forgotten, and felt vexed because she was awakened, and was now possessed by a tormenting longing to recall and bring back the frightened-off dreams.

She did not want to look at Marguerite, who had suddenly turned into an actress, thirsting for hand-clapping and making eyes at that huge monster the public ; at Mephistopheles, who stood with his right hand pressed to his breast as a token of gratitude and sincere pleasure ; nor at Faust, who suddenly looked very much like a hair-dresser, and who was sending in all directions sweet, airy kisses.

"Come, Vania!"

Ivan Mikhailovich rose and offered her his arm, and they once more repaired to the lobby. Here he treated her to tea and fruits. "It is splendid for allaying thirst!" he said, handing her an orange. And from this moment all animosity was forgotten, and peace reigned once more between them.

"Not sour, I hope?"

"No, it is very good."

Xenia Pavlovna ate her orange, and gazed at the men who passed them. "They are all different here from what they are at home," she thought ; "they are all rude, all go to their clubs, and my Vania is in reality much better than many of these men."

"How did you like Marguerite, Vania?"

"Pretty well—though, after Alma Fostrom, she is, of course——"

"Have you heard Alma in that rôle?"

"Well, I like that, really! Did we not hear her together at St. Petersburg? Have you forgotten already?"

" Ah, that was so long ago."

" Though this opera is immortal by itself, I have seen it over a hundred times, and will be glad to see it as many times more. Here one sees life as in a mirror—— Yes—— Do you remember—in the garden ? " he concluded in a low voice, leaning toward his wife.

Xenia Pavlovna's face was covered with a slight blush, and her eyes had a thoughtful, far-away look in them, which gradually grew sad and dreamy.

" All this was, but it has passed as if in a dream," her lips whispered, and her head swayed on her beautiful bare neck.

Here some acquaintances passed, and pressing their hands warmly, enquired :

" How are you ? "

" Very well, thank you. And you ? "

" Pretty well, as usual. But you, Xenia Pavlovna, still continue to grow more beautiful ! "

Xenia Pavlovna blushed, and a hardly perceptible shade of pleasure flitted over her face, and made it sweet and strong and proud.

" What are you saying ! " she replied, slightly screwing up her eyes and coquettishly fanning herself. " On the contrary, I think I am growing worse-looking with each passing day ! "

Then all the men began to protest in chorus, and the women silently fixed their coiffures with their fingers, while Ivan Mikhailo-vich looked at his wife and thought that she was really a very lovely woman, probably one of the loveliest in the whole theatre, and he also began to feel very pleased, and twirling his moustaches, he spoke proudly :

" You ought to see her portrait when she was my fiancée ! It hangs over my desk. She had a braid twice as thick as this Marguerite's——"

In the last scene a whole revolution took place in the soul of Ivan Mikhailovich. He began to imagine Xenia Pavlovna overtaken by the sad fate of Marguerite, and himself in the rôle of Faust, and grew very sorry for Xenia Pavlovna. The gloomy arches of the prison, on the grey stone floor some straw, and on it this woman, outraged, criminal, insane, and nevertheless so pure and saintly ; the low melodies so full of sadness and tenderness in which arose hazy memories of past happiness, made Ivan Mikhailovich's breath come faster. He looked at Xenia Pavlovna, and noticing tears in her eyes, felt that this woman was very dear to him and that he was somehow very guilty toward her.

Ivan Mikhailovich sadly gazed upon the stage, listened to the low strains of music, and it seemed to him at times that it was his Xenia thrown into prison, and he recalled how they first met at a ball and how he at the conclusion of it sang : " Amid the noisy ball," and how afterward they sat in the dark garden, listening to the singing of the nightingale and gazing at the silvery stars.

All this was, but it had passed as if in a dream.

They returned from the theatre with souls refreshed, overfilled with sadness mingled with joy, and it seemed to both as if all their former disputes and frictions over trivialities had vanished for ever-more, and a part of their former happiness had returned to them. They rode home dashingly in a light, new sleigh over the well-beaten road, and Ivan Mikhailovich had his arm round Xenia Pavlovna's waist as tightly as if he feared to lose her on the way. Xenia Pavlovna hid her face in the soft white fur of her collar, and only her sparkling eyes were visible from under a very becoming little hat of the same white fur, like two coals, dark and moist.

Ivan Mikhailovich wanted to kiss her, forgetting that they were in the open road, but Xenia Pavlovna screwed up her eyes, in which lurked silent laughter and slightly shook her white fur hat.

At home the samovar and Maria Petrovna awaited them.

The samovar gurgled joyfully, rising importantly in all its beauty and sparkle from the snow-white of the tablecloth ; the nice white loaves of bread smelled good and very tempting ; and fresh, soft-boiled eggs seemed just waiting to be cracked over the nose with a spoon.   And Maria Petrovna, sailing out of the nursery with her old wrap over her shoulders, spoke kindly : " Well, children, you must be quite hungry ? "

Ivan Mikhailovich did not reply.   He entered the dimly lighted drawing-room and paced it with a slow tread, smoothed his hair with the palm of his hand and purred : " Angel, Angel Marguerite ! "

Then he returned to the dining-room, approached Xenia Pavlovna, silently kissed her on the head, and again went into the drawing-room where he continued purring.

" You had better eat and leave ' Angel Marguerite ' for after," said Maria Petrovna, thrusting her head into the doorway of the drawing-room.

" In a moment ! In a moment ! " Ivan Mikhailovich replied with vexation, and continued walking, wholly surrendering himself to vague emotions and recollections and the feeling of tender sadness for the past.

Afterward they all three had tea and spoke very amiably, and a good and peaceful feeling filled their hearts.   Xenia Pavlovna changed her evening dress for a white gown with sleeves like wings, and let down her hair.   She visited the nursery several times, and, sinking on her knees before the three little beds, she gazed with a mother's passion and tenderness at the sleeping babies with their full, chubby little arms and sweet, calm faces, and it seemed to her that here were sleeping the little angels, pure, gentle, helpless, and great in their purity, that had carried Marguerite into heaven.

" You look like Marguerite in prison," remarked her husband, leaning on his arm and gazing at his wife long and attentively ; and it seemed to him as if a whole chapter of his life had disappeared, and before him was a sweet, young maiden with golden hair, whom one longed to love, to adore for ever.

And under this glance Xenia Pavlovna lowered her eyes, smiled, and felt that somewhere far down at the very bottom of her soul the broken, unfinished song of her youthful heart sounded like a mountain echo.

Ivan Mikhailovich, who, generally supping at home in his shirt sleeves, now felt constrained to take off his coat, endeavoured to lend to his gestures and motions as much elegance and grace as possible, and was amiable and courteous at table, even to his mother-in-law.

" Shall I hand you the butter ? " he asked, anticipating her wish.

" You are acting just as if you had come on a visit," Maria Petrovna remarked, and, taking the butter with a pleasant smile, said : " Thank you ! "

" Well, good night, my Marguerite ! " said Ivan Mikhailovich, approaching his wife and once more gazing attentively into her eyes ; then he kissed her hand and cheek.

" Good night, my Faust ! " jokingly replied Xenia Pavlovna, kissing her husband on the lips.

Then Ivan Mikhailovich pressed Maria Petrovna's hand and went into the bedroom.

The blue hanging-lamp flooded the chamber with a soft, tender, soothing, bluish light, and it was so peaceful and cosy. Ivan Mikhailovich undressed, and, taking off his boots, still continued to sing from *Faust* in a tender falsetto :

> 'Tis life alone to be near thee,
> Thine only, all thine own !

EUGENE N. CHIRIKOV

STRAINED RELATIONS

MISHA maintained a stubborn silence. He had had no desire whatever to speak. When he was called to dinner he refused categorically :

" I don't want any. . . ."

When he was called to tea, he replied calmly, with firm conviction in his voice :

" Have your tea or coffee, or whatever it is, but let me alone ; I don't want anything."

Misha's elder sister burst out into an unnaturally loud peal of laughter on receiving this reply and said :

" Do you think any one cares ? You can give up eating and drinking altogether if you like ; we shan't cry about it."

With this she fluttered out gaily and disappeared behind the door. Misha, however, discerned in her exaggeratedly careless reply, as well as in her gay exit, a certain sympathy with his cause. Of course, she was pretending, making believe that papa and mamma " didn't care " that he had no dinner or tea. . . . Of course they were all concerned about him, and did not know what to do to make him take his dinner and tea. . . . Let them worry. . . . It was their own fault. . . . Getting only one mark in Latin was not so terrible as to merit being disgraced before everybody and told that he was only fit to be a shoemaker . . . as for being a shoemaker, well, he did not care . . . but all the same he was not going to eat his dinner.

Misha was sitting in the drawing-room, reading a magazine and listening to what was going on in the next room. They were no doubt talking about him there, saying that he would not eat or drink, and that after all he was " a clever boy."

" Where is Michael ? . . . Still sulking ? " he hears his mother say.

" He is angry," Nina put in slowly and deliberately.

" We must leave him something, anyhow," he hears in his father's deep voice.

" Leave me something, eh ! . . . As if I want it ! " says Misha.
" Why leave things for a shoemaker ? "

" Michael ! " his father calls.

Misha is silent. His father calls again.

" What do you want ? " Misha replies with austere dignity,
bending lower over his magazine.

" Come here ! Stop sulking. . . ."

" I am not sulking ; I am reading. . . . It isn't proper for a
shoemaker to sit at table."

" Blockhead ! "

" All right then, I'm a blockhead," Misha burst out aloud, and
added softly, " You'll hear from the blockhead."

" He's angry," his sister said loudly.

" Shut up, you little fool ! " Misha whispered, and an intense
hatred towards his sister possessed him. He longed for revenge. . . .
If only his father were not there. . . . Why did she interfere ? No
one asked her opinion ! He coughed angrily, threw the magazine
on the table, and, searching in his pockets, pulled out a pencil.
Under one of the pictures representing a young man under a bench
with a young girl standing by—the text explaining that he is carving
her name underneath, it being already carved all over the top of
the bench—he wrote, " This is Nina and Volodka Petushkov ; two
big fools." He left the magazine open at this page so that every
one could see it, and went to his room. Catching sight of Nina's
hat on the table he threw it on the floor.

" I won't have this rubbish on my table ! " he shouted, though
there was no one to hear him. Misha felt at enmity with everybody.
It seemed to him that the house was divided into two hostile camps,
in one of which was himself, Misha, while the other contained the
rest of the household. Thus when the housemaid came into the
room and addressed him, he turned to her in a hostile manner.

" Michael Pavlitch ! "

" Get out ! "

" There's a visitor for you ! "

" Get out, I tell you ! "

" You've had no dinner, that's why you're angry. . . ."

Misha knew quite well that the maid had been sent in to him.
He felt sorry and wanted to make amends. . . . Yet he was not a
baby . . . Let them worry ! But he really was hungry. Should
he go down to the kitchen ? No, it was not worth it ; the cook was
sure to tell the housemaid, who would tell his parents, and they
would feel consoled.

It was better to bear his hunger. If his father or mother came
and said : " Don't be angry, Misha . . . you know that if you don't
eat and drink you'll fall ill, and that would upset us . . . I'm sorry

this has happened, it won't occur again,"—then Misha would have agreed, and would have gone instantly into the dining-room. Of course they had left something for him. There was beetroot soup that day. . . Misha swallowed the saliva that had risen, and going to the door listened for the sound of his mother's step. Father, of course, would not come, but mother might come and say she was sorry. . . .

But mother did not come, and he was hungry. Instead of the expected delegate, Falstaff, the beautiful setter, appeared at the door. With slow measured pace he walked into the room, sniffed at Misha, and wagged his tail. Falstaff was papa's favourite, and his place was under the writing-table in papa's study. Why did he come here ? Let him go to his master and wag his tail. He had eaten so much that he looked on the point of bursting.

" Get out ! " Misha said suddenly, in an angry whisper, giving the dog a kick. It whined, then shook its tail as though offended, and trotted out. And Misha was hungry. . . .

For a long time he sucked the fingers of his left hand, seriously considering his position. At last he got a brilliant idea that would deliver him from all compromise with the enemy. Ivanov, a boy in his own form, had once sold his brother's Algebra book and had bought himself a penknife with the proceeds. . . .

And Misha could sell his last year's books and get some pies and pastries at the pastry-cook's. . . . He could even go to the milk shop . . . and here they would be worrying. . . . Well, let them worry ! It was their own fault. . . . They would treat him better another time. . . .

Hunting in his bookcase, Misha pulled out a thin book. . . . " I may want it, but not very soon. . . . By that time they will have forgotten that I had it and will buy me a new one," Misha thought —and finally decided to sell it.

He did not want to go out through the dining-room . . . they were all in there, and would think that he was seeking for an excuse to make it up. . . . Not he ! . . . He could get on very well without doors. . . .

He climbed out of the window, hid the book in his bosom, and set out for the market. It was getting towards evening—the shops would be shut soon . . . it was necessary to hurry. . . . Misha flew like the wind. . . . He tried to make a short cut across some half-built houses. . . . The result was a most conspicuous hole in his boot. At another time he would have been quite upset by this accident, as the boots were new ones and had been given him with the warning that he was to take care of them. . . . Now he did not care ! Let them buy new ones ! Of course they would say he could go barefoot like a shoemaker. . . . But he knew very well they would buy them. . . . It would be too disgraceful for the son of a lawyer to be seen in torn boots. . . . There was no need to worry . . . they would buy them. . . . At last, there was the market-place. It was gay and lively. . . . What a racket . . . screaming, quarrelling . . . a perfect pandemonium.

" Hot p-p-pies ! " yelled a broad-faced, greasy-nosed peasant in a nasal voice. He looked at Misha and asked :

" Do you want any pies ? "

" What are they made of ? " Misha asked.

" Buy mine, sonny ; his are cold and mine are hot ! " squeaked a peasant woman, as she stood up holding the earthen-pots containing the hot pies. . . .

" I will buy some presently. I have no time now," said Misha, as he pushed his way through the dirty, motley crowd, to the quarter where were the second-hand book shops. In great trepidation he approached a dealer. The latter was standing by his counter in an expectant attitude ; an old man with a grave air, he looked more like a professor than a shopkeeper. Catching sight of the schoolboy, he hid himself behind the counter and, opening a book, pretended to read.

" Do you buy books ? "

" What have you to sell ? "

" Asia, Africa, and America ! quite new," Misha gasped out.

" Smirnov's ? "

" Yes."

" Had it been Europe, now, I might have bought it, but I've a lot of these," the shopman said, reluctantly taking the book from Misha.

" It is an old edition. . . . I'll give you ten kopeks for it," he added, turning over a few pages of the book.

" I was told to sell it for not less than twenty," Misha said diffidently.

The shopkeeper yawned and handed the book back to Misha.

" Fifteen then . . . it's quite new ! "

The shopkeeper made no reply.

" Very well, then, I'll take ten kopeks. "

" And a good bargain you're making," the shopkeeper said, yawning as he put the ten kopeks on the counter and threw the book carelessly on to a shelf. Then he turned back to the book he was reading.

" I may perhaps bring Europe too," said Misha, as he put the money into his pocket.

" Do . . . only is it like this one ? Any other is not worth ten kopeks. Send all your friends to me. I give better value than any one. . . ."

" I will send them."

Misha walked out of the shop and began to examine the eatables on the stalls. Before he got to the pies he was tempted by some halva and poppy seeds. He bought some for three kopeks and ate it with great relish. Then he got to the pie-woman.

" What kind are they ? "

" Mushroom, meat, and carrot."

" How much ? "

" Two for five kopeks."

" I don't like carrots. Give me one mushroom and one meat pie."

After eating the two pies he felt thirsty. With the last two kopeks he bought two tankards of some kind of pink kvas. He could hardly finish the second glass. . . . It was nasty and too sweet—still it was a pity to leave it.

" Oof ! " Misha exclaimed, finishing the second tankard with difficulty.

" What's the matter, has it gone to your head ? " the stall-keeper asked boastingly, and then went on with his loud singing cry of :

" Sweet, refreshing kvas ! "

When he got home, Misha found on his table a plate of cold meat, some bread, a glass of milk, and three muffins. The only thing that tempted him was the muffins, of which he was very fond, but his pride would not allow him to eat them. If he were sure they did not remember how many they had given him—whether it was two or three—he might have eaten one. He carefully cut off a strip from each and ate them. He took a sip of the milk. It was very nice. . . . But no ! He would not have any more. . . .

The pink kvas really got into his head, and the halva and poppy seeds, the pies of mushrooms and bad meat disturbed his stomach.

" Fooh ! Horrible ! " he exclaimed angrily, and from time to time spat on the floor.

" Where have you been ? " Nina asked, appearing at the door.

" That's my business. I don't ask you where you gad about."

In passing Nina glanced at the table where stood Misha's dinner, untouched.

" Mamma said you were to eat the meat ! "

" I've no need to eat. I'm a blockhead and a shoemaker. . . . You are all lawyers . . . and it doesn't matter about a blockhead ! "

" As you please ! "

" Very well ! You can go out for a walk with your Petushkov and leave me alone. . . ."

" Idiot ! " she snapped irritably and went out.

Misha felt capable of withstanding the siege by his enemies, and of repelling their assaults, by his complete indifference to food. The mushroom and meat pies, the halva and poppy seeds were to be his allies.

This might have continued perhaps for quite a long time, had not an unforeseen incident put an end to the mutually strained relations. Misha had a stomach-ache and it grew worse as time went on. The pain compelled him to lie face downwards on the bed. He did not want to betray his disarmed position, and for some time controlled himself and stifled his groans in the pillow. But the mushroom pies and the sweet refreshing kvas did their work. He groaned aloud and beat the pillow with his hands.

" Oh, what a punishment ! " he said plaintively from time to time, kicking his feet. Towards evening, no longer able to control himself, he cried aloud, and all his enemies rushed to his bedside— all excepting his father, who was usually at his club at that hour. His mother took his temperature, his sister Nina got the mustard- pot, the housemaid ran for the doctor, even Falstaff came to see the invalid and, making his way among the bustling enemies, looked sadly and sympathetically at Misha with large, intelligent eyes.

" What have you done ? " the mother asked in a state of alarm, fearing in the bottom of her heart that he had taken poison, as he had threatened to do at other periods of strained relationship.

" Did you take anything ? Misha, tell me ! There's a dear ! Tell me quickly ! "

" Mamma ! Oh ! oh ! oh ! Mamma, I sold Asia, Africa, and America . . . oh ! oh ! oh ! . . . and bought some mushroom pies. . . ."

" What is the matter ? Misha ! My God, he is delirious ! Send to the club for father ! Oh, my God ! "

His mother bent over Misha, put her hand on his forehead, and kissed his cheek. His sister, with tears in her eyes, ran about the room, and going up to the window looked out anxiously to see if the doctor were coming. At last the doctor arrived.

" Well, young man, where does it hurt ? Turn over, please ! " Misha turned over obediently. The doctor examined him.

" What have you eaten to-day ? "

" He hasn't eaten anything to-day, doctor. He hasn't had a bite since he got back from school."

" That is not wise. . . . All the same, young man, perhaps you have eaten something after all. Tell me frankly. . . ."

" Yes, I ate some mushroom pies. . . . I sold Asia, Africa . . ."

" What is the matter ? " asked the alarmed father in a whisper, jumping out of the cab that had brought him from his club where he had abandoned an unfinished rubber.

An hour later, all the house was still. Misha, with a poultice on his stomach, lay in bed, and near him sat his mother and sister. They both fussed around him and obediently fulfilled his most capricious wants.

The pain had ceased, and Misha began to feel entirely satisfied.

DMITRI S. MEREJKOVSKY
B. 1866

LOVE IS STRONGER THAN DEATH

THE Florentine citizens of the old family of Almery belonged from time immemorial to two different trade corporations : some of them worshipped the protector of the butchers, Saint Antony ; the others had on their banner the image of a lamb and were engaged in the woollen trade. Like their ancestors, the brothers Giovanni and Matteo Almery belonged to these corporations. Giovanni dealt in meat in the old market-place—the Mercato Vecchio ; and Matteo had wool mills on the Arno. Buyers came willingly into Giovanni's meat-store, not only because they could always find there fresh ham, tender veal, and fat geese, but also because they liked the storekeeper for his cheerful disposition and his smooth tongue. No one knew how to exchange a pointed joke with a casual passer-by, a neighbour or a customer so cleverly as the butcher Almery ; no one spoke with such ease of everything under the sun—of the diplomatic blunders of the Florentine Republic, of the intentions of the Turkish Sultan, of the plots of the French king. Very few people ever took offence at the butcher's jokes, and to those who did he cited the old proverb : " A good neighbour is not defamed by a joke, and the tongue is sharpened on a jest, like a razor."

His brother Matteo, the wool merchant, was of a different character. He was a shrewd, politic man, always somewhat stern and taciturn ; he conducted his affairs better than the careless and good-natured Giovanni, and every year two of his ships, laden with wool, left the harbour of Livorno for Constantinople. He had very high ambitions and regarded his business as the road toward a government position. He always paid court to the aristocrats— the " fat people," as they were called in Florence—and he cherished the hope of elevating the Almery family, perhaps even of seeing his name borne aloft on the wings of immortal fame. Matteo often urged his brother to give up his meat business, because it was not sufficiently aristocratic, and to add his money to Matteo's capital.

But Giovanni would not take his counsel. While he respected his brother's ability, he secretly feared him ; and though he did not say it openly, he thought : " Honey tongue, heart of gall."

One hot day Giovanni came home from his shop very tired. He ate a hearty supper as usual, and drank plenty of cold wine. Suddenly he was striken with apoplexy—for he was a very stout, short-necked man. That night he passed away, before he had had time to take the communion or to make his will. The widow, Mona Ursula, a modest, kind-hearted but rather stupid woman, entrusted her husband's business affairs to his brother Matteo, who knew how to deceive her by crafty and honeyed words. He convinced the simple-minded woman that the deceased, owing to his carelessness, had left his account books in disorder ; that he had died on the eve of bankruptcy, and that if she wished to save what was left, it was necessary to close the meat shop in the Mercato Vecchio. Evil tongues asserted that the cunning Matteo cheated the widow mercilessly, in order to direct the current of Giovanni's capital upon the wheels of the wool mills, in accordance with his old wish. However it was, one thing was certain : Matteo's affairs improved immensely from that time, and instead of two ships, he was now sending off to Constantinople five or six ships, laden with excellent Tuscan wool. He was soon promised the profitable and honourable post of standard-bearer of the wool corporation—the Florentine *Arte de Lana*.

The monthly allowance which he gave to his brother's widow was so small that she suffered much privation, particularly as she was not alone. She had a dearly beloved young daughter, Ginevra by name. In those days there were just as few suitors in Florence for a dowerless maiden as there are to-day ; but the devout Mona Ursula did not lose courage. She prayed fervently to all God's saints, especially to Saint Antony, the tireless and faithful protector of the butchers in this world and the next ; she cherished the hope that God, the defender of widows and orphans, would send to her dowerless daughter a good and worthy husband.

Besides, she had another right to expect such a thing. Ginevra was a remarkably beautiful girl. It was hard to believe that the stout, clumsy, merry Giovanni could have a daughter of such rare, tender charm. Ginevra always dressed in plain, dark clothes ; around her beautiful, long, slender neck there was a string of pearls on which hung an ancient cameo of chrysolite with the image of a centaur upon it. Her head-dress was a piece of muslin reaching to the centre of her forehead and so transparent that one could see through it the thick masses of pale golden hair. The gentle face of Ginevra was the face of the Madonna painted by Filippo Lippi, the Immaculate Virgin who appeared to Saint Bernard in the desert,

and with tender, long, wax-like fingers turned the pages of his books.
There was an expression of the same endless innocence in the childish
lips, in the calm, sad look, in the high, light eyebrows.   And though
there was about her the freshness of a convent lily, she seemed frail
and short-lived, as though not at all created for life.   When the
butcher's daughter walked to church through the streets of Florence,
modest, quiet, with lowered eyes, a prayer-book in her hands, the
gay youths hastening to a banquet or a hunting-trip stopped their
horses ; their faces at once assumed an air of importance, their
jesting and their laughter ceased, and for a long time they followed
the beautiful Ginevra with their eyes.

Uncle Matteo, on hearing the praises of his niece's virtues, conceived a design to marry her to one of the secretaries of the Florentine
Republic, Francesco dell' Agolanti.   He was an elderly man, but
one who was respected by all, and who had close connections with
the rulers of the city at that time.   Francesco was a great Latin
scholar ; he wrote his reports and documents in the bombastic style
of Livy and Sallust.   Somewhat stern and misanthropic by nature,
he was irreproachably honest, like the ancient Romans.   His face
also was like the face of a senator of the days of the Republic, and
he knew how to wear the long, dark red cloak of the Florentine
officials like a real Roman toga.   He loved the ancient languages so
passionately that when the Greek language was in vogue in Tuscany,
and the Byzantine scholar from Constantinople, Emanuel Chrizoloras,
began to lecture on Greek grammar at the studio—the university
of those days—Agolanti, notwithstanding that he was already a
middle-aged man and secretary of the Florentine Republic, was not
ashamed to sit beside small boys on the school bench.   He soon
mastered the Greek language so that he could read Aristotle's
Organon and Plato's Dialogues in the original.   In a word, the wool
merchant, with his cunning and ambitious designs, could not con-
ceive of a better or more advantageous relative.   Matteo promised
to give a fair dowry with his niece, on the condition that Agolanti
was to unite his name and coat-of-arms with the name and coat-
of-arms of Almery.

Notwithstanding all these qualities of her suitor, Ginevra opposed
her uncle's intentions for a long time and kept delaying the wedding
from year to year.   When Matteo at last demanded an immediate
and decisive answer, she announced that she had another bridegroom, whom she loved better than Agolanti.   To the great surprise
and even fright of the devout Mona Ursula, she spoke the name of
Antonio de Rondinelli, a young sculptor who had his workshop in
one of the narrow side streets, near the Ponte Vecchio.   Antonio
had made the acquaintance of Ginevra in the house of her mother a
few months before.   He had asked for permission to make a wax

cast of the head of the young girl, desiring to use Ginevra's beauty for a carved image of the holy martyr Barbara, which was ordered from him by a rich convent in the outskirts of the city. Mona Ursula could not refuse the sculptor in such a religious matter, and while the work was going on the artist fell in love with his beautiful model.   Then they met at the public festivals and at the winter gatherings, to which Ginevra was always eagerly invited, for her beauty made her welcome at every festival.

When Mona Ursula, excusing herself timidly and politely, informed Matteo that Ginevra had another bridegroom whom she loved, and when she mentioned the name of Antonio de Rondinelli, the wool merchant, although terribly enraged, assumed a calm, benevolent look, and addressing Mona Ursula, said in his quiet voice :

" Madonna, if I had not heard with my own ears that which you have told me just now, I should never believe that such a virtuous and sensible woman as you are would pay any attention to the passing whim of an inexperienced child. I don't know how it is done nowadays, but in my time young girls did not dare even to utter a single word as to the choice of a bridegroom. In everything they obeyed the will of the father or the guardian. Just consider the matter—who is this Antonio whom my niece has honoured by her choice ? Is it possible that you do not know that sculptors, poets, actors, and street-singers are people who have nothing else to do and who could not conduct a more honourable and profitable business ? They are the most light-minded and unreliable set of people to be found in the wide world, they are drunkards, libertines, idlers, atheists, squanderers of their own and other people's fortunes. As for Antonio, you surely must have heard what all Florence knows. I will simply mention to you one of his peculiarities —the round basket which hangs in his workshop on a rope, across a beam, so that one end of the rope is attached to the basket and the other to a nail in the wall. Into this basket Antonio throws all the money that he earns, without counting it. And any one who wishes, whether a pupil or an acquaintance, can come, pull down the basket without asking the owner's permission, and take as much money as he pleases—copper, silver, or gold. Do you think, Madonna, that I would intrust my money, the dowry I promised your daughter, to such a lunatic ?

" But that is not all. Are you aware that Antonio cherishes the hideous atheism of the epicurean philosophy which is sown by the devil, that he does not go to church, that he scoffs at the holy sacraments, and does not believe in God ? Good people have told me that he worships the marble fragments of the abominable pagan idols, the gods and goddesses they have recently begun to exhume ; that he worships these rather than the blessed relics and the thaumaturgical images of the saints. I have also been told by other people that at night he and his pupils dissect dead bodies which he buys for a high price from the hospital guards, in order, as he claims, to study anatomy, the construction of the human body, the nerves, the muscles, and thus to perfect himself in his art ; but in reality he does this, I think, to please his assistant and adviser, the im-memorial foe of our salvation, the devil, who instructs him in the art of Black Magic. For it is only through charms, witchcraft, and diabolical suggestions that this heretic has won the heart of your innocent daughter."

With such words as these Uncle Matteo managed to frighten Mona Ursula and to convince her that he was right. When she told her daughter that in case she should positively refuse to marry Francesco dell' Agolanti, Uncle Matteo would stop giving them their monthly allowance, the young girl, filled with untold sorrow, submitted to her fate and expressed her willingness to obey her uncle's will.

During that year a great calamity had befallen Florence, a calamity which had been foretold by many astrologers because, in the sign of the Scorpion, Saturn had come too close to Mars. Several merchants who came from the East brought the germs of the plague in their large bales of valuable Indian rugs. A solemn procession marched through the streets, singing the plaintive *Miserere* and carrying the images of the saints. Laws were made prohibiting the unloading of refuse within the limits of the city, the tanneries and the slaughter-houses were forbidden to discharge refuse into the Arno, and measures were taken to keep the sick away from the community. Under penalty of a fine, of imprisonment, and, in certain cases, of death, the people were forbidden to keep in the house the bodies of those who had died during the day until sunset, or of those who had died during the night until sunrise, even if the relatives claimed that death was caused not by the plague but by some other disease. Special inspectors went around in the city at all times of the day or night to knock at the doors, to inquire whether there were any sick or dead in the house, and even to search, if they pleased. Here and there wagons smeared with pitch were seen in the smoke of the torches, accompanied by silent people in masks and black clothes, with long hooks with which they took up the plague-stricken bodies and threw them into the wagons, from afar, so as not to come close to the corpses. There were rumours that these men, whom the people called " black devils," picked up the bodies of those not yet dead, so as not to return to the same place again.

The plague, which began to rage toward the end of summer, continued until late in autumn, and even the winter colds, which set in early that year, did not check it. And so the well-to-do people in Florence, who were not tied to the city by important affairs, hastened away to their villas, where the air was free from the germs of the plague.

Uncle Matteo, fearing that his niece might change her mind, hastened the wedding under the pretext that Mona Ursula and her daughter must leave the city as soon as possible, and that Francesco dell' Agolanti had offered to take both Ginevra and her mother to his beautiful villa on the slope of Monte Albano.

Matteo wished this, and it was so decided. The wedding was to take place within a few days. Then the ceremony was performed quietly, without any pomp, as was becoming in those sad days. At the wedding ceremony Ginevra stood pale, like a ghost, and her face was terribly calm. But her uncle hoped that these girlish whims would disappear soon after the wedding and that Francesco would know how to win the love of his young bride.

But his hopes were not to be realised. When the young bride, leaving the church, entered the house of her husband, she began to feel dizzy. Soon she sank to the ground as if dead. At first all thought that she had fainted. They tried to revive her, but her eyes remained closed, her breathing became weaker, her face and whole body turned deathly pale and her limbs grew cold. After a few hours a physician was summoned (at that time physicians were called unwillingly, for fear the rumour might spread that a plague-stricken person was in the house) ; but when he placed a mirror before Ginevra's lifeless lips not the slightest sign of a breath could be seen upon it.

Then all, seized with inexpressible grief and compassion, felt convinced that Ginevra was really dead. The neighbours said that God had punished Almery for having set the wedding at such an inappropriate time, and that the young bride of Francesco, immediately upon her return from church, had contracted the plague and died. These rumours spread rapidly, because the relatives of the girl, fearing the visit of the " black devils," concealed from everybody until the last moment the fact of Ginevra's fainting and death. But toward evening came the inspectors, who were informed by the neighbours of everything that had taken place in Agolanti's house, and they demanded that the relatives either give up the body of Ginevra or bury it immediately. Only when they were given a fair-sized bribe did they consent to leave the body in Francesco's house until the evening of the next day.

None of the relatives, however, doubted that Ginevra was dead, except her old nurse, whom everybody considered half-witted. With plaintive lamentations the old woman begged them not to bury Ginevra, asserting that the physicians were in error, that Ginevra was not dead at all, that she was sleeping ; and she swore that when she put her hand on the heart of her darling she " felt that it was beating weakly, weakly, more weakly than the wing of a butterfly."

The day went by, and as the young girl showed no signs of life, they put a shroud on her, placed her in a coffin and carried her away to the cathedral. The dry and spacious sepulchre, floored with smooth Tuscan bricks, was situated between two doors of the church, in one of the cemetery yards, under the shade of tall cypress trees, among the tombs of the noble families of Florence. Matteo paid a high price for this grave, but then the money was taken out of the dowry which was to have been given with Ginevra. The burial service was conducted in very solemn fashion. There were many wax candles, and in memory of Ginevra each of the poor was given a measure of barley and olive oil for half a soldo. Notwithstanding the cold weather and the terrors of the plague, a big crowd was present at the funeral ; some, even strangers, on hearing the sad story of the young bride's death could not restrain their tears, and they repeated Petrarch's sweet line :

Death seemed beautiful on her beautiful face.

Francesco delivered an oration over the grave, using not only Latin quotations, but also Greek from Plato and Homer, which was something new in those days and pleased many of the listeners, even those who did not understand Greek.

There was some confusion at the end of the funeral ceremony, when the coffin was borne out of the cathedral and put in the sepulchre for the last kiss. A pale man in a silk mourning cloak came over to the dead girl, and lifting the crape from her face began to gaze at her with a steadfast look. He was asked to go away, and told that it was not proper for him, a stranger, to approach Ginevra before her relatives had taken leave of her. When the pale man heard that he was called " a stranger " and that Matteo and Francesco were called " relatives " he smiled bitterly, kissed the dead girl on the lips, lowered the crape over her face, and walked away without saying a word. The crowd began to whisper, pointing at him, calling the name of Antonio de Rondinelli, the man Ginevra loved and for whose sake she died.

Twilight was closing in, and as the funeral ceremony was over the crowd dispersed. Mona Ursula wished to pass the night by the coffin, but Uncle Matteo opposed this, for she was so overcome with grief that everybody feared for her life. Only Fra Mariano, a Dominican, remained in the sepulchre, where he had to read the prayers over the dead.

A few hours went by. The measured voice of the friar, and from time to time the slow striking of the clock on the tower of Giotto,

resounded in the stillness of the night.   After midnight Fra Mariano
began to feel thirsty.   He drew forth a flask of wine, and tossing his
head back, took a few sips with pleasure, when suddenly it seemed
to him that he heard a sigh.   He listened attentively ; the sigh was
heard once more, and this time it appeared to him that the light
crape on the dead girl's face stirred.   A chill of terror shot through
his frame, but as he was not inexperienced in such matters, and
knew well that even experienced people alone with the dead at
night imagine all sorts of things, he decided not to pay the slightest
attention to the matter.   He made the sign of the cross, and
resumed reading the prayers in sonorous voice.

Suddenly the friar's voice broke off, he remained as petrified, his
open eyes fixed upon the face of the dead girl.   Now it was no longer
a sigh, but a moan that came from her lips.   Fra Mariano no longer
doubted, for he saw that the breast of the dead girl was heaving and
falling slowly, stirring the crape cover. She was breathing. Crossing
himself, trembling in every limb, he rushed toward the door, and
jumped out of the sepulchre.   Brought to himself by the fresh air
outside, and thinking once more that it was only his imagination,
he whispered an Ave Maria, returned to the door, and looked into
the sepulchre.   A cry of horror burst from his lips.   The dead girl
was sitting up in the coffin with open eyes.   Fra Mariano ran off
across the cemetery without looking back, then through the Square
of Baptisteria San Giovanni and over the Via Rikasoli.   Only his
wooden sandals striking against the ice-covered brick pavement
broke the quiet of the night.

Ginevra Almery, awakening from sleep or from the deathlike
fainting spell, examined the coffin with perplexity.   At the thought
that she was buried alive she was seized with terror.   With a desperate effort she climbed out of the coffin, and muffling herself in
the shroud went out of the door which had been left open by the
friar.

She came out on the cemetery, then on the square before the
cathedral.   The light of the moon was falling through the rapidly
moving clouds, which were rent asunder by the wind, and in this
moonlight the marble tower of Giotto stood out distinctly.   Ginevra's
thoughts were confused, her head was reeling, it seemed to her that
she and the tower would soon be carried away to the moonlit clouds ;
she could not understand whether she was alive or dead, whether it
was all a dream or reality.

Not realising whither she was going, she passed through several
deserted streets, noticed a familiar house, paused, walked over to
the door and knocked.   It was her Uncle Matteo's house.

The wool merchant, notwithstanding the late hour, was not
asleep.   He was awaiting a messenger with advices concerning two

vessels which were returning from Constantinople. Rumours were on foot that the storm had wrecked many ships not far away from the Livorno coast, and Uncle Matteo feared that his ships were among them. While waiting for the messenger he became hungry and ordered his servant Nencia, a pretty, red-haired girl, with freckles and milk-white teeth, to roast a capon for him. Uncle Matteo was an old bachelor. This night he was sitting in the kitchen by the fireplace, as it was cold in the other rooms. Nencia, red-faced, her sleeves rolled up, was broiling the capon, and the merry flame was reflected on the shiny clay of the cleanly washed pots and dishes which stood on the shelves.

"Nencia, do you hear anything?" said Matteo, listening attentively.

"It's the wind. I'll not go. You have already sent me out there three times."

"That's not the wind. Some one's knocking. That's the messenger. Go, open the door at once."

The stout Nencia began to walk down the steep wooden stairs lazily, and Uncle Matteo, standing at the head of the staircase, held a lantern over his head to light the way for her.

"Who's there?" asked the servant.

"It's I—I—Ginevra Almery," replied a faint voice from behind the door.

"Jesu! Jesu! The evil spirit is with us!" muttered Nencia. Her feet began to tremble, and to save herself from falling she clasped the balustrade. Matteo grew pale and the lantern almost fell from his hands.

"Nencia, Nencia, open the door, quick!" implored Ginevra. "Let me warm myself. I am cold. Tell uncle that it is I——"

The servant girl, notwithstanding her stoutness, rushed up the staircase so fast that the steps creaked under her feet.

"There's your messenger! I told you you had better go to sleep like a good Christian! Oh, oh! Knocking again, do you hear? The poor soul is moaning—how plaintively she is moaning! O Lord, deliver us and have mercy on us sinners! Saint Lawrence, pray for us!"

"Listen, Nencia," said Matteo irresolutely. "I'll go down and see what is there. Who knows, perhaps——"

"What else will you do?" cried Nencia, clasping her hands. "Just think of him, what a brave man! You think that I'll let you go? You feel like going to the other world, do you? There's no use of your going anywhere; stay here, and be thankful nothing worse has happened to us."

Taking down a flask of holy water from the shelf, Nencia sprinkled it on the door of the house, on the staircase, over the kitchen and on Matteo himself. He did not argue any longer with the wise servant and obeyed her, presuming that she knew better how to deal with ghosts. And Nencia pronounced an adjuration in a loud voice :

" Blessed soul, go with God—the dead to the dead. May God rest you in the world of the righteous ! "

When Ginevra heard that she was spoken of as dead, she understood that she had nothing more to expect there. She got up from the threshold on which she had fallen exhausted, and staggered away in search of shelter.

Moving her frozen feet with difficulty, she reached the adjoining side street, where her husband, Francesco dell' Agolanti, lived.

The secretary of the Florentine Republic was at this time writing a long philosophical message in Latin to his friend in Milan, Mucio dell' Uberti, who was also an admirer of the ancient muses. It was a theological treatise entitled, " A Discourse on the Immortality of the Soul, in connection with the Death of My Beloved Wife, Ginevra Almery." Francesco compared the doctrine of Aristotle with the doctrine of Plato, refuting the opinion of Thomas Aquinas, who affirmed that the philosophy of Aristotle agreed with the dogmas of the Catholic Church concerning paradise, inferno, and purgatory ; while Francesco proved by many keen and weighty syllogisms that it was not at all the doctrine of Aristotle, who was secretly a sceptic and an atheist, but the doctrine of the great admirer of the gods, Plato, that was in accord with Christian faith.

The copper oil-lamp, fastened over the smooth board of his writing-table of carved wood, with numerous drawers and compartments for paper, ink, and quills, was burning with an even flame. The form of the lamp represented a Triton embracing Oceanides, for in all matters of everyday life Francesco loved to imitate the fine ancient models. Gold figures representing the dance of cupids or angels with wreaths of paradisean flowers flashed on the valuable parchment, which was as smooth as silk and as stiff as ivory.

Francesco was just beginning to analyse from a theological point of view the doctrine of metempsychosis. He alluded wittily to the Pythagoreans, who refuse to eat beans because they contain the souls of ancestors. Suddenly he heard a soft tapping on his door. He knitted his brow, for he could not bear noise while he was at work. Nevertheless he went over to the garret window, opened it, looked down on the street and in the pale light of the moon he saw the dead Ginevra muffled in her shroud.

Francesco forgot Plato and Aristotle, and shut the window so quickly that Ginevra had no time to utter a word. Then he began to whisper an Ave Maria and to make the sign of the cross in superstitious terror, like Nencia.

But he soon came to himself; he felt ashamed of his faint-heartedness when he recalled what the Alexandrian Neoplatonists, Proclus, and Porphyry, said of the appearance of the dead. Francesco soon mastered himself completely, and opening the window again he said in a firm voice :

"Whoever you may be, a spirit of heaven or of earth, begone ! Go back to the place whence you came, for it is in vain that you seek to frighten him whose mind is enlightened by the light of true philosophy. You may deceive my physical eyes, but you cannot deceive my spiritual eyes. Go in peace—the dead to the dead."

And he closed the window, this time not to open it even though a whole legion of pitiful visions should knock.

Ginevra started off, and as she was not far away from the old market-place, she soon found herself by the house of her mother.

Mona Ursula was kneeling before a crucifix, and beside her stood the stern friar Fra Giacomo, pale-faced, enfeebled by fasting. She lifted her terror-stricken eyes to him.

"What am I to do, father ? Help me. There is no submissive-ness, no prayer in my soul. It seems that God has forsaken me, and my soul is doomed to perdition."

"Obey God in everything, to the end," the friar urged her, "Do not grumble ; calm the voice of the rebellious flesh, for your excessive love for your daughter is of the flesh, not of the spirit. Grieve not because her body died, but because she appeared before the Judgment seat of the Highest with repentance, a great sinner."

At this moment there was a knock at the door. "Mother, mother, it is I—let me in, quickly ! "

"Ginevra ! " exclaimed Mona Ursula, and she was about to rush to her daughter, but the friar stopped her.

"Where are you going ? Your daughter lies in the grave, dead, and will not rise until the great Day of Judgment. This is the evil spirit tempting you by the voice of your daughter, by the voice of your flesh and blood. Repent, pray—pray before it is too late, pray for yourself and for the sinful soul of Ginevra, that both of you may not be doomed to perdition."

"Mother, don't you hear me ? Don't you know my voice ? It is I—I am alive, not dead ! "

"Let me go to her, father, let me——"

Then Fra Giacomo lifted his hand and whispered : "Go, and remember that now you doom not only yourself, but also Ginevra's soul, to perdition. God will curse you in this world and in the next ! "

The face of the friar was so full of hatred, and his eyes burned with such a strange fire, that Mona Ursula stopped, terror-stricken, clasped her hands in prayer and fell at his feet.

Fra Giacomo turned toward the door, made the sign of the cross, and said : " In the name of the Father, and of the Son, and of the Holy Ghost ! I adjure you by the blood of Him who was crucified, fade away, disappear, accursed one ! This is holy ground. O Lord lead us not into temptation, but deliver us from evil."

" Mother, mother, have pity on me—I am dying ! "

The mother started once more and stretched out her hands toward her daughter, but the friar, inexorable as Death, stood between them.

Then Ginevra fell to the ground, and feeling that she was freezing to death, she clasped her hands about her knees, bent down her head and resolved not to rise again, not to stir, until she died.

" The dead should not return to the living," she thought, and at that moment she recalled Antonio. " Is it possible that he also would drive me away ? " She had thought of him before, but a sense of shame had restrained her, for she did not wish to go to him at night alone, having been married to another. But now she saw that she was dead to the living.

The moon had disappeared. The mountains, covered with snow, stood out pale against the morning sky. Ginevra got up from the threshold of her mother's house. Finding no shelter with her own, she went to a stranger.

Antonio had worked all night on a wax statue of Ginevra. He did not notice how the hours fled by, how the cold light of the blue winter morning was coming through the round window-panes. The sculptor was assisted by his favourite pupil, Bartolino, a seventeen-year-old youth, fair-haired and handsome as a girl.

Antonio's face was calm. It seemed to him that he was reviving the dead and giving her a new immortality. The lowered eyelids seemed ready to tremble and open, her breast seemed to rise and fall and warm blood seemed to flow in the fine veins on her temples.

He finished his work and was trying to give an innocent smile to Ginevra's lips, when there came a knock at the door.

" Bartolino," said Antonio, without leaving off his work, " open the door."

The pupil went over to the door and asked : " Who's there ? "

" I—Ginevra Almery," replied a scarcely audible voice, which sounded like the rustling of the evening breeze.

Bartolino jumped back to the farthest corner of the room, pale and quivering. " The dead ! " he whispered, crossing himself.

But Antonio recognised the voice of his beloved. He jumped up, rushed over to Bartolino and tore the key out of his hands.

" Antonio, bethink yourself—what are you doing ? " muttered the pupil, whose teeth were chattering with fright.

Antonio ran over to the door, unlocked it and saw Ginevra lying at the threshold, almost lifeless, her loose locks covered with rime.

But he was not frightened, for his heart filled with great compassion. He bent over her with words of love, lifted her and carried her in his arms to his house.

He laid her down on pillows, covered her with his best rug, sent Bartolino for the old lady from whom he rented the workroom, built a fire in the fireplace, warmed up some wine and gave it to her to drink. She now breathed more easily, and although she was still unable to speak, she opened her eyes. Then Antonio's heart filled with joy.

" The woman will be here soon," he said, bustling about in the room. " We'll arrange everything right away—only you must pardon this disorder, Madonna Ginevra."

Confused and flushing, Antonio pulled the basket down from the ceiling, took out some money, handed it to Bartolino and told him to run to the market-place and buy meat, bread, and vegetables for breakfast, and when the old woman came he ordered her to prepare hot chicken soup.

The pupil rushed as fast as he could to make the purchases in the market-place, the old woman went out to kill a chicken. Antonio remained alone with Ginevra.

She called him over, and as he knelt beside her she told him everything that had happened.

" Oh, my dear," said Ginevra when she had finished her story, " only you were not frightened when I came to you, dead—only you love me."

" Shall I call your relatives—your uncle, your mother or your husband ? " asked Antonio.

" I have no relatives ; I have neither a husband nor an uncle nor a mother. They're all strangers, all except you : for to them I am dead, to you I am alive—and I am yours ! "

The first rays of the sun began to pour into the room. Ginevra smiled at him, and as the sun was growing brighter, the colour of life came to her cheeks, warm blood flowed in the veins on her temples. When Antonio bent down to her, embraced her and kissed her on the lips, it seemed to her that the sun was reviving her, giving her a new and immortal life.

" Antonio," whispered Ginevra, " blessed be the death which has taught us to love ; blessed be the love which is stronger than death."

ZINAÏDA HIPPIUS
(MME. MEREJKOVSKY)
B. 1867

APPLE BLOSSOM

I

" WHY did she arrange it so that I couldn't live without her ?
It was she who did it ; I was not to blame."

I have written these words, and how strange I feel! I might
have been speaking of the woman I love, but I love no woman :
it was my mother who arranged it so that I am dying for want of
her. If you keep a man in the warmth all his life and then turn
him out unprotected into twenty degrees of frost, he is bound to
die. And I am dying ; I am dying because of her.

These last days have been great, significant days for me. I seem
to have arrived at something, finished the half of my life, and ahead
the path is straight and dreary and swift, and so monotonous that
it will be impossible to know whether I am going backwards or
forwards, upwards or downwards. I don't know even whether to
resign myself as usual and go along the path at all.

I am twenty-seven, but no one would believe me ; I look so old.
And I know that I am an old man. There was a time when my face
was beautiful and soft like Mother's. We used to look into the glass
together, and it seemed to us that we were wonderfully alike. Now
she would not know me. I am bent, my eyes are dull, my beard is
long, my face yellow and dark. I think I shall soon die. I have no
particular illness, but I am bound to die, for only those live who want
to live, who have the will, and my will is gone. When I realised
this during these last days and saw that nothing further awaited
me, I even thought of suicide. But I can't . . . I am afraid.

I am a musician ; not a great musician, but a passable one, as
people say. I like quiet emotions and recollections that fill the
heart with a sweet pain, and the soul with a profound stillness.
Sometimes when playing a brilliant prelude at a concert (it is long
since I have been on the platform now) I would look at some portly
man in the front row of the stalls and think, " There you are,

51

looking at me and listening intently. You know what I am
playing. Afterwards you will make some clever remark about my
' technique ' and ' expression,' but if I were to stop this prelude
and play some simple little Russian song that would bring back
the years, long gone by, and the memory of a dark, warm garden,
and two dear, forgotten eyes perhaps, you would get up and go
out to hide your unwilling tears and the sweet sadness and joy
that the prelude cannot give you. I know you will want to hide
this joy, because you will be ashamed of it. It will seem to you
that you alone feel it and the others do not understand, but all
will feel it alike and each will be ashamed, thinking he is the only
one to have it." All have some bright spot in the past. I have
one like the rest.

II

It is dull to begin from the beginning, from the time when I was
a child. However, at twenty my life was no different from what
it was at ten. At twenty I was happier, perhaps, for I had
outstripped Mother and could walk with her arm-in-arm. Our
relations, though, did not change. When a boy I would often
make a scene when Mother went away to the theatre without me.
I used to say she had no right to be enjoying herself when I was
forced to learn my lessons. She would solemnly beg my forgiveness
and was unhappy if I sulked. It was impossible for us to quarrel.
She had no one but me, and I had only her.

I never talked to my father. An old man, always occupied with
some building or other, and living, as he did, in another part of
the house, he had no interest for me. And Mother was young and
slight as a girl, with large black eyes, fresh and sparkling ; her
garments rustled with her quick movements, and a strange perfume
clung about her. I never knew what it was called, but it reminded
me of early spring.

We used to live in a large town in the South. The house was a
new one, built by my father, uncomfortable and cold. There was
a small, tidy garden with other gardens adjoining it on all sides,
so that it seemed to me endless. Our garden may be no more.
I don't know, because I don't want to know.

I was never sent to school. Who could have stopped with
Mother if I had gone ? She had many friends, but none who
paid her serious attention even though her relations to my father
were known. I think she didn't encourage them. I had the best
of masters and studied fairly well. Mother, of course, worked
with me, but lessons often wearied her, and she would say, " Shall
we chuck the books, Volodia, and go for a walk, eh ? "

And we would go—Mother in her fine clothes, happy, and I, happy to possess so pretty a mother, and to be so much like her. She never changed or grew older, and we were soon taken for brother and sister, especially when I began to cultivate a moustache and a small beard. I did not seem to change inwardly. At twenty I began to take a serious interest in music and had visions of the Conservatoire. I had passed my exams. well and had to decide on what I was to do.

" You shall certainly go to the Conservatoire in Moscow," Mother said. " You must hurry up, because you are nearly twenty. You'll be famous some day ; you'll see if you're not."

" When shall we go ? "

" In the autumn, I think. Will that do ? "

There was no question of my going without her. Whom should I have to talk to ? Who would there be to caress me and walk with me ?

I would sit in her room in the evenings on the floor, at her feet, by the fire, as I used to when a boy, and I would tell her how this and that girl was in love with me, and of how I flirted with them all, and which I liked the best. Then, it seemed to me that all the girls were in love with me, because I was so handsome, and could play the piano so well.

" Do you know, Volodia," Mother said to me once, " you are not a bit like a man ; you are just like a woman. Perhaps that is the reason we are such great friends. . . . I wonder if it was my doing," she added, reflecting. " You are never in the society of men, for example, and when I see you among women, you don't flirt with them so much as show off your own charms. I am not sure . . . but it seems to me that if you were a stranger, I shouldn't like you."

I was horribly hurt, and sulked. What did this mean ? Hadn't she said that I was like her ? And now she didn't care for me. If it is bad to be like a woman, why was she not alarmed before ?

For a long time Mother begged me to forgive her, and we made peace. I never forgot her words, though, and would often say to her afterwards, " Siromiatnikov, now, and Maremianov are manly, aren't they ? Oughtn't all the women to be in love with them ? " Mother would smile and press my mouth with her large though beautiful hand, her many bracelets jingling on the wrist.

I knew I became a coxcomb because the girls liked me ; I knew that my life was empty and my heart grown commonplace with the constant posing and the senseless desire to attract. As for myself, I didn't fall in love once. There were many girls I liked, but none of them very much. I was very pure at the time, as few men are, but in thought I was no better than the others.

III

I took very little interest in books. Before my exams. I used to read ; but since, I have only worked at my music. Music alone stirred me and made me think of that which was not. I could forget much for music.

At last we went to Moscow.   I was glad to go.   I felt instinctively that everything must be changed.

We took a pretty flat on the Malaya Nikitskaya, and lived pleasantly like two chums, going to the theatre and driving together. Friends soon appeared, relations were unearthed. But I began to work zealously, and rarely came out when Mother had visitors.

At the Conservatoire I made friends with no one except my master, who was still a young man. He used to think me strange but promising, as he said. He only solved me after I had taken him home and he had seen Mother. It was impossible to understand us apart, and when together, people said, we made a complete whole.

"Look here, young man," my master said to me once, "you must work. Something ought to come out of you, or you'll be utterly lost."

And I did work. I forgot my indolence, I never bothered about my hair or my clothes, I rarely went out ; I did nothing but practise my scales. It wasn't that I liked them ; I looked upon them as a steep ladder up which I had to climb. How I used to long for the blue sky and the earth and the flowers ! I had never longed for anything, and I didn't think that I should ever long for anything at all. Mother comforted me, but . . . this is my one sore spot— I knew that we didn't understand each other about this. Mother didn't even care for our garden ; she preferred to take her walks in the streets. She used to say that the sunlight was more soothing in the half-light of the drawing-room, and that her own perfumes were better than the perfumes of the spring.

When I reflected on it at moments, I was forced to feel that she was no longer young and that we could not really be chums ; there was now a barrier between us. But these were only moments.

I have said that I never made any friends, and that was true of intimate friends, but I picked up acquaintances. I happened on drinking bouts on various occasions, and spent nights away from home. . . .

Mother questioned me with curiosity, but without the smallest reproach. I was annoyed, though, and related the details with disgust, but not without a sense of pride.

"It doesn't matter, Volodia," Mother said. " I knew this would happen, but you mustn't forget about me. Do you understand? I must come first with you always, as you are with me. Do you understand? It would be impossible to live otherwise. Do you understand? "

I merely smiled and put my arms about her. How could she help being first? Who else could be first?

IV

Several years passed. I finished my course at the Conservatoire and appeared at concerts with success. But I was not happy. What could satisfy me in the noisy songs in which I moved my fingers quickly and all marvelled at and praised me? When should I be able to play a song which I often heard, but which invariably escaped me? On the day when I play it everything will suddenly change, and I will have the same emotions as the person listening to me. We will weep together, because the song will not pass us by, but will hold us and touch the profound and mysterious in us. . . . We will weep, and afterwards . . . nothing will matter afterwards, not even if we die; it will make no difference. I knew that as long as I had no emotion nothing would happen, and I believe beyond a doubt that if the thing that comes to all would come to me, I would be able to " speak." Instead of " to play " mentally I always used the expression " to speak to people."

Mother had to go home on two occasions and left me for several weeks. I collapsed each time; I gave up working and scarcely ate. A fearful horror took possession of me. It seemed that I was all alone in the world, that Mother was not and had never been. That she had never been was the worst! If she had never been she never could be. . . .

Why did she bind me to herself so that life without her could not go on? To say that I loved her would be meaningless. I don't love air and food, yet I can't exist without them. I know I am weak, terribly weak. I haven't strength enough to make an effort not to suffer when I am suffering. . . .

Last year when I was in Moscow my father fell ill, and Mother left me before Christmas. By the end of January I was ill myself; I threw up my work and went home. It meant an extra year, but what did that matter? I couldn't work without Mother. The evening of my arrival we spent together sitting on a couch in her room in silence. I knew she was pleased. She could no more live without me than I could without her. . . .

V

I spent the days at home playing a great deal. I had a small room with one window in it facing the garden. I put my piano by the window and looked out at the sky and the trees as I played.

In the middle of February the weather grew warm. I walked in the garden and gazed at the blue sky that peeped through the bare branches of the cherry and apple trees. How bright and golden it looked through the dark branches! The distant hills began to turn yellow—yellow, not green—with the new grass. The grass always shoots out of the earth so bright and young that it seems yellow. I love the early tiny blades. Like inquisitive children they awkwardly lift a clod of soil and peep out at the sun. Ah, Mother. . . . Why didn't she come out into the garden with me? And why didn't she love what I loved? Again a coldness flowed through my heart, again estrangement. . . .

The more the spring advanced the more I sat in the garden and the happier I was. I seemed to be growing with the yellow flowers. I abandoned my fugues; again something stirred in my soul, something brighter than any fugue; again I sought, but could not find. . . . It was there, near me, in the vernal sounds and perfumes. . . . How far away it is now! . . .

It was sitting at the end of a narrow, damp path, on a low seat, by the farthest hedge in my garden. The hedge was still dark. It never worried me that my garden ended by this hedge and did not stretch on eternally. There were trees wherever I looked, and grass and earth, and the sky above them. What mattered it that these trees belonged to other gardens, when they were as good as mine? Everything I beheld and that gave me pleasure was mine. Those rugged hills with the deep blue shadows on the distant horizon were mine, too.

The sun was sinking to the west and its rays grew colder. I knew it was time to go in, but I could not leave my seat. Suddenly I became aware of some one coming softly behind me, so softly that I scarcely heard. I looked round. A sound of footsteps came from the other side of the hedge in the next garden. It was not footsteps exactly, but a continued, rustling sound, like something being trailed along the ground. It ceased. I could have risen to see what it was, but I thought, "What does it matter? It is not worth the trouble of moving." The spring air tired me. I wanted to sit still and to doze.

But again the rustling sound was repeated and ceased. I raised my eyes and encountered two strange eyes looking at me intently and angrily. I knew they were angry by the agitation I was in.

Suddenly the expression of the eyes changed to indifference. On the other side of the hedge stood a girl I did not know. For some time we looked at each other, and were silent. I thought she would go away, but she spoke.

" Good evening," she said in an unfriendly tone. " I have seen you here a great deal. Why do you always sit here ? "

" I like it," I replied shyly, as though apologising. " I have never seen you."

" I've seen you from the distance. I live over there." She pointed to a house concealed by the trees, some way from the hedge.

When she moved her arm, I noticed for the first time that her garments were strange, quite unlike the dress of an ordinary girl. She appeared to be dressed for a masquerade at a first glance, and then it struck me that her dress was simple ; in fact, the only possible dress she could have worn. It was a loose garment of some soft, white material, as broad at the top as at the hem (I could see the whole of her then, for she was standing near the hedge), with a narrow dark-red girdle round her waist. I realised what had made the strange rustling sound when she walked. The dress had a long train—hardly a train, it was a large piece of material, falling in negligent, beautiful lines behind. The sleeves were long and came down almost to the fingers.

" Why do you wear such a strange dress ? " I asked.

She was not astonished at my question.

" It's more becoming. Since no one sees me, I take care to look well for myself."

" I like it," I said. " What is your name ? "

" Marta."

" Marta ? Aren't you Russian ? "

" Oh, yes, I'm Russian. My surname is Koreneva. I live here with my mother. Haven't you heard of her ? Madame Koreneva, the blind millionairess ? "

I recollected that I had heard something about Madame Koreneva the blind millionairess, and her young daughter, who studied hard and never went out.

" I have heard," I said slowly. " How strange that we should be neighbours and meet only for the first time."

" I don't like going out," she said hastily. " You seemed surprised that I was called Marta. My real name is Martha, but I like being called Marta best, because it's prettier."

" You are altogether beautiful," I said pensively, as though speaking to myself.

" Really ? " she said simply. " I think so, but then some people say I'm not. They can't understand."

Our conversation did not astonish me. I couldn't realise that Marta was a girl and that I was paying her compliments. She seemed to me beautiful like the sky between the trees, like the mild, fragrant air, like the rosy cloud near the setting sun. She seemed to go so with everything, with the very twilight hour ; I had no desire to talk or to wonder ; I merely wanted to enjoy it all.

She, too, was silent.

"Good-bye," she said at last. "You may come here," she added haughtily, though with condescension. "You don't spoil the garden."

And once more I heard the continued rustle of her dress. She was gone. Her words did not astonish me. Her thoughts were the same as my own. One is astonished only at the things that are foreign to one, that are outside of one, and not at things that are within.

I was in a strange mood for the rest of the evening. I tried to play, but the sound of the piano irritated me. It seemed so harsh and pronounced. I went in to say good-night to Mother, but I did not tell her a word of what had passed. For the first time in my life her perfumes did not smell to me of the real spring.

VI

For two days I did not go into the garden.

I don't know what it was that I feared. Perhaps I felt that it would never be so charming again, and I did not wish to spoil the memory of it. Mother remarked on several occasions that I looked pale and did not play much. My father was still in bed, so that she was busy the greater part of the day.

"What is it, Volodia ? Shall we go for a walk this evening ? "

My reply was languid and apathetic. I had no desire to walk about the streets.

At last, on the third day, I decided, and, in the manner of weak people, I hastily took up my hat, and went into the garden with resolute strides.

There were many changes. The paths were drier, yellow anemones crept around the water-butt, and the buds on the apple trees were whiter and larger. Even on the hedge, here and there, tiny green leaves were visible. I had barely time to sit down and to collect myself, when I heard the familiar rustling sound, and Marta came up to the hedge.

"Good evening," she said.

I rose and drew near to her. She wore the same dress, or perhaps another one like it, but it had a golden girdle instead of a red one.

" Why haven't you been here ? " she asked. " I told you you might come. However, I know why you didn't come."

" Why, then ? "

" It doesn't matter . . . I know."

Was it the rays of the sun that fell on her in a peculiar way, or was it my imagination ? It seemed to me that her dress was tinged with a faint pink, like the colour of apple blossom.

A strange face had Marta. I cannot recall it. I know only that there was nothing dark or vivid about it. The hair, twisted at the back into a simple knot, almost carelessly, seemed to mingle with the greyness of the air surrounding it ; the oval face was pale and delicate ; the eyes, too, were light-coloured and transparent like pure water. I can't remember their colour, but at mid-day, when the sky was very blue, they must have been dark.

I remember every feature, the delicate, straight brows, the bright-red, compressed lips, but the face as a whole escapes me. I can almost be glad that it does, for the more intangible a memory, the more complete it is.

" I know where the sun will set to-day," Marta said. " There, behind the bend of that hill. It set more to the left yesterday ; a good deal more to the left. I know where the sun is going to set every day. These are my days, mine ! " She spoke these words solemnly. " Would you like to know what changes there will be in the garden to-morrow ? Would you like me to tell you what night the apple trees will burst into bloom ? "

" How do you know ? " I asked softly.

" I know all about the garden, the spring, the sun and the flowers, because I love them."

And I believed that she knew.

" What do you think that acacia tree over there is feeling ? "

" Joy, I think."

" What joy ? "

" The same joy that you and I. . . . Joy from the sun."

" Yes, we all rejoice, all. . . . Sometimes I hear you play," she added after a pause. " I like the sound from here ; it's not harsh. . . ."

I remembered that the piano had sounded very harsh to me during these days.

" You won't be angry with me ? " Marta continued ; " but you sometimes play such complex things, with so many different notes. That is not what you want ; you ought to get away from other people's ideas, and listen here " ; she waved her hand through the air ; " and put yourself in harmony with this, in unison with everything. . . ."

She stopped, in obvious difficulties to explain her meaning, but, of course, I understood.

"I have always thought that. I shall do it. I am so glad you think as I do. It must be right."

"Can't you play something slower and simpler ? I once heard a song, often sung and played at concerts, but not in the way I like it. It goes, ' Not a word, my friend, nor a sigh.' I have no voice, but I am going to sing it, because I want you to know the motif."

And she sang softly, as though she were speaking. I listened and asked her to repeat it.

"Even the words are beautiful," she said ; "but I don't understand their meaning now. These are my days," she repeated once more. "When the spring has gone. . . ."

Her voice fell. It suddenly occurred to me that I had not seen her smile.

"Do you never smile, Marta ? " I asked.

"The sun is about to set," she said solemnly. "I laugh in the morning."

At this moment, sitting in my St. Petersburg flat, with its dark, curtainless windows and sagging, grimy ceiling in the middle of which is a large, austere-looking hook, it seems to me that this never was, and could never have been. Had I dreamt it ? But the thing that happened afterwards was not a dream—the loathsome, horrible, impossible thing for which I am dying. And the one depended so completely on the other.

That evening, after my second meeting with Marta, I put out the candles in my room, opened the window, and sat down to play. I tried to recall the motif of Marta's song. It was a sweet, simple motif, composed of a few simple notes. I did not add an unnecessary chord, nor a single scale. I repeated it again and again, and each time it came out different and better than the last, bringing back the vernal sounds and the yellow afterglow.

I didn't know what had come over me, but I felt it was something good. I went to the window and looked below ; unconsciously, I opened the door, walked down the dark staircase, and went out into the garden.

It was lighter there than in the room. A hazy mist hung, shimmering ; the new moon had set, and only the stars were out.

At the bottom of the path Marta's white dress gleamed dimly. I knew she would be there. It was right that she should listen. . . .

"It was good," she whispered when I was near her. "Don't speak loudly. I was waiting for you. I wanted to ask you something. Don't come to the garden to-morrow ; come the day after to-morrow, at sunset, and stay a long time. That night the

apple buds will come into bloom. We shall see the first blossom
. . the first blossoms. . . . Would you like to ? will you come ? "
" I will come," I said, also in a whisper.
She nodded, moved away from the hedge, and was gone.
I remained alone.

VII

The next day I got up late. I went lazily into the dining-room
and lazily drank half my coffee. Recalling Marta's request, I did
not go into the garden, but sauntered lazily about the rooms. I
had no energy to do anything.

I had a desire to go in to Mother and sit down beside her in
silence. Despite the haziness of my existence during these days, I
was ill at ease and missed something—I had not seen much of
Mother. I had no desire to tell her anything ; she did not care
for the garden, and it was all connected with the garden. But
Mother was as necessary to me as my very self. I had only then
realised that she did not feel as I felt, nor the same things that I
felt. Why had she deceived me for so long ? Why had she
arranged it so that I couldn't live without her ?

I sat through dinner languid and pale, without eating anything.
All at once I felt some one's gaze fixed on me, and I turned. Mother
was glaring at me with darkening eyes, in which there was so much
unexpected anger and hate that I shuddered, and my heart grew
cold, before I had had time to think or to reflect. Was I dreaming ?
was it my imagination ? A heavy weight seemed to oppress me.
I shrank and grew smaller ; I was conscious of my own body, and
my limbs seemed to be in the way.

I went straight from the dining-room to Mother's dressing-room,
but she wasn't there. I waited. I knew she would come.

And she came. She didn't look at me ; she sat down in a big
arm-chair in silence. I, too, was silent, suffering inexpressibly ; the
pain was so unlooked for, so senseless, so hopeless.

" I know everything, Volodia," she said at last.

I was relieved at the sound of her voice, but I couldn't take in her
words.

" What ? " I asked with an effort.

" I know and understand everything. You are in love. Some
people would say it was bound to come, but it mustn't. I won't
have it, I won't have it ! I have tried my utmost, and you won't
get away from me ! "

I regarded her mad outburst in blank desperation. Her anger
frightened me, but I did not pity her.

" What are you driving at ? I don't understand."

She grew calmer, and continued more quietly.

" You are in love with Martha Koreneva. I know you meet her in the garden. You go about half dazed. Do you want to marry her, by any chance ? I must tell you then that the lady of your choice is an eccentric person. She's corrupt since childhood. She's either a fool, or much too clever. Take care. You needn't have kept it from me ; I know just the same."

My thoughts were confused, my tongue would not obey me. I, in love with Marta ? It couldn't be ! I, want to marry her ? I, to marry ? Either one of us must be mad, or we are all mad. I began to stammer out confused words, scarcely knowing what I said. I spoke of the garden, the spring, and the apple trees—of Marta, saying that she was a living garden to me,—also of the sky and the wind. In despair I suddenly realised that Mother couldn't understand me unless she had felt what I had felt. . . .

An instinctive fear shot through my heart that I was alone, that Mother had deserted and hated me, and I couldn't be alone. I would have lied at that moment, if lying had been of any use. I had never lied before. Mother, I think, saw how I suffered.

" I see," she said, " that you never suspected anything ; but you must bear in mind, Volodia, that our relations are not such that I could ever be a passively affectionate mother. I have given up the whole of my life to you, and you must give up the whole of your life to me—every bit of it. That is what I have aimed at. I have never left you ; I made you myself, for myself. I may have done a wrong thing, but I don't care. There is justice in it. I am not capable of self-sacrifice ; besides, it is too late now. However you might love your wife, or your mistress, or how much she might love you, you could not live without me ! "

She spoke these words viciously and got up. I approached her, put my arms about her, and looked into her eyes.

" Don't torture me," I said. " I know I am yours ; I can't live without you. I don't want any wives ; I love no one. I don't understand why you . . . It was the garden and the flowers I cared about . . . and the music. . . . Forgive me."

She pressed me closely to herself and said, " You must promise me not to go into the garden, or to see Marta again. You are not in love with her yet, but . . . don't interrupt. . . . I feel it's impossible. . . . I know that you are weak enough to break your promise, my dear, but keep up your patience only for to-morrow. . . . Early on the day after, we shall go away. Eh ? "

To-morrow ! To-morrow the apple trees were coming into bloom !

" Silent ? Don't you want to ? "

Again she knit her brows.

I promised. It was painful, and I cried. I did so love the flowers.
. . . But I knew I could give them up for her. I thought, though
I did not understand why, that it was impossible to go. . . .

VIII

Preparations for the journey began in the morning. Our house-
keeper could not come with us, for my father was still ill. Mother
energetically did everything herself. I was as one dead, and sat
about with half-shut eyes. The sun looked in at my window,
bathing me in its warm rays, but it frightened me, so I got up and
pulled down the blind. It was not my sun.

Hours passed. The gnawing at my heart was dull and incessant.
I suffered, wondering, but submitted, having neither the strength
to choose nor to decide.

At the hour of sunset I wanted to go to Mother, to press closely
against her, and to sit with my eyes shut, losing all count of time.

I went into the drawing-room and looked out of the window.
The sun was large and round, and seemed as big as the side of the
grey hill. I almost ran into Mother's room. It was empty. I
passed through the anteroom ; no one was there. In the corridor
I came across a housemaid. " Where is your mistress ? " I asked.

" Madame has gone to order the carriage for to-morrow. She
asked me to tell you, sir, that afterwards she was going to the
Polotskys and would be back late. If you feel well enough, sir, she
wants you to go to the Polotskys about nine ; if not, she wants you
to go to bed early. . . ."

I didn't wait for the maid to finish. This was cruel, beyond my
strength to bear. Alone at that moment with my promise and an
aching desire to go into the garden once more and to feel the spring,
to hear what the apple trees would say. . . . I always submit without a struggle to things that are stronger than I, and then, too, I
submitted to the inevitable. I looked at the sun again with a wan
smile, and without so much as a glance back, or a moment of
hesitation, I went into the garden.

IX

When I had banged the gate behind me and taken a few steps
among the trees, I suddenly came to myself. I forgot everything.
Each moment my relief was greater and my gladness grew. The
mingled perfumes, various and many-toned, overwhelmed me. I
had come back to my friends, ashamed that I had deserted them
for so long. Unconsciously I walked to the end of the path.

Marta was there, not on the other side of the hedge, but on the seat. She sat with hands clasped on knees and looked at me severely.

"I'm sorry, Marta," I said, "the sun has set."

"Not yet, it is not beyond the horizon yet ; it is only behind the hill. It doesn't matter."

I sat down beside her. She was paler than usual, but her dress— I could no longer be mistaken—was not white, but had the faintest touch of pink about it.

"We must wait," Marta said. "They will open to-night. Do you notice how white the moon is ? It looks like a small cloud. When it gets brighter and the sky rises higher, they will open."

"What makes you like this, Marta ? " I asked. "You seem to be at one with them."

"You are the same, are you not ? I know you are. That is why I am glad you are with me and that I love you."

"I love you, too, Marta," I said. "I love you as I do the garden, as everything."

"As everything ? " she repeated, growing pensive.

The short twilight passed. The moon came out, casting a timid light on the path, shy and hazy. The scent of earth and anemones grew stronger. The strong branches of the apple trees threw their shadows, and everything that until then had been silent and motionless, murmured and moved. An almost imperceptible mist or vapour glided over the moonlight. The shadows crept along and left the flowers. The sky and the moon rose higher, higher, and colder.

A weird sensation of fear came over me. I waited intent, absorbed in my expectancy. Marta did not look at me. She felt cold.

She moved towards me, and unconsciously I put my arm about her, merely to be nearer to her.

"We must be very, very calm," she said, laying her white hand on mine. "We mustn't get excited. We must wait in perfect stillness. Without stillness in the heart, you can't get near *her*."

I knew she meant Nature.

"And we must be near to each other, eh, shall we ? " she continued hastily, looking into my eyes. "You and I . . . at one with her. . . ."

I had never felt so "at one with her " as I did then. This was happiness, if it could only last.

A faint, new scent came towards us. We both became aware of it at the same time, and knew in a moment whence it came.

"The first bud has opened," Marta said. "Don't look at it. Wait until others come. . . ."

She spoke in a whisper, solemnly. I pressed her closer against me. I wanted to speak, but she murmured, "Not a word," looking at me beseechingly. I was silent, and glad to be silent. I did not want more than I had ; this was happiness in itself.

A strong, new perfume filled the whole garden. The moon declined ; the apple trees did not grow dark ; they were white, but not with the moonlight.

At the moment when all around us grew clearer and colder, and the sky turned green and the dawn broke, I looked into Marta's face. She was sitting in the same attitude, closely pressed against me. She raised her eyes and smiled.

" It is time now," she said. " The sun is going to rise, and the apple trees will bloom."

A pang shot through my heart. I remembered. I turned pale ; my heart grew heavy and cold.

Marta looked at me anxiously.

" What is it ? "

" Marta, I am unhappy. . . . Pity me. . . . I must go away. . . ."

" Go away ? " she repeated slowly, without surprise. " So soon ? Stay a little longer. There is no hurry. Stay till they begin to fall."

" I can't, I can't. . . . It is not I. . . They want me. . . ."

" Oh, others," she said calmly. " They always spoil everything. Don't be unhappy. Go. I didn't want it to be so soon. . . ."

I looked into her eyes in despair. They were wide open and calm, but full of tears. Had she moved her lashes or her glance, the tears would have fallen.

I got up. She remained on the seat, but did not look at me.

" Good-bye," I said.

" Good-bye, don't forget. . . ."

" What ? "

" Everything. I shall not forget. We both know now how to live. . . ."

" Marta ! Others. . . ."

" Yes, others ! Aren't you able . . . can't you. . . . But you won't forget, will you ? "

I looked at her, then at the green sky, now quite bright ; I looked at the apple trees that seemed covered with snow.

" I won't forget," I said. " Good-bye."

She nodded. I went away.

X

What happened afterwards I will tell briefly, because it is too painful for me to linger over it. To revenge herself, Mother did it on purpose, I know. She grew worn and haggard that night, it is true, but it must have been from the violent hatred she felt towards me. Everything helped. I knew that she wouldn't forgive me, that she couldn't forgive me. I never said a word to her. I seemed to be dead. She ordered me to go away alone, and said that she would never forgive me, or see me again. She must have known that she wouldn't be able to bear this, and that she would forgive me when she saw that I couldn't live without her, so she died on purpose, not to break her word.

Some man approached me and gave me a long handshake. He asked me to bear up and said, " Your mother was a wonderful woman. What a shock her death must have been to you ! Your relations to each other were so wonderful. . . ."

I laughed in an unnatural way and said, " Yes, you are right." And this time it was I who shook the man's hand.

After the funeral I went away. What could have kept me there ? I did not ask about Marta and did not go into the garden. . . .

How many years have passed since then ! I have lost count of them. Sometimes I recall the night when the apple trees burst into bloom, and I sit down by the piano and play the little song, " Not a word, my friend, nor a sigh," and my heart grows lighter. But that happens very rarely. I seldom remember. . . . With every hour my life becomes more burdensome. I live because I haven't the strength even to die. I live in St. Petersburg, alone in this gloomy flat, give useless music lessons, and return aimlessly to my home. How much longer will it go on ?

There is a hook in the middle of the ceiling in the large room. I have already mentioned it. . . . Why shouldn't I take a cord from the trunk in the hall and throw it over the hook ? No one would know, particularly as it is night. . . . My old cook is asleep. What harm could there be in my throwing the cord over the hook ? I could take it down and put it back in the hall again if I chose. There would be no harm even if I were to make a noose. I wouldn't hang myself. I'm not bound to hang myself simply because I make a noose ! Hanging is so horrible, so ugly. . . . How far away I am from Marta ! Am I really going to ? . . . No, no ; it's only to try. No one need know. I will only try. . . .

SKITALITZ
(A. PETROV)
B. 1868

THE LOVE OF A SCENE-PAINTER

THE scene-painter Kostovsky had gone on the spree just at a time when he should not have done so : preparations were afoot for the presentation of a spectacular play, the success of which wholly depended upon the beauty of the set scenes. The posters were already displayed all over the city ; it was necessary to hurry forward the different arrangements and to paint the new scenery, and now something happened that the stage-manager had feared all along ; Kostovsky went on the spree.

This always occurred just at a time when he was indispensable. As if an evil spirit prompted him just at such times, and the forbidden liquor became more tempting than ever, he felt an unconquerable longing to experience a feeling of guilt, to act against the will of every one, against his own interests, but certainly not against the promptings of the Evil One, who had, for the time being, wholly taken possession of him.

His impetuous nature, full of talent, could not exist, it seemed, without powerful impressions ; and he found them only in carousing. The days of revelry were for him always full of interesting encounters and strange adventures peculiar only to himself. But as soon as he came to his senses and sobered up, he took to his work with a sort of furious energy : everything around him at such times was at a fever-heat of excitement, and he himself was burning with the fire of inspiration. Only because he was a wonderful scene-painter, a genius of his craft, he was not discharged. He hurt the reputation of the company with his scandals, adventures, and careless, soiled dress, his whole plebeian appearance ; but for all that, from his brush came the most exquisite, artistically executed scenes, for which the public often called the painter before the curtain, and about which the press remarked afterwards.

Behind the scenes the members of the company kept aloof from

67

Kostovsky, and no one wanted to be on intimate terms with him ; the chorus-singers " drank," too, but considered themselves of a higher class than the workman-painter, and did not want him in their society ; and the chorus-girls and ballet-dancers treated him like some sexless being, kept aloof from him, and looked at him with a grimace of disgust.　He, on his part, also took little interest in them.

He admired only Julia, a little ballet-dancer, and even her he loved only as an artist, when she danced on the stage enveloped in the rays of the limelight which he himself manipulated.　He liked the turn of her pretty little head, and he admired her, distinguishing her in the crowd of the other ballet-dancers by an exceptionally bright ray.　In real life he never spoke to her, and she pretended that she did not notice his attentions at all.

Living in a strange solitude, without love or friends, not having the sympathy of any one in the company, but being at the same time indispensable to it, he felt deeply injured, and caroused, as happened now when he was so badly needed.

The stout stage-manager stood on the stage after rehearsal and spoke about Kostovsky with the business-manager of the troupe, an elegant, dark-complexioned man of Hebrew type.

The broad, fat face of the stage-manager expressed wrath, anxiety, and sorrow.

" Well, just tell me, please," he spoke tearfully, while in his heart a storm was raging, " what am I to do now ?　What am I to do n-o-w ? "

And, crossing his fat hands helplessly on his paunch, he wrathfully and sorrowfully looked at his companion.

" Hoggishness, that is all ! " replied the business-manager.　" He started to drink on the steamer when we were coming here and has not sobered up yet.　And do you know, he fell into the sea on the way here !　That was a joke !　I was suddenly awakened by the cry : ' Man overboard ! '　I sprang to my feet. ' Who is it ? ' ' Kostovsky ! ' ' Ah, Kostovsky, and I thought it was—some one else ! '　And I went back to bed as if nothing had happened, because, in my opinion, Kostovsky is not a man, but a pig."

" How did he come to fall into the water ?　Was he drunk ? "

" Of course he must have been drunk.　He fell asleep on the deck and was forgotten.　The vessel lurched and he rolled over."

" Ho-ho-ho ! " the stage-manager's deep laugh rang out.

" He-he-he ! " chorused the business-manager in his thin, piping laugh.　" But what is still funnier, the sea would have none of him, and he was fished out even before he had time to become entirely awake.　A wonderful accident, really !　Even the sea refused to swallow such a rascal ! "

" But where is he now ? " inquired the stage-manager after he had ceased laughing, and a little softened by the story of Kostovsky's mishap at sea.

"Here. He is sobering up a little in a dressing-room. They searched for him all over town, and at last they found our friend in a tavern, engaged in a hot battle with some apprentice ; they did not even allow him to finish the fistic argument, but pulled them apart, and brought him here. Now he is nursing a beautiful black eye."

"Bring him in here, the rascal."

The young man ran briskly across the stage and vanished behind the scenes. And immediately the empty theatre loudly resounded with his piping voice :

"Kostovsky ! Kostovsky ! "

"He will come at once," the man said on returning, and winked his eye as if to say : "The fun will begin immediately."

A slow, unsteady step was heard approaching, and upon the stage appeared the man who had caused so much bad blood and ill-feeling, and whom even the sea would not accept.

He was of middle height, sinuous, muscular, and slightly round-shouldered, dressed in a coarse blue blouse full of paint spots and girded by a leather strap ; his trousers, bespattered with paint, were tucked into his high boots. Kostovsky had the appearance of a common workman, with long, muscular hands like those of a gorilla, and probably of great strength ; his far from good-looking but very characteristic face, with its prominent cheek-bones and long, reddish moustaches, breathed of power. From under knitted brows gloomily, and at the same time good-naturedly, looked out a pair of large blue eyes. The main peculiarity of this face was an expression of impetuousness and energy ; his left eye was embellished by a large discoloration—the mark of a well-aimed blow—and his coarse, reddish locks bristled out rebelliously in all directions. On the whole, Kostovsky impressed one as a bold, untamable being.

He bowed, at once shamefacedly and proudly, and did not offer any one his hand.

"What are you up to now, Kostovsky ? Eh ? " the stage-manager spoke in a freezingly cold manner. "The play is announced for to-morrow and we shall have to withdraw it ! What are you doing me all this injury for ? Is it honest of you ? Why are you drinking ? Just look what an ornament you have under the eye ! You ought to be ashamed of yourself ! "

Kostovsky took a step backward, thrust his long fingers through his locks, and suddenly became alight with a passionate, indomitable emotion :

"Mark Lukich ! " he exclaimed in a dull, husky, but convincing voice : "I drank ! That is true ! But now—— I will make everything necessary ! To-day is Saturday and there is no performance.

I shall not go out of here till to-morrow! I shall work the whole night through! I! I—— Great God!"

Kostovsky waved his hands in the air, and it seemed that he was suddenly possessed with a desperate energy. He longed for work as for expiation.

"But do you understand what there is to be done? Entirely new scenery must be painted, and well painted, too! Do you understand?"

"I shall paint it well, no fear of that!" exclaimed Kostovsky enthusiastically, once more running all his ten fingers through his coarse locks. After musingly pacing the stage for some moments, he stopped before the stage manager.

"Please tell me all about it, what sort of scenery is wanted, and for what it is needed," he said in a calmer voice.

"You see, this will be the second act. Two people are lost in the steppe at night. The place must be a dull, obscure wilderness; a terrible fear possesses them, and supernatural things take place there. You must paint for us this steppe; everything must be in it: the impression of remoteness, the darkness and clouds, and so vividly that a shiver of dread should run through the public."

"That is enough!" interrupted Kostovsky. "I shall paint you the steppe. I will work the whole night on the stage by lamplight and to-morrow everything will be ready. Have you the materials?"

"Everything is ready; all that is necessary is to work!" put in the business-manager.

But Kostovsky already felt the inspiration of the artist. He turned away from his superiors, no longer even aware of their presence, and standing in the centre of the stage he shouted in a powerful, imperious voice:

"Here, Pavel, hurry there! Vanka, here with you! Lively there, you sons of the devil, Kostovsky means to work now!"

The workman Pavel and the apprentice Vanka, a nimble, slouchy fellow, passionately devoted to the stage, came rushing in and immediately began to bustle about, spreading the enormous canvas and bringing forward the paints and brushes.

"Well," said the business-manager to the stage-manager, "thank God, he has come to his senses at last; we shall not be compelled now to withdraw the play! Let us go and have our dinner. He must not be interfered with now."

The whole night the stage was brightly illuminated, and in the empty theatre reigned the quiet of the grave. Only the tread of Kostovsky could be heard as, with his long brush in his hand, he continually approached and retreated from his canvas; all around stood pails and pots of paint.

He made rapid strides in his work. With a blue mark under his
eye, dirty with paint, with bristling hair and moustaches, he accom-
plished with his enormous brush a titanic kind of work. His eyes
were ablaze and his face looked inspired. He created.

At eleven o'clock in the morning the whole company, which had
gathered for the rehearsal, stood agape before the creation of
Kostovsky. The actors, chorus-singers, male and female, and the
ballet-dancers gazed at the enormous canvas from the stage and
afterward from the orchestra, and freely expressed their opinions.
The whole background of the stage was occupied by the gigantic
picture. It was the steppe. On the edge it was overgrown with
tall, dense burdocks and other steppe-grass, farther could be seen a
desolate-looking steppe-grave, thickly overgrown with grass, and
still farther unrolled the cheerless, dull steppe with a wonderful,
immeasurable perspective, a steppe out of the fairy-tales, out of the
times of knighthood—pathless and unpeopled. It seemed to the
onlookers that suddenly the famous Knight of the Russian fairy-
tale, Ilia Muromets, would appear from behind the mound and
would bawl out : " Is there a live man in this field ? " But the
bleak steppe was silent, terribly, gloomily silent ; looming up
against the sky were dark grave-mounds, and sinister, black, bushy
clouds were gathering. There was no end to these clouds and
grave-mounds, and the measureless vista of this steppe. The whole
picture breathed gloom and oppressed the soul. It seemed as if
something terrible would immediately take place, that the grave-
mounds and the clouds had a symbolic meaning, that they were in a
way animated. True, when one stepped up too close to Kostovsky's
scenery one could not make out anything : one saw a mere daub and
splash made with the large brush—hasty, bold strokes, and nothing
more. But the farther the spectator retreated from the canvas the
clearer appeared the picture of the enormous steppe, spiritualised by
a powerful mood, and the more attentively he looked at it, all the
more was he possessed by the feeling of uncanny dread.

" Well, what do you say to this ? " hummed the crowd. " Devilish
fellow, Kostovsky ! A real talent ! Just see what devilry he has
let loose ! "

" Well, that is nothing ! " he replied naïvely. " We are simple
workmen : when we work we work, but when once we are bent on
having a good time we take our fill—that is how we are
made ! "

They all laughed at him, but they spoke about him the whole
day : he had never succeeded so well as at this time.

And he continued at his work ; it seemed as if his energy had only
just now become aroused. While the rehearsal was going on, he
painted a Hindu Temple, shouted at his assistants, and in the heat

of inspiration even railed at the stage-manager, who wanted to draw his attention to something.

He was untamable, irresponsible, and great. Dirtier and more unkempt than ever, he strutted through his workroom at the back of the stage, painted the superbly beautiful, fantastic Temple, and lived through the happiness of inspiration. His whole appearance, excited by the sleepless night full of inspiration, was the embodiment of power and passionate energy : the pale face with the blue discoloration under the eye, the bristling locks, and the flaming eyes that seemed to emanate blue rays—all this showed that the inspiration of Kostovsky did not flash up for a moment, but that it burned long and steadily with an inexhaustible, even light.

He was wholly engrossed by his Temple, when he suddenly felt close to him some one's light step, and an exquisite perfume was wafted to where he stood. He turned around—before him stood Julia.

She wore the costume of a ballet-dancer, that is, almost no costume, as she had to dance at the rehearsal. She was a pretty little thing in pink tights, white satin slippers, and short gauze skirts ; her high, strong bosom heaved tranquilly and peacefully, and her creamy face smiled. Her black, almond-shaped, languid eyes looked tenderly and promisingly at Kostovsky. In the costume of a ballet-dancer she looked like a being just out of fairyland, and it was difficult to imagine a being so totally different from Kostovsky as was this fairy. She was all exquisite grace and litheness ; he, ungainly, dark, and big, stood before her abashed and confused, and gazed at her with delight and admiration ; the long brush was lowered to the floor to her feet.

Kostovsky forgot his work, and Julia broke into a ringing laugh, and, sparkling with her sharp little teeth, she came nearer to him with her light, graceful step, and, stretching out to him her beautiful little hand, she boldly said : " How do you do, Kostovsky ! "

.   .   .   .

Several months passed. The enormous opera-house was crowded to the doors. Behind the scenes they were hot at work, crowding one another, bustling and pushing. Through the curtain came the hum of the public and the solemn waves of the orchestra music.

The stage-carpenters ran about like men possessed, adjusting and shifting the scenery, and from somewhere in the darkness above rose and descended enormous canvases, the walls of temples, steeples, woods, and sea-waves.

All this work was superintended by Kostovsky. He was unrecognisable, his face looked years younger and brighter, his blue eyes were alight with joy and happiness, his feet were encased in shiny patent-leather boots, and he wore a well-fitting, elegant velvet jacket ; his fair locks were no longer bristling.

" Let down the bottom of the sea ! " he commanded in a ringing voice.

The enormous canvas on which was depicted the bottom of the sea was lowered. The painter retreated a few steps and once more looked lovingly at the " sea bottom." This was his latest creation.

" Listen, Pavel ! " he shouted, " when the mermaids begin to swim, you will let Julia come first and lower than all the rest ; let her down to the very bottom ! "

" It shall be done ! "

At last everything was ready for the mermaids to swim over the bottom of the sea. Kostovsky was already perched high, with the electric reflector turned on the stage ; he himself had to manage the lighting up of the scenery and the actors. The Bottom of the Sea became suffused with a tender, poetic light. This greenish-silvery light seemed to penetrate the water as if with the bright sunlit day above. And here at the bottom everything lived knowing no light. In the distance stood a coral-reef, and everywhere half-alive vegetation greedily stretched its branches over the water, and all around floated slimy jelly-fish.

Underneath, the first thing to meet the eye was the yawning mouth of a submarine cave, from which were thrust out the arms of a hideous, enormous devil-fish that, without moving, glared out of its two green eyes.

And from amid this primitive, abnormal world appeared a wonderfully beautiful woman with flowing hair and bare shoulders, with the form of a fish below the waist, covered with shining, silvery scales. The loveliness of her head and the beauty of her shoulders were enhanced by the ugliness of the submarine world.

She swam like a fish, easily and gracefully, turning and twisting, her scales sparkling and glittering ; she was followed by another mermaid, a whole school.

Lighted by the rays of the reflector, at the will of Kostovsky, they became marvellous, fairy-like beauties.

But they were all eclipsed by one. She swam lower than all, and was distinguished from all by the radiance of her beauty. She was lighted better and more alluringly than the rest, the tenderest rays of the reflector warmly and lovingly fell upon her, ran after her, and lovingly caressed her graceful body, adding a seductive expression to her face and making her eyes shine like stars. She seemed to be created of light, and this light changed with every moment, and she changed with it, garbed in thousands of different tints. A veritable queen of the deep.   She felt that the artist-enchanter had bestowed on her a marvellous loveliness, that the delighted public was ready to break forth into a storm of applause in honour of this beauty, and, swimming close to the painter, she gratefully waved her sparkling fish-tail, over which, by the will of the enamoured magician, suddenly fell a shower of many-coloured diamonds.

She swam behind the scenes, and he, rising on tip-toe and smiling happily, sent her an airy kiss from behind the reflector.

All in the company knew of this love affair behind the scenes : Julia always left the theatre in the company of Kostovsky, they stayed at the same hotel, and his room adjoined hers.   Kostovsky was always with her, enjoying to the full the pleasure that the contemplation of her beauty afforded him, while she willingly allowed him to pay court to her.   He followed her like a faithful dog, and waited long and patiently at the door of the women's dressing-room while she leisurely removed the make-up from her face, dressed, and chatted with the other girls.

This time, after the conclusion of the performance, he had to wait particularly long at the foot of the stairs ; one after another the closely wrapped little figures came down the stairs and went off with the men who were awaiting them, just as the scene-painter was awaiting Julia.   But *she* was not to be seen.

Sad and troubled, Kostovsky stood at his place, looking about him indifferently, and continually throwing expectant glances at the door of the dressing-room.   And the door opened less and less often, as almost all the women had already departed.

At last Rosa, a vivacious Jewish chorus girl, came out.   " What are you standing here for ? " she drawled, lifting her brows in surprise and making a sly grimace.   " I am the very last one, there 's no one else, and Julia left long ago.   It seems you did not notice when she went out."

" What, is she gone ? " asked Kostovsky, and on his face appeared a pained expression.

" Ha, ha, ha ! " Rosa's silvery laugh rang out ; " very simply, she left before the end of the performance in the company of her new admirer, and you, my sweet one, have tired her long ago ! "

The scene-painter stepped back and caught himself by the head. " It is not true ! " he said in a dull voice.

" Well, I like that ! " Rosa said excitedly, " and it is your own doing, too !   She only wished to be pushed ahead.   You always light her up so that the whole front row is second to her !   She has made a career for herself, and does not need *you* any longer."   And Rosa ran laughingly down the stairs.

Kostovsky stood long motionless in the same place, and, enveloped in the quiet and darkness of the empty theatre, he felt that, little by little, then stronger and stronger, his breast was filled with acutest pain.

When Kostovsky knocked at the door of Julia's room she received him very coldly. Her moist eyes looked indifferently and tranquilly from under her thick, black eyelashes ; her black hair, carelessly pinned, lay like a luxurious crown, and two thick curls fell over her full cheeks. She wore a wide kimono of some cheap material, and light slippers.

" Julia," whispered Kostovsky, breathless with excitement.

" Sit down ! " she said carelessly, not noticing anything special in his appearance, and added, " and try to occupy yourself with something. I really haven't any time to entertain you."

" Julia ! "

She half-leaned upon the bed and became wholly absorbed in her book.

He was irritated by this woman's unnecessary artfulness ; why use these artifices, which offended him the more, because she could easily tell him outright and settle it ?

" Julia, you speak to me as to a visitor who has to be entertained ? Why this ceremony ? "

" There is no ceremony about it ! " she replied in a displeased tone. " It—simplifies our relations, that is all : every one occupies himself —with what he pleases. I am—reading. And you occupy yourself with something else, and if you feel ennui—go away."

She was driving him out.

Kostovsky was beside himself with rage at this " simplifying of relations."

" Listen to me," he said, in a voice full of irritation. " I wish to speak to you, and will not wait till you finish reading."

She did not reply, and, half reclining on the bed, she continued looking at the open book. A painful silence ensued.

Kostovsky sat at the table and quietly gazed at Julia. Leaning on her elbows on the pillow, she had thrown herself into a graceful, kittenish pose ; her little feet encased in their tiny, light slippers, impishly hid under the folds of her kimono, and from their hiding-place teased Kostovsky. The lovely curves of her body showed through the thin dress, the wide sleeves left visible her chubby arms to the elbow ; and she was, as a whole, so sweet and graceful that Kostovsky, hating her at this moment, longed to take her in his arms.

He turned his eyes away from her. The room was poorly furnished—a cheap hotel room, lighted by electricity. Near the door stood the wardrobe with her costumes, in the centre the table, and near the window the dresser and a mirror. On a rack close to the entrance into the room hung her plush jacket, trimmed with tiny cats' paws. He looked long and with hatred at this jacket with its cats' paws, and recalled how amiably she used to meet him before, forcing him into a chair and smoothing his bristly locks tenderly, and how pleasant it was to feel the tender touch of the little hand.

She quickly flung away her book, and angrily rose from the bed. " You have nothing to speak to me about ! " she exclaimed, reddening. " Everything has been said already ! It is time to end this spoony love affair, this sentimental drivel ! "

" Spooniness—sentimental drivel," he repeated bitterly. " Julia ! What has come between us ? "

" There is nothing between us, nothing could be ! " she energetically declared. " We have nothing in common—nothing whatsoever—and—we must put an end to our acquaintance ! "

She gave the table a push and sat down in the darkest corner of the room, looking at him from there with her large, black eyes. Her eyes had always the same expression ; no matter at whom they looked, they seemed to be inviting and promising something without the knowledge of their possessor. Spurning him, she at the same time lured him on.

" I understand ! " he spoke sadly, and pushed his chair close to her. " You wish to part with me ; they say you have another—some one from the first row of the orchestra. Well, let us part. But why all this subterfuge and why quarrel ? I do not wish that all this should end so badly—with a quarrel. I wish at least to keep the memory. But, Julia, know that all those—from the first row —despise you—humiliate you—love in you only the flesh. And I —— Why, I—l-o-v-e you, the devil take you, accursed one ! "

He grasped her arm above the elbow and shook her with his large paws.

" Ah ! How rude ! He abuses me ! Let me go ! Let me go, I say ; you will dislocate my arm ! Ruffian ! "

She longed to quarrel with him. And he, on his part, felt a flood of ferocious wrath, a passionate longing to tear, lacerate, beat, and throw her out.

He grasped her arms still tighter. His eyes turned a greenish colour, his teeth gave out a grating sound.

" Ai ! " she cried. But he fell on his knees before her.

" Sweetest, dearest, my golden one, my sun, my joy ! You are my all ; all my thoughts, all my feelings, everything is for you, from you, and about you ! Oh, I am rude ; I am a brute, but I love you ! Without you there is no life for me ; I shall again sink to the bottom from which you raised me ! Well, darling, well, my happiness, forgive me. You see I kiss your hands, your dress. Forgive ! "

And on his bent knees this big, powerful man caught the tiny hands of the tiny woman and kissed them, kissed her dress, and wept.

When he lifted his head he suddenly caught her glance directed toward him, a strange, attentive glance.   In this glance of her moist, black eyes there was no love, nor pity for him ; nor even contempt, but something offensive, resembling curiosity, but more heartless than curiosity.   It was the curiosity of a vivisectionist, the curiosity he exhibits when dissecting a live rabbit, or that of a naturalist when he sticks his pin through a rare beetle, and looks on at its contortions.   He even now interested her, but only as something primitive, original : his sharp transitions from rudeness to tenderness, the strangeness of the declaration, the sudden fits of ferocious rage only to humble himself before her and to weep a moment later —all this was very interesting.

But Kostovsky's mind was suddenly illumined as if by lightning : he understood all at once the real relation of Julia toward him, and felt that he had received a deadly wound at her hands, that she was only interested in him, but she had never loved him, could not love him ; that she was a being from a world other than his ; that he was a total stranger to her.   The words died away in his heart.   He grew silent, caught his hat, and without another glance at Julia rushed out of the room and the hotel.

Kostovsky found himself suddenly in a dirty dram-shop, where his steps had almost unconsciously led him.   He had not drank for a long time, but now he felt a terrible necessity for the dram-shop, the noise, the clinking of the glasses, and the smell of bad vodka.

He sat in a corner of the dram-shop, alone, at a small table.   Before him stood a large bottle of vodka and the noxious side-dishes peculiar to such resorts.   The dirty table-cloth was stained with vodka and beer, and the paraffin hanging-lamp dimly lighted the room, filled with tipsy people.   They were all bawling, drinking, and clinking their glasses ; the pale-faced waiters ran about, serving the drinks, and in the adjoining room cracked the billiard-balls, and some one of the players, whenever he hit the ball, sang out in a merry tenor voice a popular song : " Wherever I go, or stroll, I see only Ju-li-a, only Ju-li-a."

" Oh, the devil ! " muttered Kostovsky, pouring out the tenth glass, and gloomily draining it.   He was irritated because, even here in the dram-shop, *she* was persecuting him.   He had decided to forget her for evermore : he hated and despised her, and did not wish to remember her at all.

The dram-shop enveloped him in its sounds and smells, and eased his suffering with its well-known colouring of something intimate, free, something he had lived through in the past.

But little by little his thoughts withdrew from the dram-shop, and *she* appeared once more, and would no longer leave him.

She was now in the costume of a mermaid, with the body of a fish covered with silver scales, radiant under the many-coloured rays of the reflector, seductively beautiful. She lured him after her with enticing smile, and swam away far, far into the boundless sea. And the man in love with a mermaid felt that he was perishing, that he could never more return to his former carelessness, power, and strength of soul. And he recollected his former life before he knew the mermaid and her kisses. True, he had caroused then, but that was not drunkenness, it was dare-devilry, his power was seeking a free outlet. His heart was athirst for dash and merriment. So, like the legendary fisherman, he had found in his net a mermaid. He lifted her in his arms, kissed and caressed her, and—good-bye to careless life ! The man was ruined by the mermaid !

" Oh, the devil ! " Kostovsky roared, draining his glass, and thinking thereby to drive off the troublesome thoughts ; but *she* continued to torture him pitilessly, appearing before him every moment in another costume, now as a fairy, a shepherdess, and again as a mermaid ; or she swam close to him in a wide homely gown, and her thick, black curls fell over her forehead and upon her full, pink cheeks. And her whole figure was as if flooded by radiant, poetic rays.

" And when with friends I drain the wine-red bowl, I see before me none but Julia "—came from the billiard-room the merry tenor voice. Gradually the dram-shop filled with a mist, through which the lights burned very low, and the noise of the revellers sounded indistinctly and seemed far off, resembling far-away sea-breakers. The dram-shop filled with sea-waves, which rose and fell. And from the waves swam out a mermaid who was laughingly luring Kostovsky.

For a moment he lifted his head, and again saw before him the bottle, poured out another glass, and drained it ; the mist became denser, rolled before his eyes. But he still saw, rising amidst the wine-vapours high over the bottle, her poetic, sweet image.

·   ·   ·   ·   ·   ·   ·

When Kostovsky was at last found, after a search of several days in the different dram-shops of the city, and brought to his senses, the opera, with its sea-bottom and mermaids, was again produced.

Now Kostovsky once more looked his old self : the unkempt, carelessly dressed scene-painter was even more gloomy than before ; his locks bristled and his moustaches stood on end worse than ever.

He stood gloomily on his platform behind the scenes, lighting up the mermaids with the rays from his reflector. His soul was filled with cold and gloom and obduracy. Now he himself kept aloof from everybody, hated the whole troupe, and lived alone.

And the mermaids swam over the sea-bottom.

But it was no longer the former radiant, poetic light which shone upon them ; the light which the artist threw upon them now was a sad, pale light, and under its rays they seemed inanimate, sickly, and half dead.

But when Julia appeared, swimming as formerly lower than the rest, sinister, dark-blue rays came pouring upon her, and she looked more like a fury than a mermaid. Her face was blue, horrible, with black lips and black cavities instead of eyes, and the slippery fish-body was as if covered with a loathsome slime.

A mutter of disgust ran through the theatre.

And the painter also lit up with the same light the sea-bottom with all its monsters ; and like a symbol of nightmare and sadness the green-eyed devil-fish came out of the darkness, and the noxious octopuses began to move around.

The blue body of Julia seemed to swim in this loathsome mass, and at last blended with it into one living, monstrous, deformed creature.

The scene-painter slowly turned the glasses of the reflector, gazed upon the work of the light he had created, and it seemed to him that he had destroyed for ever the former charm of the woman, and that she whom he had loved had never been beautiful ; and it seemed to him that only now he saw her in her real light, and that she only became divinely beautiful when lighted by the bright rays of his love.

MAXIM GORKY
B. 1868

TWENTY-SIX MEN AND A GIRL

THERE were twenty-six of us—twenty-six living machines shut up in a damp cellar, where from morning till night we kneaded dough and made it into krendels and sushkas. The window of our cellar looked on to a brick area, green and mouldy with the moisture. The window was protected from the outside by a close net of iron bars, and the light of the sun could not penetrate through the panes covered with flour dust. Our employer had bars placed in front of the window so that we should not be able to give a piece of his bread to a passing beggar, or to one of our comrades who might be out of work and starving. Our employer called us rogues and gave us half-rotten tripe to eat for dinner instead of meat. It was close and stuffy for us cooped up in that stone box, beneath the low, heavy ceiling covered with steam and cobwebs, and within the thick walls, grimy with dirt and mildew. We would rise at five o'clock in the morning, only half awake, and at six, dull and listless, we were already seated at the table making krendels out of the dough that had been prepared for us by our comrades while we were asleep. And the whole day, from early morning till ten o'clock at night, some of us would sit at the table rolling the yielding dough with our hands, while the others were kneading the flour with the water. And the whole day long the simmering water in the pot where the krendels were cooking sang low and sadly, and the baker's shovel scraped harshly and viciously against the oven as the pieces of boiled dough were thrown on to the hot bricks. And from morning till night the wood burned in the stove, and the red reflection of the flames danced over the walls of the bakehouse, as though silently mocking us. The giant stove looked like the misshapen head of some fairy-tale monster—it seemed to thrust itself out of the ground, open its broad jaws, full of living fire, and breathe heat upon us, and look at our endless work with its two dark ventilators over the oven. These two ventilators were like eyes—the dispassionate, pitiless eyes of a monster.   They always looked at us with the same dark gaze, as though they were weary of seeing the eternal slaves, and without expecting anything human of us, scorned us with the cold scorn of wisdom.

Day after day, in the flour dust, in the dirt we brought in with our feet from without, in the hot heavily laden atmosphere, we rolled the dough into krendels, moistening it with our sweat.   We hated our work with a poignant hatred and never ate what we made with our hands, preferring krendels made from rye dough.   Sitting at the long table facing each other—nine facing nine,—mechanically, through the long hours, we would move our hands and fingers, and were so used to the work that we had no need to follow our movements.   And we had looked at one another for so long that each of us knew every wrinkle on the face of his comrade.   We had nothing to talk about, we had exhausted every topic of conversation, and were silent most of the time, unless we abused each other—one can always abuse a man, especially if that man be a comrade.   But even that happened rarely.   How can a man offend you if he be half dead, if he is like a stone, if all his feelings have been crushed out of him by the weight of his labours ?   But silence is very painful to men like us who have said all there is to say—it is only for those who have not yet begun to speak that silence is simple and easy. . . . But sometimes we would sing, and our song would begin in this way : in the midst of our work one of us would heave a deep sigh, like the sigh of a tired horse, and then begin softly humming one of those slow airs, the sweet plaintive motive of which always lightens the heart of the singer.   One of us would sing and the rest would at first listen silently ; the song would tremble and die away beneath the dark ceiling of our cellar, like a tiny camp-fire in the steppes on a damp autumn night, when the grey sky spreads over the earth like a leaden roof.   Another voice would join in—and two voices would now be floating softly and plaintively in the thick atmosphere of our over-crowded pit.   And suddenly, several more voices would join, and the song would rise like a wave ; it would grow louder and louder and almost seem to move the heavy grey walls of our stone prison. . . .

The whole twenty-six would be singing, our powerful harmonious voices filling the bakehouse until it seemed too small to hold so much sound.   The song would beat against the stone walls, wailing and moaning, filling the heart with a sweet, stirring pain, opening old wounds and awakening despair.   The singers would sigh deeply and heavily ; one man would suddenly stop in his song and sit for a while listening to his comrades, then again his voice would mingle with the general wave.   Or one would cry out desperately, " Ah ! " then go on singing with his eyes closed, the rich wave of sound perhaps seeming to him like some distant path, a broad sunlit path along which he himself was walking.

But the flame was still flickering in the stove, the baker was still scraping with his shovel, the water was still simmering in the pot, and the reflection of the fire was still dancing on the walls in silent mockery. And in other men's words we sang of our dull grief and of the leaden despair of living men deprived of the sun, the despair of the slave.

Thus we lived, the twenty-six of us, in the cellar of the large stone house, and our burden was as heavy as though the whole weight of the three storeys of the house were resting on our very shoulders. But we had something else that was good besides the singing— something that we loved and that perhaps took the place of the sunshine we lacked. On the second floor of our house was a gold-embroiderer's shop, and in it, amongst the many girls who worked there, lived Tania, the sixteen-year-old maid-servant. Every morning her little rosy face with the sparkling blue eyes would peep through the little window of the door leading into the passage, and her caressing, ringing voice would call out to us :

" Prisoners ! have you any little krendels for me ? "

We would all turn at this clear, joyous sound so familiar to us and gaze good-humouredly at the little maiden face, smiling so sweetly. We liked to see the little nose pressed against the glass, the tiny white teeth, shining between the rosy lips, parted in a smile. We all rushed to open the door for her, tumbling over each other. And she would come in—the gay little thing—and stand before us, smiling and holding up her apron. Her long-nut-brown plait that was jerked over her shoulder lay across her breast. And we, black, dirty, misshapen, would look up at her (the threshold being higher than the floor by several steps) and bid her good-morning in specially chosen words we kept only for her. When talking to her our very voices grew softer and our jokes came more easily. There was something special in everything we did for her. The baker would thrust his shovel into the oven and take out the brownest krendels he could find, which he deftly threw into Tania's apron.

" Take care the master does not catch you ! " we always cautioned her. She would laugh roguishly, call out gaily, " Good-bye, prisoners ! " and vanish like a little mouse.

That was all. . . . But long after she was gone we enjoyed talking about her to each other ; we said the very same things we had spoken yesterday and the day before, because both she and we and everything around us was the same as yesterday and the day before. It is hard and painful for a man when nothing around him changes, and if it does not have the effect of destroying his soul utterly, then the longer he lives the more painful becomes the monotony of his surroundings. In our talk of women, our coarse, shameless words would sometimes disgust even ourselves. It may be that the women we knew were not worthy of other words. But we never spoke badly of Tania. Not a single man among us would have dared to touch her with his hand, and we never made a loose joke in her presence. Perhaps it was because she never stayed long enough with us, for, like a falling star, she would flash out for a moment and vanish, or it may be that she was so small and pretty, and beauty inspires respect even in the coarsest of men. And besides, though the hard work had deprived us of will-power, we were nevertheless men, and needed something to worship. We had no one better than Tania, no one but Tania ever paid the least attention to us inhabitants of the cellar, though there were scores of people in the house. And the most important thing of all is that we looked upon her as belonging to us, a being that seemed to exist solely by virtue of our krendels. We made it a duty to keep her supplied with them, piping hot ; it became a daily offering to our idol, an almost holy rite, that bound us closer to her day by day. In addition to the krendels we used to give Tania advice, such as that she ought to put on warmer clothes, that she ought not to run quickly up the stairs, nor to carry heavy bundles of wood. She would listen to us with a smile, reply to our words with a laugh, and never take the least notice of what we said. This in no way offended us ; we were merely anxious to show her that we cared for her.

Frequently she would come to us with some request, such as asking us to open the heavy cellar door or chop some wood, and with a kind of pride and joy we would do all that she demanded of us.

But when one of us asked her to mend his one and only shirt, she sniffed disdainfully and said, " What an idea ! as if I could ! "

We laughed at the bold man and never made any further demands on her. We loved her, and that is saying much. A man always wants to bestow his love on some one, even though he sometimes spoils and sullies his love, even though he may ruin the life of another, because he loves without respecting the beloved. We could not help loving Tania because we had no one else to love.

Sometimes one of us would begin to criticise our attitude in this fashion :

" Why do we spoil the girl ? What is there in her after all ? We seem to take a lot of trouble over her."

The man who had dared to speak thus was soon rudely cut short. We had to love some one and we had found some one to love. The being we loved—the whole twenty-six of us—must be apart' and sacred for each ; he who violates this thought is our enemy. Perhaps the thing we loved was not really good, but, then, there were twenty-six of us, and because of that we wanted the thing that was dear to us respected by all alike.

Love is no less oppressive than hate ; perhaps that is why some clever people maintain that hate is more flattering than love. But if it is as they say, why do they run after us ?

Besides the krendel bakery our employer had a bread bakery in the same house, separated from our pit by a single wall. There were four bread bakers, but they avoided us, considering their work cleaner than ours. They never came to visit us, and made fun of us whenever we met in the yard. Neither did we visit them. Our employer forbade us to do so, fearing that we might steal some milk rolls. We did not like the bread bakers because we envied them ; their work was easier than ours, they were better paid and better fed than we were, they had a larger, brighter room than ours and were all such robust, clean-looking fellows, while we were sorry, yellow creatures. Three of us suffered from disease, one was covered with scabs, another completely deformed by rheumatism. In leisure hours and in the holidays the bread bakers would put on their smart pea-jackets and squeaky boots (a couple of them had concertinas too) and go out walking in the park, while we would wear our dirty rags, remnants of boots or bast shoes, and the police would not let us into it. No wonder we did not like the bread bakers !

One day it came to our ears that one of the bread bakers had got drunk, and that the master had sacked him and engaged another man. This man was reputed to be a soldier who went about in a satin waistcoat and wore a gold watch chain. We were curious to see this wonder and kept running out into the yard one after another in the hope of catching a glimpse of him.

But he came to us of himself. With a kick he opened the door, and, standing on the threshold, smiling, he said to us :

" God be with you. Good-morning, mates ! "

The icy air, coming in a dense cloud at the door, played about his legs ; he stood on the threshold looking down at us, and his yellow teeth shone beneath his fair, well-twisted moustache. He certainly wore some peculiar waistcoat of a bluish shade, embroidered with flowers ; it seemed to shine and sparkle, and the buttons were of some red stone. The chain, too, was there.

He was handsome, this soldier, tall and robust, with rosy cheeks, and a clear kindly expression in his bright blue eyes. On his head was a starched cap, and from beneath his clean apron that had not a single crease in it there peeped the pointed toes of his highly polished boots.

Our own baker deferentially requested him to close the door, which he did slowly, and then began asking us questions about our employer. Vying with each other, we told him that our master was a sweater, a scoundrel, a blackguard—everything, in fact, that it behoves one to say of an employer, but it is impossible to set it down here.

The soldier listened, curling his moustache and looking at us with his bright tender eyes. . . .

" Are there many girls here ? " he asked suddenly.

Some of us began to laugh deferentially, while others with knowing grimaces explained to him that there were nine girls in all.

" Do you make the most of your opportunities ? " the soldier asked with a wink.

Again we laughed, a soft, confused laugh. . . . Many of us would have liked to make the soldier believe that we were fellows just as smart as he was, but not one of us could do it ; not one of us knew how. Some one even confessed as much, saying softly :

" That is not for the likes of us. . . ."

" Yes, it would be difficult for you, certainly," the soldier remarked with assurance, looking us up and down. " It's hardly in your line. You have no bearing . . . no figures, no presence, so to speak. A woman is particular about a man's appearance. His figure must be good and he must be well dressed. And then a woman admires strength in a man. He should have an arm, like this, see ! "

The soldier pulled his right hand out of his pocket and showed us his arm, bare to the elbow. It was a white powerful arm, covered with shining, golden hair.

" The leg, the chest—everything must be firm. And, again, a man must be decently dressed to show off his good looks. Take me, for instance ; all the women love me. I don't raise a finger to beckon them, but they throw themselves at my head, five at a time. . . ."

He sat down on a sack of flour and went on telling us how all the women loved him and how gallantly he treated them. At last he went away, and when the door shut after him with a squeak we were silent for a long time, thinking of the soldier and of his tales. But suddenly we all began to speak, and it was soon evident that we had taken a fancy to him one and all. Such a nice simple fellow he was—he came and sat and talked to us. No one ever came to see us, or spoke to us in such a friendly way. And we talked of him and of his future conquests among the embroidresses, who, when meeting us outside, would sidle by us or walk straight at us as though unaware of our presence. And always we never more than dared to admire them, out of doors or when they passed our window, in the winter dressed in peculiar coats and caps, and in the summer in hats with many coloured flowers and parasols in their hands. Still, among ourselves, we talked of these girls in such a way that had they heard us they would have gone mad with shame and vexation.

"I hope he won't spoil our Tanushka!" the baker remarked suddenly with concern.

None of us spoke, struck by his words. We had forgotten about Tania ; the soldier had hidden her from us, as it were, with his big handsome figure. Then a dispute arose, some maintaining that Tania would not degrade herself so far, others that she would not be able to resist the soldier, and a third lot declared that if the soldier began to worry Tania we should have to break his ribs for him. At last we all decided to watch Tania and the soldier carefully, and to warn the girl against him. This ended the dispute.

A month went by ; the soldier baked his bread, walked with the embroidresses, often came to visit us, but never spoke about his conquests among the girls ; he would only curl his moustache and lick his lips. Tania came to us every morning for " the little krendels," and was just as sweet, merry, and friendly to us as usual. We tried to talk to her about the soldier ; she called him a " goggle-eyed calf " and other funny names, and this allayed our fears.

We were proud of her, seeing how the embroidresses ran after the soldier. Tania's attitude towards him seemed to raise us all, and we, as though responsible for her attitude, began to assume a scornful air in our relations to the soldier. And we grew to love Tania still more, and still more gladly and good-naturedly did we greet her in the morning.

But one day the soldier came to us a little the worse for drink, and, sitting down, began to laugh, and when we asked him what he was laughing about, he explained.

"Two of the girls have quarrelled over me. . . . How they did knock each other about ! ha, ha ! One seized the other by the hair and threw her on the floor in the passage and sat on her . . . ha, ha, ha ! They scratched and tore . . . you would have died ! Why can't a woman fight fair ? Why must she always scratch and pull ? "

He sat on the bench, robust and clean and joyous—sat there and laughed. We were silent. We did not like him just then.

" How the women do run after me, to be sure ! It's really funny. I've only to wink and they come—the devil ! "

He raised his white hands covered with the shining hair and

slapped them down on his knees. He looked at us with such a pleasantly surprised air, as though he himself were frankly astonished at the happiness he found in his success with women. His fat rosy cheeks shone with self-satisfaction, and he kept on licking his lips.

Our baker gave a quick angry scrape with his shovel over the hearth and suddenly said with derision :

" It doesn't take much to cut down a little sapling, but you try a big pine tree."

" Is that for me ? " asked the soldier.

" Yes, you."

" What do you mean ? "

" Nothing. . . . It slipped out."

" But wait. What is it all about ? What pine ? "

Our baker did not reply, but kept on quickly plying his shovel, putting in the boiled krendels, taking out the baked ones and throwing them noisily on the floor, where the boys were busy stringing them together. He seemed to have forgotten both the soldier and the conversation. The soldier, however, suddenly fell into a state of restlessness. He rose and walked up to the stove, very nearly knocking himself against the handle of the shovel the baker was flourishing wildly in the air.

" But you must tell me what you mean. I am hurt. Not a single girl can resist me, I assure you, and you say such offensive things."

He was genuinely hurt ; it may be that besides the capacity for leading women astray there was nothing else he could be proud of ; perhaps this capacity was the only living thing about him, the only thing that enabled him to feel himself a man.

There are some men in whom the best and highest in life appears only as a kind of malady of the soul or the body which they carry about with them all their lives, living by it, suffering from it, complaining about it, and by their complaints attracting the attention of others towards them. It is their only means of gaining the sympathy of their fellows ; they have no other. Deprive them of this malady, cure them and they will be unhappy, because you take away from them their only hold on life and leave them quite empty. A man's life is sometimes so empty that he involuntarily prizes his vice and lives by it ; one might almost say that men are often vicious from sheer boredom.

The soldier was offended, and again demanded loudly of our baker :

" You must tell me what you mean ! "

" Shall I ? " the baker turned to him suddenly.

" Well ? "

" Do you know Tania ? "

" Yes, what then ? "

" Well, try her, that's all ! "

" I ? "

" Yes, you."

" Pooh ! That's as easy as winking ! "

" We shall see."

" You will see ! ha, ha ! "

" She will send you . . ."

" Give me a month."

" What a braggart you are, soldier ! "

" Give me two weeks ! I'll show you ! And who is Tania, anyway ? Pooh ! "

" Get away . . . you hinder me ! "

" Two weeks and it's done. You are a . . ."

" Get away, I tell you ! "

Our baker was seized with a sudden fit of fury and brandished his shovel in the air. The soldier edged away from him quickly, in astonishment. He looked at us in silence for a moment and then said quietly and maliciously :

" Very well." Then he left us.

We were so interested in the dispute that none of us had spoken, but when the soldier had gone, a noisy animated conversation arose among us.

Some one called out to the baker :

" It's a nasty job you've started, Pavel ! "

" You get on with your work ! " the baker replied angrily.

We felt that the soldier had been touched to the quick and that Tania was threatened by danger. Yet, in spite of this, we were seized by an agreeable burning curiosity to know what would happen. Would Tania resist the soldier ? And almost all cried out confidently :

" Tania ! Of course she will ! It would take more than the bare hands to get Tania ! "

We were seized by a passionate desire to test the strength of our goddess. With intensity we tried to convince each other that our goddess was invincible and would come out of the ordeal victorious. It seemed to us now that we had not sufficiently provoked the soldier. We feared that he might forget the dispute, and resolved to wound his vanity still further. Our life from that day became peculiarly tense and exciting. We argued with each other all day ; our brains seemed to have grown clearer and we had more and more to talk about. It seemed to us that we were playing some game with the devil and that the stake on our side was Tania. And when we heard from the bread bakers that the soldier had begun " courting " Tania, such a painfully sweet sensation came over us, and life seemed to us so interesting that we did not even notice when our employer, taking advantage of the general excitement, added another fourteen poods of dough to the day's work. The whole day the name of Tania did not leave our lips. And every morning we waited for her with a kind of peculiar impatience. Sometimes it seemed to us that she wanted to come right into our room—and that would not have been the old Tania, but some one quite new and strange to us.

However, we told her nothing of the current dispute. We asked her no questions and treated her kindly and considerately as usual. But something new and strange had crept into our feelings towards her, and this new thing was a poignant curiosity, sharp and cold as a steel knife.

" The time is up, mates ! " our baker announced one morning, stopping in his work.

We knew quite well without his reminding us, but nevertheless we all started.

" Look at her well . . . she is coming soon," our baker continued. And some one remarked sorrowfully : " As if you could see that with the eye ! "

And again a heated noisy discussion arose among us. To-day we should know at last how pure was the vessel into which we had poured all that was best in us. This morning, for the first time, we realised that we were really playing a great game, that this test of her purity might end by depriving us of our goddess altogether. We had heard how persistently the soldier had been pursuing Tania during the whole fortnight, but not one of us had thought of asking her how she behaved towards him. And she continued coming each morning for the krendels and was just the same to us as ever.

On this day, too, we soon heard her voice :

" Prisoners ! Here I am ! . . ."

We opened the door, and when she came in, contrary to our usual practice, we greeted her in silence. With all our eyes fixed on her we did not know what to say or what to ask of her. We stood before her, a dark, silent crowd. She was evidently taken aback at this unaccustomed reception. We saw her suddenly turn pale ; she grew uneasy, and shifting about in her place asked in a depressed tone of voice :

" Why are you . . . like this ? "

" And you ? " the baker demanded of her solemnly without taking his eyes off her.

" What about me ? "

" Nothing."

" Well, be quick and give me the krendels ! "

Never before had she hurried us.

"You've got plenty of time!" the baker said, without moving from the spot, or taking his eyes off her face.

But she suddenly turned and vanished through the door.

The baker took up his shovel and said quietly, as though addressing himself to the stove:

"I suppose it's done! That blackguard of a soldier! The scoundrel!"

Pushing past each other like a flock of sheep, we sat down silently at the table and lazily continued our work. Soon some one began:

"But perhaps it is . . ."

"Shut up, do!" the baker cried out.

We all knew that he was a man of common-sense, and cleverer than we were. We took his cry as a sign of the soldier's conquest. We were sad and uneasy. . . .

At twelve o'clock, during the dinner hour, the soldier came in. He was as clean and well dressed as usual, and as usual looked us straight in the eye. To see him made us uncomfortable.

"Well, my good people, would you like to see what a soldier can do? Go into the passage and peep through the crack. . . . Do you understand?"

We went out tumbling over each other and glued our faced to the crack in the wall leading into the outer vestibule. We had not long to wait. Soon, with hurried step and anxious face, Tania came walking along the yard, skipping over the puddles of melted snow and mud. She vanished into the door of the cellar. Not long after, slowly and humming an air, the soldier followed her. His hands were thrust into his pockets and his moustache was quivering. . . .

It was raining. We saw the drops of rain fall into the puddles and make rings in them as they fell.

It was damp and grey—a dull, depressing day. The snow still lay on the roofs, and the earth was already covered with dark patches of mud. The snow on the roofs, too, was soft and brown and dirty. The rain fell slowly with a dull, monotonous sound. The waiting was cold and dreary.

The soldier was the first to come out of the cellar. He walked along the yard slowly, his moustache quivering, his hand in his pockets—the same as we had always seen him.

Then Tania came out. Her eyes were sparkling with joy and happiness and her lips were parted in a smile. She walked as though in her sleep, with uncertain tread, swaying from side to side. . . .

This was more than we could bear. We all rushed out of the

door into the yard and began hissing and shouting at her, maliciously and wildly.

She started when she saw us and stopped still as though thunder-struck, stopped in the mud beneath her feet. We surrounded her and malignantly, unrestrainedly, began pouring abuse on her in our filthy, shameless words.

We did not make much noise about it, we did not hurry, seeing that she could not escape us. We just surrounded her and mocked her to our heart's content. I do not know why we did not strike her. She stood in our midst, turning her head this way and that, listening to our insults while we, more and more fiercely, went on bespattering her with the filth and poison of our words.

The colour left her cheeks. Her blue eyes, so happy a moment ago, opened wide ; her breath came quick and sharp and her lips trembled.

And we surrounding her, punished her as though she had robbed us. She belonged to us ; we had lavished on her the best that was in us, and though this was no more than a beggar's crumb, still, there were twenty-six of us and she was alone, and because of that we could not think of torments enough that would match her guilt. What insults we poured on her while she stood there wild-eyed, staring at us and shaking like a leaf. We laughed and bellowed and roared. Other people joined us from somewhere. One man pulled Tania by the sleeve.

Suddenly her eyes flashed ; she raised her arms slowly and straightened her hair, then she said slowly and calmly, looking straight into our faces :

" You miserable prisoners ! "

And she walked straight at us as though we were not there barring her way. And in fact no one barred her way, for we all moved aside to let her pass.

Walking out of our midst, without so much as a turn of the head, she said loudly and with an indescribable contempt :

" You brutes ! . . . You scum of the earth ! "

And was gone.

We were left in the yard in the mud and rain, beneath the grey sunless sky.

Soon we too went back to our stone pit. The sun as before never peeped in at our window and Tania never came to see us again.

MAXIM GORKY

COMRADES

I

THE hot July sun shone brightly over Smolkina, bathing the old huts in its bounteous, brilliant rays.   It poured down with particular force on the roof of the elder's hut, recently re-covered with smoothly-planed deal boards, yellow and fragrant.   It was Sunday, and the whole population were in the street, thickly overgrown with grass and strewn with clumps of dried mud.   A large crowd of peasants—men and women—gathered about the elder's hut ; some were sitting on the earthen seat, others on the ground, and still others were standing.   In and out among them, chasing one another, ran the little children, receiving now a cross word, now a blow, from one of the elders.

In the middle of the crowd was a tall man with a large over-hanging moustache.   From his tanned face, covered with a thick, bristly beard and a net of bluish wrinkles, from the tufts of grey hair that peeped out beneath his straw hat, one would have guessed that the man was fifty.   He was staring on the ground ; the nostrils of his long, gristly nose trembled, and when he raised his head to glance at the elder's hut one could see that his eyes were sad and solemn ; they were deep set in their orbits and the bushy eyebrows cast a dark shade over them.   He was dressed as a lay-brother, in a brown, torn cassock that barely covered his knees, and was pulled in at the waist by a piece of cord.   A wallet was slung over his shoulder, in his right hand he carried a long staff with an iron tip, his left hand was thrust into his bosom.   The people surround-ing him eyed him suspiciously, with derision and contempt ; they were manifestly overjoyed at having caught the wolf before he had brought any harm to their flock.   When passing through the village he had gone up to the elder's window and asked for a drink. The elder had given him some kvas and tried to enter into conversation with him, but contrary to the habit of most strangers he had replied to the elder's questions unwillingly.   The elder asked for his papers, but it turned out that he had none. And the man was detained, it being decided to take him to the volost. The elder chose the village policeman as his convoy, and was now in the hut getting him ready for the journey while the prisoner remained outside amid the laughter and jeers of the crowd.

The prisoner had been placed by a willow, and he stood there leaning his bent back against it.

A mole-eyed old man with a foxy face and a grey pointed beard appeared on the doorstep. Sedately he lowered his legs, in long boots, from one step to the other, and his round belly shook solidly beneath his long printed cotton shirt. Behind his shoulder the square, bearded face of the policeman could be seen.

" Do you understand, Efimushka ? " the elder asked of the policeman.

" It doesn't take much understanding—I know all. I, the Smoliansky policeman, have got to take this man to the magistrate, and nothing more ! " He said these words slowly, with a comic solemnity, and winked at the crowd.

" And the paper ? "

" The paper is in my bosom."

" All right, then ! " the elder said approvingly, then scratching his side violently, he added : " Go, then, and God be with you ! "

" Shall we go . . . march, eh, Father ? " The policeman said, smiling to the prisoner.

" They might let us have a cart at least," the latter responded. The elder laughed.

" A cart ? What next ? There are many of your feather tramping through the fields and villages . . . there are not enough horses for you all. You can get there very well on foot. The idea ! "

" Never mind, Father, let us start," the policeman said encouragingly. " We haven't got far to go ; only about a score of versts in all, with God's will. Not so much, perhaps. We'll get there quickly enough, you and I—and then you can rest . . ."

" In a cell," the elder added.

" Never you mind," the policeman went on hastily ; " a man can rest even in prison when he's tired. And then a cell is very cool after a hot day—not at all bad, I assure you ! "

The prisoner looked his convoy up and down ; the latter was smiling with a frank, jolly smile.

" Come along, good Father ! Good-bye, Vasil Gavrilitch ! Come along ! "

" God be with you, Efimushka . . . Keep your two eyes open."

" See with your three ! " some young fellow in the crowd called after the policeman.

" Do you think I'm a baby ? "

They started, keeping close to huts in the strip of shade. The man in the cassock walked ahead, languidly at first, and then in the brisk gait of a person accustomed to the road. The policeman, with a stout stick in his hand, followed behind him.

Efimushka was a short, thick-set peasant with a broad, kindly face, encircled by a flaxen, tufty beard that began from his clear grey eyes. He was nearly always smiling for some reason, exposing his strong yellow teeth and screwing up his nose as though he wanted to sneeze. He was dressed in an overcoat, the skirts of which were tucked into his belt so that they should not impede the movement of his legs ; on his head was a dark green cap without a peak, pulled low over his forehead in front and looking very like a prisoner's cap.

His companion walked on without taking the least notice of him, as though he were absolutely unconscious of his presence behind. They were walking along a narrow winding lane through a sea of waving rye, and their shadows crept over the golden ears.

On the horizon was the blue crest of a wood ; to the left, away in the endless distance, stretched the sown fields ; a village lay like a dark patch in the middle, and beyond, again fields, lost in the azure mist.

To the right, behind the clump of willows, was a newly tinned church spire that had not yet been painted, sparkling so brightly in the sun that it was painful for the eyes to behold.

The larks were singing in the sky, the cornflowers shone among the rye—it was hot, oppressive. The dust rose from beneath the pedestrians' feet.

Efimushka was bored. A terrible gossip by nature, he could not be silent long. Expectorating on the ground, he suddenly began singing in a drawling falsetto voice :

" ' Oh—oh, why-y . . . Oh, why—does my heart ache so . . . ? '

" No voice to-day, damn it ! And there was a time when I could sing well . . . One Vishinsky schoolmaster used to say to me, ' Go on, Efimushka, begin ! ' And how we used to sing together, he and I. A splendid fellow he was ! "

" Who was he ? " the man in cassock asked in a hoarse voice.

" The Vishinsky schoolmaster."

" Is Vishinsky his name ? "

" Vishinsky is a village, brother. The schoolmaster's name was Pavel Michailovitch. A first-rate man he was. He died three years ago."

" Was he young ? "

" Barely thirty."

" What did he die of ? "

" Grief, I suppose."

Efimushka's interlocutor gave him a sidelong glance and smiled.

" It was like this, you see, my good man. He taught and taught for seven whole years and then he began to cough. He coughed and grieved, and grieved and coughed, and from grief I suppose he took to drink. And Father Alexai did not like him, and when he began to drink he sent a letter to the town saying this and that—that the schoolmaster's drinking was a temptation to others. And a reply came from the town to the schoolmistress. A tall, bony woman she was with a big nose. Well, Pavel Michailovitch could see that the game was up. And he grieved the more. ' I taught and taught . . . and this is the end, confound it ! ' He went straight from the school into the hospital, and in five days his soul had passed away to God . . . That is the whole story. . . ."

For a time they walked on in silence. The wood was getting nearer and nearer with each step, rising up before the eyes of the travellers and turning from blue to green.

" Are we going through the wood ? " Efimushka's companion asked.

" For a mile or two on the edge. But why do you ask ? Ah, you ! You are a goose, my good Father, when I look at you ! "

And Efimushka laughed, shaking his head.

" What do you mean ? " the prisoner asked.

" Oh, nothing. Ah, you ! ' Are we going by the wood ? ' he asks. You are too simple, my good man ; another would not have asked at all. A man cleverer than you would have gone straight into the wood and . . ."

" What ? "

" Nothing. I can see through and through you, brother, with all your trickeries. You just give up that idea about the wood, for you have to reckon with me. I can manage three men like you single-handed. Did I guess right ? "

" You did, you fool ! " the prisoner replied, curtly and expressively.

" I did guess right, you see ? " Efimushka said triumphantly.

" What did you guess, you scarecrow ? " the prisoner asked with a crooked smile.

" About the wood . . . I understand. ' When I come to the wood,' you said to yourself, ' then I will hack him to pieces . . . that is me . . . and bury him in the fields or in the wood.' Wasn't that it ? "

" You fool . . ." the prisoner said, shrugging his shoulders. " Where could I escape to ? "

" Where you liked, of course . . . that is your own affair."

" But where ? " Efimushka's companion asked this partly in

anger and partly it seemed in curiosity, as though he really wanted his convoy to tell him where he was to go.

"I have told you, wherever you like!" Efimushka said calmly.

"I have nowhere to escape to, brother, nowhere!" his companion said softly.

"Oh, well! . . ." the convoy pronounced the words incredulously, with a wave of the hand.

"There is always somewhere to run. The earth is wide enough. A man can always find a place in it somewhere."

"But what has that to do with you? Do you want me to run away?" the prisoner queried with a smile.

"How you do talk, to be sure! Do you call it reason? If you run away, whom do you think they will put into prison? Me, of course! No, I only said that for the sake of talking. . . ."

"You are a simpleton . . . however, you seem a decent sort of peasant . . ." Efimushka's companion said, with a sigh.

Efimushka was not slow in agreeing with him.

"You are right; some people do call me a simpleton . . . and as for being a decent peasant, that is also true. I am simple by nature, that is the main reason. Some folk are always ready to take advantage of you by all manner of cunning, but what has that to do with me? I am all alone in the world. A man may live by cunning and he dies, he may live a straightforward life and he dies also. And I am always on the side of straightforwardness."

"That is well said!" Efimushka's companion remarked indifferently.

"What else should I be? Why should I blacken my soul when I am all alone here? I am a free man, brother, I live as I like—I spend my life according to my own lights . . . yes . . . What is your name? . . ."

"What? . . . Well . . . Ivan Ivanov, if you like."

"So . . . Are you of the clergy?"

"N-no . . ."

"Really? And I thought you belonged to the clergy . . ."

"Was that because of my clothes?"

"Why, yes . . . In appearance you are something like a runaway monk or a deposed priest . . . But as for your face, that is different. Your face looks more like a soldier's. . . . God knows what sort of a man you are!" And Efimushka cast a glance at the stranger full of curiosity. The latter sighed, straightened the hat on his head, and wiping the perspiration from his brow, asked:

"Do you smoke?"

"Why, of course! No need to ask!"

He pulled a greasy pouch out of his bosom and, bending his head, began filling a clay pipe, without arresting his walk.

" There, smoke it ! "

The prisoner stopped, and leaning over towards the match his convoy had lighted, took a deep pull at the pipe. The blue smoke floated through the air.

" Then what kind of people do you come from ? Are you a burgess ? "

" A nobleman," the prisoner replied curtly, expectorating to one side on the ears of corn, already covered with a golden sheen.

" Oh, oh, really ? Then how do you come to be walking about without a passport ? "

" Because I want to."

" Well, well, did you ever ? . . . The gentry is hardly used to this kind of wandering life, eh ? You unfortunate man ! "

" Stop your gossip . . . we've had enough now," the unfortunate man said drily.

But Efimushka, with an increasing sympathy and curiosity, looked at the passportless man and, shaking his head pensively, continued :

" Dear, dear ! How fate plays with a man, if you only stop to think of it ! I believe you must belong to the gentry ; you have such a fine carriage. Is it long since you've led this sort of life ? "

The man with the fine carriage gave Efimushka a severe look and shook him off with his hand, as one would a troublesome wasp.

" Shut up, I tell you ! Why will you bother me like a woman ? "

" Don't you be angry with me," Efimushka said soothingly. " I ask out of sheer kindness . . . I have a very kind heart. . . ."

" That is your good fortune. . . . And the fact that your tongue keeps on wagging incessantly is my misfortune."

" All right, I won't talk. A man can be silent when some one does not want to listen to his conversation. But you haven't any cause to be angry . . . It isn't my fault that you've had to live like a tramp, is it ? "

The prisoner stopped and pressed his teeth so firmly together that his cheek-bones stood out sharply and his grey beard bristled. He stared Efimushka up and down from head to foot with half-closed eyes that flashed fire.

But before Efimushka had had time to observe this dumb show, he was again measuring the distance with his long strides.

The face of the talkative policeman expressed a bewildered sadness. He stared up at the sky, at the twittering larks, whistled to them through his teeth, and marched on rhythmically, beating time with his long stick.

They reached the edge of the wood. It stood immovable, like a dark wall, and not a sound was borne from it to the travellers. The sun has set, and his slanting rays bathed the tops of the trees in

purple and gold.   A fragrant moisture came from the trees, and the
darkness and tense stillness reigning in the wood created a weird,
uncanny feeling.

When a wood stands before the eyes dark and immovable and
wrapt in a mysterious stillness, when each tree appears to be straining
for some sound, it gives you the impression that the whole place is
full of living creatures who are only in temporary hiding, and you
wait for the moment when suddenly something vast will emerge, incomprehensible to the human brain—something that will speak in a
powerful voice of the mighty mysteries of creative nature. . . .

II

When they reached the edge of the wood Efimushka and his companion decided to rest for a while, and sat down on the grass by the
broad stump of an oak.   The prisoner slowly took his wallet from his
shoulder, and turned to the policeman casually :

" Would you like some bread ? "

" I will eat it, if you give it me."

And silently they both began to chew bread. · Efimushka chewed
his slowly, sighing and staring fixedly at some spot on the fields to
the left, while his companion, completely absorbed in the process of
appeasing his hunger, ate quickly and munched loudly, measuring
the remaining piece with his eyes.   The fields were getting darker ;
the corn had already lost its golden hue and turned to a reddish
yellow ; to the south-west rugged clouds were floating in the sky,
casting their shadows on the fields and creeping over the ears of corn
till they touched the spot where the two human forms were sitting.
The trees, too, cast their shadows over the earth, bringing a feeling
of sadness into the heart.

" The Lord be praised ! " Efimushka said, gathering together the
remaining crumbs into the palm of his hand, and licking them up
with his tongue.   " God gave the bread and no eye has seen, or
having seen has not offended !   Shall we rest here for an hour or so,
friend ? We'll get to the cell in time, eh ? "

The friend nodded.

" Well, now . . . what a nice place this is, to be sure. I know it
well. . . . Over there to the left used to be the Tuchkov's estate—
gentry of these parts. . . ."

" Where ? " the prisoner asked quickly, turning to the spot indicated by Efimushka.

" Over there . . . beyond that jutting-out bit. All the land
around here used to be theirs.   Rich gentry they were, but they went
to pieces after the emancipation. . . . I belonged to them too ; all
the peasants here belonged to them.   They were a large family

. . . There was the Colonel himself, Alexander Nikititch Tuchkov, and his children, four sons. I wonder where they are all now? The wind seems to bear people away like leaves in the autumn. Only one of them remains. . . . It is to him that I am taking you. . . . He is our magistrate—an old man now. . . ."

The prisoner laughed with a curiously choking, inward laugh; his bosom and belly were shaking, but his face was set, the hoarse rasping sounds issuing from between his parted teeth.

" What is the matter? What ails you, eh?"

" Nothing; it will soon pass off, the prisoner replied abruptly, though kindly. " Go on with your story. . . ."

" Yes. . . . Well, you see, it was like this. . . . There lived these Tuchkovs, and now they are no more . . . some of them died, others disappeared, so that not a breath or a trace of them remains. There was one in particular, the youngest . . . Victor he was called . . . Vitia. He and I used to be chums. . . . At the time of the emancipation we must both have been about fourteen years old. . . . What a boy he was, to be sure, the Lord have pity on his soul! As pure and impetuous as a stream! Where is he now? Alive or dead, I wonder?"

" What was so particularly nice about him? " the prisoner asked softly.

" Everything! " Efimushka exclaimed. " His beauty, his mind, his kindness of heart. If only you could have seen the two of us, you dear, strange man. Dear, dear! What games we used to play, to be sure! How jolly it was! How we enjoyed ourselves! He had a gun—a birthday present from his father—I used to carry it sometimes. We would disappear into the woods for two or three days at a time, and when we'd get back there would be a scolding for him and a whacking for me. But we'd be off again the next day just the same. ' Efimka, let's go and gather mushrooms! ' he would say. We must have gathered poods of these mushrooms, and as for birds, we killed thousands of them. And then he used to collect butterflies and beetles and pin them down in a box . . . It was great sport. And he taught me to read. . . . ' Efimka,' he said, ' I'm going to teach you to read.' ' All right! ' I said, and he began. . . . ' Say A,' he said, and I shouted, " A, A!" and we both laughed. At first I treated it as a joke—what is the use of reading to a peasant? But he would scold me. ' Your freedom has been given you,' he said, 'so that you may learn. If you can read,' he said, ' then you'll know how to live and where to look for the truth. Children, as we know, are very imitative '; he must have heard his elders say that and repeated it. It is all nonsense, of course; learning is in the heart and the heart will point to the truth . . . the heart is all-seeing. . . . And he took to teaching me, got so fond of it, in fact, that he gave me no peace. He would wear me out. ' Vitia,' I would say to him, ' it's no good ; I can't learn to read, I can't ! ' Then he would bawl at me : 'I'll get father's cane if you don't begin at once ! ' ' All right, all right ! I'm ready ! ' One day I jumped up from my lesson and ran straight away. He searched for me the whole day with his gun, and wanted to shoot me. ' I would have shot you if I had found you that day,' he said to me afterwards. That's the sort of boy he was ! Fiery, self-willed—a real gentleman. . . . He used to be fond of me. . . . One day my father was belabouring my back with the straps when Vitia came into our hut and saw him. My word ! You should have seen what followed ! He turned deadly pale and shaking all over, clenched his fists and went for my father. ' How dare you ! ' he said. ' I'm his father,' my father said. ' Ah ! we shall see, father ! I can't manage you alone, but your back will one day be like Efimka's.' After these words he burst into tears and ran out of the room. And what do you think, Father ? He kept his word. He must have told the servants, for one day my father comes home groaning ; he wants to take his shirt off, but it has stuck to his skin. . . . He was furious with me that day. ' This is what I've suffered for you, you hanger-on ' . . . and he gave it me, too. . . . As for being a hanger-on, I was never that . . ."

" No, Efim, never ! " the prisoner said resolutely, trembling all over. " As I see you now, you could never have been a hanger-on," he added hastily.

" That's just it ! " Efimushka exclaimed. " I simply loved that boy Vitia. . . . He was such a clever child ; every one loved him, not only I. . . . What things he used to say ! I can't remember them all—more than thirty years have gone by since then. . . . Oh, Lord ! Where is he now ? If he is alive he must be either in a very high position or in the very lowest depths . . . such is human life ! It boils and bubbles and no sensible mess comes out of it. . . . And people go on perishing . . . how sorry one is for them, mortally sorry ! " Efimushka gave a deep sigh and hung his head on his breast . . . there was a short pause.

" Are you sorry for me, too ? " the prisoner asked gaily. His tone was particularly gay and the whole of his face was lighted up by a gentle, kindly smile.

" What a funny man you are ! " Efimushka exclaimed. " Why shouldn't I be ? Who are you, to be sure ? Since you roam about as you do it is plain that you have nothing belonging to you in this world, not a corner or a bite. . . . And who knows but what you may be carrying some big sin about with you . . . you are an unfortunate man, to be sure. . . ."

" Yes," the prisoner said.

Again they were both silent. The sun had already set ; the

ka had a brass medal hidden in his bosom. Efimushka rose to his full height, picked up his stick, exposed the medal on the very middle of his breast, and said severely :

"Come, get up ! "

"I won't."

Efimushka stared wide-eyed in perplexity and was silent for a moment, failing to understand the prisoner's sudden playful mood.

"Come, don't be lazy now," he said, more gently.

"I won't come ! " the prisoner repeated resolutely.

"You won't come ! What do you mean ? " Efimushka shouted with rage and astonishment.

"Nothing. I want to stop the night here with you . . . go along . . . light a fire. . . ."

"Stop the night, indeed ! As for a fire, I'll make your sides burn so that you will need no fire ! " Efimushka said threateningly. But in the depths of his heart he was nonplussed. A man refuses to come and seems to offer no resistance, he does not attempt to struggle, but just lies there quietly on the ground. What was he to do ?

"Don't shout, Efim," the prisoner counselled calmly.

Efimushka was silent once more, and shifting from one foot to the other he stared down at the prisoner with his large wide-open eyes.

The latter looked up at him and smiled. Efimushka was at a loss to know what to do.

Why had this tramp who had been so solemn and cross all the time suddenly become so indulgent? What if he were to fall upon him, tie his hands and give him a couple of blows on the neck? And, in the severest of official tones that he could command, Efimushka said :

"Get up, now, you loafer, or I will bind you and then you will have to come ! Do you understand ? Look sharp or I'll strike you ! "

"Me ? " the prisoner asked, with a smile.

"Do you think I couldn't ? "

"Would you strike Vitia Tuchkov, Efim Grislov ? "

"Be damned to you ! " Efimushka exclaimed in amazement. "What's the matter with you ? What the devil are you up to ? Get up, I say ! "

"Stop shouting, Efimushka, it is time you recognised me," the prisoner said with a calm smile, rising from the ground. "Aren't you going to greet me ? " Efimushka stepped back from the hand extended to him and stared at the prisoner's face with wide-open eyes. His lips trembled and his face twitched. "Victor Alexandrovitch . . . is that really you ? " he asked in a whisper.

"I will show you my papers if you like, or better still, I will remind you of some things of the past. . . . Do you remember how you fell into the wolf-trap in the Kamensky Wood ? Or how I got caught on the branch of a tree when hunting for birds' nests and hung with my head down ? Or how we stole the cream from the old dairywoman, Petrovna, and the tales she used to tell us ? "

Efimushka sat down heavily and began to laugh confusedly.

"Do you believe me now ? " the prisoner asked, sitting down beside him ; he looked into his face, and put his hand on his shoulder. Efimushka was silent. It was now quite dark around them. A faint rustling and murmuring could be heard in the wood ; somewhere in the thicket a night bird cried mournfully ; a cloud crept over the wood with a scarcely visible motion.

"Well, Efim. . . . Aren't you glad to see me ? Or are you quite overcome ? What a splendid chap you are ! Just the same as you were when a boy, Efim. Won't you speak, Efim ? "

Efimushka blew his nose violently into the skirt of his overcoat.

"Dear, dear, dear ! " the prisoner said, shaking his head reproachfully. "Well, really, you should be ashamed of yourself ! Nearly fifty years old and to carry on like this ! Stop now ! " He put his arm on the policeman's shoulder and shook him gently. The policeman gave a trembling laugh and then began to speak without looking at his companion.

"It is nothing. . . . It is only because I'm glad. . . . Is it really you, you ? I can hardly believe it. You . . . Vitia . . . and in this guise ! Going to a cell. . . . No passport . . . nothing but bread to eat. . . . No tobacco. . . . My God ! Is that as it should be ? If only I were in your position and you the policeman. . . . It would be more fitting. But what has happened ? How can I look you in the eyes ? It was always a joy to think of you. . . . ' Vitia.' I used to think to myself sometimes . . . and the heart would nearly stop still. And now . . . My God . . . people wouldn't believe me if I told them. . . ."

He mumbled his broken phrases, his eyes fixed on his legs while his hand now clutched at his breast, now at his throat.

" Don't tell people anything about it ; there's no need. And never mind. . . . It is not your fault, is it ? Don't you worry about me . . . I've got my papers all right ; I didn't show them to the elder because I didn't want to be recognised here. My brother Ivan will hardly put me in a cell ; on the other hand, he will probably set me up again. . . . I shall live with him and you and I can go and hunt together again. . . . See how well everything will turn out ! "

Vitia spoke these words soothingly, in the tone that grown people use when comforting a crying child. The moon had risen above the wood and seemed to float towards the cloud, lighting up its edges with silvery delicate opal shades. The quails screamed in the corn, somewhere a rail-bird cackled. The darkness drew denser.

" That is true," Efimushka began softly. " Ivan Alexandrovitch will be pleased to see his own brother again . . . and you will adapt yourself to the life once more. That is so . . . and we will go out shooting together. . . . Only it is not what I expected. I thought you would do things in life . . . and now, what has it come to ? . . ."

Vitia Tuchkov laughed. " Oh, oh, Efimushka ! I have done enough things in life. . . . I have squandered my inheritance, thrown up my work ; I've been an actor, a clerk in a timber merchant's business ; I've kept actors myself . . . tasted everything to the dregs . . . got head over ears in debt and was mixed up in some affair. . . . Oh dear ! It has all been and gone ! "

The prisoner waved his hand and laughed good-humouredly.

" I'm not a gentleman any more, Efimushka . . . I've got cured of that. What fine times you and I are going to have together, eh ! Come, wake up ! "

" Don't mind me . . ." Efimushka said in a depressed tone of voice : " I feel ashamed. I have talked such a lot of rubbish and nonsense to you . . . just like a peasant. . . . So you want to stop the night here ? Shall I light a fire ? "

" Yes, go on ! "

The prisoner stretched himself on the ground on his back and the policeman disappeared into the thicket, whence a rustling and crackling of branches could soon be heard. In a little while Efimushka reappeared with a bundle of brushwood, and soon a tongue of flame was creeping gaily over the little mound of dry twigs.

The old comrades looked at it musingly as they sat opposite each other, in turn taking a pull at the clay pipe.

"Just like old times," Efimushka said sadly.

"Only the circumstances are different," Tuchkov said.

"Life is becoming more and more difficult. . . . See how it has broken you. . . ."

"We can't tell yet whether it has broken me or it . . ." Tuchkov said with a smile. A silence ensued.

"My God, Vitia! What a dilemma, to be sure!" Efimushka exclaimed sadly.

"Never mind. . . . What has been, has been," Tuchkov comforted him philosophically.

Behind them rose the dark wood like a wall, murmuring softly to itself; the flames crackled merrily in the fire around which the silent shadows danced, and an impenetrable darkness lay across the fields.

MAXIM GORKY

SIMPLE FOLK

I WALKED leisurely along the soft grey road among the corn that reached up to my chest. The road was so narrow that the crushed and broken ears lay in the ruts besmeared with tar.

The heavy ears swayed to and fro ; the mice ran noisily in the corn. In the sky overhead, larks and swallows could be seen, a sign that not far off there were a river and human habitations. My eyes, wandering over the sea of gold, searched for the sign of a steeple raised to the sky like the mast of a ship ; searched for trees that in the distance would look like sails ; but nothing could be seen except the rugged steppes that rolled down in soft inclines to the south-west —deserted like the sky and just as tranquil.

In the steppes you feel like a fly on a plate—when in its very heart you feel that the earth is the centre of the universe, embraced by the sun, surrounded by the stars, blinded by its beauty.

There it was—so vast—clothed in red—majestically dropping into the distant blue horizon among the snow-white clouds. The corn was sprinkled with the golden dust of the setting sun, the corn-flowers were already dark, and in the early evening stillness you could plainly hear the song of the earth.

The sky was covered with rosy, fan-shaped clouds—one of them touched my breast and, like Moses' rod, called to life a host of peaceful thoughts. I wanted to embrace the evening earth and whisper loving words to her, words such as had never been spoken before.

The heavens were sprinkled with stars and the earth was a star— the earth was sprinkled with men and I was a man ; roaming fearlessly over every path, seeing all the sorrow and joy of life, drinking the bitter and the sweet like the rest of mankind.

. . . I was hungry, and there had not been a scrap of bread in my wallet since morning. That hindered thought and was some-what annoying. The earth was so rich, man had spent so much labour on her, yet some one was hungry. . . .

Suddenly the road turned to the right—the walls of corn moved asunder, exposing a valley, at the bottom of which flowed a blue stream. A new bridge, as yellow as a turnip, stretched across it and was mirrored in the water. Seven white huts stood out against the slope beyond the bridge, and some tall thick poplars threw a deep shadow over them ; a cropped stallion wandered among the silver-grey trunks, flapping his tail. There was a strong smell of smoke, tar, damp hempseed ; the cackling of chickens ; a baby cried wearily—soon it would go to sleep. Were it not for these sounds one might have thought the scene was the hasty sketch of some clever artist—the soft, tender colours he had used already fading in the sun.

In the half circle was a hut, a well, and next to it a small red chapel, tall and narrow, looking like a one-eyed sentry. A crane was bending to the earth, uttering its long cry ; a peasant woman all in white was drawing water, stretching herself and raising her bare arms—she looked as though she might float away at any minute like a cloud. The well was surrounded by shiny black mud that looked like crushed velvet, and two boys of about three and five, naked to the waist, were silently kneading the mud with their yellow feet as though they wished to mix the red rays of the sun into it. This good work engaged my attention ; I looked sympathetically at the boys, with real interest—the sun was at home in the mud, the deeper it penetrated the earth, the better for the earth and for man !

From above I could see everything as plainly as the palm of my hand. Seven huts on the farm—no work was to be had there—still it would be pleasant to gossip with the good folk in the evening. I walked over the bridge filled with the passionate desire to tell these people gay and wonderful stories—for you know this is as necessary to man as the bread he eats.

Coming towards me from under the bridge—as though a lump of soil had come to life—there rose up a powerful, unkempt, unshaven man, wearing baggy blue trousers and an open rough linen shirt, grey with dirt.

" Good evening ! "

" The same to you. Where are you going ? "

" What river is this ? "

" This ? Why, the Sagaidak, of course."

On his large round head the grey curls floated in the wind ; his moustache was clipped short, the ends hanging down like a Chinaman's. His little eyes stared at me sharply and distrustfully, obviously taking note of the numerous holes and patches in my garments. Sighing deeply, he pulled a long red-stemmed clay pipe out of his pocket and, screwing up his eyes, looked carefully into the black bowl and asked :

" Have you got a match ? "

" Yes."

" Any tobacco ? "

" A little."

He stood pensive for a while and looked towards the sun sinking among the clouds.   Then he asked :

" Is it Moscow tobacco ? "

" No, it's from Romensk-Rimorinka."

" Oh," he said, stroking his wrinkled nose ; " good tobacco that ! "

I could not very well go into the hut without the host, so I stood by his side until he should have finished his slow questions as to who I was, whence I came, where I was going, and for what reason——I was growing a little impatient, being anxious to approach him in some way.

" Work ? " he drawled through his moustache.   " There is no work here.   What sort of work could there be now ? "

He turned away and spat into the river.

On the opposite bank, waddling gravely, came mother goose, followed by her downy goslings ; two little girls came behind them : one, somewhat larger than the goose, wore a red kerchief and had a stick in her hand ; the other, white, fat, bandy-legged and staid, looked just like the bird.

" Yufim ! " a piercing, unseen voice called out.   The man turned his head and said approvingly :

" What a throat ! "

Then he began to wriggle his dirty toes with their cracked skin, looked down at their broken nails, and at last said :

" Perhaps you can read and write ? "

" Why do you ask ? "

" Because if you can, you could read the book over a dead man."

This idea seemed to please him.   A gay smile rippled over his flat face.

" Don't you consider that work ? " he asked, turning to hide the twinkle in his eye.   " I would give you ten kopeks and the dead man's shirt into the bargain."

" And—food ? " I mused aloud.

" Naturally ! "

" Where is the dead man ? "

" In his hut.   Will you come ? "

We walked towards the back of the garden whence issued the cries.

" Yufim ! Yufim ! "

The shadows crept over the soft road towards us ; behind the bushes, by the river, I could hear children's voices and the splashing of water ; some one was planing a plank ; the sound of sobbing floated into the air.   The old man remarked leisurely :

" There was an old woman here who used to read ; she was a marvel ! They took her to town and she lost the use of her legs—a pity it was not her tongue. She was very useful—only too quarrelsome. . . ."

Just then a black puppy—about the size of a large frog—ran up to me, lifted its tail and legs and yapped threateningly, sniffing the air with its pink puppyish nose.

" Down ! "

From behind somewhere, a young barefooted woman shot out and, clapping her hands angrily, cried out :

" Yufim ! I keep calling and calling you ! "

" As if I did not hear ! "

" Where have you been ? "

My companion silently showed her a yellow pear and led me into the yard belonging to the hut next door. The barefooted woman remained behind, sending a volley of abuse after us.

Two old women were sitting by the door of the little hut : the one, round and untidy—like an ill-used leather ball ; the other, bony, bent in the back, with a dark, cross face. At their feet lay a huge dog as big as a sheep, with tangled coat, red watery eyes, and rough tongue hanging out. Yufim related every detail of our meeting, and told them of what use I could be. Two pairs of eyes regarded him silently ; one of the old women craned her dirty neck, the other, having listened to the end, said to me :

" Sit down ; I'll get you some supper."

The little yard was overgrown with plantains and other weeds ; in the middle stood a black cart without wheels. The cattle were being driven home, and from the farm-yard there floated a stream of subdued sounds ; from every corner of the yard grey shadows crept over the grass.

" We must all die some day," Yufim remarked with quiet conviction, knocking out his pipe against the wall. The barefooted, rosy-cheeked woman stood by the door and asked in a lowered voice :

" Are you coming or aren't you ? "

" I must finish this business first, then . . ."

I was given a hunk of bread and a basin of milk. The dog rose, and, resting her old dribbling jaw on my knees, looked into my face with lustreless eyes as though asking :

" Is it nice ? "

The hump-backed old woman's voice was heard in the yard, mingling with the evening breeze that stirred the dry grass.

" You beg and pray for God to save you from sorrow, and it falls on you twice as heavily. . . ."

Dark as Fate, she craned her long neck, and rocking herself with

a measured motion she fell slowly to the ground at my feet, murmuring monotonous rambling phrases :

"There are some who work when they like, or not at all when they
don't choose to ; but our people work till they have no strength left,
yet they get no reward. . . ."

The old woman's soft mutterings were heard in the yard :

"The Mother of God rewards every one. . . . She rewards
all. . . ."

A moment's deep silence.

Deep and weighty it seemed, pregnant with meaning ; it seemed
to augur the birth of great thoughts and momentous words.

"I must tell you," the old woman said, trying to straighten her
back, "that among many enemies my old man had one friend.
Andrey was his name. When we could no longer live at my grand-
father's down by the Doritsa, and people began to worry and abuse
him until he couldn't say a word and the tears came to his eyes,
Andrey came to him and said : 'Hadn't you better go away,
Yakov ? You have hands, the earth is big ; a man can live anywhere. If people are spiteful here it is because they are herded
together and stupid ; don't judge them, but live simply ; let them
go about their business and you about yours ; let them live according to their lights and you according to yours. Live quietly and
submit to none ; then you will conquer all.' Thus my Vassil used
to affirm often : 'They are they . . . and we are we !' A good
word, you know, never dies—wherever it is born it flies over the
whole world like a lark."

"That is true," Yufim affirmed. "That is quite right. As we
say, 'A good word is Christ's and a bad one the priest's.' "

The old woman lifted her head sharply, and cried out :

"Not the priest's, but yours. . . . Yufim, Yufim, your hair is
already grey, and still you say things without thinking. . . ."

At this moment Yufim's wife appeared, waving her arms and
scattering abuse :

"My God ! what a man ! He doesn't answer, doesn't listen, only
stands there barking at the moon like the dog."

"Oh dear !" Yufim drawled. "There she goes. . . ."

In the west the clouds began to rise, like blue smoke and fire ; it
seemed as though the whole steppes would instantly burst into flame.
In the east it was already dark and the black sultry night was
creeping up.

The warm odour of the dead man issued from the window of the
hut just over my head. The dog's nostrils and grey ears trembled,
the eyes, blinking pitifully, looked towards the window. Yufim,
looking up at the sky, seemed to assure himself :

"It will not rain ; no——"

" Have you a psalter ? " I asked.

" What ? "

" A book, a psalter ? "

All were silent.

Faster advanced the southern night, sweeping the light from the earth as though it were dust.   How pleasant to sleep in the fragrant hay till sunrise !

" Perhaps Panka has one," Yufim said confusedly.   " With his little ones. . . ."   Whispering, they went into the hut, and the little round old woman said to me with a sigh

" Go in and look at him if you want to.'

Her dear little head was bent humbly.   Folding her arms across her breast she whispered :

" Most Holy Mother. . . . Most pure. . . ."

The dead man looked stern and important.   His thick grey beard was parted in a deep crease down the centre, his nose was buried in his thick moustache, his protruding eyes were half open, so was his mouth.   It seemed as though he were thinking deeply ; that angry thoughts occupied him ; that at any moment he would utter some last significant sentence.   Over his head burnt a taper whose blue smoke flickered nervously ; it cast but a faint light, and only enhanced the hollows under the eyes and the deep wrinkles in the cheeks of the dead man.   On the grey shirt, like two mounds, lay his dark bony hands, the fingers clenched even in death.   A current of air blew in from the window to the door, bringing with it an unpleasant odour of rank grass and of decay.   More ardent and clearer came the old woman's murmur as she sobbed dryly ; through the small square of sky seen through the window the afterglow loomed threateningly, and when the bluish evening light streamed through the window into that room, cramped as a coffin, the yellow candle-light seemed to fly away, the grey hair on the corpse sparkled like fish scales, and the face seemed to frown austerely.   The old woman's murmur was deeper ; cold was her heart, and without soothing her affliction the old words rose bitterly to her mind :

" Do not mourn for me, mother, seeing me in the coffin.   I will arise when . . ."

He would not arise.

The thin old woman came in and announced that there was no psalter on the farmstead, but there was another book if that would do.

The other book turned out to be a grammar of Church Slavonic. The first few pages were missing, and it began with the words :

" Friend, Friends, of the Friend. . . ."

" What are we to do ? " the poor little old woman asked sadly when I told her that the grammar was of no use to the old man ; her childish little face trembled and her swollen eyes again filled with tears.

" A man lives on and on," she said, sobbing, " and in the end does not earn for himself a decent burial."

I told her that I would read all the prayers and psalms I knew, over her husband, only she must go out of the hut. I was not used to this kind of work and could not remember all the prayers if any one were listening. She either did not understand or did not believe me, for she stood for a long time by the door, sniffing, and wiping her worn face with her sleeves. After a time she went out.

The afterglow shone in the black sky down to the horizon where the steppes met the sea ; a blue mist pervaded the hut, silently bringing with it the sultry darkness of the night ; the candle glimmered timidly. The man lay and with half-shut eyes looked out on the flickering shades running over his chest, the white walls, and the ceiling. I looked carefully at him out of the corner of my eye (one could not tell what a dead man might do) and conscientiously intoned in a soft voice :

" Forgive us our sins though we be worse than beasts. . . ."

But at the same time came thoughts denying them :

" It is not sin that is difficult and bitter, but truth ; our conscious and unconscious sins ; those due to youth and bad teaching ; those due to wantonness and despair. . . ."

" This hardly applies to you, brother," I reflected.

Blue stars twinkled in the fathomless darkness of the heavens—who besides myself was watching them at that hour ?

From the distance came a sound of thunder and everything trembled in the afterglow.

Pit-pat, pit-pat went the dog on the clay floor ; it kept walking to and fro, sniffing my legs, growling softly and then going out again. It was probably too old to mourn for its master with despairing howls as dogs are wont to do. When it went out, the shadows seemed to follow it ; they flowed out at the door and fanned my face with a cold breeze. The candle-light seemed to wish to tear itself from the candle and fly away to the stars as small and pitiful as itself. I did not want it to vanish, and followed its flicker with such intensity that my eyes ached. It was painfully stuffy in the hut. I stood at the dead man's head, immovable, listening intently to the silence. . . . A desire for sleep, difficult to overcome, possessed me. With a great effort I recalled the beautiful hymns by Makari, by the great Zeatoust, by Damaskin, and in my head, buzzing like flies, were the words of the Sixth Rule to those about to fall asleep :

" If you find a soft pillow leave it, and put a stone there for Christ's sake. If you would sleep in the winter . . ."

In order to keep awake I hummed a hymn of praise :
" My Lord, save my soul which is weakened in all terrible
sins. . . ."
Behind the door I heard the dry faint murmur :
" Merciful Mother of God . . . take my soul. . . ."
Her soul seemed to me as grey as a dove and just as timid.
When it should fly to the throne of the Mother of God and She
stretched out Her soft white hand, this little soul would start,
flutter its little wings and, with a fearful joy, would die.
Then the Mother of God would say to Her Son :
" See how terrified Your people are upon the earth. They are
unaccustomed to joy. Is this well, my Son ? "
And He would reply :
" I do not know."
In His place I would have been confused.
Through the deep stillness an answer seemed to come, also in
song. The stillness was so intense that the distant sound sinking
in it seemed unnatural, a fantastic echo of my own voice. I ceased
and listened. The sound was nearer and clearer ; some one, with
heavy dragging feet, was approaching and murmuring :
" N-no. . . . It will not rain. . . ."
" Why are the dogs not barking ? " I thought, wiping my eyes.
It seemed to me that the dead man's brow twitched and that a
solemn smile trembled on his lips.
Outside, I heard a heavy voice :
" What ? Ah, old woman . . . I knew that he would die. Well,
be silent ! Men like him always stand up until the last hour and
then lie down never to rise. . . . Who ? . . . A stranger ? . . .
Ah. . . ."
Something large and formless, like the darkness itself, knocked
against the door and lurched into the hut, filling it to the very
ceiling. With a broad wave of his arms this man crossed himself
in the candlelight, stumbled forward, and, almost touching the feet
of the corpse with his forehead, said softly :
" Well, Vassil ? " and then burst out into sobs.
There was a strong smell of vodka. The old woman stood in the
door begging him :
" Father Demid, give him the book. . . ."
" Why should I ? I'll read myself ! "
His heavy hand lay on my shoulder ; his large hairy face bent
towards mine.
" You are young yet. Are you in the Church ? "
His head was enormous, like a cask, and his long thick hair shone
like gold even in the flickering candle-light. He reeled and shook
me to and fro ; he emitted a strong smell of vodka.

"Father Demid," the old woman said tearfully and obstinately.

He interrupted her threateningly.

"How many times have I told you that a deacon is not addressed as 'father'? Go away. Go to bed. This is my business. Go away. . . . Light another candle, I can't see anything."

Sitting down on the bench and putting the book on his knees he asked :

"Will you have a drink ? "

"There's nothing here."

"What's that ? " he said severely. "Well, I've a bottle here, see ? "

"It is not fitting to drink here."

"That is true," he muttered pensively. "I must go out. . . . That is true."

"What are you going to do, sit down and read ? "

"I ? I don't want to read. You read. I don't feel myself—— 'My enemies have crushed me as though many fought me from on high,' and into the bargain I am somewhat drunk."

He threw the book at me and shook his head heavily :

"People die off and the earth is still overcrowded . . . people die without seeing any good. . . ."

"This is not a psalter," I said, examining the book.

"You lie ! "

"Look at it ! "

He bent back the cover, and passing the candle over the page read the scarlet letters : "Ocktoich. . . ."

He was surprised.

"The Ocktoich ? . . . How does it come here . . . even the sizes are different . . . the psalter is a small fat book, and this . . . it must have been because I hurried so."

The mistake seemed to have sobered him. He got up, went over to the old man and stroking his beard leant over him :

"Forgive me, Vassil . . . what can I do ? "

Raising himself, he shook back his thick hair, and taking the bottle from his pocket, put the neck to his lips, and sucked the spirit for a long time, breathing through his nose.

"Do you want some ? "

"I'm sleepy. If I drink I shall fall asleep."

"Well, fall asleep, then ! "

"And the prayers ? "

"What use is it to any one here for you to murmur words that no one understands ? "

He sat down on the bench, and bending over, rested his head in his hands and lapsed into silence.

The July night was already melting away ; the darkness quietly receded to the corners.   Through the window came a breath of the early morning dewy freshness.   The light of the two candles seemed paler ; their two flames looked like the frightened eyes of a sick child.

" Had you been alive, Vassil," the deacon muttered, " I should have had a place to go to, but now my best friend is dead, and I have nowhere to go. . . . Lord, where is Thy righteousness. . . ."

I sat by the window, my head in the open, smoking, dozing, listening to the heavy plaint :

" They have consumed my wife and they will devour me as a pig does cabbages. . . . Is it right, Vassil ? "

The deacon again pulled out his bottle, sucked at it, wiped his beard, and leaning over the dead man, kissed his forehead :

" Good-bye, my friend. . . ."

He turned to me, and with sudden strength and clearness said :

" He was a simple man, this ; didn't stand out from the others ; seemed a rook amongst rooks.   But he was not a rook, he was a white dove, and no one knew it except I . . . yes . . . ' And now he has departed from the bitter toil of the Pharaohs '—and I am alive—and only my enemies remain."

" Have you had a great sorrow ? "

He did not reply at once, and then said earnestly :

" Every one has more sorrow than is necessary . . . and I have so much . . . if you sleep . . . your sorrow follows you into your dreams."

He stumbled and fell against me, saying :

" I want to sing, and I mustn't now.   People would wake up and grumble . . . but I would like to sing ! "

Softly he hummed in my ear :

> To whom shall I tell my sorrows ?
> To whom of my sorrows sing ?
> Whose h-h-hand . . .

His stiff beard tickled my neck and I moved away.

" You don't like it ?   Well, the devil take you !   Go to sleep ! "

" Your beard tickled me."

" Shall I shave it off for you, my honey ? "

He sat down on the floor and was pensive a moment.

" Well, you read ; I'll go to sleep ; only don't run off with the book, for it belongs to the Church.   I've had experience of tramps before !   Why do you run all over the place ?   Why do you tramp about ?   After all, where are you going ?   What draws you ?   Go on your way.   Say that a poor deacon here is ruined—tell some person who will pity me.   Diomid Kubasov, deacon, that is I . . . beyond salvation. . . ."

He fell asleep. Opening the book at random, I began to read :
" The uncultivated land which has become the nourisher of all,
which opens its hand, and by its benevolence feeds all living
creatures. . . ."
The " nourisher of all " lay stretched out before me, covered with
dry, fragrant grass. Sleepily I looked out upon its dark, enigmatic
face, thinking of the man who had walked his furrow so many times,
his only care being that the dead should come to life. Strange
thoughts rose in my mind. I saw a man stalking over the bare,
deserted steppes. He had a thousand hands that held the earth in
wide embrace ; in his tracks the dead steppes came to life and bore
fruit, villages and towns sprung up, and still he went on, incessantly
sowing life—human life. The earth regarded all men kindly ; all
the mysterious strength in them was called up to conquer death,
eternally transforming the dead into life ; all walked along mortal
paths to immortality ; men ate of the seed of death but did not die.
Many thoughts came knocking at my heart ; the beating of their
wings produced a joyful sensation ; I wanted to ask many questions
of someone who would answer simply, fearlessly, honestly.
Around me, the dead and the sleeping, and in the sheds outside,
signs of life ; but it did not matter ! There were many human
beings on the world, and sooner or later I would find the long-sought
one. . . .
I imagined myself out of the hut, on the open steppes, looking back
at it, a mere speck on the earth. The huts were close together, their
windows all dark except this one, in which faintly glimmered a
captive light over the dead man's head. . . .
That was the heart that had ceased to live. . . . I realised that
only an ordinary little man had died, but when I thought of all his
work it seemed infinitely big. . . . I remembered the unripe,
crushed corn lying in the ruts on the steppes, the larks up in the
blue sky over the golden grain, the steppes themselves, stretching
over the earth. . . .
I heard a flapping of wings ; the shadow of birds passed over the
light grass outside, silver with dew.
The cocks crowed—five of them—the geese awakened, the cows
began to low, and somewhere a wattle hedge creaked. I longed to
be out on the steppes ; to go to sleep on the warm, dry earth. The
deacon was asleep at my feet ; he lay on his back and exposed his
broad chest. His fiery hair shone like a halo, his red face was puffed
out angrily, his mouth was open, and his moustache moved slightly.
His hands were long, and he had fingers like the prongs of a garden
fork.
Involuntarily I imagined this man embracing some woman ; her
face would be buried in his beard, and she would laugh and throw her

head back as it tickled her. I wondered how many children he had.

It was unpleasant to think that he carried sorrow in his heart where joy should have been.

The old woman's kindly face peeped in at the door, and through the window I caught the first rays of the rising sun.

A light, silky, transparent mist hovered over the river, and the trees had that strange immobility which makes one think they are about to burst into song and tell the understanding soul about the great mysteries of nature.

" Such a good man," the old woman whispered, gazing down sorrowfully at the deacon's big body.

As though reading from a book I could not see, she told me, in simple words, the story of his wife.

She had sinned with a certain man. People got to know of it and told her husband, and when he forgave her, laughed at them. From that day, to hide her shame, she had never left the house—and he had taken to drink. . . . It was two years now . . . and he would probably lose his place soon. The old woman said that her husband never drank and tried to dissuade the deacon from it. " Ah, Demid," he would say, " don't let people get the upper hand of you ; live simply ; let them go about their business and you about yours. . . ."

The tears fell from her dim little eyes and dissolved in the wrinkles of her swollen cheeks. The little head shook like a faded autumn leaf ; it was pitiful to see this kindly face so worn with age and sorrow. I sought in my soul for some word of consolation, but could find none, and felt hurt.

I recalled the words I had read somewhere, a long time since :

" The servants of God should laugh, not weep ; weeping is offensive to man and to God."

" I must go on," I said in confusion.

" Ah ! "

It was a hasty exclamation as though my words had alarmed her. With trembling hand she tried to find the pocket in her skirt, her lips meanwhile moving silently.

" I don't want money, mistress ; give me some bread if you have any. . . ."

" You don't want a copper ? " she asked incredulously.

" Of what use would it be to me ? "

" As you please," she agreed pensively. " As you please . . . go on your way . . . thank you ! "

Before me, in the blue sky, the sun was proudly displaying its rays over the earth like a peacock its tail. I winked at it ; I knew it well ; in an hour or two its smile would burn like fire, but for the moment, at any rate, we were pleased with one another. I walked among the corn, singing its praise—the Lord of Life.

> Inaccessible Nature
> Let me reach thee !
> Let me bathe in thee !
> Light up my soul !
> And lead me on with thee
> Beyond all good and evil.

.   .   .   .

We live simply. . . . Let them go about their business and we about ours.

MAXIM GORKY

MAKAR CHUDRA

A COLD, damp wind was blowing from the sea, wafting over the steppe the melancholy melody of the splashing of the waves which struck against the shore, and of the rustling of the bushes close by. From time to time the gusts of wind brought along toward us chilled, shrivelled, yellow leaves and flung them into the pile of burning wood, stirring the flame, from which the surrounding darkness of the autumn night quivered, and retreating shyly, disclosed the vast steppe on the left, the endless sea on the right, and opposite me the massive figure of Makar Chudra, the old gipsy, who was watching the horses of his camp, which had pitched its tents some fifty yards away from us.

Not paying the slightest attention to the cold waves of the wind which threw his coat open, bared his hairy, bronze chest and beat against it mercilessly, he reclined in a fine, free, strong pose, his face turned toward me ; he puffed methodically at his huge pipe, emitted heavy volumes of smoke from his mouth and nose, and fixing his eyes over my head into the dead quiet darkness of the steppe, talked to me without pausing, and without making a single motion to protect himself from the boisterous wind.

"So you are wandering around ? That's good ! You have chosen a fine lot for yourself, falcon. That's the proper thing to do : wander and look on ; when you have seen enough, lie down and die —that's all !

"Life ? . . . Other people ? " he went on, after he had listened sceptically to my retort. "Eh ! What have you to do with that ? Are you not life yourself ? Other people live without you, and without you they will go through life. Do you think that you are of any use to anybody ? You are neither bread nor a staff, and no one needs you.

"To study and to teach, you say ? Can you learn how to make people happy ? No, you cannot. First become grey, then say that it is necessary to teach. To teach what ? Everybody knows what he needs. Those that are wiser take what there is, those that are foolish get nothing, and everybody learns for himself.

" They are very queer, your people. They have huddled themselves together in crowds and crush one another, and yet see how much room there is on earth." He pointed toward the steppe. " And they're for ever working. What for ? For whom ? No one knows. You see a man ploughing, and you think : here he will by degrees waste away his strength tilling the soil in the sweat of his brow, and then he will lie down and die in it and decay. Nothing will remain after him, he will see nothing of his field, and he will die, as he was born, a fool.

" Was he born but to dig the earth a little, and then to die before he had time to dig a grave for himself ? Does he know freedom ? Does he understand the vast expanse of the steppe ? Does the whispering of the waves of the sea gladden his heart ? Eh ? He's a slave all life long—that's all there is to it !

" Look at me ! At fifty-eight I have seen so much that if you were to write it out on paper you could not get it into a thousand bags like the one you have there. Well, tell me, where have I not been ? You can't. You have never even heard of some of the places I have seen. That's the way to live : wander, wander— and that's all. Don't stay on in one place too long—what's there in it ? Just as day and night are for ever chasing each other around the earth, so you should run from thoughts about life, in order not to cease loving it. For when you muse over it, you'll cease loving life. It is always the case. That's the way it was with me. Eh ! That's the way it was, falcon.

" I was in prison in Galichin. ' Why do I live on earth ? ' I somehow thought to myself for weariness—it's so tedious in prison, falcon. Eh, how tedious ! And my heart was seized with anguish when I looked out of the window toward the field—it was clutched as with smith-tongs. Who can say wherefore he lives ? No one, falcon ! It is not necessary to question yourself about it. Live, and that's all there is to it. Go around and look on about you, then sadness will never seize upon you. . . ."

He spat into the bonfire and fell silent, again filling his pipe. The wind howled plaintively and softly, the horses were neighing in the dark, and a tender, passionate song came soaring from the camp. The beautiful Nonka, Makar's daughter, was singing. I knew her voice, which was of a deep, throaty timbre, and always rang with queer discontent and pretension, whether she sang a song or asked after your health. The haughtiness of a queen was fixed on her swarthy, dull face, and in her eyes flashed a consciousness of her fascination and of the irresistibility of her beauty, and her abhorrence of everything that was not herself.

Makar handed me the pipe. " Smoke ! Does the girl sing well ?
I should say she does ! Would you want such a girl to fall in love
with you ? No ? Good ! That's right ; don't trust them, and
keep at a distance from them. Kissing is more pleasant to a girl
than smoking a pipe is to me ; but when you have kissed her, your
freedom is dead in your heart. She will tie you to herself with
certain cords which are invisible and which cannot be torn, and you
will give up to her all your soul, and only the rest will remain for
you. It's true ! Beware of the girls ! They lie, the reptiles.
' I love you,' she says, ' better than anything in the world ' ; but
try to stick her with a pin, and she'll tear your heart. I know it.
Eh, how well I know it ! Well, falcon, if you wish I'll tell you a
true story. You had better remember it, and if you do remember
it you'll be a free bird all your life long. . . .

" There was once a young gipsy, Zobar by name—Loiko Zobar.
All Hungary and Bohemia and Slavonia and all around the sea knew
him—he was a fine, brave fellow ! There was not a village around
that neighbourhood where some one did not take a vow to kill
Loiko ; but he lived, and when Zobar took a liking to a certain
horse he was sure to caracole on it, even if a whole regiment were
to guard it. Ah ! Was there any one he was afraid of ? Even if
Satan came to him with his entire suite Zobar would surely pick a
quarrel with him, and if he could not strike him with a knife, he
would have kicked each and every one of the devils—that's certain !

" And all the gipsy camps knew him or heard of him. He loved
nothing but horses, and even these he did not love long. He would
ride a horse a little, and then he would sell it ; and as for the money
—whoever wanted it could have it. Nothing was sacred to him ; if
you needed his heart he himself would have torn it out of his chest
and would have given it to you, just to help you. That's the kind
of man he was, falcon !

" Our camp was wandering at that time over Bukovina—that was
some ten years ago. Once—it was a night in spring, I remember—
we were sitting, I, and soldier Danila, who fought together with
Kossuth, and old Nur, and Radda, the daughter of Danila, and the
rest of us.

" Do you know my Nonka ? She's a queen-girl ! Well, and yet
you can't compare Radda with her—it would be too much honour
for Nonka ! You can't describe Radda in words. Perhaps her
beauty could be played on a violin, but only by one who knows the
violin as his own soul.

" Many a valiant fellow's heart she broke. In Morave a certain
old magnate once noticed her and he became dumbfounded. He
sat on his horse and stared at her, trembling as with fever. He was
handsome like the devil on a holiday ; his coat was trimmed with

gold ; on his side a sword flashed like lightning. Whenever the
horse stamped his foot the old nobleman's sword, set with precious
stones, and the blue velvet of his cap, looked like a bit of the sky.
He was a man of importance ! He stared and stared, then he said
to Radda :

" ' Here, kiss me ; I'll give you a bagful of money.'

" And she turned aside, that's all.

" ' Forgive me if I insulted you ; grant me at least a gentler
glance.' The old fellow at once lowered his crest, and flung the
wallet filled with money at her feet—it was a big wallet, dear ! She
pushed it with her foot into the mud, and that's all !

" ' Eh, what a fine girl ! ' he sighed, and whipped the horse ; only
a cloud of dust remained.

" On the next day he came again. ' Who's her father ? ' he
thundered over the camp. Danila came out. ' Sell me your
daughter ; take as much as you want ! '

" And Danila said to him : ' Only you noblemen sell everything,
from your hogs to your conscience. But I fought along with
Kossuth, and I don't deal in anything ! '

" The old baron roared and grasped his sword, but one of us put
a burning cinder into the horse's ear, and the horse carried him away.
We started off at once. We wandered one day and another—but
he caught us.

" ' Hey, you,' he said, ' my conscience is clear before God and
before you. Give me the girl in marriage. I'll share everything
with you—I am very rich ! '

" He was burning, and, like feather-grass tossed by the wind, he
was shaking in his saddle. We grew thoughtful.

" ' Well, my daughter, speak,' said Danila, under his breath.

" ' If an eaglet were to go to a raven's nest of her own will, what
would become of her ? ' Radda asked us.

" Danila laughed, and we all laughed with him. ' Good, my
daughter ! Did you hear, sir ? The thing doesn't work ! Look
for doves ; they're more yielding.' And off he went.

" And the old magnate seized his cap, threw it to the ground and
darted away ; he galloped so that the earth began to tremble. Such
was Radda, falcon.

" Yes ! So one night we were sitting and listening to music which
was soaring over the steppe ; beautiful music it was ! It made the
blood warmer in the veins and it lured us somewhere. We felt that
this music made us wish for something, after which it would be no
longer necessary to live, and if to live, then as kings of the whole
world ; that's the kind of music it was, falcon.

" And the music came nearer and nearer. Soon we discerned a
horse in the darkness, and on it sat a man playing as he advanced

toward us. He paused at the wood-pile, stopped playing and looked at us with a smile.

" ' Eh, Zobar, you ! ' exclaimed Danila joyously. ' So that was Loiko Zobar ! '

" His moustaches reached to his shoulders and mingled with his locks ; his eyes were burning like bright stars, and his smile was like the sun, by God ! He looked as if he had been cast of one block of iron together with his horse. He stood there in blood-colour, in the flame of the wood-pile, laughing, his teeth flashing. Eh, may I be accursed if I did not love him already as I loved myself, before he even said a word to me or noticed that I, too, lived in the white world !

" You see, falcon, what kind of people there are in the world ! He'll look into your eyes and make your soul a prisoner, and you're not a bit ashamed of it—you even feel proud of it. With such a man you at once become better yourself. There are few such people, my friend ! And it is better that there are but few of them. If there were much good in the world it would not have been considered as good at all. That's the way it is ! But listen :

" Radda said to him : ' You play well, Loiko. Who made you such a well-sounding, delicate violin ? '

" He began to laugh. ' I made it myself, and the strings I twisted out of the heart of a young girl I loved dearly. The violin is still a little false, but I can manage the bow well ! You see ? '

" Of course, a young fellow will try at once to befog a girl's eyes, so that they should not consume his heart, while he himself is seized with longing for her. Thus it was also with Loiko. But he didn't strike the right girl.

" Radda turned aside and said, yawning : ' And people told me that Zobar was wise and clever. That's the way they lie.' And she went away.

" ' Eh, beautiful girl, your teeth are sharp ! ' Loiko flashed his eyes and dismounted his horse. ' Good-evening, brethren ! I have come to you ! '

" ' We welcome our guest, O eagle ! ' said Danila in reply to him.

" We lived for some time in the same place ; things went well, and Zobar stayed with us. He was a comrade ! And he was wise, like an old man ; he knew everything. He knew how to read and write Russian and Hungarian. Sometimes he would start to talk—I would give up sleeping for an age, and rather listen to him. And then he played ; may the lightning strike me if any one in the world ever played as Zobar ! He would whisk the bow over the strings— and your heart would begin to quiver ; he would run the bow over the strings once more—and your heart would become petrified listening, while he played and smiled. One felt like crying and laughing at the same time, listening to his songs.   Now some one was moaning bitterly from under his bow, moaning, begging for help, and cutting your heart as with a knife.   Now the steppe was telling fairy tales to the skies—sweet, sad fairy tales.   Now a girl was crying, escorting her departing lover.   Now the lover called the girl for a rendezvous in the steppe.   And suddenly—hey !—a gay, free melody would resound like the crash of thunder, and it seemed as if the sun itself would soon dance to the tune of that melody.

‘ " Every vein of your body understood that melody, and you yourself became its slave.   And if Loiko would cry out at that time, ‘ To knifes, comrades ! ’ we would all draw our knives and go against anybody he would point out.   He could do everything with a man, and everybody loved him, loved him intensely.   Only Radda did not look at him, and she even mocked him.   She stung Zobar to the quick !   Loiko gnashed his teeth, tugged at his moustaches ; his eyes were darker than the abyss, and sometimes something flashed in them which made one fear for one's soul.   Loiko would go far away at night into the steppe and until morning his violin would weep there, burying his freedom.   We lay and listened, thinking of what was to be done.   We knew that when two rocks are rolling against each other we must not stand between them—they'll crush us.

" Once we all gathered and discussed matters.   It became tedious. Danila asked Loiko :

" ‘ Sing a song, Zobar ; cheer up our souls ! ’

" Zobar glanced at Radda, who lay a little distance away from him, gazing at the sky, and then he started.   The violin began to speak as if it was really a maiden's heart !   Loiko sang :

" Hey-hop !   In my heart a fire is burning, and the steppe is vast,
   Like the wind, my steed is swift, and my hand is firm.

" Radda turned her head, and, raising herself a little, smiled to the singer.   He flushed like the dawn of day.

" Hey, Hey-hop !   Come, my comrade !   Shall we gallop away ?
   The steppe is clothed in stern gloom, and yonder the break of day awaits us !
   Hey-hop !   Let's fly to meet the day.
   Rise upward, but let your mane not touch the beautiful moon !

" How he sang !   No one ever like that now !   But Radda said, as though filtering water :

" ‘ You had better not fly so high, Loiko, for you may fall down. Look out, you may fall with your nose into a ditch, and you'll dirty your moustache.’

" Loiko glanced at her like a beast, but said nothing—the brave fellow restrained himself and sang on :

"Hey-hop!   Soon the day will come, and we are still asleep.
Ey, Hey!   Then you and I will be consumed by the fire of shame!

" ' That's a song for you ! ' said Danila.   ' I have never before heard such a song ; may Satan make of me a pipe for himself if I lie ! '

" Old Nur twitched his moustaches and shrugged his shoulders, and we were all delighted by Zobar's fine song.   Only Radda did not like it.

" ' A mosquito buzzed like this one day, mimicking the cry of an eagle,' she said, as if throwing snow on us.

" ' Perhaps you want the knout, Radda ? ' Danila stretched himself toward her, and Zobar, as black as the earth, flung his cap to the ground and said :

" ' Hold on, Danila !   A wild horse needs a steel bridle !   Give me your daughter for a wife ! '

" Danila smiled.   ' Take her,' he said, ' if you wish and if you can ! '

" ' Very well,' said Loiko, and turned to Radda.   ' Well, girl. listen to me awhile, and don't be haughty !   I have seen many girls—eh, many !   But not one of them touched my heart as you have done.   Eh, Radda, you have made a prisoner of my soul ! But what of it ?   What is to be, will be—and—eh, there isn't a horse on which one can run away from himself !   I take you as my wife before God, before my honour, before your father and all these people.   But look out ; my freedom is not to be thwarted.   I shall continue to be a free man, and to live as I please.'   And he came up to her, his teeth firmly set, his eyes flashing.   We saw how he outstretched his hand to her.   Now, we thought, Radda has put the bridle to the horse of the steppe.   Suddenly we saw that Zobar threw up his hands, and struck the ground with the back of his head——

" What had happened ?   It was as though a bullet had hit the brave fellow's heart.   Radda has lashed his feet with a huge leather knout and then tugged it to herself ; that is why Loiko fell.

" And soon again the girl lay on the ground, motionless, silent, smiling.   We were waiting to see what would happen.   Loiko sat on the ground, clasping his head with his hands, as though fearing lest it should burst.   Then he got up quietly and went away into the steppe, not looking at any one.   Nur whispered to me, ' Watch him ! ' and I crept after Zobar into the steppe in the darkness of the night.   That's the way it was, falcon ! "

Makar threw out the ashes from his pipe and began to refill again. I muffled my top-coat more tightly about me and, lying, looked at his old, black, sunburnt, weather-beaten face. He shook his head sternly and muttered something under his breath ; his thick grey moustaches were stirring, and the wind waved his hair. He looked like an old oak which had been struck by lightning, but which was still mighty, and proud of its might. The sea kept whispering to the shore as before, and the wind wafted this whisper over the steppe. Nonka had stopped singing, and the clouds which had overcast the sky made the autumn night still darker and more terrible.

"Loiko walked step by step," went on Makar, "his head hung, his arms dangling like whips, and when he came down to the valley, near the brook, he seated himself on a rock and heaved a sigh. He sighed so that my heart began to bleed for pity, but I did not go over to him. You can't help one in misery with a word ; isn't it so ? He sat an hour, another and a third, without stirring from his place.

"And I lay a little distance away. The night was light, the moon covered the entire steppe with silver, and one could see far away.

"Suddenly I noticed Radda coming hastily from the camp. I began to feel cheerful—eh, how cheerful ! 'Radda's a fine, brave girl,' I thought. She walked over to him, but he did not notice her. She put her hand on his shoulder ; Loiko shuddered and raised his head. Then he jumped up and clutched his knife ! 'Oh, he'll kill the girl ! ' I thought, and was about to call to the camp, and run to them, when I heard Radda's voice :

"'Drop that ! I'll break your head ! ' Radda held a pistol in her hand and she aimed straight at Zobar's forehead. That was a Satan of a girl ! 'Well,' thought I, 'they're now equal in strength ; what will happen now ? '

"'Listen ! ' Radda thrust the pistol into her belt and said to Zobar : 'I have come not to kill you, but to make peace with you. Drop that knife ! '

"He dropped it and looked into her eyes morosely. It was terrible, my friend ! Two human beings stood and faced each other like beasts, and both were so good and brave. Only the bright moon looked down on them, and I—that's all !

"'Well, listen to me, Loiko ; I love you ! ' said Radda. He merely shrugged his shoulders, as though he was bound hand and foot. 'I have seen brave fellows, but you are braver and handsomer in soul and face than all. Each and every one of them would have shaved off his moustaches if I were but to give a single wink to him ; they would all fall at my feet if I only wished it. But what's

the use ? They're not too brave as it is, and I would have made
women of them altogether. There are but few brave gipsies left
in the world—very few, Loiko. I have never loved any one, Loiko,
but I love you. And then I love freedom ! I love freedom, Loiko,
more than I love you. And I cannot live without you, just as you
cannot live without me. Therefore I want you to be mine—soul
and body—do you hear ? "

"Zobar smiled. ' I hear ! It cheers my heart to hear your
words ! Go ahead, speak on ! '

" ' And there's another thing, Loiko : no matter how you turn
about, you'll be mine. Therefore don't waste any time in vain ;
my kisses and caresses are awaiting you. I will kiss you passionately, Loiko ! Under my kiss you will forget your valiant life, and
your gay songs which delight the brave gipsies will no longer
resound over the steppe. You will sing tender songs of love to
me, your Radda. Don't waste your time in vain. I have said it ;
that means that to-morrow you will yield to me as to an older
comrade. You will bow to my feet before the whole camp, and
you will kiss my hand—and then I will be your wife ! '

" That's what the devilish girl wanted ! Such a thing was
unheard of in our days. Only long ago there was such a custom
in Montenegro, but among gipsies—never ! Fraternity with a girl !
Well, falcon, try to invent something more ridiculous than that !
You'll break your head for a year, and you will not invent it !

" Loiko jumped aside and shouted over the whole steppe, like
one wounded in the chest. Radda shuddered, but she did not
betray herself.

" ' Well, then, good-bye till to-morrow, and to-morrow you'll do
as I bid you. Do you hear, Loiko ? '

" ' I hear ! I'll do it ! ' moaned Zobar, and outstretched his
hands to her. She did not even look at him, and he staggered, like
a tree broken by the wind, and fell to the ground, sobbing and
laughing.

" That's how the accursed Radda harassed the brave fellow. It
was with difficulty that I brought him to himself.

" Eh, who needs that people should be afflicted with misery ?
Who is it that loves to hear how a human heart, rent by grief, is
moaning ? There, think about it !

" I returned to the camp and told everything to the old people.
They thought it over and decided to wait, to see what the result
would be. And this is what happened. When we all gathered
around the wood-pile next evening, Loiko also came. He was
agitated, and he had become terribly thin overnight ; his eyes were
sunk ; he lowered them to the ground, and without lifting them,
said :

" ' It's this way, comrades : I looked into my heart last night and I did not find in it the place of my old free life. Radda alone lives there. Here the beautiful Radda is smiling like a queen ! She loves freedom better than she loves me, while I love her better than I love my freedom, and I decided to bow to Radda, as she bade me, so that every one shall see how her beauty conquered the brave Loiko Zobar. And then she will become my wife and will caress me and kiss me, so that I shall not feel like singing any songs for you any longer, and I'll not feel sorry for my freedom. Isn't it so, Radda ? ' He lifted his eyes and looked at her.

" She nodded silently and sternly, and pointed at her feet with her hand. And we looked on and understood nothing. We even felt like going away, if only not to see how Loiko Zobar would kneel before a girl—even if that girl was Radda. We felt ashamed, we felt sorry and sad.

" ' Well ! ' cried Radda to Zobar.

" ' Eh ! Don't be in a hurry, you'll have time, you'll grow tired of it yet,' he laughed. And his laughter was like the sound of steel. ' So here's the whole affair, comrades ! What remains to be done ? It remains for me to find out whether my Radda's heart is really as strong as she has shown it to me. I'll try, then—forgive me, brethren ! '

" Eh ! We had not time yet to conjecture what Zobar was about to do, and Radda lay already on the ground, and Zobar's crooked knife stuck in her breast up to the very handle. We were dumb-founded.

" Radda drew out the knife, threw it aside, and stopping up the wound with a tuft of her black hair, she said with a smile, in a loud clear voice : ' Good-bye, Loiko ! I knew that you would do it ! And I died—'

" Do you understand the girl, falcon ? That's the kind of a devilish girl she was, may I be accursed for ever and ever if it isn't so ! Eh !

" ' Eh, I will make a low bow to you, proud queen ! ' cried Loiko over the whole steppe, and throwing himself to the ground, he pressed his lips to the feet of the dead Radda and lay as petrified. We bared our heads and stood in silence.

" What can you say in a case like this, falcon ? Nur was about to say, ' We must bind him ! ' But our hands would not move to bind Loiko Zobar, and Nur knew it. So he waved his hand, and stepped aside. And Danila picked up the knife which Radda had thrown aside, and he looked at it for a long time, stirring his grey moustaches. Radda's blood had not yet dried up on the crooked, sharp knife.

" Danila walked over to Zobar and stuck the knife into his spine right opposite the heart.

" ' That's the way ! ' said Loiko, turning to Danila, and he went off to overtake Radda.

" We looked on.   Radda lay, pressing with her hand the lock of her black hair to her heart, and her open eyes were fixed on the blue sky, and near her feet lay the outstretched form of the brave Loiko Zobar.   His locks fell on his face and covered it.

" We stood absorbed in thought.   Danila's grey moustaches were quivering, his heavy eyebrows knitted.   He looked at the sky in silence, and old Nur, white as snow, laid himself down on the ground, face downward, and began to sob so that his old shoulders twitched up and down.

" There was something to cry about, falcon !

" You are wandering ?   Well, then, go your way ; don't turn aside.   Go straight.   Maybe that you will pine away in vain. That's all, falcon ! "

Makar became silent and, hiding his pipe in his tobacco-pouch, he covered his breast with his coat.   It was drizzling : the wind became stronger, and the sea grumbled dully and angrily.   One by one the horses came over to the dying flame of the wood-pile, and staring at us with large, intelligent eyes, stopped, motionless, surrounding us in a close ring.

" Hop, hop ! ehoy ! " Makar shouted to them gently, and clapping his favourite black horse on the neck, said, turning to me : " It's time to go to sleep ! "

And he covered himself with his coat over the head, and outstretching himself on the ground, fell silent.   I did not feel like sleeping.   I looked into the darkness of the steppe toward the sea, and in the air before my eyes soared the majestically beautiful figure of Radda.   Her hand pressed a lock of black hair to the wound in her breast, and through her thin, swarthy fingers blood was trickling drop by drop, falling to the ground in fiery red stars. And behind her, at her feet, soared the brave Loiko Zobar ; his face was covered with heavy black locks, and from under them cold, large tear-drops were dripping. . . .

The rain was increasing, and the sea was singing a gloomy and solemn hymn to the pair of beautiful gipsies—Loiko Zobar and Radda, the daughter of old soldier Danila.

And they both whirled about silently and easily in the darkness of the night, and the beautiful singer Loiko could not overtake the proud Radda.

MAXIM GORKY

IN THE STEPPES

WE left Perekop behind us in the very worst of moods—hungry as wolves and angry with the whole world. During the space of twelve hours we had been deliberately plying all our strength and resources to steal something or earn a little money, but when we were at last convinced that neither the one nor the other was possible we decided to move on farther. Where? Farther at all events. It was a unanimous decision, and we communicated it to each other in words. In every respect we were ready to continue on the path of life along which we had trodden so long. This, too, each decided for himself, and though no word was uttered it could yet be seen plainly in the solemn glances of our hungry eyes.

There were three of us ; we had not known each other long ; we had all met at Herson, in a tavern on the banks of the Dnieper.

One of us had been a soldier of a railway battalion and later a superintendent on a piece of railway in Poland. He was a red-haired, muscular man with cold grey eyes ; he could speak German, and had an intimate knowledge of prison life.

A man of our stamp rarely likes to talk about his past life, always having a more or less well-grounded reason for not doing so ; thus it was that we all believed each other—at any rate, outwardly we believed each other, while inwardly each man believed but poorly in himself.

When our second companion, a dry little man with thin lips always pressed sceptically together, spoke of himself and said that he had once been a student of a Moscow University, we took it as a fact. In reality it mattered little to us whether he had been a student or a spy or a thief, the only thing that counted was that during our acquaintanceship he was our equal. He suffered hunger as we did, was under strict police surveillance in the town and under suspicion with the peasants in the country, and hated the one and the other with the hatred of a defenceless, hunted, hungry animal, dreamt of universal revenge against all,—in a word, by his mood and his position among the kings of nature and the lords of life, we were birds of a feather.

Misfortune is the very strongest cement for binding people together even of the most opposite natures, and we were all convinced that we had a right to consider ourselves unfortunate.

The third was myself. From a sense of modesty inherent in me from earliest infancy I will not say a word about my virtues, and not wishing to appear naïve I will be likewise silent about my vices. But just to give a general idea of my character I will merely say that I always considered myself better than other men, and will go on thinking so to the end of my days.

And so, we left Perekop and walked on farther, having as our aim that day the shepherds of the steppes, from whom one can always beg a piece of bread and who rarely refuse it to a passing stranger.

The soldier and I walked abreast, the "student" following behind us. On his shoulders was a kind of pea-jacket, on his pointed, angular head, closely shaven, were the remains of a broad-brimmed hat; grey trousers, covered with many-coloured patches, encircled his legs; on the soles of his feet was a gear he called sandals, made out of an old boot-leg, picked up in the road, and the lining of his coat torn into strips. His small greenish eyes flashed as he walked on in silence, raising the dust behind him. The soldier had on a red fustian shirt, which he had "acquired with his own hands in Herson," according to his own words; besides this shirt he wore a warm waistcoat lined with wadding; on his head was a military cap of an uncertain hue, put on according to the military rule, "the crown tilted a little to the right brow"; coarse baggy trousers were on his legs, and he was barefooted.

I, too, was barefooted.

And around us as we walked, on all sides, in a broad sweep, stretched the steppe beneath the blue sultry dome of the cloudless summer sky, looking like a huge, round, black platter. The dusty road that burnt our feet cut across it like a broad band. In places the stubbly strip of cut corn bore a close resemblance to the soldier's long unshaven cheeks.

The soldier walked, singing in a hoarse bass:

> ...and praised be Thy holy Sabbath...

During his service in the army it had fallen to his lot to be a kind of chanter in the battalion chapel, and consequently he knew many troparions and hymns, which he misused on every occasion when our conversation happened to lag.

The soft purple and rosy outlines of some forms became discernible in the distance on the horizon.

" I suppose it's the Crimean mountains," the " student " said in a dry voice.

" Mountains ! " exclaimed the soldier. " It's soon, too soon, my friend, for you to see mountains. It's a cloud . . . only a cloud. Don't you see ? It looks just like huckleberry kissel and milk."

I remarked that it would certainly be pleasant if the cloud were really composed of kissel. This instantly made us think of our hunger and brought back the bitterness of our days.

" Ah, the devil ! " cursed the soldier, spitting on the ground ; " if we could only meet some one ! Not a living soul ! . . . We shall have to suck our own paws like the bears in the winter."

" I told you we should have to try a peopled part," the " student " announced instructively.

" You told us ! Of what use is your learning if you cannot talk ? What peopled parts are there here ? The devil knows where they are ! "

The " student " was silent, biting his lips. The sun had set, and the cloud on the horizon was one mass of indescribable colour. There was a salt, earthy smell. And this dry, pleasant smell increased our appetites the more.

There was a gnawing in the pit of the stomach, a strange, disagreeable sensation that seemed to draw the strength out of every muscle in the body, making it lose its suppleness. A stinging, acrid taste was in the mouth, the throat was parched, the head swam, and dark spots danced in front of the eyes. Sometimes these spots took the form of steaming lumps of meat or chunks of bread, and the memory gave these " visions of the past, visions mute," each its particular smell, and then it seemed as though a knife had been thrust into the stomach.

We walked on, however, describing our sensations to each other, straining our eyes for the sight of a sheep trail and our ears for the sound of a Tartar's cart carrying fruit to the Armiansky market.

But the steppes were silent and deserted.

The day before this unfortunate day the three between us had eaten four pounds of rye bread and five water-melons, on which we had walked forty miles (" the expenditure in excess of the income "), and going to sleep in the market square of Perekop we were awakened by violent pangs of hunger.

The " student " was right when he advised us not to sleep, but to take advantage of the night and go about our business. . . . In decent society, however, it is not permissible to discuss schemes for the violation of private property, so I will be silent on this point. I merely want to be just and not coarse for the sake of my own interests. I know that people are becoming more tender of heart in these highly cultured days, and that even when taking a man by the throat with the object of strangling him, it is done with all possible politeness and due observation of all the proprieties fitting to the occasion. The experience of my own throat makes me observant of this moral progress, and with a pleasant feeling of confidence I maintain that everything evolves and perfects itself in this world. In particular this remarkable progress is largely visible in the yearly growth of prisons, taverns, and thieves' dens.

And thus, swallowing our saliva and by friendly conversation trying to ignore the pain in our stomachs, we walked along the silent, deserted steppes, beneath the red rays of the setting sun, vaguely hoping for something to turn up. In front of us was the setting sun, sinking gently into the soft cloud, ablaze with its rays, and behind us a blue mist was rising from the steppes to the sky, narrowing the unfriendly horizon.

" Collect everything you can for a camp-fire, mates," the soldier said, picking up a small log from the road ; " grass and twigs and everything ! We've got to spend the night in the steppes . . . and there'll be a dew."

We separated on all sides, and began collecting dry grass and everything we could lay our hands on that would burn. With every bending movement towards the ground, a passionate desire took possession of the whole body to cast oneself down and lie immobile and eat of the black, abundant earth,—eat and eat until one could eat no more, then close one's eyes and sleep. It mattered not if it meant sleep for ever, so long as one could chew, and feel the thick, warm mess in the mouth slowly descending down the parched throat into the greedy, gnawing stomach, burning with a desire for food.

" If we could only find some roots . . ." the soldier sighed. " There must be some edible roots. . . ."

But there were no roots in the dark, ploughed soil. The southern night came on quickly ; the last rays of the setting sun had barely faded when the stars began to twinkle in the dark blue sky, and around us the shadows grew closer and closer, shutting out the endless plane of the steppes. . . .

" Mates," the " student " whispered, " a man is lying over there, to the left. . . ."

" A man ? " the soldier asked doubtfully. " Why should he lie there ? "

" Go and ask. He must have bread with him to station himself in the steppes . . ." the " student " explained.

The soldier looked in the direction where the man lay, then expectorating resolutely on the ground said :

" Come, let us go to him ! "

Only the keen green eyes of the " student " could have distinguished that the dark mass lying about a hundred yards to the left of the road was a man. We hastened towards him, quickly stepping over the lumps of ploughed earth, and feeling how the newly born hope of food quickened the pangs of our hunger. We were quite near, but the man did not move.

" Perhaps it is not a man," the soldier said gloomily, giving expression to the general thought. But our doubt vanished that very instant, for the mass on the ground suddenly moved, seemed to grow, and we saw it was a real, living man, kneeling down, with his hand stretched towards us. And he was saying in a hoarse, trembling voice :

" Don't come near, or I'll fire ! "

A dry click resounded in the turbid air.

We stopped as at a military command and for several seconds we were silent, dazed by the unfriendly greeting.

" Confound the beast," the soldier muttered expressively.

" A revolver, to be sure," the " student " said pensively ; " an adventurous fish one can see. . . ."

" Hi ! " the soldier called out, evidently resolving on something.

The man was silent and did not change his attitude.

" Hi, there ! We won't touch you . . . only give us some bread . . . something to eat. For Christ's sake, mate ! . . . Be damned to you, you devil ! "

The latter was added under his breath.

The man was mute.

" Do you hear ? " the soldier went on, trembling with rage and despair. " Give us some bread. We won't come near you ; throw it to us. . . ."

" Very well, . . ." the man said curtly.

" My dear brothers," he might have added, and had he put into these three Christian words the purest and holiest of feelings they would not have roused us more or made us more human than his curt " Very well."

" Don't be afraid of us, my good man," the soldier went on gently, with an ingratiating smile on his face, though the man could not have seen his smile, for all that he was lying no more than twenty paces away from us ; " we are peaceful fellows . . . tramping from Russia to Kuban. . . . We got short of money on the road . . . and sold everything we possessed. . . . It is now the second day since we tasted any food."

" Catch ! " the good man said, with a swing of his arm. A black lump flew through the air and fell some little distance from us on the ploughed soil. The " student " hastened to get it.

" Catch again, again ! That is all ; I haven't any more. . . ."

When the " student " had collected the objects given in this original way it appeared that there were about four pounds of stale wheaten bread. It was covered with earth and very hard. The first did not engage our attention, the second was very fortunate for us, as stale bread is more satisfying than new, it containing less moisture.

" There—there—and there ! " the soldier said, solemnly giving each our portion. " But stop—they are not equal. As for you, scholar, I must break a piece off yours, or else he will have too little."

The " student " without a word submitted to about an ounce of his bread being taken from him. I took the piece and put it into my mouth. I began to chew it slowly, slowly, scarcely able to control the convulsive movements of the jaws that were ready to crunch stones. I experienced a keen pleasure in feeling the quick convulsions of the throat and being able to satisfy it a little, drop by drop. Mouthful after mouthful, warm and inexplicably, indescribably delicious, the food penetrated into the burning stomach and seemed at once to turn to blood and brain. A joy, such a strange, peaceful quickening joy made the heart warm, in the same measure that the stomach was filled, and a feeling of drowsiness came over me. I forgot about these days of chronic hunger, forgot about my comrades engrossed in the pleasures of the same sensations that I had experienced. But when with the palm of my hand I put the last crumbs of bread into my mouth I realised that I was still deadly hungry.

" I daresay the fiend has some more bread, or some meat perhaps . . ." the soldier mumbled, sitting opposite me on the ground and rubbing his hands over his stomach.

" No doubt he has ; the bread smelt of meat. . . . At any rate he is sure to have some more bread . . .," the " student " said, then added softly : " If it were not for the revolver. . . ."

" I wonder who he is, eh ? "

" A man of our complexion, I suppose. . . ."

" The dog ! " the soldier said viciously.

We were sitting close together, casting sidelong glances at the spot where our benefactor lay with the revolver. Not a sound or a sign of life reached us from him.

The night closed around us with its powers of darkness. A deadly silence reigned in the steppes ; we could hear our own breathing. From time to time the melancholy squeak of a marmot could be heard. The stars—the living flowers of the sky—shone brightly above our heads. . . . We were hungry.

It is not without a feeling of pride that I say that on this extra-ordinary night I was no better and no worse than my comrades. I suggested to them that we should go boldly up to the man and without doing him any harm eat all the food we found about him. Even if he attempted to fire only one of us would fall, and it was possible that the shot would not be absolutely deadly.

" Come on ! " the soldier exclaimed, jumping up.

The " student " rose more slowly.

And we started almost at a run, the " student " creeping behind us.

" Comrade ! " the soldier rebuked him.

We were met by a dull murmuring and a sharp click. There was a flash and a shot rang out.

" Missed ! " the soldier exclaimed joyfully reaching the man at one bound. " Now, you devil, you will get it from us. . . ."

The " student " rushed for the wallet.

The " devil " rolled over from his knees to his back, and throwing up his arms began to wail.

" What the devil ? . . ." the soldier exclaimed in astonishment, his foot ready in the air to give the man a kick. " What is he howling about ? Hi, what is the matter with you ? Have you hit yourself, eh ? "

" Here's bread and meat and cakes . . . quite a lot ! " the " student's " voice could be heard exultantly.

" Well, die there, damn you ! . . . Let us eat, mates ! " the soldier cried.

I snatched the revolver out of the man's hand. He had ceased his moaning and was now lying motionless. Only one cartridge remained in the chamber.

Again we were eating, eating silently. The man was also silent, not moving a single limb. We paid no attention to him.

" And was it really only food you wanted, mates ? " a hoarse, trembling voice asked suddenly.

We all started. The " student " nearly choked, and bending down, started coughing violently.

The soldier, chewing, began to abuse him.

" You dog ! May you burst like a dry twig. Did you think we wanted your skin. What use would it be to us ? Confound your ugly face ! To fire at people like that ! . . ."

He went on eating while the abusive words fell from his lips, losing most of their force and expressiveness in consequence.

" You wait till we've finished eating, then we'll settle with you," the " student " announced viciously.

Then the stillness of the night was suddenly broken by a moaning and sobbing that frightened us.

" How should I know, mates ?   I fired . . . .because I was afraid. I was coming from Kovy Afon . . . in the Smolensk Government. . . . Oh, Lord !   A fever came upon me . . . when the sun set.   Woe is me ! I left Afon because of the fever there. . . . I am a carpenter in Afon . . . a carpenter . . . I have a wife . . . and two little girls at home . . . it is more than three years since I've seen them . . . you can eat everything you find, mates. . . ."

" We will do that without your invitation," the " student " said.

" By the Lord, had I known that you were such quiet, decent folk, I would not have fired.   And you know, mates, in the steppes here. . . . Am I to blame, eh ? "

He wept as he spoke, or rather he gave forth a kind of trembling, timid wail.

" What a worm, to be sure ! " the soldier said contemptuously.

" I expect he's got some money with him," the " student " announced..

The soldier half shut his eyes and looked at him with a smile.

" Right, mate. . . . Well, now let us light a fire and go to sleep."

" And he ? " asked the " student."

" The devil take him !   We can't roast him, can we ? "

" He deserves to be roasted," the " student " said, with a shake of his pointed head.

We went to fetch the materials that we had thrown down where the carpenter had stopped us with his threatening cry, brought them back quickly, and were soon seated around a camp fire.   It rose with a gentle heat in the still night air, illuminating the small space on which we sat.   We were inclined to sleep, though we could still have supped once more.

" Mates ! " the carpenter called out to us.   He was lying three paces away, and at times it seemed to me that he was muttering something to himself.

" Yes ? " the soldier said.

" Can I come to you . . . to the fire ?   Death is on me . . . my bones seem all broken. . . . My God ! I shall never get home, never. . . ."

" Crawl over here," the " student " said.

The carpenter, slowly, as though fearing to lose an arm or a leg, moved over the ground to the fire.   He was a tall, terribly emaciated man ; everything seemed to hang on him, and his large glazed eyes reflected his consuming pain.   His contorted face was haggard, and even by the light of the camp fire it appeared yellow and ghastly. He was trembling in every limb, and aroused in us a scornful pity.

He stretched his long arms to the fire and rubbed his bony fingers, the joints of which bent slowly and languidly. He was disgusting to look at.

"Why do you travel on foot in the condition you are in? Are you too mean to spend the fare, eh?" the soldier asked severely.

"They advised me not to go on the water, but to go by the Crimea; the air would do me good, they said. But I cannot walk any more. . . . I am dying, mates! dying alone in the steppes. . . . My flesh will be food for the birds, and no one will know. . . . My wife . . . my daughters . . . are expecting me . . . I wrote and told them I was coming . . . and my bones will be washed by the rain of the steppes. . . . Oh Lord, oh Lord!"

He howled with the forlorn cry of a wounded wolf.

"Shut up, you devil!" the soldier shouted in a rage, jumping to his feet. "Why do you whine? Why can't you leave a man in peace? If you must die, then be quiet about it. . . . Of what good are you, anyway? Hold your peace!"

"Give him a knock on the head," the "student" suggested.

"Let us go to sleep," I said. "And as for you, if you want to remain by the fire, then you had better stop whining, or I expect . . ."

"Do you hear?" the soldier asked furiously. "Understand once and for all! Do you think we are going to pity you and bother about you because you threw some bread at us and tried to fire a bullet into us? Confound you! Other men would . . . fugh! . . ."

The soldier ceased and stretched himself on the ground.

The "student" was already lying down. I, too, lay down. The scared carpenter shrank into a heap, and drawing nearer to the fire, fixed his eyes upon it in silence. I lay to the right of him and could hear his teeth chattering. The soldier, lying on his back with his arms under his head, was staring up at the sky.

"What a night, eh? So many stars . . . warmth . . .," he turned to me after a short silence. "The sky is more like a blanket. I love this wandering life, my friend. It's a cold, hungry life, but free, very free. . . . There is no one over you . . . you are master of your own fate. . . . If you want to bite your own head off, no one can say you nay. . . . It is good. . . . How hungry I was these last days and vicious, but now, here I am lying down and looking up at the sky. . . . The stars are winking at me, as though to say: 'It doesn't matter, Lakutin; roam over the earth, learn all there is to learn, and don't submit to any one.' . . . Yes, and the heart feels good. . . . And you, carpenter, how do you feel? Don't be angry with me for being cross, and don't be afraid of anything.

. . . If we ate your bread, we meant no harm—you had bread and we hadn't, so we ate yours. . . . And you, like a savage, fired bullets at us. . . . Don't you know that bullets are dangerous? I was very angry with you. If you hadn't fallen down I should have paid you out for your impudence. And as for the bread—to-morrow you can get as far as Perekop and buy some more there. I know you've got money. . . . How long is it since you've had the fever?"

For a long time the soldier's heavy bass and the trembling voice of the ailing carpenter droned against my ear. The night, dark and dense, descended closer to the earth, and the fresh, fragrant air was pleasant to breathe.

The camp fire gave out an even light and a delicious warmth. . . . The eyes closed, and, through the drowsiness, something soothing and purifying hovered in front of them.

.   .   .   .

"Hi, get up, quickly! We must be off!"

With a start I opened my eyes and jumped quickly to my feet, assisted by the soldier, who, with a tug at my arm, pulled me up from the ground.

"Make haste! March!"

His face was solemn and anxious. I looked around me. The sun was rising, and a red ray lay across the immobile, blue face of the carpenter. His mouth was open, his eyes started out of his head with a glassy expression of horror. The garments over his breast were torn asunder, and he lay in an unnatural, contorted position. The "student" was nowhere to be seen.

"Well, have you seen enough? Be off, I tell you!" the soldier said significantly, pulling me by the arm.

"Is he dead?" I asked, shuddering with the keenness of the morning air.

"Of course he is. If some one were to strangle you I suppose you would be dead," the soldier explained.

"Was it . . . the 'student'?" I exclaimed.

"Who else then? Was it you or I? Yes. He finished him off nicely, the scholar, and left us both in the lurch. Had I only suspected it I would have killed that 'student' yesterday. I would have killed him at once—with one blow of my fist. There would have been one blackguard the less in the world! Do you realise what he's done? We must take care that not a living soul sees us in the steppes. Do you understand? The carpenter may be discovered to-day, and they will see that he's been strangled and robbed. They will look out for men of our sort . . . and want to know where we are going and where we spent the night. They will catch us, though you and I have nothing . . . but this revolver I have in my breast. A pretty thing ! "

" You had better throw it away," I counselled.

" Throw it away ? " he asked musing. " A costly thing it is. . . . And they may not catch us after all. No, I won't throw it away. Who knows that the carpenter carried firearms ? I won't throw it away. . . . It must be worth three roubles at least, and then there is a cartridge in it. How I should like to put it through that ' student's ' head ! The dog ! I wonder how much money he walked away with ? The cursed pig ! "

" And what about the wife's little girls ? " I ventured

" Little girls ? What girls ? Oh, the carpenter's ! They will grow up and get married, I suppose. Besides, they have nothing to do with the case. Let us get away quickly, mate. . . . Which way shall we go ? "

" I don't know. . . . It makes no difference."

" And I don't know, and I know that it makes no difference. Let us go to the right—the sea must be there."

We walked towards the right.

I turned back. At some distance from us, a dark little mound rose in the steppes with the sun shining on it.

" Are you looking to see if he's risen ? Have no fear, he won't run after us. That scholar of ours managed the job well. . . . A nice comrade, to be sure ! He tricked us jolly well ! Ah, mate ! men grow worse and worse from year to year ! " the soldier said sadly.

The steppes, silent and deserted, and bathed in the bright morning sun, spread out before us, touching the sky at the horizon, so clear and gentle and glorious that all dark and unjust deeds seemed out of place amidst the vast space of this free plain, covered by the dome of the blue sky.

" I want to chew something, mate," my comrade said, rolling a cigarette out of some cheap tobacco.

" What and where and how shall we eat to-day ? That's a problem."

.   .   .   .

With these words my neighbour in the hospital ward finished his story, saying to me :

" That is all. I got very friendly with that soldier, and we walked together as far as the Karsky province. He was a good, practical, kind-hearted fellow, a typical, barefooted tramp. I had a great respect for him. We walked together as far as Asia Minor, and there we lost sight of each other. . . ."

" Do you ever think of the carpenter ? " I asked.

" As you see—or as you have heard. . . ."

" Nothing more ? "

He laughed.

" What must I feel about it ? I am not to blame for what happened to him, any more than you are not to blame for what happened to me. And no one is to blame for anything, even though we are all brutes."

MAXIM GORKY

BOLESLOV

THIS is what a friend of mine told me one day :

While I was studying at Moscow I lived in a little house where a strange girl was my neighbour. She was Polish ; her name was Teresa. She was tall, strong, brown, with heavy eyebrows and vulgar features, as if carved with an axe. Her eyes looked dull, she had a deep voice, and her manners were those of a prize-fighter. Heavy and muscular of body, her whole appearance was fearfully ugly. We had opposite rooms in the garret. I never opened my door when I knew she was at home. Sometimes I met her on the stairway or in the yard, and she smiled at me with a sort of cynical smile. Often I saw her coming home with red eyes, her hair in disorder. At such times she met my gaze with an impudent stare. Then she would say : " Hullo, student ! "

Her stupid laugh was disgusting. I would have changed my rooms to avoid meeting her ; but the place was so pleasant, with the unobstructed view over the city, and the street was so quiet, that I stayed.

One morning, after I had dressed and was lying on my bed, the door opened suddenly and Teresa appeared on the threshold.

" Hullo, student ! " she said in her deep voice.

" What do you want ? " I asked.

I looked at her. Her face wore an expression of confused shyness, something I had never noticed before.

" Student," she said, " I want to ask you a favour. Please don't refuse it ! " Lying there on my bed, I thought, " This is only a pretext." But I said nothing.

" I should like to write a letter home," she continued.

" What the deuce is she driving at ? " I thought. I jumped up from the bed, took a seat at the table, got paper and ink, and said, " Come in ; sit down and dictate."

She entered, sat down cautiously and shot a keen look into my eyes.

" Well, to whom shall I write ? " I asked.

"To Boleslov Kaschput, who lives at Swenziani, on the Warsaw Railroad."

"What do you want me to write ? Go ahead——"

"My dear Boles—my sweetheart—my love—my soul—may the Blessed Virgin protect you ! My dear, why have you not written for so long a time to your little dove, Teresa, who feels so sad ? "

I could hardly help laughing at her. To think of this " sad little dove," almost six feet high, robust, with fists like an athlete, and a face as black as if the " dove " had done nothing all its life but sweep chimneys !

But I kept my face straight and asked : "Who is this Boleslov ? "

"Boles, sir ? " she replied, with an air of astonishment, as if it was inconceivable that any one should not know who Boleslov was. "Boles is my betrothed——"

"Betrothed ? "

"Why should you be so surprised, student ? Can't a young girl like me have a sweetheart ? " she said.

"A young girl "—what a joke ! "Maybe," I said. "Everything is possible. How long have you been engaged ? "

"For ten years."

Well, I wrote a letter for her, so full of love and tenderness that I myself would have liked to be in Boleslov's place, if the message had come from any one but Teresa.

"Thank you with all my heart, student," said Teresa. She appeared deeply moved. "Can I do something for you ? "

"No, thanks."

"I can mend your shirts and clothes, student." That annoyed me somewhat, and I assured her briefly that I did not need her services. So she left.

Two weeks went by. One evening I was sitting at the window, whistling and wondering what I might do for some distraction. It was awful weather outside, and I did not like to go out. Suddenly the door opened.

"For heaven's sake ! " I thought. "Somebody is coming."

"Student, are you very busy just now ? " It was Teresa. Well, I would rather have seen somebody else.

"No. Why ? "

"I wanted you to write another letter for me."

"All right. To Boles ? "

"No. I want his answer——"

"What ! " I exclaimed.

"Excuse me, student ; I'm stupid. I didn't express myself clearly. It is not for me, but for one of my friends—that is, not a friend, but an acquaintance. He does not know how to write—he has a betrothed like me——"

I glanced up at her. She looked ashamed ; her hands trembled and she was confused. I thought I understood.

" Listen, my girl," I said. " All that you tell me about yourself and Boleslov, and so on—all this is pure imagination ; you were lying. It is only a pretext for coming here. I do not want to have anything to do with you any more ; you understand ? "

I saw that she was frightened. She blushed and tried hard to say something. I began to feel that I had misjudged her. She had not come, after all, with the grotesque idea of leading me from the path of virtue. There was something behind this. But what ?

" Student——" she began ; but with a sudden gesture she turned on her heel and went from the room.

I remained with an uneasy feeling in my heart. I heard her close her door with a bang. She was angry. I reflected for a moment and resolved to call her back. I would write the letter. I felt sorry for her.

I went to her room. She sat at her table, her face in her hands.

" My girl," I said, " you——"

When I come to this point in my story I always feel deeply touched. She jumped up, came straight to me, her eyes shining, put her arms on my shoulders and sobbed as if her heart would break.

" What—what—difference—does it—make to you—to—to— write these—few—lines ? Oh—you—looked like such a—good— fellow ! Yes—there is no—Boleslov—and—no—Teresa. There is only—me—me alone ! " " What ! " I said, quite dumbfounded by her words. " Then there is no—no Boles at all ? "

" No."

" And no Teresa ? "

" No—that is—I am Teresa."

My head was in a whirl. I looked at her in astonishment. One of us was surely crazy. She went back to the table, fumbled in the drawer and brought out a piece of paper.

" Here," she said, coming back to me ; " here, take back this letter you wrote for me. You do not want to write a second one. Other people with kinder hearts will do it."

She held in her hand the letter I had written for her to Boleslov. What in the world did it mean ? " Listen, Teresa," I said. " What is all this ? Why do you want other people to write letters for you when you haven't posted this one ? "

" To whom should I post it ? "

" Why, to Boleslov—your betrothed ! "

" But—there's no such person ! " I gave it up. The only thing I could do was to go away. But she began again :

" No, he does not exist ; there is no Boleslov "—with a gesture that indicated how impossible it was to explain. " But, *I want him to live.* I know I am not like others—I know what I am—but it does not harm anybody if I write to him."

"What do you mean ? To whom ? "

"Why, to Boleslov ! "

"But you told me just now," I interjected, still puzzled, " that there was no such person."

"Oh, Mother of God ! What do I care if there isn't ! There *is* nobody, but I *imagine* that there is a Boleslov. I write to him as if he were real, and he answers ; I write again, and he answers again——" At last I understood. I felt guilty, ashamed, with a shock as if of physical pain. Beside me, almost within arm's reach, lived a poor human being who had not a soul in the world to show her the least affection ; no parents, no friends, nothing ! And this poor creature had invented a lover, a bridegroom, for herself !

She went on in her deep, monotonous voice : " This letter you wrote for me to Boleslov—I asked somebody else to read it aloud to me. I listened and imagined that Boleslov lived. And then I asked for a reply from Boles to his Teresa—to me. I feel almost sure that Boleslov lives—somewhere—I don't know where—and so I can manage to live. It is not so hard, so terrible, so lonely ! "

Well, from that day on, twice a week regularly, I wrote letters from Teresa to Boles and from Boles to Teresa. I give you my word, they were full of passion, especially the replies. And she—she listened to the reading, sobbed, laughed, and was happy. In return she took care of my clothes, mended my shirts and socks, cleaned my shoes, and brushed my hat.

Three months later she was arrested on some suspicion and put in gaol. I have never seen her again. She must have died.

ALEXANDER I. KUPRIN

B. 1870

PSYCHE

November 23rd.—One might ask me the simple question as to why I have taken to keeping a diary again after giving it up for five years ; and really there is nothing more absurd than keeping a diary or writing one's autobiography. In the first place, they all begin alike, the author's first duty being to assure the reader, by all that is holy, that he is not writing for the public, but merely for his own personal amusement. Or they say, " So that I, a grey-haired old man, surrounded by a crowd of rosy-cheeked children, may re-live the past and feel again what I felt as a blossoming youth, and that the solitary tears of reminiscence . . .," or something like it. But long before they have attained their grey hairs they flourish it about and show it off. Many times will such a one re-read his recollections—of no interest except to himself— to some timid, ethereal, provincial creature who will tremble with the rush of unknown sensations—and quietly yawn behind her pocket-handkerchief. How vulgar it is that really intelligent people should be ready to parade their petty personal sensations, and consider it sensible and in good taste !

As for me, my diary is far too important for me, and, needless to say, I shall not read it to any one.

To-day the doctor informed me that if I continued the life I have been leading for the past three years—that is, constant starvation, insomnia, and working like a horse—I would have a complete nervous breakdown. The young doctor did not mince matters with me. He advised a holiday in the Crimea, when I haven't even the money for a pair of goloshes ! However, I understood quite well that he inferred that I was going mad ; the more so as many of my worthy ancestors were drunkards and lunatics. In this book I shall set down all my thoughts until I begin to feel the signs of abnormality, and then . . . either the hospital or, if I have sufficient will-power left, a bullet through my brain.

November 26th.—Whose fault is it ? I am certainly possessed of great talent and originality ; there is no need to show off before myself. I am, of course, not confirmed in this opinion because I have been given a gold medal by the academy council with whom I happen to disagree on questions of art, nor by the praise of newspaper critics. I am no longer a boy, and can gauge things at their true value, for " human honour is as senseless as a dream." But I feel myself in the presence of an intense and mighty creative force ; my observation is keen, I can catch quickly the smallest details of objects, and above all I have never had to strain my imagination, as many artists have to when hunting for subjects. Gigantic thoughts, each bolder and more original than the preceding, come crowding into my head, so fast as to make me feel afraid. And above all, during the process of creation, as though in a religious ecstasy, I feel the sweet consciousness of an unknown god within me. My head is on fire, cold waves run down my back, my hair turns cold and stands on end, my spirit exults. And mocking fate, as though on purpose, has placed me in the sad position of not being able to complete a single one of these precious images. Fighting for one's daily bread is incompatible with free creation ! Sometimes, with danger to life and reason, one must veer from dreams of fame to the perspective of death by starvation. Hunger is the very worst food for inspiration. But then, with my uncontrollable rush of fantasies and the inner activity that exhausts me, I cannot become a clerk or a shoemaker !

November 27th.—To-day I finished my twelfth Pushkin. I have got so used to modelling them that I could work with my eyes closed, and they all come out as like as peas. Pushkins sell easily just now on account of some 50th celebration or other, but the dealer to whom I take my statues is not satisfied with my work. " You lack variety," he says dryly. " What we want is a varied series ; the public taste differs so." I am sometimes nauseated at the thought that it may be necessary to change over to this dreary daily work. I notice sometimes, with horror, that after a week's work on my funereal profile busts of warriors they begin to take on the same characteristics, like a director of a department or a merchant of the first guild. But what is to be done when ten or twenty roubles enable me to be the master of my inspirations for a whole month !

November 28th.—For some reason or other it is generally assumed that a drunkard borders on the state of idiocy. An astonishingly wrong conclusion ! Meanwhile I must confess that I have got into the habit of drinking vodka in these cursed lodgings, that, thanks to my carelessness, are never heated. At first I limited the amount to two or three glasses, merely to warm myself. Now I am almost drunk while writing. My brain is very active and remarkably clear ; it notices subtle little details of its sensations that would certainly have been lost to a sober brain.

Only my tongue and legs do not obey me, and my eyes work badly ; all objects lose their clear form and seem to be besprinkled with sand. But that signifies nothing. It is a well-known fact that many great masters created their immortal works when in the very same condition in which I am now. I wanted to work ; I have a certain great thing in view, but continued lying on the miserable couch that my landlady calls a bed, and dreamt of fate.

November 29th.—I awoke about mid-day with a terrible headache. I had a strange dream last night. I saw myself standing somewhere on the outskirts of the town. It seemed to be in autumn. The wind whistled through the telegraph wires, and a fine cold rain, that came in sharp gusts, covered all objects in a dull grey veil. Dusk began to fall and my heart was oppressed with a sensation of impending misfortune. . . . Suddenly, behind me, there was the sound of the stamping of many horses. I turned, and saw a strange sight. Ten or twelve horsemen, dressed in black from head to foot, were hurrying forward at terrific speed. Their horses wore black caparisons with round eye-holes. The horsemen came onwards quickly, turning neither back nor to one side. Each carried in his hand a tarred torch that burned with a red, smoky flame. I gathered that it was a funeral, and in fact, from some corner there appeared a hearse drawn by three pairs of horses, so swiftly as to keep up with the riders. The black coffin was covered with bright crimson roses. I ran after this strange procession and together we reached the cemetery. This was a very desolate place. The bare trees groaned and shook, throwing off their cold spray on to the earth ; there was a smell of earth and rotting yellow leaves.

The horsemen took the coffin and began lowering it into the grave, but the lid was not shut and I saw in it a marble statue of a girl of extraordinary, divine beauty. She reposed on a bed of bright green grass and was covered in red roses and camellias. I do not know how it was, but I recognised her instantly—it was sleeping Psyche !

I threw myself at the men who were lowering the coffin and shouted and cried in my endeavour to tell them that the being in the coffin was alive, but they laughed and pushed me away roughly. Again I managed to get to the coffin, put my arms round the beautiful cold body and found myself, together with it, in the grave. From above they were shovelling the earth on me . . . deeper and deeper.

At last, I could no longer breathe. I wanted to cry out, but my voice sounded no more than a whisper ; I made a desperate movement—and awoke.

November 30th.—Another wasted day. My " warriors " annoy me for some reason or other, I cannot endure to look on their coarse,

healthy muscles ! Then why have I worked at them with such affection for months on end, and why did I go to the ice factory, where for
twenty kopeks I got two fellows to fight each other ? Instead, I
thought the whole day of the wonderful statue with whom I
had lain in the grave.   Where have I seen this beautiful calm face,
this body as tender as a girl's, the breasts scarcely formed, lissom and
graceful yet naïve for all its nakedness ? And why was it Psyche in
particular, and not Daphne or Flora ? I am interested in the psychology of dreams and have read a great deal on this subject.   I knew
very well that one does not see anything in a dream that one has
not seen some time or other in reality.   Probably I have seen my
Psyche.

But where ? I go over all the classics in my mind yet fail to recall
that face, strangely familiar yet impossible to describe.   There is
something in the highest degree fine about it, yet at the same time
it is absurdly simple ! When I want to conjure up the image of it in
my mind, I cannot get it on any account, yet I have only to think
of something else for a moment and it floats before my eyes.

December 2nd.—I have scarcely the time to wash the clay from
my hands to write a few lines in this stupid notebook.   This is the
third day that I have been modelling my Psyche.   My nerves seem
alive, the work goes easily and quickly, and when I go to bed each
night I have the feeling of perfect balance of mind and heart—a
condition near to blessedness.   Some sculptors depict Psyche as
an absolutely developed woman—an incomprehensible mistake !

Psyche is almost a child ; she is slight of stature and must
produce the impression of a beautiful creature, vaguely and timidly
realising her transformation from a child into a maiden.

Besides this I have made a still greater discovery.   No other
body but a virgin's should ever be cast, modelled or carved in any
material, because sculpture is the purest, the highest, and certainly
the most chaste of all the arts.   For this reason, a sculptor when
working should avoid having before his eyes either natural or lay
figures, and particularly should conquer his carnal part.   If the
idea to be made incarnate in marble is mixed with vulgar reality,
instead of the idea you get a travesty of it.   It is not in vain that
in our ancient art only the simplest instruments are used—hands
and modelling sticks.

This notebook will not be read by any one but myself, so I can
speak openly.   Phidias, Canova, and Thorwaldsen, in spite of all
their genius, could not separate themselves from the common
everyday feelings of their private lives.   A sculptor is only in a
condition to create something great when he is himself pure and
chaste.   I am representing Psyche asleep.   It is said that figures
lose something in a lying posture, but that does not deter me.

December 4th.—My God! what tortures! what hellish labour, and nothing, nothing has come of it! Do what I will, I cannot remember the Psyche of my dream. From morning to night I work until I feel mad and exhausted, with no result! Before me is not the sleeping Psyche but a piquante subject with a sweet languor.

Yes! I have certainly overworked myself. Of course you cannot go on for eight days without taking off your working overall. I must try and rest.

December 6th.—What accursed rest is this? For two days I have not risen from the couch and am tortured by most horrible nightmares. All the events of the last few days are mixed up in my brain in the most incomprehensible manner. There are moments when I cannot make up my mind as to whether a certain event happened this morning or yesterday, or a week ago, or if I have read it in a book, or seen it in my sleep.

In general I have noticed more than once that my memory becomes clouded quickly, particularly since I dropped all my acquaintances and scarcely ever speak aloud. Like an old man, I can still remember clearly all that happened in my childhood, but about the present my memory is confused and hazy. For the greater part of the day I sleep and have a hundred dreams, but in these dreams I also see myself lying on the couch, usually repeating a thousand times over some stupid phrase and not knowing what to do from despair. These trivial dreams are so interwoven with trivial reality that I sometimes wonder with horror where the one begins and the other ends. At moments I seem to become sober and with despair I want to tear myself away from this cursed semi-consciousness. I want to shake myself, to distract myself a little, but in a short time the vortex of sleep again begins to suck me down.

The night is full of horror. I do not fall asleep until daylight, and, sometimes with terror, sometimes with amazement, I contemplate the tremendous file of pictures, statues, faces familiar and unfamiliar, that appear before my eyes without any action of my will and which disappear again against my desire. Some of the faces are simply hideous. They make horrid grimaces, roll terrible eyes, and put their tongues out. When one of them approaches my face I grow as cold as at the approach of death.

To rid myself of these hallucinations I drink several glasses of vodka and begin to feel better. Ought I to see a doctor?

December 8th.—Accidentally I happened to see myself in the mirror. I had not seen myself for three weeks and simply grew horrified when there looked out at me that long, yellow, terribly thin face with cheeks as drawn as those of a corpse, and sunken eyes, with black hollows beneath them. I positively hate my own appearance. Man is supposed to be the glory of creation, but at this moment I undoubtedly belie that statement.

December 10*th.*—Can I describe what took place last night ? I still cannot come to myself from the mass of sensations I have gone through. Words cannot convey a hundredth part of it, still I will endeavour to set out everything in order.

In the middle of the night I awoke feeling that some one had called me by name. This frequently happens with me when the moon shines full on my face. My room was filled with a silver-green light and seemed quite unfamiliar ; the walls seemed to have grown and receded ; every object looked strange and suspicious. I seemed to feel by instinct that some event of tremendous importance would take place instantly—at that very moment. My glance fell on Psyche. She lay on the floor ; her body, covered over with damp cloths and bathed in a dead, soft light, seemed transparent. Mechanically seizing the modelling sticks I put in a few fine lines . . . and suddenly I cried out and trembled with joy : before me lay the same Psyche I had seen in my dreams, whose image I had tried so hard to recall ! No words can express the wild joy that rose in my heart. At last I understood why her face had seemed so simple and familiar. It was the prototype of that divine beauty and harmony a striving for which is hidden in every man's breast from the day of his birth and which humanity has christened by the much hackneyed name " the ideal." Fate has granted us artists the means of reaching it, but until this momentous night we had all tormentingly and fruitlessly run after its shade. And I, I, a pale, ugly, weary sculptor, had reached it, had caught what until now seemed the impossible and had embodied it in a palpable form. Oh ! I understand quite well that my talent had nothing to do with it and that my hand had been led by chance. It is for this very reason that no one but myself must ever see Psyche, because if man ever develops art to such a degree, it will only be in a thousand years to come. First of all, man will get to know and conquer all those forces of nature that at the present time enslave him, and then when he reaches the goal, this eternal truth and beauty, he will cease to be man. God only knows what consequences might follow upon the public appearance of my Psyche. She must lie in the ground for a hundred years, like the works of the ancient Greeks, until her time comes and fate takes her out like a beacon that must light up the hill-top.

Not dated.—I have written nothing for the past few days because of an unbearable headache. There are moments when some one seems to be hammering on my skull, and every movement causes excruciating pains. By the way, to-day I spent all the money I had on plaster of Paris.

No date.—As soon as it began to get dark in the room I carefully drew the curtains, lit the lamp, and stood for a long time silently contemplating the unearthly beauty of my creation that lay before me.

This is what is so wonderful : everything that man has pursued to madness from time immemorial—fame, sensuality, patriotism, all earthly pleasures—one can get tired of, but the ecstasy that I now experience can never pall ! I wonder what would happen if she were a living woman ! It seems to me that one would have to kill her just as I am going to cover her with earth in a few days. But until then she is entirely mine, and her beauty belongs to me alone.

Mine ! Ah, if that word had not become so common by a thousand human desires !

My fate is wonderfully strange. I am thirty-five years old and absolutely weary of life. But even in the days of my youth there did not exist for me the charm of feminine caresses. Perhaps with my particularly abnormal organism I had no need of them. When women plainly avoided all contact with me, I was not in the least hurt, but soon grew pleased. I had never known women, nor kisses, nor caresses, nor affectionate glances. And this fate, as though out of a sense of justice, has sent me the most incredibly high happiness, —a happiness that can never be experienced by those defiled by the impure love of women. But this is not all ; I know, I have a presentiment, that a greater happiness is in store for me, clothed for the time being in secrecy ! Ah ! Now I have finished the mould in plaster of Paris, and it lies before me, blinding in its whiteness.

December 15th.—I have forgotten to put dates in my diary as I had other things to think about. My landlady informed me that as to-day was the 15th of December, it was exactly three months since I had paid for my lodgings. The poor woman it seems is partly sorry for me and partly afraid. However, what can one expect ? It is not for nothing that to common people the word " artist " has come to be a synonym for madman or blackguard.

I write and am bothered by a curious circumstance. At moments I forget certain letters and it costs me a great deal of pains to recall them. Why is this ? But it is of no consequence. A great thought has occurred to me. If the proverb accords every lord the right to his fancy, who can forbid a free artist to enjoy his for once in his life ? This is my idea. . . . I do not remember whether I recorded in my diary the dream in which I saw *her* first, in the coffin. I think I did. I want to resurrect entirely into reality that first impression, that is, to place her in a nice fir coffin lined with dark velvet and strewn with green. But where can I get the money ?

December 16th.—To-day Slivinsky, one of my Academy colleagues, came to see me. He is a very curious man. At a first meeting he conveys the impression of a madman ; his hair is always dishevelled, his glance now wanders about aimlessly, now suddenly becomes fixed on the face of the person who happens to be talking to him, though Slivinsky neither sees nor hears him, but is occupied with his own thoughts. Sometimes he interrupts you by some question that has no relation to the subject under discussion, and is merely some conclusion he has arrived at in his own train of thoughts. He is terribly absent-minded, a passionate lover of women—a fact that frequently disgusts me—and is always hunting for adventures. In every-day affairs he is quite a child, and if, in his presence, the conversation turns on worldly matters he sits silently biting his nails. His hobby-horse is psychology in general and psychology of woman's heart in particular. I love talking to him because sometimes such amazing ideas occur to me that seem absurd to all but him. He understands at once and knows beforehand what I am going to say—he has an extraordinary gift that way. At times, when we happen to see much of each other, we dig down so deeply into the innermost recesses of our hearts and disclose such awful filth that we become the worst of enemies. I heard his voice on the stairs and wanted to send someone to say that I was not at home, but it was too late ; I had scarcely time to drag the sheet from the bed and cover Psyche with it. Not a single human being shall see her as long as I live !

"What is the matter with you !" Slivinsky said, before we had barely exchanged greetings, and in a most unceremonious manner looked me up and down.

"What do you mean ? Have I grown horns on my forehead that you stare at me like that ? " I asked rudely, on purpose to draw his attention from a certain direction.

"No, not horns. Had there been horns there would have been cause to wonder indeed, but your face looks like a squeezed lemon, and there are purple lines under your eyes."

I was silent.

"And do you know what I think, brother ? " Slivinsky asked suddenly, with some agitation. "I suppose it never enters your head that you are going to die soon ? "

"Leave off, please."

"You don't believe me ? But I plainly see in your face the lines of a peculiar spiritual beauty. Do you understand ? I often noticed when I was in the hospital that with nervous people, a few weeks before death, the soul, freeing itself, destroyed its prison. However, let us drop it. What are you doing now ? Are you working ? "

Ah ! I must be cunning ! However, I knew what would happen, and I replied so indifferently that I even surprised myself ; not one of our clever actors could have controlled his voice so naturally.

" I lie on the couch, think a little of immortality, gossip with my landlady ; on the whole I pass the time interestingly and usefully."

Slivinsky fixed his heavy gaze on my face.

" You lie, brother," he concluded suddenly. " You have some inner ebullition. But never mind ; I do not ask for frankness. I came to you for this purpose. Do you know, spiritualism when you study it closely is not such arrant charlatanism as one is led to think. . . ."

And with his usual enthusiasm and eloquence he began to explain his incredibly bold theory of media, yet not without a touch of humour. Taking advantage of a momentary silence I asked :

" And what have you been doing all this time ? Why don't you tell me about yourself ? "

" I haven't done a thing," he replied, dropping his spiritualism. " And do you know why ? In the first place, because I seem to have a vocation for women rather than for sculpture ; it must have been love of woman's body that made me study our art. In the second place, and I mean this quite seriously, our art is a very poor one ; it is as cold as marble, to which it is allied, and just as pure. I may be mistaken, but in my opinion a sculptor who is destined to create an immortal work must be just such an anchorite and as abnormal as you are. . . ."

How strange ! This man always utters the thoughts that I can never decide to put into words ; it is not for nothing that I call him my conscience. It would be interesting to know by what different paths we reach the same conclusions.

" Do you know," Slivinsky continued, and instantly I knew by the gentle tone of his voice that he was going to talk on his beloved theme, " earlier, I might have turned out to be of use, but lately I have been so lax morally as to be ruined for art. I am not content with this severe purity of line, this lifeless plaster of Paris. I could still perhaps become a painter, only because a painter has the arrangement of paints, colour, and shade. Painting is more sensual. But I have no desire to join any such company. Youth is given to men only once, and of course not with the purpose of destroying it or burying it, as you have done, entirely in one art."

" To combine these objects is the ideal of sensation hunters—I am not of their number."

" I don't know what to do with myself, but meanwhile I wisely enjoy all the gifts that beneficent nature and quick wits have bestowed on man, and in doing so I place woman, of course, in the foreground—lovely woman."

" And don't you think this vocation will bore you after a time ? "

" Never ! Don't you see, my boy, that I belong to the chosen people who have developed in themselves such a subtle receptiveness that they enjoy most the details, the accessories of love, so to speak, rather than love itself in the coarse, vulgar sense of the word.   And as these accessories are as varied as human nature itself, it follows that there will always exist for me the charm of novelty.   Ah ! what a pity you are such a degenerate and cannot understand me. Do you know, for instance, the mysterious unfathomable charm there is in the gradual process of becoming intimate with a woman ? Those timid hints when the eyes have told all, those quarrels and oppressive bursts of jealousy, the first confusion. . . . But of course you understand nothing of this."

" I understand quite well that it is a gastronomic corruption ! " I interrupted with displeasure.

Slivinsky looked at me with amazement.   He seemed to think me incapable of such a reply.

" Perhaps you are right," he drawled pensively, but instantly brightened again.   " Yes ; but do you know the struggles involved in this corruption ? How often one has to use all one's brain, all one's strength ? Listen ! Do you know to what lengths a man's will may carry him ? Have you ever considered the question ? "

This time I noticed that Slivinsky awaited my answer with interest.

" I cannot pretend to understand your question thoroughly," I replied, " but if by the word ' will ' you imply, as I do, every desire in life, then as you know I have always considered it more convenient to man to deny this same ' will.' "

" Oh ! do leave your Schopenhauer alone ! " Slivinsky exclaimed with annoyance.   " I meant ' will ' in the worldly sense of the word, that is, as meaning the strength of the most prosaic desires.   In my opinion the intensity of man's desires, yours and mine, can endow us with such gigantic powers that nothing need be impossible for us in this world ! "

It seems according to Slivinsky that the will can be cultivated by a form of constant and persistent gymnastic exercises consisting in acting against one's desires every minute of the day.   If at a given moment I am hungry I must endure it as long as I can, if I want to lie down I must walk about, if I like to sleep on a soft bed I must train myself to sleep on stones, and so on.   When in this manner man has completely subjected his will, then all those around him, men and beasts, will involuntarily and imperceptibly become subordinate to his desires.   For that man there will be no obstacles except those presented by time.

" Don't you see," Slivinsky continued enthusiastically, " that by constantly following one idea I cannot only become Pope of Rome or Emperor of China, but even the greatest genius or scholar.   Have

you heard of the negro slave who, unable to read or write, developed
his memory to such a degree by concentration that he could repeat
off by heart five hundred ciphers of eight meanings that had been
dictated to him ? But that is nothing. I can give you better
examples. How do you think Napoleon rose from a simple
lieutenant to one of the greatest emperors in history ? You think
it was only fortune ? No doubt it was partly fortune, because in his
undertakings there frequently happened favourable combinations of
circumstances—but principally it was the strength of his desires.
Where you and I allow our chances to escape us tens of thousands
of times, the man who firmly resolves to make use of them is not
deterred by risks, sacredness of tradition, or the number of his
victims. Strength of desire and confidence ! That is everything—
that is the famous lever of Archimedes. In the Scriptures it is
said that those that have faith may remove mountains, and such
faith is attainable by all whose desires are unusually concentrated.
The Fakirs heal the sick and make the dead to rise. . . ."
   I did not recognise Slivinsky ; he seemed to have grown taller
and more imposing ; his eyes shone with the fires of inspiration and
his voice sounded solemn and enraptured.
   " I wonder that with your theory, you have so far remained a
simple mortal," I said, after a time.
   " Why ? Because I don't want anything else, but I have tried
my will on women, on whom I want to draw the conversation.
Remember my great apophthegm—when you come to write your
reminiscences about me, it will be useful to you ; there is no man
who, possessed of a strong and flexible will, cannot subdue and obtain
for himself the love of a woman. And not only a woman with a sick
imagination or what we call a temperament, but even one as in-
accessible as a goddess and as cold as marble."
   " Do you think then that an actual statue could be thus
hypnotised ? "
   In putting this question I felt my cheeks turn pale. It was
as though I had looked into a dark abyss—it was painful and
gay.
   " It is possible," Slivinsky replied seriously. " You remember
the story of Galatea, and, as you know, there is not a single myth
without some foundation. I have already said that there is nothing
impossible to a strong will. And in the end, even if you do not
actually bring the statue to life, you yourself, do you see, you yourself *will believe that you have done so !* "
   Slivinsky rose to leave and in going out asked, " What is that you
have covered with a sheet ? May I have a look ? "
   Had I obeyed my first impulse and flown at his throat, this
extraordinary man would have been sure to have got my secret

forcibly.   As it was I did not move from my place, but extending
my hand in the parting, replied, gathering my wits together :
 "It is only a piece of rubbish lying about."

I did not suspect myself of such a store of cunning and self-
possession ! Directly after Slivinsky's departure I made a screen
with the sheets and hung it over *that* corner.

No date.—My head whirls, my hand trembles, and refuses to obey.
I do not know whether I am in a fit state to collect my thoughts
and set out correctly all that has happened.   When night came I
drew the curtains and lit the lamp.   The room seemed suddenly to
become solemn and mysterious.   I could not tear my eyes from the
white screen that enclosed the corner ; it seemed that behind it
was some silent, invisible life.   I was irresistibly drawn behind the
screen, but I lingered, and as in a fever tried to drag out the burning
expectancy as long as possible.

At last my agitation became insufferable and I resolved to put an
end to it.

Holding my breath, I approached with cautious tread the sheets
that hung from the ceiling, and put them aside with trembling
hands.   In this tiny enclosure, no more than three paces wide,
there reigned the sweet silence of a sanctuary.   *She* lay on the
broad piece of coarse linen, covered from head to foot in a sheet
which faintly indicated her wonderful form.   She lay on her back,
her left leg a little bent ; her head leaning a little to one side rested
on her left arm, and the right hung negligently down to the ground.

I do not say that I was afraid ; had she at this moment raised
herself from her stone couch and spoken to me, I should not have
been afraid ; I even seemed to expect it ; but I controlled my
limbs with difficulty ; they seemed heavy—as though buried in
sand ; countless, tiny glowing points danced before my eyes with
amazing rapidity.   But all the time I closely followed every one of
my sensations and clearly noticed that the sheet covering her breasts
slowly rose and fell, trembling with her soft breathing.   My heart
beat like a drum and was filled with a fatiguing delicious pain. . . .

After that I lose the thread.   I only remember how I quietly fell
on my knees, bending my head to the ground ; how I carefully
raised the sheet ; how my lips drew near to her body. . . . But
when my lips came in contact with her cold form, the unbearably
sweet pain in my heart burst out and spread like a flame on which
alcohol has been poured. . . . For a moment it seemed to me that
it was death.   I must have fainted, for when I opened my eyes the
daylight was creeping in round the edges of the curtain.

What does it all mean ? Was Slivinsky right when he said that I
would die soon ? Well, what of that ? I am prepared to meet death
like a beloved guest, for could life tempt me with anything after

that moment of ecstasy I experienced last night ? Ah, how I bless that which in my childhood seemed to me such a terrible misfortune, that caused my comrades to turn from me with contempt ! It only protected me against corruption, and, denying me the principal human joy, had given fate the possibility of rewarding me abundantly.

No date.—To-day, for the first time in two months, I went out into the street. I must have produced a very strange impression on the passers-by, for all looked me up and down. The frosty air intoxicated me, the snow, sparkling in the sun, caused my eyes to fill with tears, and my legs, grown unaccustomed to walking, bent under me and shook my feeble body from side to side. Added to this, my coat was covered with down and the lining of wadding showing copiously in places completed the general impression. I wandered about in vain all day and failed to secure a single kopek. I must put off the idea of the coffin. My God ! What is happening to me !

The same.—Why do not Slivinsky's enthusiastic words go out of my mind ? I keep thinking the whole day, and the conclusions I come to, frighten me. Slivinsky said that to the will nothing was impossible. Consequently, one must be able consciously to concentrate the will, to desire obstinately, persistently, and untiringly. I know very well that an object made of stone could not of itself, of its own volition, rise from its place and come to me. But then, are there not hypnotised subjects roaming over field and flood which do not exist in reality ? Perhaps people search for what does not and cannot exist. However, the devil himself could not solve this question !

The same.—I again awoke during the night with an unexpected shock and sat up quickly in bed. The moon was shining with unusual brightness and her beams seemed charged with a monotonous murmur.

Had I seen something in my sleep, or had I, during the day, been thinking on some important matter ? It seemed to me that I had forgotten something of the utmost importance, and tried to recall what it was. And suddenly, like lightning, the terrible thought flashed through my mind, " One must know how to desire ! " I got off the bed with difficulty, and again with that sweet trembling of the heart stole behind the curtain. My body shook with agitation, cold, and weakness ; my jaws chattered unpleasantly. Slowly and cautiously, fearing to disturb Psyche's light slumber, I pulled the sheet off her ; she did not move a muscle, but her breast rose and fell with a scarcely perceptible motion.

Oh, what omnipotent beauty there was in her calm face, in her gentle, semi-transparent, naked body ! I gathered together all my will-power, clenched my hands so that the nails cut into the flesh, controlled myself with an effort, and said commandingly and confidently :

" Awake ! "

And suddenly, through the murmur of the stillness, there sounded a deep, broken sigh. The immobile face lit up with a smile, the eyes opened and gently met mine ! The acute, rapturous sensation in my heart again burst out and flowed wonderfully through the whole of my being. I cried out and fell down, but before losing consciousness I felt two cold, naked arms entwine themselves around my neck. . . .

The same.—I do not understand what is the meaning of this dark room with the grating from which peep strange, long-whiskered faces—or is it that prison from which Slivinsky said my soul must escape ?

The same.—My God ! How hard is victory ! At times I beat my head against the walls of my prison, pluck out my hair, and tear the flesh from my face.

When will it all end ?

No date.—Victory ! My hands will no longer obey me, my lungs take in less air with each breath. But in the unattainable height, midst waves of radiant light, I already see your gentle smile, my goddess, my Psyche !

ALEXANDER I. KUPRIN

LENOTCHKA

ON his way from St. Petersburg to the Crimea, Colonel Voznitsin of the General Staff purposely stopped for two days in Moscow, where he had spent his childhood and youth.

It is said that the higher animals, when feeling the approach of death, revisit their familiar haunts as though bidding them good-bye. An early death did not threaten Voznitsin—with his forty years he was still strong and well preserved. But in his tastes, feelings, and relations to the world at large there had taken place that imperceptible change which marks the decline to old age. His round of joys and pleasures shrunk almost of itself; the habit of retrospection appeared together with a sceptical disbelief in all "movements"; the unconscious, silent, unreasoning love for nature disappeared, giving place to a refined taste for beauty; the fascinating charm of women ceased to disturb him, and, above all— the first sign of spiritual decay—the thought of his own death no longer came to him in the former light-hearted transient manner as of old, when it used to seem that not he but some other person of the name of Voznitsin was to die sooner or later. Now it came with a cruel, irrevocable, merciless clearness that at night caused a shudder and made the heart fall apprehensively.

And thus he was drawn to revisit the old places for the last time; to revive in his memory the dear, painfully-sweet poetic recollections of his childhood; to open his soul to the sweet pain of the brightness and purity of the first impressions of life that had gone for ever beyond recall.

And that is what he did. For two days he went about Moscow visiting the old haunts. He drove over to the boarding school in the Gorohovy fields, where from the age of six he had been educated on the Froebel system by worthy old dames. There everything was changed; the boys' section no longer existed, but in the girls' class-room, as of old, there was the pleasant, alluring smell of the polished ash tables and forms mingled with the still more enticing smell of goodies, particularly apples, that, as in former days, were stored in a special locked cupboard. Afterwards he went to the cadet corps and the military school. He also visited the house chapel at Kudim, where, as a boy cadet, he had served at the altar, handing the incense to the priest and coming out to the Evangel in a surplice. There also he had stolen the ends of wax candles, drunk the "tepid-water" after Communion, and with various grimaces made to sprinkle the absurd deacon, for which act he was once chased from the altar by the portly, majestic elder, who was wonderfully like the image of our Lord in the Cavaoth altar-piece.

He walked past the houses where he had experienced the first naïve, half-childish languor of love, went into the garden and up the stairs, and scarcely recognised anything, so changed and rebuilt was all, after a quarter of a century of absence. But to his grief and amazement Voznitsin observed that his desolate spirit and stale soul remained cold and unmoved, and did not reflect in itself the former familiar sadness respecting the past—such a bright, gentle, pensive, humble sadness. . . .

"Yes, yes—it is old age," he said to himself, shaking his head sadly. "Old age, old age, old age. . . . There is nothing to be done !"

After Moscow, some business matter took him for a day to Kiev, and he reached Odessa at the beginning of Passion Week. But a spring storm arose on the sea, and Voznitsin, who was not a good sailor, decided against taking ship. It was only on the morning of Passion Saturday that the weather grew calm and the sea still.

At six in the afternoon the steamer *The Grand Duke Alexei* left the Praktichiskoy Harbour. No one came to see him off, which pleased him very much. He could not endure the usually hypocritical and always tiresome comedy of saying good-bye, when, God only knows why, for the space of half an hour you stand on board smiling in a forced manner at the anxious people below on the dock, calling out every now and then senseless meaningless words in a theatrical tone, as though for the entertainment of the bystanders, kissing your hand to them, and at last, with a sigh of relief, feeling that the boat is slowly and heavily moving off.

The passengers that day were very few and these mostly third class. In the first class beside Voznitsin, as his valet informed him, there was only a lady and her daughter. "Excellent," the colonel thought with relief.

Everything promised a calm and comfortable voyage. He had an excellent cabin—large and light, with two couches standing in the corners and no upper berths. The sea, grown calm after the wild storm, was still covered with small waves, but no longer tossed the ship. Towards evening, however, it grew cold on deck.

That night Voznitsin slept, with open porthole, more soundly than he had done for months, not to say years. In Eupatoria he was awakened by the sound of the steamer's sirens and the noise of feet on the deck. He dressed quickly, ordered some tea and went above. The steamer was bathed in a semi-transparent, rosy-white mist mingled with the gold of the rising sun. The flat yellow banks could be seen shining in the distance, and the sea washed softly against the sides of the steamer. There was a pleasant odour of fish, seaweed, and tar. From a large barge that stood alongside the *Alexei* they were unloading bales and barrels.

" Raise ! Higher up ! Stop ! Lower ! Stop ! "

The words of command rang out clearly in the morning air. When the barge moved off and the steamer had started on its way, Voznitsin descended into the dining-room. A strange sight awaited him there. The tables, placed alongside the walls, were gaily decorated with real flowers and covered with Easter fare. Roast snipe and turkeys stretched their hideous bare heads on long necks supported by wire frames. These thin necks, bent into the shape of question marks, shook and nodded with the motion of the ship, looking like rare antediluvian animals as they are drawn in pictures, lying on large dishes with their feet bent under them, glancing around and bending their heads down with an anxious and comic cautiousness. The bright rays of the sun streamed in through the skylights, casting round patches of gold on the tablecloth, changing the colour of the Easter eggs to purple and sapphire, lighting up with a living glow the hyacinths, forget-me-nots, violets, tulips, and pansies.

A lady came in to breakfast. Voznitsin glanced at her quickly in passing. She was neither young nor beautiful, but had a well-preserved, high, somewhat round figure, and was simply dressed in a plain grey wrap, the collar and cuffs of which were embroidered in silk. Her head was covered with a light-blue, almost transparent, gauze scarf. She drank her tea, reading a book at the same time, a French one, Voznitsin decided, judging by its compact size and yellow cover.

Something about her struck Voznitsin as strangely familiar yet remote, not so much in her face as in the bend of her neck and the raising of her eyebrows as she turned her gaze upon him. But this subconscious impression instantly vanished and was forgotten.

Soon it grew hot, bringing a desire to go on deck. The lady passenger went up and sat down on a seat on the leeward side. Now she would read for a while, now rest the book on her lap as she gazed out to sea at the whirling dolphins and the distant, broken, reddish bank covered on top with scanty vegetation.

Voznitsin paced the deck. Once when he passed the lady she again looked at him intently with a kind of questioning curiosity, and again it seemed to him that they had met somewhere. Little by little this impression grew disturbing and persistent. And above all the colonel was now convinced that the lady had the same feeling about himself. But his memory refused to obey, no matter how much he taxed it.

Suddenly, coming up to the lady for the twentieth time, he abruptly, almost unexpectedly to himself, stopped near her, raised his fingers to his military cap and slightly clinking his spurs, said :

" Excuse my presumption . . . but I keep on thinking that we know each other or rather . . . that we knew each other a long time ago."

She was not at all beautiful—a browless blonde almost auburn with grey threads in it, which thanks to the lightness of her hair were not noticeable at a distance ; and light eyelashes over blue eyes, and a withered freckled skin. Only her mouth was fresh, rosy, and full with beautiful curved lines.

" And I, too, would you believe it, sit here and wonder where we could have met," she replied. " My name is Lvova. Are you any wiser ? "

" I am afraid not. . . . My name is Voznitsin."

The lady's eyes lit up with such a gay and familiar smile that it seemed to Voznitsin that he would recognise her at any moment.

" Voznitsin ? Kolya Voznitsin ? " she exclaimed joyfully, extending her hand.

" Don't you know me now ? Lvova is my married name. . . . But surely, you must remember. Don't you remember Moscow, Povarsky Street, Borisoglebsky Lane—the church house ? And your chum in the corps, Arkasha Urlov. . . ."

The hand that held the lady's trembled and closed more tightly. The instantaneous gleam of recollection seemed to blind him.

" My God. . . . Is it really Lenotchka ? I beg your pardon . . . Elena . . . Elena. . . ."

" Vladimirovna. You have forgotten. . . . And you are Kolya, the same Kolya, awkward, shy, and sensitive. How strange ! What a strange meeting ! Won't you sit down ? I am so glad. . . ."

" Yes." Voznitsin uttered some foreign phrase about the world being so small that people couldn't help running across each other.

" Well, tell me about yourself. How is Arkasha ? And Alexandra Millievna ? And Oletchka ? "

In the corps, Voznitsin had made great friends with one of his comrades by the name of Urlov. Every Sunday, unless he was denied a furlough, he spent with Urlov's people, and also Easter and Christmas ; in fact, all his holidays. Before entering the military school Arkasha was taken very ill and the Urlovs had to go to the country. From that time he had lost sight of them. Many years ago he had heard that Lenotchka was for a long time engaged to an officer with the curious name Jenishok—the accent on the first syllable—who for some absurd reason unexpectedly shot himself. . . .

" Arkasha died in the country in the year ninety," Madame Lvova said. " He had sarcoma in the head. Mamma only survived him two years. Oletchka finished her medical course and is now county doctor in Serdobsk. Before that she was assistant surgeon at Jmakin. She wouldn't marry for any consideration, although she had many excellent offers. I have been married for twenty years "—she smiled sadly at one corner of her mouth—" I am an old woman now. . . . My husband is a landowner and a county magistrate. Not very brilliant, but an honest man, good to his family, not a drunkard, a gambler, or a debauchee, as so many are nowadays . . . for which God be thanked. . . ."

" Do you remember how I was once in love with you, Elena Vladimirovna ? " Voznitsin interrupted. She laughed, and her face seemed suddenly to grow younger. Voznitsin got a momentary glimpse of the numerous gold stoppings in her teeth.

" What nonsense ! A mere boyish attraction. And not even that. You were not in love with me at all, but with the Sinilinkov girls—with all four of them in turn. When the eldest married, you laid your heart at the feet of the next, and so on. . . ."

" Ah ! So you were jealous of me a little ? " Voznitsin remarked, with a playful complacency.

" Not a bit. . . . To me you were no more than my brother Arkasha. Later, when we were both about seventeen, then perhaps I was a little annoyed that you transferred your attentions. You know, it is funny, but girls, too, have women's hearts. We need not at all be in love with the silent adorer, but are jealous of him nevertheless. However, this is all nonsense. Tell me instead how you are and what you do."

He told her about himself, about the academy, his staff career, the war, and his present service. No, he had not married ; at first he had feared poverty and the responsibility of a family, and now it was too late. Of course there had been various attractions as well as some serious attachments.

Then the conversation languished, and they sat silently looking at each other with affectionate, tear-bedimmed eyes. In Voznitsin's memory there quickly rose up images of that past separated from him by thirty years. He had first met Lenotchka when neither of them had yet reached their eleventh year. She was a thin, capricious little girl, provoking and quarrelsome, not at all pretty, with her freckles, her long arms and legs, light eyebrows and red hair, of which two thin straight strands, separated from the rest, always fell on either side of her cheeks. Ten times a day there were quarrels and reconciliations between her, Voznitsin, and Arkasha. Sometimes they would come to blows. Oletchka never joined in ; she was always noted for her good temper and common sense. In the holidays they always went to dances, theatres, the circus or skating. Together they got up Christmas parties and children's performances, made coloured eggs for Easter and dressed up for Christmas. They often worried and teased each other like young puppies.

Thus three years went by. Lenotchka went away for the summer as usual to their country place at Jmakin, and when she returned to Moscow in the autumn, and Voznitsin saw her again for the first time, he opened his eyes and mouth in amazement. She was still not beautiful, but there was something about her more wonderful than beauty, that bright, rosy bloom of early maidenhood that comes suddenly, God only knows by what miracle, and in one day transforms a clumsy, long-legged, long-armed child that looks like an over-grown puppy into a charming girl. Lenotchka's face still retained the deep, rosy, country complexion beneath which one felt the hot blood circulated merrily : there was a suggestion of hips and a clear firm outline of breasts ; the whole of her body had grown supple, lithe, and graceful.

And their relations suddenly changed. It happened after one of their Saturday parties when Lenotchka and Voznitsin, playing together in the half-dark room, took to wrestling. The window was still open ; from the front garden came a clear, fresh smell of autumn, and a faint odour of decayed leaves ; slowly, stroke by stroke, there floated in the rare, sad note of the large bell of Borisoglebsky church.

They wound their arms about each other, tightly pressing their bodies together, and breathing into each other's faces. But suddenly, blushing so deeply that it was noticeable even in the twilight, and dropping her eyes, Lenotchka whispered abruptly, angrily, and confusedly :

" Let me alone. . . . Let me go. . . . I don't want to . . ." and added with an angry glance of her sparkling eyes, " Nasty, horrid boy ! "

The nasty, horrid boy stood with trembling hands that hung down. Even his legs trembled, and his forehead was bathed in perspiration. He had only just felt in his arms her slender, docile, feminine body, broadening so wonderfully at the hips, and the touch of her firm, yielding, maidenly breasts against his chest ; he perceived the scent of her body, that joyful, intoxicating scent like that of poplar buds, or young black-currant shoots on a clear damp evening in the spring after a shower, when the sky and the fields sparkle in the setting sun and the May beetles are buzzing in the air. Thus there began for Voznitsin that year of languishing, turbulent, and bitter dreaming and solitary tears. He grew shy, and became awkward and rude as a result of his unbearable shyness. Never a moment passed but he would catch his foot in a chair and upset it, or his hands, like rakes, would catch in anything soft, or upset cups of tea or milk at the table. " Our Kolya has grown quite wild," Alexandra Millievna would say of him good-naturedly.

Lenotchka laughed at him. He would stand quietly at her back when she was drawing or embroidering, and gaze at her bended head with a wonderful sensation of pain and gladness. He would look at the white neck with the light wavy golden hair ; or watch how the brown school bodice on her breast would now be slightly crinkled as she breathed, and then become smooth, round, and full as she filled her lungs.

And the sight of the naïve bracelets on her white maidenly arms and the fragrant odour of poplars followed him everywhere—to school—to church.

All his exercise-books and the covers of his text-books were scored with the beautifully interwoven initials E. U., and they were also carved on the lid of his box in the centre of a pierced, burning heart. With a woman's instinct the young girl was aware of his silent adoration, but in her eyes he was too much of the family, too customary. For him she had suddenly changed into a blossoming, dazzling, fragrant, marvellous being, while he remained for her the same impetuous boy with the bass voice, hard, rough hands, narrow military coat, and broad trousers. She flirted innocently with the schoolboys of her acquaintance and with the priest's sons in the churchyard, but, like a cat sharpening its claws, it sometimes amused her to fire Voznitsin with one of her quick, clever, ardent glances. But if, forgetting himself, he pressed her hand a little too tightly, she would threaten him with a rosy finger, saying significantly :

" Look out, I'll tell mother everything ! "

And Voznitsin grew cold with unfeigned terror. Needless to say, at this stage Kolya remained for a second year in the sixth form, and of course that very same summer he had managed to fall in love with the eldest of the Sinilinkov sisters. But it was at Easter that his heart, overflowing with love, attained a moment of heavenly bliss. . . .

He had gone with the Urlovs to the midnight Easter service at the Borisoglebsky church, where Alexandra Millievna had a special place with a special rug and a soft folding chair. It seems that Alexandra Millievna and Oletchka remained behind for the blessing of the bread and Easter cake, while Lenotchka, Arkasha, and Kolya left the church together. But on the way Arkasha suddenly—and no doubt diplomatically—vanished as though the earth had swallowed him. The two youngsters remained alone.

They walked along arm in arm, adroitly making their way through the crowd, and keeping time with their young, obedient legs. Everything intoxicated them on this glorious night : the joyful singing, the numerous candles, the kissing, laughter, and movement in the church and in the street—the numerous, unusually animated people, the dark sky with the large twinkling spring stars, the scent of the young leaves from the garden behind the fences, this unexpected nearness and the feeling of being lost among the crowd at so late an hour. Pretending that it was done by accident, Voznitsin pressed her elbow against his side. She gave a scarcely perceptible response. He repeated this secret caress, and again she responded. Then, in the darkness, he sought out the tips of her slender fingers and stroked them gently ; the fingers made no resistance, did not get angry nor escape.

Thus they got to the gate of the house. Arkasha had left the gate open for them. To reach the house it was necessary to walk along a narrow wooden bridge—placed there on account of the mud—between two rows of limes a hundred years old. But when the gate banged behind them he seized her hand and began to kiss her fingers,—so warm, soft, and animated.

" Lenotchka, I love you, love you. . . ."

He put his arm about her waist, and in the darkness kissed her somewhere near the ear. His cap slipped back and fell on the ground, but he did not trouble to pick it up. He continued kissing her cold cheeks and murmuring as in a fever :

" Lenotchka, I love you, love you. . . ."

" Don't ! " she said, also in a whisper, and by this he found her lips. " Don't. . . . Let me go. . . . Let . . ."

Such sweet, burning, half-childish, naïve, inexperienced lips ! When he kissed her she did not resist, but did not respond to them, and breathed in a peculiarly touching manner—quickly, deeply, submissively. Tears of joy streamed down his cheeks, making them cold. And when he tore himself away from her lips and looked up at the sky, the stars, shining through the branches of the lime trees, danced, multiplied, and broke away through his tears.

" Lenotchka . . . love you. . . ."

" Let me alone."

" Lenotchka ! "

And suddenly she exclaimed in unexpected anger :

" Let me go, you nasty, horrid boy ! You will see ! I shall tell mamma everything. I shall certainly tell her ! "

She did not tell her mother, but from that night never remained alone with him. And then the summer came. . . .

. . . .

" And do you remember, Elena Vladimirovna, how two young people once kissed each other by the gate of the church-house on a certain beautiful Easter night ? " Voznitsin asked.

" I remember nothing . . . you nasty, horrid boy," she replied with a sweet laugh. " However, look, here comes my daughter. I must introduce you. Lenotchka, this is Nikolai Ivanovitch Voznitsin, an old, old friend, a friend of my childhood. And this is my Lenotchka. She is exactly the same age as I was on a certain beautiful Easter night."

" Big Lenotchka and little Lenotchka," Voznitsin said.

" No, old Lenotchka and young Lenotchka," Madame Lvova corrected him without a trace of bitterness.

Lenotchka was very much like her mother, only prettier than the latter had been in her girlhood. In place of her mother's red hair she had chestnut hair with a metallic sheen about it : the dark brows were delicately and boldly outlined, but the mouth was a little coarse and sensual, though beautifully fresh and pretty.

The girl was interested in the floating lighthouses, and Voznitsin explained their use and construction. Then he went on to talk about the depths of the Black Sea, about the work of divers, about ship-wrecks. He was a good talker, and the girl listened to him, breathing through parted lips, and not taking her eyes off him.

And he, the longer he looked at her, the more his heart filled with a soft, bright sadness—of compassion for himself, joy for her and this new Lenotchka, and a gentle gratitude to the past. It was the very feeling for which he had longed in Moscow, only more intense and almost entirely altruistic.

And when the girl left them to look at the Hersonesky Monastery he took the hand of Lenotchka the elder and kissed it.

" Life is wise after all ; one must obey its laws," he said pensively. " And besides, life is beautiful. Life is one constant resurrection of the dead. You and I will pass away, vanish, but from our bodies, from our thoughts and acts, our minds, inspirations, and talents there arise, as out of dust, another Lenotchka and another Kolya Voznitsin. All things are bound and linked together. I go away, yet I remain. One can only love life and submit. We all live together, the dead and the resurrected."

He bent over once more to kiss her hand and she kissed him affectionately on his grey temple. And when, after this, they looked at each other, their eyes were moist and smiled with a sweet, weary, sad, smile.

ALEXANDER I. KUPRIN

THE SLAVONIC SOUL

THE more I burrow into my memory of the past and reach back to the events of my childhood, the more incredible and confused become my recollections. Undoubtedly many things I seem to remember were told me later, in more conscious years, by those who, with love and care, watched my first steps ; much could not have happened at all, but, having been read or heard somewhere, must have sunk deeply into my soul. Who can say in these reminiscences where facts end and fancy begins ; fancy that has long ago turned to truth ; and still more, where the two become indissolubly intermingled ?

Particularly clearly there arises before me the original figure of Yass and his two comrades—I might even say friends—on life's path, Matska the old cavalry gelding, and Bouton the yard-dog.

Yass was distinguished by his deliberate speech and action, and always gave the impression of a man centred in himself. He spoke very rarely, always weighing his words, and tried to make his language as Russian as possible ; only in moments of strong spiritual upheavals did he resort to Little Russian abuses and even whole sentences. Thanks to his clothes of sedate cut and dark colour, his solemn, somewhat sad, clean-shaven face, and his significantly compressed thin lips, he looked very much like a retainer of the old school.

Of all men, excluding himself, Yass, it seems, only honoured my father with respect. To us children, to mother, and to all his own as well as our acquaintances he bore himself respectfully but with a certain degree of pity and contemptuous condescension. The reason for his immeasurable pride was always a source of mystery to me. It sometimes happens that servants, with well-known insolence, take to themselves something of the glamour of power that belongs to their masters. But my father, a poor doctor in a little Jewish town, lived so simply and quietly that he could not have given Yass cause to look down on others. Likewise Yass had none of the motives for insolence in a servant ; neither city polish, nor foreign phrases, nor the self-confident conquest of neighbouring housemaids, nor the sentimental art of strumming romances on a guitar—an accomplishment that has already ruined many inexperienced hearts.   He spent all his leisure hours lying in complete inaction on his box.   Not only did he read no books, but he openly despised them.   All books except the Bible were in his opinion utterly false and only written for the purpose of getting money from people, so he preferred his own long trains of thought that he turned over in his mind during the hours that he lay on the box.

Matska was dismissed from military service for his numerous vices, that reached most alarming proportions ; besides which his forelegs were bent, and at the joints, his body was decorated with flabby growths, while his hind-legs were stiff.   His head, with its camel-like profile, he always strained upwards, displaying his Adam's apple, and this, coupled with his huge size, unusual leanness, and the absence of one eye, gave him a sad and absurdly serious expression.   Such horses that strain their heads upwards are called " star-gazers " in the army.

Yass treated Matska with greater respect than he did Bouton, who sometimes showed a frivolity not at all in keeping with his years.   He was one of those large, long-haired, shaggy dogs that partly remind one of a ratter, only ten times as big, and partly of a poodle, and he was a born watch-dog.   At home he conducted himself with a lofty seriousness and reasonableness, but in the street he behaved in a very unbecoming manner.   If he went out with father he would never run humbly behind the carriage as all well-behaved dogs do.   He would attack all the horses he met and jump at their jaws, and would only run off when with agitated snort they bent their heads to bite him.   He would penetrate into strange yards and come tumbling out head over heels, followed by a dozen furious dogs ; and what was worse, he would make friends with dogs that had long earned for themselves very doubtful reputations.

In our Podoly or Voliny nothing gives a man greater chic than a good turn-out.   A squire who has long ago mortgaged and remortgaged his estates, and is daily expecting a visit from the lawyers, will go to church on a Sunday in a light tarantas drawn by four or sometimes six beautiful fiery horses, and when he reaches the square of the little town will invariably say to the coachman, " Whip up, Joseph ! " I am convinced, however, that not one of the neighbouring rich landowners ever turned out in such pomp as Yass turned out father whenever he happened to go anywhere. In the first place, Yass himself put on a high patent-leather hat with a square brim, and a broad yellow girdle.   Then Matska,

harnessed to the old springy travelling carriage, was led away a
hundred paces from the house. No sooner did my father appear
at the door than Yass triumphantly cracked his whip ; Matska
would wave his tail pensively for some time and then set out in a
slow trot, throwing out and lifting up his hind legs like a cock.
On arriving at the porch, Yass behaved as though he was with
difficulty holding back the impatient horse, pulling at the reins
with all his might. All his attention was taken up by the horse,
and Yass would not have turned his head whatever happened.
No doubt it was all done for the glory of our family honour.

In every way Yass had a very high opinion of my father. It
sometimes happened that a poor Jew or peasant would be waiting
his turn in the antechamber while father was engaged with other
patients. Yass would often enter into conversation with them for
the sole purpose of making my father more popular as a doctor.
" What do you think ? " he would say, taking up a superior attitude
by the hearth and looking the patient over from head to foot while
the latter stood humbly before him. " You may perhaps think
that you have come to see the district clerk or the inspector. My
master, brother, is not only higher than the inspector, but he will
even be higher than the superintendent. He knows everything
there is to know in this world, I assure you. What is the matter
with you ? "

" I've got a pain . . . in my heart here," the patient would blurt
out confusedly, " and in my chest and kid . . ."

" Well, there you see ! And why ? And how to cure it ? You
do not know and I do not know. But my master has only to look
at you and he will say in an instant whether you are going to live
or die."

Yass lived very carefully and used all his money to buy various
domestic articles, which he stowed away carefully in his big tin-
bound box. Nothing gave us children greater pleasure than his
permission to watch him tidy up these things. The inside of the lid
was stuck all over with prints of the most various subjects. Here,
side by side with severe patriarchal-looking generals with green
moustaches, were such things as " The Soul under Trial," gravures
from Niva of studies of female heads, and the Nightingale robber on
the oak-tree, carefully opening his right eye to receive Elya-
Muronitsa's arrow. Then gradually there would be taken out of the
box a whole collection of coats, waistcoats, great-coats, sheep-skin
caps, cups and saucers, ancient boxes decorated with glass beads and
flowers, and small round mirrors. Not infrequently, from a side
pocket would appear an apple or some other delicacy that always
seemed to taste particularly nice to us.

On the whole, Yass was very methodical and painstaking. One day he broke a large ewer and my father scolded him for it. The next day Yass appeared with two new ones. " It doesn't matter ; perhaps I may break another, and anyway they will be useful in the house," he explained. In the rooms he had introduced and maintained a model cleanliness. He jealously guarded his rights and duties, and was firmly convinced that no one could clean floors better than he could. One day a heated discussion arose between him and the new housemaid, Yeoka, as to which could clean the rooms better. We were appealed to as experts, and from a desire to tease Yass gave our verdict in favour of the girl. We children, not understanding the human soul, did not suspect what a blow we had given him by our cruel decision. He went away without saying a word, and the next day every one in the little town knew that Yass had got drunk.

This happened with him about two or three times a year usually, and caused him as well as all the family much unhappiness. There was no one to chop the wood, feed the horses, or carry the water. For five or six days we neither saw nor heard anything of him. On the seventh day he appeared terribly unkempt, hatless, and coatless. Thirty paces behind him followed a motley crowd of Jews ; the street urchins shouted and grimaced. All knew that an auction was about to take place, and in fact in a few moments Yass ran out of the house holding in his arms almost all the contents of his sacred box. The crowd quickly surrounded him.

" Well ? So you won't give me any vodka ? " he shouted, shaking the trousers and waistcoats hanging over his arms. " What ! I have no money, haven't I ? And what is this ? And this ? And this ? "

And one after another his garments flew among the crowd that seized them with greedy hands.

" How much will you give ? " Yass shouted at some Jew who held one of his coats. " How much will you give, mare's-head ? "

" Well . . . I can give you fifty kopeks," the Jew said.

" Fifty ? Fifty ? " Despair brought Yass to extreme measures. " I don't want fifty ! Give me twenty kopeks. Give me . . Well ? Skinflints, give me ten kopeks for the lot ! May your eyes burst from your heads ! May the plague devour you ! May you have been strangled in childhood ! "

There were police in our town, their only duty being to be present at christenings, but on occasions such as the present, while not joining the disorder, they played the part of the humble, silent guest. My father, seeing the plunder of Yass's belongings, and no longer able to contain his anger and contempt (the idiot had got drunk, so he must pay for it !), threw himself disinterestedly among the greedy crowd. In a moment there remained on the scene only Yass and my father, the latter holding a shabby razor-case in his hand. For a moment or two Yass reeled from astonishment, raised his eyebrows helplessly, and suddenly threw himself on his knees. " Master ! Master ! What have they done with me ! My dear master ! "

" Go into the shed ! " my father said angrily, pushing Yass from him as the latter seized the skirts of his coat and began to kiss them. " Go into the shed and sleep ! And let there be no trace of you here to-morrow ! " Yass went submissively into the shed, and then there began for him painful hours of drunkenness made infinitely worse by the pangs of remorse. He lay face downwards, support-ing his head on the palms of his hands, his eyes fixed on one point in front of him. He knew exactly what was taking place in the house at that moment. He pictured us clearly, pleading with father on his behalf, and saw how father waved us impatiently aside. He knew perfectly well that this time my father would not be shaken.

From time to time, out of curiosity, we would listen at the door of the shed, whence issued strange sounds as of moaning and sobbing.

At these periods of despondency and sorrow Bouton considered it his moral duty to visit the suffering Yass. The intelligent dog knew that in ordinary sober moments Yass would never have permitted the slightest suggeston of a familiar relationship. For this reason, whenever he met the severe servant out of doors, Bouton always pretended to be looking intently at something in the distance, or to be anxiously engaged in catching a fly. One circumstance always puzzled me ; we often caressed and fed Bouton, pulled the prickles from his coat—a proceeding he bore in stoic silence in spite of his obvious sufferings—on these occasions we even kissed his cold wet nose, yet all his sympathy and affection belonged entirely to Yass, from whom he knew nothing but blows. Alas, now that cruel experience has taught me to judge things more thoroughly, I begin to suspect that the source of Bouton's attachment was not so mysterious after all. It was not I but Yass who used to take him out the dish with the dinner leavings.

In times of peace, I repeat, Bouton would never have risked appeal-ing to Yass's feelings, but in days of sorrow he would walk boldly into the shed, sit down by the prostrate Yass, stare into a corner, and begin breathing heavily and sympathetically. If this did not help, Bouton would lick his protector's face and hands, at first timidly, and then more and more boldly. Finally, Yass, sobbing, would throw his arms round Bouton's neck, while Bouton would whine softly, and soon their voices would mingle in a strange, touching duet.

On the following day Yass came into the house before it was light. He was depressed and dare not raise his eyes. He made the floor and furniture shine brilliantly before my father's appearance, the very thought of which made Yass tremble. But father was un-moved. He gave Yass his passport and wages and ordered him to clean the kitchen as quickly as possible. Prayers and entreaties proved futile.

Then Yass played his last card.

" You really want me to go, sir ? " he asked boldly.

" Yes, and quickly too ! "

" Well, I won't go. You can throw me out if you like, but without me you will all die off like flies. I won't go."

" The police will make you go."

" Make me go ? . . ." Yass asked in confusion. " Very well, let them do so. Let the whole town see how Yass, after having served you well and faithfully for twenty years, is then taken to the police station. Let them take me ? It will not be I, but you, sir, who will be ashamed ! "

And Yass really did remain. Threats had no effect on him. Paying no attention to them, he worked incessantly, trying to make up for lost time. At night he did not go to bed in the kitchen, but lay down in the stall near Matska, while the horse stood all night pawing the ground and fearing to step on Yass. My father was a good-natured, indolent man, somewhat of a slave to his habits and environment. By the evening he had already forgiven Yass.

In his own way Yass was quite handsome—a dark, melancholy type of Little Russian. The girls would eye him, though not one of them, when chasing a quail across the yard, would dare to nudge him coquettishly or give him an encouraging smile ; he was too haughty and had too cold a contempt for the fair sex. The charm of family life likewise had little attraction for him. " When a woman enters the hut," Yass would say squeamishly, " the air immediately becomes foul." Once, however, he made an attempt in that direction, when he surprised us more than ever.

One evening when we were at tea, Yass entered the dining-room, sober but in great excitement, and pointing mysteriously over his shoulder at the door, asked in a whisper : " Can she come in ? "

" Who is there ? " father asked. " By all means let her come in." In a state of expectancy we fixed our eyes on the door, through which a strange being slowly emerged. It was a woman of at least fifty, ragged, drunk, and crazy.

" Give us your blessing, sir ; we want to get married," Yass said, falling down on his knees.

" Get down, you fool," he shouted at the woman, pulling her roughly by the sleeve.

Father was so amazed that he only realised the situation after some difficulty. For a long time he explained to Yass that only a madman could marry such a worthless creature. Yass remained on bended knees listening silently ; the crazy woman, too, did not rise.

" Then you won't let me get married, sir ? " Yass asked at last.

" Of course not," father replied ; " and what is more, I am sure you will not do it."

" So let it be, then," said Yass resolutely.   " Get up, you fool," he turned to the woman.   " Do you hear what the master says ? Be off with you ! "   With these words, and holding the unexpected visitor by the scruff of the neck, he quickly disappeared out of the dining-room with her.

This was Yass's only attempt at matrimony. Every one explained it their own way, but none got any further than guessing at his motives ; and when he was asked about it Yass would merely wave his interrogator aside with annoyance.

Still more mysterious and unexpected was his death.   It happened in such a sudden, incomprehensible manner, and apparently had so little connection with the ordinary events of Yass's life, that I feel a certain awkwardness in having to write about it.   I guarantee, however, that all I have related not only took place, but has not been overdrawn one bit for the purpose of creating an impression.

One day, at the station that was three miles from our little town, a well-dressed man, not old, was found hanging in the lavatory. That very day Yass asked permission to go to see the suicide. He returned in about four hours and walked straight into the dining-room, where there happened to be visitors, and stopped by the door. It was some days after his penitence in the shed, and he was perfectly sober.

" What do you want ? " mother asked.

" Ha, ha, ha," he burst out.   " His tongue was hanging out . . . the gentleman's tongue . . ."   My father instantly ordered him to the kitchen. The visitors remarked about Yass's peculiarities, and soon the little incident was forgotten.

On the following day, as he passed the nursery at about eight o'clock in the evening, Yass went up to my little sister and kissed her.

" Good-bye," he said, stroking her hair.

" Good-bye, Yass," she answered, without raising her eyes from her dolls.

Half an hour later Yeoka came running into my father's study, pale and trembling.   " Sir, . . . there in the garret . . . hanging . . . Yass . . ."   She fell down unconscious.

In the garret hung Yass, suspended from a thin cord.

When the examining magistrate cross-examined the cook, it appeared that on the day of his death Yass behaved very strangely.

" He stood before the looking-glass," she said, " squeezing his neck with both hands until he went red in the face and his tongue hung out of his mouth and his eyes stood out of his head. . . . He was evidently trying to see what he would look like."

The magistrate put down the suicide as due to an unsound mind.

The day after Yass was buried—in a place set apart for such cases on a slope in the woods—Bouton could not be found anywhere. It appeared that the faithful dog had run off to Yass's grave and had lain there whining, mourning the death of his solemn friend. Afterwards he disappeared, leaving no trace.

Now, when almost an old man, I sometimes review my past, and my mind turns to Yass, the same thought occurs to me each time : What a strange soul—faithful, pure, contradictory, absurd yet large —a real Slavonic soul—inhabited the body of Yass.

ALEXANDER I. KUPRIN

AS AT HOME

IT was . . . well, really, it seems to me sometimes that it must have been about thirty years ago, so many events, people, towns, successes, failures, joys, and sorrows, lie between the present and those days. I lived at the time in Kiev, at the very beginning of Padola, below Alexandrovsky Goskoy in a room in the Dneprovskaya Gavan kept by a former ship's cook who had been discharged for drunkenness, and his wife, Anna Petrovna, who had a perfect genius for cunning, greed, and spite.

There were six of us permanent lodgers, all solitary folk. Room 1 was inhabited by the eldest tenant. At one time he had been a merchant and had kept an orthopædic and corset shop Then he took to gambling and lost his business. Later he had been a clerk somewhere, but a passion for card-playing had taken him out of the ordinary rut. Now he lived in God only knows what kind of an absurd manner. He slept all day, and late in the evening stole away to some secret gambling den or other, of which there are many on the banks of the Dnieper near the large river-port. Like all gamblers who play more for sport than for gain, he was broadmined, affable, and attractive.

In Room 3 lived an engineer by the name of Butkovsky. If one were to believe him, he had been through the courses on forestry, mining and civil engineering at technical schools, besides a number of higher schools abroad. And really, in general knowledge, he was something like a stuffed sausage or like a trunk which has been hastily packed for a long journey—one throws all sorts of rubbish into it until it closes only with difficulty, and when it is opened the things come flying out. He would discourse freely—even without being asked—on such varied topics as pilotage, aviation, botany, statistics, dendrology, politics, petrology, astronomy, fortifications, birdbreeding, kitchen gardening, town colonisation. He got drunk about once a month for three whole days, during which time he would only speak French and write French notes to his former colleagues about money. Then for five days he would lie under his blue check, English plaid and perspire. He did nothing else except write numerous letters to newspapers everywhere and on all possible occasions, such as on the draining of a bog, the discovery of a new star, artesian wells, and so on. If he happened to possess any money he would distribute it in the various books on his shelves, and discover it later as a surprise. I recollect how he often would say in his lisp :

"My friend, will you be good enough to take Elisa Hakla from the shelf—volume four. Between pages two and three hundred there is a five-rouble note that I owe you."

He was quite bald, and had a white beard and grey fan-like side whiskers.

I lived in Room 8. In No. 7 there was a student with a round hairless face who stammered. Now he is a famous public prosecutor. In Room 6 there was the German, Karl, specialist in road-making and confirmed beer-drinker. Room 5 was occupied by the woman Zoya, whom the landlady respected more than the others. In the first place, she paid more for her room than we did, and paid in advance ; in the second, she was a very quiet lodger, as she rarely brought home guests, and then only of an aged, " respectable," quiet type. She spent most of her nights in strange hotels.

I must say that we were all acquainted yet somehow not acquainted with each other. We lent and borrowed from each other such things as tea, charcoal, cotton, hot water, newspapers, ink, and stationery.

There were only nine rooms in the house ; the remaining three were let to strange couples for brief periods. We did not object, we had grown accustomed to everything.

. . . .

The southern spring had come quickly. The ice had gone from the Dnieper. The river rose so high that the low bank on the left was covered to the very horizon. The nights were dark and warm, and at intervals there were short, sharp showers. One day the buds on the trees were scarcely grey, and when you woke the next day you saw how they shone suddenly with the tender, bright green of the new leaves.

Easter, too, came with its beautiful, joyous, great night. I had nowhere to go for the festival, and simply strolled about the town by myself, went into church, watched the processions and illuminations, listened to the noise and singing, admired the sweet faces of women and children lit up from below by the warm glow of the candles. An intoxicating sadness filled my soul—sweet, light, and soft, as though I mourned, without pain, the departed purity and simplicity of my childhood.

On returning home, I met our porter, Vaska, a snub-nosed, cunning young fellow. We gave each other the Easter greeting.

Grinning from ear to ear, and showing his teeth and gums, he said to me :

" The young lady from No. 5 wants you to go and see her."

I was rather surprised, not being at all acquainted with the young lady.

" She sent you a note," Vaska continued ; " there it is, on the table."

I found a ruled sheet of paper torn from a notebook, and beneath the printed heading " Cash Received," read the following :

" Dear No. 8—If you are free and have no objection, I should like you to come to my room to break the Holy Easter fast.   One who is known to you.   ZOYA KRAMARENKOV."

I knocked at the engineer's door to ask his advice. He was standing before the looking-glass trying with his fingers to smooth his stiff, obstinate, unkempt grey hair.   He wore a shiny frock-coat that gave him an air of importance, and a white necktie around an old frayed collar.   He had also received an invitation, so we went in together.

Zoya met us at the door, with blushes and apologies.   She had the typical face of a common Russian prostitute ; soft, good-natured, characterless lips, somewhat broad nose, browless protruding grey eyes.   But her smile—her present smile—so homely, un-affected, modest, tender, and womanly, made Zoya's face charming for the moment.

The gambler and Karl were already there.   With the exception of the student, all the permanent lodgers of the Dneprovskaya Gavan were gathered together.

Her room was just as I had imagined it to be.   On the chest of drawers were empty chocolate boxes, absurd pictures, greasy powder, and hair curlers.   The walls were lined with photographs of curly-haired barbers, conceited actors in profile, and severe soldiers with bare swords.   On the bed was a mountain of pillows under a lace coverlet.   But the table, spread with a paper cloth cut into a lace pattern, was resplendent with Easter cake, rolls, eggs, a leg of ham, and two bottles of some mysterious kind of wine.

We exchanged Easter greetings with her, kissing on both cheeks in the chastest manner, and sat down to table.   I must say that we must have presented a most strange sight at that moment ; four men at the ends of lives of hunger and misfortune, four weather-beaten old horses who counted two hundred years between them, and the fifth—our hostess—a Russian woman of the streets, no longer young, that is to say, the most unfortunate, stupid, naïve, characterless, and kind-hearted being in the world.

But how pleasant and awkward she was ! So modest in her hospitality, so friendly, so delicately simple !

" Take it," she said affectionately, handing a plate to one of us. " Take it, and eat, please ; No. 6, I know you like beer, Vaska told me so. There is a bottle near you, under the table. And for you, gentlemen, I have some wine. It is very good wine, from Teneriffe. A sailor whom I know always drinks it."

We four had seen enough of life, and of course knew the price of this Easter feast that had been prepared for us, including the wine, but this knowledge did not warp or offend us.

Zoya told us her impressions of the night. In Bratsva, where she had been for the midnight service, it was very crowded, but she had been fortunate enough to get a good place. The academy choir had sung beautifully, and the Evangel was read by the students themselves, in every language under the sun—in French, German, Greek, even in Arabic. And when the bread and Easter cake were blessed outside, there was such a commotion that the pilgrims got their supplies mixed up and began to quarrel amongst themselves.

Then Zoya grew pensive. She sighed, and began telling us about Easter week in her native village.

" We used to gather little flowers that we called ' sleep,' little blue ones, the first to open, and used to make a concoction from them with which to dye the eggs. They would come out a beautiful blue.

" To get yellow, we would wrap the eggs in onion-skin and boil them. And then we used to dye them with coloured rags. For the whole week we went about the village, beating egg against egg, at first with the ends and then all over ; the one whose egg got broken first would lose. One young fellow got an iron egg from somewhere in the town, and of course beat everybody. But he was found out and all his eggs were taken from him, while he got a thrashing into the bargain.

" Besides this, we used to have swings the whole week. There were the common swings in the middle of the village, and then each little gate had its own swing, just a board and two ropes. The whole week the boys and girls would swing and sing, ' Christ is risen ! ' It is very nice in our village ! "

We listened to her silently. Life had for so long and so cruelly struck us hard blows that we had altogether forgotton our recollections of childhood, of family life, of mother, and the Easters of the past.

Meanwhile the calico curtains over the windows were turned a cold blue by the dawn, then they grew darker and turned to yellow and suddenly became rosy from the rising sun.

" If you are not afraid, gentlemen, I will open the window," Zoya said.

She drew the curtain and pushed back the casement. We all
followed her to the window.

It was such a bright, pure, festive morn as though some one during
the night had with careful touch washed and put in place each
object ; the blue sky, the white, fleecy cloud, the tall poplars, the
trembling, fragrant, green leaves. The Dnieper spread out before
us in immense space, blue and terrible at the banks, calm and silver
in the distance. All the church bells were ringing.

And suddenly we all turned round. The engineer was crying.
Holding the window-sill and his head pressed against the frame, his
whole body was shaking with sobs. God only knows what was going
on in the lonely wounded heart of the unfortunate old man. I knew
but little of his past life, things I had gathered by stray remarks :
an oppressive marriage, a dissolute wife, embezzlement of state
money, a revolver shot at his wife's lover, longing for his children
who had followed their mother.

Zoya sighed pitifully, put her arms about the engineer, placed
his purple, bald head, with its sparse grey hairs, on her breast, and
began quietly to caress his shoulders and cheeks.

" You poor, dear thing," she said in a sing-song voice. " I know
how difficult it is for you all to live—you are all like scattered grains
of sand . . . old and lonely. But, never mind. . . . Be patient,
my dears. . . . God will make it right in the end and all will be
well. . . . My poor, dear thing. . . ."

With difficulty the engineer pulled himself together. His eyes
were red, and his swollen nose had turned almost blue.

" Damm ! Damm it ! " he said, angrily turning to the wall. And
by the sound of his voice I knew that he was trying to restrain his
tears.

Five minutes later we took our leave, each respectfully kissing
Zoya's hand. The engineer and I were the last to leave, and, as it
happened, we were met at Zoya's door by the student, who had just
returned home from a party.

" Ah ! " he exclaimed with a smile and a suggestive move of his
eyebrows, " so that is where you have been ? . . . Hm. . . .
Enjoyed yourselves, I see ! "

In the tone of his voice was the usual vulgarity. But the engineer
slowly looked him up and down from the crown of his head to his
boots, and, after a pause, said over his shoulder with unutterable
contempt :

" You blackguard ! "

ALEXANDER I. KUPRIN

A CLUMP OF LILAC

NIKOLAI YEVGRAFOVITCH ALMASOV scarcely waited till his wife opened the door, and without removing his overcoat or cap strode into his study. As soon as his wife saw his gloomy face with its heavy frown and the nervous biting of the lower lip, she understood that a great misfortune had befallen him. . . . She followed her husband silently. In the study Almasov stood for a while on the same spot gazing absently into a corner of the room. Then he dropped the portfolio he held in his hand—it flew open as it fell—and threw himself into a chair, clenching his hands viciously.

Almasov, a poor young officer, had just returned from a lecture at the Staff College. To-day he had shown the professor the last and most difficult piece of practical work—a local survey.

Until now all his examinations had gone off happily and only God and Almasov's wife knew what labours they had cost him. It began at the very beginning—his very entrance into the college had seemed impossible at first. For two years on end he had solemnly tried to get through, and it was only at the third attempt he had, with incessant labour, overcome all obstacles. Had it not been for his wife he would never have found enough energy and would have given up the attempt long before, but Verotchka would not allow his spirits to droop, and helped him keep his courage up. She had learnt to meet every failure with a clear, almost gay, countenance. She had deprived herself of every luxury in order to surround him with a comfort which, though modest, was essential to a man engaged in brain work. According to the need she would in turn copy his papers, draw his plans, be his reader, prompter, and memorandum book.

Five minutes of heavy silence passed, broken only by the cracked ticking of the alarm clock, a sound wearisome and familiar : one, two, three—two clear strokes, the third a cracked one. Almasov, without removing his coat or cap, sat turned to one side. . . . Vera stood two paces away from him, also silent, with a look of suffering on her handsome, nervous face. She was the first to speak and used

182

that caution that only a woman can command at the sick-bed of a dear one. . . .

" Kolya, was your work . . . unsatisfactory ? "

He shrugged his shoulders and made no reply.

" Kolya, have they rejected your survey ?   Tell me, don't mind ; we can talk things over together."

Almasov turned quickly to his wife and began in that heated, irritable manner people usually employ when giving vent to a long pent-up sense of wrong.

" Well, then—they rejected it, if you wish to know.   Can't you see for yourself ?   To the devil with the whole business ! . . . All this rubbish "—he kicked the portfolio containing the plans viciously —" all this rubbish may as well be thrown into the fire now !   This is the end of the college !   In a month I shall be back again in the regiment and in disgrace too.   And all for the sake of that cursed spot . . . damn it ! "

" What spot, Kolya ?   I don't understand."

She sat down on the arm of his chair and put her arms round his neck.

" What spot, Kolya ? " she asked again.

" Oh, an ordinary spot of green.   You know how I worked until three o'clock last night to get it finished.   The plan is well drawn and coloured : they all say that.   Well, as I was sitting tired out last night, my hand trembled and I made a spot.   Such a thick, greasy spot !   I tried to rub it off and made it worse.   I sat thinking and wondering what to do when it occurred to me to draw a clump of bushes over the spot. . . . It came out very well, the spot was quite covered.   I took it to the professor to-day.

" ' Ah, yes-s. . . . How did you get these bushes here, Ensign ? '

" I should have told him there and then how it happened.   He might only have laughed. . . . However, I don't think he would have laughed—he's much too stiff an old German pedant.   I said to him, ' But there is a clump of bushes there.'   ' No,' he replied ; ' I know the place as well as the palm of my hand ; there are no bushes there.'   A long discussion ensued and a good many of our officers were present.   ' If you are so convinced of that clump, we must ride over to-morrow and inspect the place. . . . I will show you that you were either very careless or drew the plan from a three-mile map. . . .' "

" But why is he so sure that there is no clump of bushes there ? "

" Oh dear ! what a childish question to ask !   Because for twenty years he has known that place better than his own bedroom, and because he is the most disgusting pedant in the world, and a German into the bargain. . . . In the end it will come out that I lied, and, besides. . . ."

While speaking he kept taking the burnt matches from the ash-tray near by and breaking them between his fingers, and when he had finished threw the bits viciously on the floor. It was evident that this powerful man felt a strong desire to cry.

Husband and wife sat thinking heavily without saying a word. Suddenly Verotchka, with an energetic movement, jumped down from the chair.

" Listen, Kolya, we must go this minute !   Get ready quickly ! "

Nikolai Yevgrafovitch frowned as though from physical pain.

" Oh, don't be absurd, Vera. Do you think I can go and apologise ? It would be like signing my own death warrant.   Don't do anything foolish, please."

" I don't want to do anything foolish," Vera said, stamping her foot.   " I don't ask you to go and apologise . . . simply if those stupid bushes are not there, we must go and plant some at once."

" Plant ? . . . Bushes ? . . ."   Nikolai Yevgrafovitch opened his eyes wide.

" Yes, plant them.   If you told a lie, we must put it right.   Get ready quickly—give me my hat and coat . . . no, not there, look in the cupboard . . . my umbrella."

While Almasov was finding her hat and coat and trying to object uselessly, Vera was quickly opening all the drawers of the tables and chests, pulling out baskets and boxes, opening them and emptying their contents on the floor.

" Earrings. . . . Only rubbish. . . . They won't give anything for them. . . . And this ring with the expensive stone . . . we must get it back again somehow. It would be a pity to lose it. Bracelet . . . they won't give much on that either—it is too old. . . . Where is your silver cigar case, Kolya ? "

In five minutes all her treasures were gathered together in her bag.   Vera, already dressed, cast a last glance round to see if she had forgotten anything.

" Come along," she said resolutely.

" But where to ? " Almasov protested.   " It is getting dark, and that place of mine is five miles away."

" Nonsense !   Come along ! "

The Almasovs first drove over to the pawnbroker's. The man who valued their things was long accustomed to the daily sight of human misfortune, and their plight did not at all touch him.   He examined the things so long and so methodically that Vera began to lose patience. She was particularly hurt when after testing the brilliant in her ring with an acid, and weighing it, he offered her three roubles.

" It is a real stone," Vera protested.   " It is worth thirty-seven roubles at least."

The man closed his eyes with an air of weary indifference.

" It makes no difference to us, madam. We don't go in for stones," he said, throwing the last article on to the scales. " We only value metals."

To make up for this, the old bracelet was valued highly, to Vera's astonishment. Altogether they managed to get about twenty-three roubles, which was more than enough.

When the Almasovs drove up to the gardener's, the white St. Petersburg night was already spread over the sky and air in a milky blue. The gardener, a little old Southerner in gold spectacles, had just sat down to supper with his family. He was very much astonished and annoyed at these belated customers and their strange request. He must have suspected some mystery, and to Vera's obstinate questions, answered dryly :

" I am sorry, but I cannot send labourers so late at night and so far away. If to-morrow will do, I am at your service."

There was only one thing to do and that was to tell the gardener the whole story about the unlucky spot, which Verotchka did. The gardener listened incredulously, almost unfriendly, but when Vera got to the point when it occurred to her to plant the bushes, he became more attentive and smiled approvingly from time to time.

" Well, there is nothing else to be done," he agreed when she had finished. " What kind of bushes do you want to plant ? "

However, none of the bushes he possessed seemed suitable, and whether they would or not, they had to have a clump of lilac.

It was in vain that Almasov tried to persuade his wife to return home. She persisted in accompanying him, and all the time the bushes were being planted, fussed and worried and hindered the gardeners, and only consented to go home when she was quite sure that the turf around the bushes could not be distinguished from the rest of the grass.

On the following day Vera could not sit at home, and went out to meet her husband. When he was still some way off she could tell by his vigorous, sprightly gait that the story of the bush had ended happily. . . . And, in fact, although Almasov was covered with dust, and could scarcely stand on his legs from fatigue, his face shone with the triumph of victory.

" It was fine ! It was capital ! " he called out when still ten paces away, in answer to his wife's anxious look. " Try and picture to yourself how we got to the clump. He looked and looked, and even tore off a leaf and bit it. ' What kind of a tree is this ? '- he asked. ' I don't know, Your Excellency.' ' It must be birch,' he said. ' It must be birch, Your Excellency,' I replied. Then he turned to me and extended his hand. ' I am sorry, Ensign, I must be getting old to have forgotten these bushes.' A nice old man he is, and so clever.

It seems a shame to have deceived him. He is one of our best professors. His knowledge is simply wonderful, and he is so quick and accurate at surveying, it is simply marvellous ! ''

But it was not enough for Vera to hear the story once. She made him tell her again and again every detail of the conversation with the professor. She was interested in the smallest detail ; what was the expression of the professor's face, in what tone of voice he had said he was getting old, what Kolya himself felt at the moment. . . .

And they walked home together as though they were alone in the street, holding hands and laughing without cause. The passers-by stopped in amazement to look at this strange couple.

Nikolai Yevgrafovitch had never dined with such appetite as on that day. After dinner, when Vera went into her husband's study with a glass of tea, husband and wife burst out laughing at the same time and looked at each other.

" Why are you laughing ? " Vera asked.

" And why are you ? "

" Tell me first, and I'll tell you afterwards.''

" Oh, it was only nonsense. I was thinking about the lilac bush. And you ? "

" I, too, was thinking of the lilac bush. I wanted to say that henceforward lilac will always be my favourite flower.''

LEONID N. ANDREYEV
1870-1919

THE THIEF

I

FIODOR YURASOV, a thief who had served three sentences, set out
to visit his old mistress, a woman who lived about seventy miles
from Moscow.   At the station, he sat in the first-class refreshment
room, eating pies, drinking beer, and being waited on by a man in
dress clothes.   Later on, when every one began to move towards
the carriages, he mingled with the crowd, and, unintentionally as
it were, taking advantage of the general commotion, abstracted a
purse from the pocket of an old gentleman who happened to be near
him.   Yurasov was not in need of money, he had plenty in fact, and
this casual, unplanned theft could only have done him harm.   But
it happened.   The gentleman must have suspected the theft, for
he stared curiously and fixedly at Yurasov, and though he did not
stop, turned round several times to look back at him.   The second
time Yurasov saw the gentleman was from the window of the
carriage.   Looking excited and perplexed, he was walking quickly
along the platform, hat in hand, staring into people's faces, then
turning back and looking for some one in the carriages. Fortunately,
the final signal was given and the train started.   Yurasov looked
out cautiously : the gentleman, his hat still in his hand, was standing
at the end of the platform carefully peering into the passing carriages
as though he were counting them ; and even in his fat, awkwardly
posed legs there was the same expression of perplexity and excitement.   He stood still, but it must have seemed to him that he was
walking, his legs were in such a funny position.

Yurasov drew himself up, straightened out his knees, and, for
some reason or other, felt himself to be taller and straighter, a
smarter fellow than usual.   Tenderly he stroked his moustache with
both hands ; it was long, fair, and beautiful, and hung, like two
golden crescents, down either side of his face.   While the fingers
enjoyed the pleasant sensation of the soft, thick hair, the grey eyes
gazed down with an aimless, naïve austerity on to the winding rails

187

of the neighbouring lines.   With their metallic sparkle and silent twisting they looked like quickly running serpents.

Counting the stolen money in the lavatory—it amounted to some twenty-four roubles—Yurasov squeamishly turned the purse over in his hand.   It was old and greasy, did not shut well, and into the bargain smelt of some perfume or other, as though it had been in the possession of a woman for a long time.   This odour, somewhat stale but exciting, reminded Yurasov pleasantly of the woman he was going to see.   Smiling, gay, and careless, disposed for friendly conversation, he went into the carriage determined to be like the other passengers, polite, formal, and unassuming.   He wore a coat made of real English cloth, and boots of brown leather, and he believed in them, his coat and boots.   He was convinced that every one would take him for a young German clerk from some big commercial house.   He always followed the financial news in the papers, knew the current price of the important stocks, and could talk about business matters.   It sometimes seemed to him that in reality he was not the peasant Fiodor Yurasov, a thief who had served three sentences, but a respectable German, Heinrich Walter by name.   The woman to whom he was going called him Heinrich and his mates called him " The German."

" Is this seat engaged ? " he asked politely, though at a glance it could be seen that the seat was free since there were only two other passengers in that section of the compartment, an old retired officer and a lady with many parcels, who was obviously up from the country shopping.   Neither replied, and with affected accuracy he dropped down on to the soft springy seat, carefully stretched out his long legs, showing his brown boots, and took off his hat.   Then with a friendly look he glanced at the old officer and at the lady, and laid his broad white hand on his knee so that the ring on his finger—with its large stone—could be plainly seen.   The stone was not a real one and shone garishly ; they did in fact notice it but said nothing ; they neither smiled nor grew more friendly.   The old man turned to another page of his paper, and the lady, young and beautiful, stared out of the window.   With a vague feeling that he was discovered, that again he was not taken for a young German, Yurasov quietly withdrew his hand that seemed to him too large and white, and in a respectful voice asked :

" Are you returning to your country-house ? "

The lady, pretending not to hear, put on a preoccupied expression. Yurasov was familiar with this expression when a man or woman became distant, annoyingly distant, and, turning to the officer, asked :

" Would you be good enough to look in your paper and see how Ribinsky stands ; I can't remember."

The old man put his paper down slowly, pressed his lips together severely, and looked at him with an offended air.

" What was that ?   I did not hear."

Yurasov repeated his question, pronouncing his words slowly and distinctly, while the old man stared at him disapprovingly as at a nephew who had got into a scrape or at a soldier who had neglected some duty.   Gradually his anger began to rise ; the skin on his head beneath the thin grey hair grew red, his chin trembled.

" I don't know," he bawled.   " I don't know.   There is nothing of the kind in the paper.   I can't think why people will ask senseless questions ! "

And he returned to his paper, lowering it every now and again to shoot an angry glance at the annoying man opposite.   It seemed to Yurasov that every one in the compartment was ill-natured and distant, and he felt it strange that he should be sitting in a second-class compartment on a soft, springy seat.   With dull despair and anger in his heart, he recalled how everywhere among respectable people he met with this, sometimes hidden and often unconcealed direct enmity.   He wore a coat of real English cloth, brown boots, and a costly ring, but they did not seem to notice these things, and, instead, saw something else, something he failed to see when he looked at himself in the glass or into his consciousness.   In the glass he looked like other men only, perhaps, handsomer ; it was not written across his face that he was the peasant Fiodor Yurasov, a thief who had served three sentences, and not a young German by the name of Heinrich Walter.   This incomprehensible treacherous something that was apparent to all except himself aroused in him the usual dull despair and fear.   He wanted to run away, and looking round sharply and suspiciously—not at all like an honest German clerk—he walked out of the carriage with long, heavy strides.

II

It was early in June ; everything before the eyes, right up to the distant immovable stretches of woodland, was young and strong and green.   The grass was green, the leaves on the trees were green, the little plants in the bare kitchen-gardens were green ; everything was so wrapped up in itself, so deeply immersed in silent, creative thought, that if the grass and the trees had had faces they would all have been turned to the earth, would have been preoccupied and distant ; all lips would have pursed in deep silence.   Yurasov, sad and pale, standing alone on the rocking little platform, felt all this in a vague, troubled way.   The beautiful, silent, enigmatical fields

were just as coldly estranged from him as the people in the carriage.
High above the fields was the sky, also pre-absorbed ; somewhere
behind him the sun was setting, its straight broad rays spread over
the earth, but no one looked at it in this benighted place, no one
thought about it, no one cared.   In the town where Yurasov was
born and had grown up, the houses and streets had eyes, and they
looked at people.   Some were unfriendly and malicious, others were
good and kind, but here no one noticed him, no one knew him.
The coaches too were pensive ; the one in which he was travelling
was running along, rocking to and fro with an angry motion ; the
one behind ran neither faster nor slower, as though it were alone,
and it also seemed to be gazing at the earth and listening.   Beneath,
under the coaches, there was a rumble and noise as of many voices,
now like a song, now like a piece of music, now like some strange,
incomprehensible conversation, but all distant and alien.   People
could be seen, looking small in the distance, and all seemed active
and unafraid.   They even seemed to be gay, for every now and
again the fragment of a song could be heard, drowned in the rumbling
noise of the wheels.   There were tiny houses too, scattered about
freely, and their windows looked straight out into the fields.   If at
night you were to look out from these windows you would see the
fields, the open, free, dark fields.   That day, the day before, every
day and every night, trains passed there, and always there were
those quiet fields with the little people and the little houses.   The
day before, at that hour, Yurasov had been sitting in the " Progress "
restaurant and had not even thought of any fields, yet they were
there just as then, just as quiet, beautiful, and pensive.   Over there
was a copse of large old birches with rooks' nests in their green tops ;
and while he had been at the " Progress " restaurant drinking vodka
with his chums or looking at the aquarium with its sleepless fish,
the birches had stood there just as quietly and calmly, with the
same darkness above and around them.

With the strange thought that only the town was real and that
this was an illusion, and that one had only to close one's eyes and
open them again to find it gone, Yurasov closed his eyes tightly and
stood perfectly still.   Instantly such an unusually pleasant feeling
came over him that he did not wish to open them again ; doubt and
thought and dull despair had vanished ; his body swayed involuntarily and pleasantly with the motion of the carriage, and a warm,
soft, gentle breeze from the fields fanned his face.   With a confident
gesture he stroked his thick moustache ; there was a ringing in his
ears, while from beneath there came that rhythmic murmur of the
wheels that sounded like music, like song, like distant conversation,
sad and sweet.   He vaguely imagined that from his very feet to his
bowed head he could feel the vibration of the soft, empty space ;

that before him stretched a blue-green abyss full of gentle, timid, secret caresses, and strangely, somewhere in the distance, a soft, warm rain was falling.

The train slackened and stopped for a minute, for one single minute. Immediately Yurasov was enveloped by an immense, wonderful stillness as though it were not one minute that the train stood still, but a year, a dozen years, an eternity. All was quiet ; the dark, greasy, little stone lying against the rails, the corner of the low red roof of the deserted platform, the grass on the slope. There was an odour of birch leaves, of meadows, of fresh manure, and this too seemed invested with that immense stillness. Awkwardly catching hold of the rail, a passenger alighted from the neighbouring carriage and walked away. He seemed strange and unusual in this stillness, like a bird that had always flown and suddenly took to walking. Here he should have flown, not walked. The path was long and obscure, and his steps were short, and he lifted his feet absurdly in this immense stillness.

Gently, as though ashamed of its own noise, the train moved off, and it was only about a mile farther on that all the parts of its iron body got into swing. Yurasov, tall, thin, and supple, paced the platform in agitation. Unconsciously twirling his moustache, he gazed upwards with sparkling eyes, clinging eagerly to the iron bar on that side of the carriage where the large red sun was disappearing beneath the horizon. He had discovered something ; he realised something now that had escaped him all his life, and that had made of it an uncouth, clumsy business like the passenger who walked instead of flying. " Yes, yes," he affirmed, serious and preoccupied, and resolutely shaking his head, " of course it is so, of course."

And the wheels reaffirmed in chorus, " Of course it is so, of course ; of course it is so, of course."

It seemed to him that not speech but song was appropriate, and he began to sing, softly at first, then louder and louder until the sound of his voice mingled with the rumbling of the wheels. The rhythm of his song was that of the wheels, and the melody was a pliant, clear wave of sound. There were no words, no time or form ; distant and vague and terribly vast like the fields, they ran off with mad swiftness, and the human voice freely and lightly followed them. The voice, first high, then low, spread over the earth, gliding over the fields, piercing through the woods, and lightly losing itself in the limitless sky. So should a bird fly when Spring calls it ; so, without aim or path, trying to embrace all, to feel the whole ringing breadth of the vast heavens. Thus, no doubt, the green fields would have sung had they been endowed with voices ; thus in quiet summer evenings sing the little people as they move about in the distant green stretches.

Yurasov sang, and the purple reflection of the setting sun lit up his face, his coat of English cloth, and his brown boots. He sang, accompanying the sun, and his song grew sadder and sadder, like a bird that, feeling the vastness of the heavens, trembles with some unknown despair and calls to it knows not whom.

The sun had set, and a grey web lay on the quiet earth and over the tranquil sky. The grey web lay on his face, effacing the last reflections of the sunset and making it look deathly. " Come to me ! Why don't you come ? The sun has set, the fields grow dark. Why don't you come ? It is lonely and painful for my solitary heart, so lonely, lonely ! Come ! The sun has set, the fields grow dark. Come then, come ! " Thus his soul wept, and the fields grew darker. Only in the sky over the setting sun it grew brighter and deeper like a beautiful face turned to the beloved that is quietly, quietly disappearing.

III

The inspector passed through, and the conductor, slipping out, said roughly to Yurasov :

" You musn't stand on the platform ; go into the compartment." He went away, slamming the door angrily behind him, while Yurasov called after him : " You blockhead ! "

It seemed to him that the coarse words, the slamming of the door, were all due to the respectable people in the carriage, and again feeling himself the German Heinrich Walter, he shrugged his shoulders with an irritable, offended air and said to an imaginary, portly gentleman :

" What a ruffian ! People always stand on the platform, and he says you mustn't ; the devil knows why ! "

Then there was a halt with its sudden, powerful stillness.   At night the grass and the woods smelt stronger and the people walking about did not seem so absurd ; the transparent twilight seemed to endow them with wings, and two women in light dresses seemed not to be walking, but floating like swans. Again he felt both happy and sad, and wanted to sing, but his voice would not obey, his tongue uttered dull, commonplace words, and the song would not come. He wanted to dream, to weep sweetly and unconsolably, but instead he could only see a portly gentleman, to whom he remarked carefully : " Have you noticed how the Sormovsky stock is rising ? "

And the dark, moving fields again became preoccupied, incomprehensibly cold and distant. Dissonant and unintelligible were the sounds of the wheels, and it seemed that they wrangled and hindered each other's progress. Something was knocking amongst

them ; there was a rusty squeaking, scraping ; it was like a crowd
of drunken, foolish, gibbering lost souls. They began to divide up
into groups, all dressed in gaudy costumes. They moved forward,
and in drunken, dissolute voices burst out in chorus :

" Malania, my goggle-eyed girl . . ."

With such disgusting clearness did Yurasov recall this song that
was sung in all the town gardens, that he and his chums had sung,
that he tried to ward it off with his hand as something living, as a
stone flung at him. And these painfully senseless words, persistent
and insolent, possessed such a cruel power that the whole of the long
train, the hundreds of rolling wheels, took them up :

" Malania, my goggle-eyed girl . . ."

Something monstrous and formless, turbid and clinging, attached
itself to Yurasov with a thousand thick lips and kissed him with
impure wet kisses. It cackled and bawled with a thousand throats,
it whistled and roared and whirled round the earth like a mad thing.
The wheels seemed like hideous round faces, and through the
shameless laughter borne along in that frenzied whirlwind, each
hammered and roared :

" Malania, my goggle-eyed girl . . ."

Only the fields were silent. Cool and calm, deeply absorbed in
their pure creative thought, they knew nothing of the distant stone
towns where men lived, and those disturbing, stupefying thoughts
were foreign to their souls. The train was bearing Yurasov forward,
and this vulgar senseless song was calling him back to the town,
pulling at him roughly and cruelly like a poor runaway prisoner
caught at the prison gates. He still leaned forward, stretching
out his hand to the unknown happy vastness, while before him rose
his inevitable fate, the cruel picture of bondage amid stone walls
and iron railings. The cold indifference of the fields, their refusal
of help, their distance, filled him with utter loneliness. He felt
afraid, so unexpected, so big and terrible was this feeling of being
discarded from life like a dead man. Had he been asleep for a
thousand years and awakened in a new world among new people,
he could not have felt lonelier than then. He wanted to recall
something near and dear to him, but there was nothing, and the
shameless song roared in his tired brain, giving birth to sad and
painful recollections, throwing a shadow over his whole life. He
saw the garden where they had sung that song. He had stolen
something there and they had hunted for him. They had all been
drunk, both he and those who hunted him with shriek and cries.
He had hidden in some dark corner, and they had lost him. He
had sat there for a long time, near some old planks full of nails,
beside a barrel of quicklime. He had felt the freshness and
fragrance of the earth, and the strong odour of young poplars ;

on the paths near by gaily-dressed people had walked about, and
the band had played. A grey cat had passed by, pensive and
indifferent to the voices and the music—so unexpected in such a
place. He had called her " Puss, puss ! " and she had come up,
had purred and rubbed herself against his knees ; had let him kiss
her soft mouth that smelt of fur and herring. His kisses had made
her sneeze, and she had gone off majestic and indifferent like a
society lady, and then he had come out of his hiding-place and had
been caught. On that night there had been a cat at any rate,
but now there was nothing but the complacent fields, and Yurasov
began to hate them with all the strength of his loneliness. Had
he had the strength he would have stoned them, he would have
gathered together thousands of people and ordered them to stamp
out that soft treacherous green that brought joy to all except him ;
that drained from his heart the last drop of blood. Why had he
left the town ? Had he not come, he would have been sitting in
the " Progress " restaurant, drinking wine, talking, and laughing.
And he began to hate the woman to whom he was going, the
wretched impure partner of his unclean life. She was rich now ;
she had adopted him and gave him as much money as he wanted.
When he got there he would beat her black and blue, beat her
until the blood would flow. Then he would get drunk and cry ;
he would clutch his throat and, sobbing, sing :
    " Malania, my goggle-eyed girl . . ."
The wheels no longer sang. Like sick children they grumbled
plaintively and seemed to press against each other as though
seeking caresses and consolation. From above, the austere,
starry sky looked down on him ; the severe, virgin darkness
surrounded him ; and the solitary, scattered lights were like the
tears of pure pity on a beautiful, pensive face. In the distance
twinkled the red lights of a station whence was borne on the warm,
fresh night air the sweet, soft strains of music. The nightmare
vanished, and with the customary lightheartedness of a man who
has no place on the earth, Yurasov instantly forgot it and listened
excitedly, trying to catch the familiar melody.
    " They are dancing ! " he said, smiling ecstatically, his laughing
eyes peering round, and rubbed his hands.
    " They are dancing ! Curse it ! They are dancing ! "
He braced his shoulder, unconsciously swayed to the measure of
the familiar dance, and absorbed the rhythm. He was very fond
of dancing, and when he danced was good and kind and gentle ;
he was no longer either the German Heinrich Walter, or Fiodor
Yurasov, the thief who had served three sentences, but a third
person of whom he knew nothing. When the gusts of wind carried
the sounds away over the fields, he was alarmed, fearing they had

gone for ever, and almost cried. But louder and more joyful, as though they had gathered strength in the dark fields, the whirling sounds returned and Yurasov smiled happily.

"They are dancing ! Curse it ! They are dancing ! "

IV

They were dancing near the station. The local people had got up a dance and had engaged a band. Round the wooden platform had been hung red and blue lanterns, which chased the darkness from the very tops of the trees. Youths, girls in light dresses, students, a little young officer in spurs—so young that it looked as if he were only dressed up for fun—all were whirling smoothly over the broad platform. The dresses blew out with the wind and the dust rose beneath their feet. In the dim mysterious light of the lanterns all the people seemed beautiful, and the dancers seemed ethereal and touching in their purity. Around them was night, and they were dancing ; if you moved only ten steps away from the crowd, the vast all-powerful darkness swallowed you—and they were dancing, and the band played for them so pensively, softly, and sweetly. The train stopped for five minutes, and Yurasov mingled with the onlookers. In a dark, colourless ring they surrounded the platform, holding the wire fence ; so colourless and out of place. Some smiled with a strange, guarded smile ; others were gloomy and sad with the peculiar wan sadness of people who watch the gaiety of others. But Yurasov was gay ; with the enthusiastic glance of the connoisseur he appraised the dancers, while he tapped lightly with his foot. Then he decided suddenly :

"I shall not go on. I shall stop and dance."

From out the circle, making their way leisurely through the crowd, came a couple, a girl in white and a youth almost as tall as Yurasov himself. Past the sleepy carriages at the end of the platform where the darkness stood like a sentinel, they walked, beautiful and seeming to carry with them some of the light. To Yurasov it seemed that the girl shone, so white was her dress, so dark the brows on her fair face. With the confidence of a good dancer, Yurasov caught them up and asked :

"Can you please tell me where I can get a ticket for the dance ? "

The beardless youth, with a severe glance at Yurasov over his shoulder, replied :

"It is a private dance."

"I am a stranger passing through ; my name is Heinrich Walter."

"I have told you it is a private dance ! "

" My name is Heinrich Walter, Heinrich Walter."

" Look here ! " the youth began threateningly, but the girl pulled him on. If she had only looked at Heinrich Walter ! But she did not deign to, and shining as a cloud does against the moon, she shone white in the darkness and then dissolved in it.

" I don't care ! " Yurasov whispered proudly after them, but in his soul it grew white and cold as if snow had fallen there—pure, white, dead snow. The train was still standing there for some reason, and Yurasov paced up and down past the carriages, so handsome, solemn, and majestic in his cold despair, that no one would have taken him for a thief who had served three sentences in prison. He was quite calm ; he saw and understood everything ; only his feet—as though they were made of rubber—did not feel the ground ; and in his soul something was dying, quietly, softly, without pain, without a flutter. Then it was quite dead. The music was still playing, and mingled with it there floated to him a strange, alarming conversation :

" I say, conductor, why doesn't the train go on ? "

" There is a reason, I daresay. Perhaps the driver has joined the dance."

The passengers laughed and Yurasov walked on further. On his way back he overheard two guards talking :

" They say he is in this train."

" Who saw him ? "

" No one saw him. The gendarme said so."

" Your gendarme is mistaken, let me tell you. There are people quite as clever as he is."

The bell rang. Yurasov was undecided for a moment, but from the dance there came the girl in white on some one's arm, so he jumped on to the little platform of the coach and went to the other end of it. Thus he no longer saw the girl in white or the dancers ; the music, however, burst out for a moment in waves of rich sound and then died away in the darkness and stillness of the night. He was alone on the rocking platform, with the faint shadows of the night ; everything was moving, everything had its own mission, strange and phantom-like as in a dream.

v

Pushing Yurasov with the door, but not noticing him, the conductor walked quickly across the platform, a lantern in his hand, and disappeared. Neither his footsteps nor the slamming of the door were heard above the rumbling of the train, but his anxious appearance and hasty offensive movements produced an impression as of sharp, broken cries.   Yurasov turned cold ; something flashed through his brain as quickly as lightning, one terrible thought possessed him—" They are hunting for me."   They had received a wire about him, he had been seen and recognised, and now they were hunting for him in the carriages.   " He," the man of whom the conductor had spoken, was Yurasov himself.   How terrible it was to find yourself in that impersonal " he " uttered by strangers.

Now they were talking about " him," hunting for " him."   Yes, they were coming from the last carriage, he could scent them like a wild animal.   There were three or four of them with lanterns ; they looked at the passengers, peered into the dark corners, awakened the sleepers.   They whispered among themselves, and step by step they were coming nearer to " him," to Yurasov, to the man who, standing on the platform, listened with outstretched neck.   The train flew along with raging swiftness, and the wheels no longer sang and talked together.   They screamed with iron tongues, whispered secretly and austerely, then shrieked in a wild frenzy of malice—a maddened crowd of infuriated singers.

Yurasov clenched his teeth and stood motionless, thinking.   To jump off with the train going at that pace was impossible ; the next station was a long way off ; he must get to the front part of the train and wait there.   While they were hunting through the other carriages something might happen—a stop or a slackening of speed —and he would jump out.   He went through the first door with an affected polite " pardon " ready on his lips, to avoid suspicion if necessary, but in the half-dark third-class carriage it was so crowded, everything was so confused in the chaos of bundles, trunks, and projecting limbs, that he lost hope of reaching the farther end and gave way to a new terror.   How was he to get past this barrier ?   The passengers were asleep, but their legs stuck out into the gangway barring his way ; they projected from below, they hung down from above, knocking against his head and shoulders ; they moved about sleepily from one seat to another, strangely unfriendly in their efforts to get back to their old places and positions.   Like springs they bent and unbent, knocking against him with their dead weight, terrifying him with their unconscious, alarming opposition.   At last he was at the door, but guarding it like two iron bolts were two legs in a huge pair of knee-boots ;   as he spurned them viciously, so they returned to the door obstinately and dully, pressing against it, bending as though they possessed no bones, and finally he managed to squeeze through the small opening.   He thought it was the platform, but it turned out to be only another part of the carriage with the same stack of bundles and limbs.   When, with head down like a bull, he managed to get to the platform, his eyes had the vacant look of a bull, and the dark terror of a hunted animal at bay seized him. He breathed heavily, and listened, crouching like an animal, for the steps of his hunters amidst the rumble of the wheels. Conquering his fear, he approached the dark, silent door. Again there was the unconscious struggle, again the unconscious threatening opposition of malicious human legs. In a first-class compartment he came across a group of passengers who had not been able to sleep. They all knew one another and were gathered together in the narrow little corridor by the open window. Some were standing, others were sitting ; a young lady with wavy hair was looking out of the window. The wind blew back the curtain, moving the lady's ringlets, and it seemed to Yurasov that it was laden with the scent of costly perfume from the town.

" Pardon ! " he said in despair.   " Pardon ! "

The men moved away, slowly and reluctantly, looking at him in an unfriendly manner ; the lady by the window did not hear. Another lady, smiling, touched her round shoulder. At last she turned round, and before stepping aside, looked at him for a terribly long time, at his brown boots, at his coat of real English cloth.   In her eyes was the darkness of night ; she half closed them as though deliberating whether she should let him pass or not.

" Pardon ! " he said appealingly, and the lady, with her rustling silk dress, unwillingly backed against the wall.

And then more of those terrible third-class compartments—it seemed as though he had passed through dozens, hundreds of them—more platforms, more stubborn doors and clinging, malicious, infuriating legs. Finally he reached the last platform, and after that was the plain dark wall of the luggage-van. Something ran past him and he went cold all over ; there was a rumbling, the floor was rocking beneath his trembling legs. Suddenly the cold hard wall against which he was leaning seemed to be pushing him away. Softly and determinedly it pushed and pushed again, like a living, cunning, cautious foe that had not the courage to come out openly. All Yurasov had gone through, blended in his brain into one mad picture of a huge, merciless hunt. It seemed to him that the whole world, till now distant and indifferent, had risen up, and, choking with rage, was hunting him ; the complacent fields, the pensive lady by the window, the massed, lifeless, obstinate legs. Those legs had been limp and sleepy, but now they were active, and in one stamping mass they would give chase, dancing, jumping, crushing everything that came in their way. He was alone and they were in thousands, in millions—the whole world ; they surrounded him and he could not escape.

The coaches whirled on, rocking madly from side to side, knocking against each other and seeming like mad iron monsters who chased each other on their short legs, crouching cunningly and pressing against the earth. It was dark on the platform and nowhere was there a glimmer of light ; one could only see things in a vague, incomprehensible way. There were shadows on long legs that walked backwards ; phantoms that now came right up to the train and then disappeared into the ever limitless darkness. The green fields and woods were inert, only their ominous shades hung over the roaring train. And slowly, stealthily, they were searching, a few carriages away, perhaps four, perhaps only one. Three or four of them, with lanterns, they were carefully examining the passengers, exchanging glances, whispering together, and with painful, barbarous slowness they were moving towards him. Now they had opened one door—now another. . . .

With a final effort Yurasov calmed himself, and looking round slowly, climbed on to the roof of the carriage. He stood up on the narrow iron strip that covered the entrance, and crouching down, threw up his arms. His hands slid about on the slippery iron roof ; he caught hold of the gutter, but it crumpled up like paper ; his feet sought support, but the brown boots, as hard as wood, slipped hopelessly along the rail. At one moment he had the sensation of falling, but wriggling in the air like a cat he managed to change his direction and fell on to the platform. He felt a violent pain in his knees, that had hit against something, and there was a sound of tearing cloth. It was his coat that had caught in a projection and had got torn. Forgetting the pain and everything else, he examined the rent as though it were of the greatest importance, then shook his head sadly and pursed his lips impatiently.

After his unsuccessful attempt, Yurasov was exhausted ; he had a desire to cry out, to lie down on the floor and say, " Take me." He had already chosen the spot where he would lie down, when he recalled the carriages and the tangle of legs, and he heard clearly those three or four men with lanterns coming towards him. Again that unreasoning animal fear possessed him and threw him about the platform like a ball, from one side to the other. He tried again, almost unconsciously, to climb on to the roof of the carriage, when a fierce, hoarse shriek that was neither whistle nor cry, that was unlike anything he knew, assailed his ears and benumbed his mind. It was the whistle of the engine, signalling to an approaching train, but to Yurasov, in his terror, it seemed something infinitely horrible and irrevocable, as though the world had hunted him down at last and with its multitudinous voices was yelling one enormous " Ah-a-ah ! " . . .

And when out of the darkness in front the answering cry was

borne towards him, and the stealthy lights of the oncoming train crept along the neighbouring rails, he threw away the iron bar and jumped out on to the zigzagging lighted rails. His teeth struck something sharply and he rolled over several times. When he raised his face with its crushed moustache and toothless mouth, over him, straight over him, there hung three lanterns, three dim lamps with round lenses. But he did not realise their significance.

LEONID N. ANDREYEV

THE ANGEL

I

SOMETIMES Sashka felt a desire to have done with that which is commonly called life. His fancy pictured to him the delight of not having to get up in the morning and wash himself in cold water, so cold that thin sheets of ice sometimes floated on its surface ; of not having to go to school, where everybody quarrelled with him and swore at him ; of never again feeling the pain in his loins and all over his body when his mother had kept him on his knees in the corner for a whole evening.

As he was but thirteen years old, however, and did not know the means whereby grown-up people achieve their wish of getting through with life, he was forced to continue going to school and spending hours on his knees in the corner. It seemed to him that life would never end. One year would pass, then another and another, and still Sashka would be going to school and spending hours on his knees at home. And since Sashka's spirit was bold and insubordinate, he could no longer endure the cruelty that life had brought to him without taking summary vengeance. He thrashed his comrades whenever and wherever he could, said rude things to policemen, tore his school-books, and lied incessantly— at school to his teachers, at home to his mother. Only to his father he never lied. If his nose was battered in valiant combat, he shed no tears, but howled so loudly and piercingly that all who heard him stopped their ears in pain and anger. After he had roared enough he would stop suddenly, thrust out his tongue at whoever happened to be near, and draw a caricature in his copy-book showing how he had bawled in the face of the headmaster until that worthy man had stopped his ears in sheer desperation, while the victor stood trembling with fear. The whole copy-book was filled with caricatures, the predominant theme being a very short, stout woman striking with a rolling-pin at a young boy as thin as a match. Underneath, heavily pencilled in uneven letters, appeared the legend : " Beg my pardon at once, you puppy ! " and following this, the answer : " Not if I know it ! "

Shortly before Christmas, Sashka was expelled from school, and when his mother gave him an unusually severe drubbing in honour of the occasion he bit her finger. This event brought about his emancipation ; and he stopped washing himself in the morning, ran about all day with the street boys, and had only one fear, that of hunger ; for his mother stopped feeding him, and only his father secretly provided him with bread and potatoes. In these circumstances Sashka found life tolerable.

On the Friday before Christmas he played with the boys until they went home and the rusty gate creaked its cold, grating sound upon the last of them. It was already growing dark, and a thick grey cloud hung over the field at the end of the dark alleys. Across the street, in the low, dark building at the corner, burned a steady, reddish light. The air was frosty, and when Sashka entered within the bright circle made by the light of the lantern he saw bright little snowflakes slowly dropping from the sky. It was time for him to go home.

" Where have you been loafing all day, you dog ? " cried his mother, shaking her fist at him, but not striking. Her sleeves were tucked up, displaying white, fat arms ; and beads of sweat stood on her flat, browless face. When Sashka passed her he recognised the familiar odour of vodka. His mother scratched her head with the short, dirty nail of her forefinger, and as she had no time to enter into a discussion she only spat and shouted :

" Think they know too much, both of them ! "

Sashka sniffed contemptuously and passed in the next room, in which he heard the heavy breathing of his father. Ivan Savvich, who was always cold, was trying to warm himself by sitting on the stove-couch and tucking his hands underneath him.

" Sashka, the Sviechnikovs want you to go and see their Christmas tree ; their servant was here," he muttered.

" Now you're putting it on, Daddy," said Sashka, with an air of incredulity.

" On my word ! The old woman didn't tell you on purpose, but she has your coat ready for you."

" You're lying," said Sashka, with still greater astonishment. The rich Sviechnikovs, who formerly paid his fees at school, had forbidden him to come into their house after his expulsion. His father assured him once more that he was telling the truth, and Sashka fell to thinking.

" Well, move along a bit, will you ? Just see how you have spread yourself out ! " said he to his father, jumping on the low stove-couch ; and he added : " Won't go to those devils, you may be sure ; that is just where they would like to have me, I know ; ' You good-for-nothing scoundrel ! ' " Sashka drawled, in imitation of a familiar voice. " The holy, fat, self-satisfied dogs ! "

" Ah, Sashka ! " exclaimed his father, trembling with cold, " no good will come of you."

" And has any good come of you ? " rudely retorted Sashka. " I'd keep my mouth shut if I were you. Afraid of the old woman, you sleepy loafer."

The father sat still and trembled. A feeble light penetrated through the white chink between the partition wall and the ceiling, and threw bright patches on his high forehead under which the eye-sockets burned deep and dark. At one time Ivan Savvich had been a heavy drinker and then his wife had feared and hated him. But when he began to spit blood and was not able to drink any more, she in her turn began to drink and gradually accustomed herself to vodka. Then she took revenge for everything she had suffered from the tall, narrow-chested man who used big words that she did not understand, who was thrown out of one position after another for drunkenness and obstinacy, and who brought home people with long hair and as haughty as himself. Unlike him, the more she drank the stouter she grew and the heavier were her fists. Now she said whatever she pleased, brought home the men and women she liked, indulged in wild revelry in the house ; while he lay behind the partition wall trembling with a continuous chill, and brooded over the injustice and cruelty of human life. And no matter to whom she spoke, the wife of Ivan Savvich always complained that she had no worse enemies in the world than her husband and her son, both of whom were stuck-up statisticians— for the father had once held a position in the statistical department of the Province.

An hour later the mother said to Sashka, " I tell you that you shall go ! " and at every word Theoktista Petrovna pounded the table with her fist so that the glasses on it jumped and rattled.

" And I tell you I am not going," answered Sashka drily, as the corners of his mouth trembled under his desire to show his teeth. In school he was nicknamed " The Wolf " for this habit.

" I'll beat you black and blue ! Oh, how I'll beat you ! " screamed his mother.

" Go on ; hit me, then ! "

Theoktista Petrovna knew that since her son had begun to bite it was out of the question to beat him, and if she turned him out of the house he would sooner freeze to death in the street than go to the Sviechnikovs' ; so she had recourse to the authority of her husband.

" H'm ! Calls himself a father ! Nice father you are—can't protect your wife from insults."

" She is right, Sashka ; you ought to go. You oughn't to be so capricious," said the father. " Maybe they will fix you up again ; they are good people."

Sashka smiled with an injured air. In past years, before he was born, his father had been a teacher at the Sviechnikovs', and he had always declared that they were the best people in the world. It was then that he secured his position in the local government office. He had to break off his relation with his old friends after he married the daughter of his landlady, who was about to become the mother of his child. Then he began to drink and gradually sank so low that he was often picked up on the street and taken to the police station. But the Sviechnikovs continued to help him with money, and although Theoktista Petrovna detested them as she detested books and everything that was connected with the past life of her husband, she valued their acquaintanceship and often boasted of it to her friends.

" Maybe you will bring me something, too, from the Christmas tree," continued his father. This was a bit of artifice. Sashka understood it and felt a contempt for his father's weakness and lying, but he was suddenly seized with a desire to do something for the sick, suffering man. He knew that his father had been a long time without good tobacco.

" Well, all right," he suddenly blurted out, " give me my jacket. Have you sewed the button on ? Oh, I know you well ! "

II

The children were not yet allowed to go into the hall where the Christmas tree stood, so they remained in the nursery and chatted. Sashka listened to their naïve prattle with haughty contempt, and felt in his trousers pocket the already broken cigarettes that he had carried off from the master's study. Then the youngest of the Sviechnikovs, Kolya, came up, and standing in front of Sashka drew in his toes and put his finger at the corner of his puffy lips. Some six months ago the boy had been persuaded by his family's insistent efforts to renounce the ugly habit of putting his finger in his mouth, but he had not yet been able to leave off the gesture completely. His yellow hair, cut straight across his forehead, his curly locks hanging down over his shoulders, and his blue, wondering eyes produced a general appearance that immediately put him into the class of youngsters whom Sashka had made the special object of his persecutions.

" Are you an ungrateful boy ? " he asked Sashka. " Mama told me that you are, and that I am a good boy."

" Don't think you could be better if you tried," Sashka answered, looking at the child's neat velvet knee-breeches and his large, flat collar.

" Do you want my gun ? Here, you can have it," and the little fellow handed Sashka a toy gun with a cork attached to it. The " wolf " aimed at the nose of the unsuspecting Kolya and pulled the trigger, discharging the cork. It struck the boy's nose and rebounded. Kolya's blue eyes opened still wider and grew moist. He removed his finger from his lips to his nose. His eyelids twitched convulsively and he said in a confused voice :

" You bad, bad boy ! "

A beautiful young lady, with hair parted smoothly on both sides and drawn over her ears, entered the nursery. She was a sister of the hostess and a former pupil of Sashka's father.

" This is the boy I was speaking about to you," she said to the bald-headed gentleman who came in with her, pointing to Sashka. " Say good-evening, Sashka ; it is not nice for such a big boy as you are to be so impolite."

Sashka, however, greeted neither her nor the bald-headed gentleman. He knew—although the beautiful lady had no suspicion of his knowledge—that his unhappy father had once loved her, and that she had married somebody else ; and although his father's marriage had taken place first, Sashka could never forgive her for her betrayal of his father.

" Bad blood," sighed the beautiful young lady. " Is it not possible for you to find a place for him ? My husband thinks that a technical school would be more suitable for him than the elementary. Sashka, would you like to go to a manual-training school ? "

" No ! " answered Sashka savagely. He had heard the words " my husband," and this had made him surly.

" Why, what do you want to become, my little fellow ?—a swineherd, maybe ? " asked the gentleman.

" No, not a swineherd," answered Sashka, somewhat insulted.

" What then ? "

Sashka did not know. " It's all the same to me," he answered, after some reflection. " I'll be a swineherd, for all I care."

The bald-headed gentleman looked at the strange boy and shook his head. When he raised his eyes from Sashka's patched shoes to his face, the boy put out his tongue and drew it in again so quickly that the lady, who had momentarily turned aside and did not notice the gesture, was greatly surprised at the shocked appearance of the old gentleman.

" Yes," said Sashka decidedly. " I want to go to the manual-training school.

The beautiful lady was greatly pleased at this. The thought passed through her mind that old love never dies.

" I don't think we can find a place for you very soon ; there is no room in the manual-training school just now," said the old gentleman, as he smoothed down a rebellious lock of hair on his neck. " However, we'll see what we can do."

The children were excited and talked noisily in expectation of what was coming. The experiment with the gun, initiated by Sashka, who enjoyed special respect on account of his size and reputation as a bad boy, was generally imitated, and many a snub nose soon grew very red. The girls folded their hands and rocked with laughter at seeing their boys receive the blows of the discharged gun without so much as making a wry face, valiantly defying all fear and pain.

Suddenly the door of the hall opened, and a voice called out, " Come, children ! Hush, not so loud ! "

With eyes wide open and bated breath, the children filed in solemn procession, two by two, into the hall, and walked slowly round the Christmas tree that towered high above them in its brilliancy. A strong, almost overpowering light fell on the round, wide-open eyes and parted lips of the children. For a few minutes a profound, unbroken silence of astonishment reigned in the room ; then suddenly there resounded a loud chorus of delighted, joyous children's voices. One of the little girls, no longer able to restrain her ecstasy, began to jump up and down, while her short plait of hair, tied with a blue ribbon, struck her shoulders at each motion.

Sashka looked sombre and downcast. Evil was at work in his wounded heart. He too was blinded by the brilliant light of the many tapers that burned on the beautifully decorated Christmas tree, but its very beauty estranged him and filled him with the same animosity as the neat, tidy, beautiful children. He wanted to kick down the tree and hurl it, with all its extravagant ornament and dazzling radiancy, upon the heads of the merry children. It was as if an iron hand clutched his quivering, childish heart, pressing and squeezing the last drop of warm blood out of it. He sat down in a corner behind the piano, and, hardly conscious of what he was doing, broke to pieces all the cigarettes in his pocket. It came into his mind that he too had a father and a mother and a home, and yet why was it that he seemed not to have them, and that there was no place where he could celebrate his own Christmas Eve as these children did ? Suddenly he thought of a little penknife that he had obtained some time ago by trading with other children, and that he loved very much. It was already old and ugly, the points of the blades were broken, and the white plate on the handle was almost half gone. To-morrow, he thought, he would put the finishing touches to it and throw it away, and then there would be nothing more for him to love or enjoy.

Suddenly his eyes lighted up with interest, and, as if by a magic spell, the usual, bold insolent and self-confident expression of his face took on a tinge of hesitating admiration.

On the side where he sat the Christmas tree was but feebly illumined, and as he stared aimlessly into the dim light, he suddenly perceived something that his soul had missed in all the plays and pictures that he had seen before, and compared to which everything around him was so empty and colourless that it seemed to him as if the people whom he saw and with whom he spoke were not really alive, and as if there must be some better people somewhere, whom it was impossible to see. The boy's longing, his slumbering sense of beauty, had recognised this object instantly. It was a little wax angel, lightly attached by a rubber band to a thick branch of the fir tree. It seemed to be floating in the air. Its transparent wings trembled softly in the brilliant light, and it appeared to be alive and soaring. The rosy little hands with their tiny fingers were outspread with an expressive upward gesture, and beneath them the beautiful little head was radiant in the halo of its golden hair —like Kolya's.

But Sashka saw in this little head something more, something different from what he saw in either Kolya's or any other child's face, or indeed in any object that he had ever before known. The little angel was neither cheerful nor melancholy ; but there was an expression on its face that could neither be translated into words nor comprehended by the mind ; if could only be felt and enjoyed. Sashka would have been unable to say what it was that so powerfully attracted him to the little angel ; yet he was certain that he had always known and loved it—loved it more than his penknife and his father—more than everything in the world. Filled with still doubting admiration and with anxiety but vaguely understood, he muttered :

" Dear, dear little angel ! "

And the longer he looked the more significant and momentous seemed to him the expression of the little angel. It was so infinitely distant and different from everything that surrounded it ! The other playthings seemed to be proud of being so beautifully decorated, and of hanging on the brilliant Christmas tree ; but the little angel looked sad, as if it feared the intrusion of the dazzling light, and purposely hid itself in the dark green to avoid being seen. A feeling of profound reverence took possession of Sashka ; his heart went

out with loving admiration to the angel.   Even to touch its delicate
little wings were sacrilege, an act of sheer madness !

" Dear, dear heavenly creature ! " muttered Sashka.

His brain was on fire.   He clasped his hands behind his back,
and prepared to do mortal combat in defence of the little angel ; he
paced up and down with cautious, stealthy steps, not daring to look
at it for fear of attracting attention, but pervaded with its presence,
and feeling certain that it had not yet flown away.

Her ladyship appeared at the door, a tall, stately dame with a
towering coiffure of dazzling white hair that encircled her head like
an aureole.   The children surrounded her and gave vent to their
delight in loud, noisy ejaculations, while the little girl who had been
jumping up and down now hung heavily on the lady's hand, and
despite her heroic efforts could scarcely keep her drowsy eyes from
closing.   Sashka stepped up to the lady, and there was a lump in
his throat when he began to speak.

" Aunt—listen, aunt ! " he said, endeavouring to give his voice
its softest expression, but succeeded only in making it seem even
coarser than usual.   " Aunt ! "

With the swarm of children around her she did not hear him,
and Sashka tugged at her dress impatiently.

" What do you want ? Why do you pull my dress ? " the stately
lady asked in astonishment.   " That is not the way to act ; it is
rude."

" Auntie, dear auntie ! Give me—that little angel on the tree ! "

" No, I cannot let you have anything from the Christmas tree,"
replied the lady indifferently.   " New Year's Day is the time when
the tree is bared.   Besides, you are no longer a baby, and you can
call me by my name like the other children.   Marya Dmitriyevna
is my name."

Sashka felt as if he were being hurled into an abyss, and he
determined to resort immediately to extreme measures.

" I am sorry—I will work hard," he blurted out.   But this
formula, which always worked wonders at school, seemed to make
no impression at all upon the stately dame.

" That will be a very good thing for you, my friend," she answered,
with the same indifference as before.

" Then give me the little angel ! " said Sashka rudely.

" I told you you cannot have it," answered the lady.   " Can't
you understand what is said to you ? "

Sashka understood absolutely nothing, and when the lady turned
to go he followed her, with his eyes fixed in a blank, rigid stare on
her rustling velvet gown.   Into his fevered brain came the memory
of a classmate at school who asked his teacher to give him a higher
mark, and, when the latter declined to do it, threw himself on his

knees, clasped his hands as if in prayer, and wept bitterly. The teacher was greatly annoyed, but gave him a better mark. This episode had been immortalised at the time in a scathing caricature by Sashka, but in the present emergency he knew of no other expedient. He pulled the lady's dress again, and when she turned he fell down with a thud upon his knees before her, and held up his hands in a prayerful attitude ; but he could not weep.

" Are you out of your senses ? " cried the lady. " What is the matter with you ? "

Still on his knees, with his hands stretched out imploringly, Sashka looked with burning hatred into her face and said rudely, " Give me the little angel ! "

The look in Sashka's eyes as he kept them riveted on the lady's face in order to catch her first word boded no good, and she hastened to say, " Very well, very well, you shall have it. You stupid youngster ! I am very glad to let you have it, though you do ask for it in such a strange manner. But why could you not wait until New Year's Day ? Stand up ! And you must never," she continued didactically, " never go down on your knees. It lowers a person's dignity. Kneel only before God ! "

" Talk away ! " thought Sashka. He stepped on her dress as he ran off behind her.

When she took down the plaything Sashka drank in the sight of it with all his eyes, while he wrinkled his nose as if in sharp pain, and spread out his ten fingers. He trembled lest the little angel should fall and be broken.

" What a pretty little thing ! " said the lady, who was now sorry to part with the plaything. " Who hung it up there ? Listen ; really, what do you want this for ? You are too big for a thing of that kind. We have some picture books here. Take them ; they are more suitable for you. I have promised this angel to Kolya ; he asked me for it," she concluded, with a deliberate lie.

Sashka's anxiety was becoming insupportable. He set his teeth convulsively. The stately lady hated and feared scenes more than anything else in the world. She slowly handed him the little angel.

" Well, there you have it," she said in a displeased tone. " What a queer, obstinate child you are ! "

Sashka received the little angel in his two hands, which he kept locked together like two steel gates, but at the same time he held it with such a gentle, cautious touch that the angel must assuredly have thought it was still floating in the air.

" Ah—h ! " A long, gentle, dying sigh escaped from Sashka's breast, and in his eyes appeared two small tears, which remained there, not being accustomed to come out into the light. Slowly

clasping the little angel to his beating heart, he kept his beaming
eyes fixed on the lady and smiled a soft, gentle smile, faint with the
emotion of an unearthly joy. It seemed as if the moment the angel's
wings touched his breast something glad and luminous would happen
—such as had never yet been upon this sad, suffering earth.

" Ah—h ! " Again he uttered the same blissful, dying sigh as
the little angel's wings touched his breast. Before the radiance of
this happy child's face even the splendour of the Christmas tree
seemed pale. The laughter of the stately lady resounded merrily ;
but the dry face of the bald gentleman quivered strangely, and the
children stood motionless in reverent silence. All were touched by
the infinite exultation of pure human happiness. And in this brief
moment all became aware of the remarkable likeness between the
awkward, clumsy schoolboy in his outgrown clothes and the delicate
wax angel, created by the hand of an unknown artist.

The next moment, however, the picture changed completely.
Sashka gathered himself together like a panther about to leap, and
looked around as if to see who would venture to approach the
little angel.

" I am going home," he said drily, pushing his way through the
children, " to my father."

III

The mother was already asleep, exhausted with the day's labour
and with drink. A kitchen lamp burned in the little space behind
the partition wall, and its feeble light penetrated with difficulty the
darkened window, casting weird shadows upon the faces of Sashka
and his father.

" Is this all right ? " asked Sashka in a whisper. He held the
little angel out of his father's reach.

" Yes, but there is something peculiar about it," whispered his
father, regarding it thoughtfully. His face began to assume the
same expression of concentrated attention and joy as that of his son.
" Look, it will soon fly away."

" Haven't I seen it already ? " answered Sashka triumphantly.
" Do you think I am blind ? Just look at its wings ! Look out !
Don't lay your hands on it ! "

The father drew his hand back quickly, and with dim eyes studied
every detail of the angel's body, while Sashka remonstrated in an
undertone :

" What an ugly habit you have, father, of touching everything
with your hands. Why, you might break it ! "

On the wall were traced sharp, dark shadows of two heads close
together—a great shaggy one and a little round one. In the great

head a strange, tormenting, yet joyous work was going forward. Its eyes looked without blinking at the little angel, and under their searching gaze it grew larger and larger. The room grew brighter, and the little angel's wings moved swiftly, quietly ; the soot-covered wooden wall, the dirty table, and Sashka melted into one even grey mass, without light or shadow. And it seemed to the ruined man as if he heard a pitying voice from that strange world in which he once had lived, and from which he had been cast out for ever. *There* they knew not of dirt and coarse, abusive language, of the blind, dismal, cruel war of egotism ; *there* they knew not the agony of the man who is picked up in the street and abused by the rough hand of the policeman amid the laughter of the onlookers ; *there* all is pure, cheerful, and bright. And all this purity had found a retreat in *her* soul, in the soul of her whom he loved more than his life and whom he had lost, while his useless life remained. Some elusive aroma united with the odour of wax that emanated from the toy, and the ruined man seemed to see her dear fingers touching the delicate little angel—those dear, sweet fingers that he longed to kiss one after another until death should lock his lips for ever. It was this that made the toy so supremely beautiful, so wondrous, so transcendent, beyond the power of human expression. The little angel descended from the heaven that was her soul, bringing thence a ray of light into the dark, smoky chamber, and into the dark soul of the man from whom everything had been taken away—love, fortune, joy.

And beside the eyes of this man of the past beamed the eyes of the youth just entering upon life, and looked caressingly at the little angel. And for these eyes the past had no existence, and the present and the future vanished before them—the ever-sorrowful, pitiable father, the coarse, insupportable mother, and the whole black waste of humiliation, abuse, and abasement, of irate, hopeless longing. Formless, misty, and vague were the dreams of Sashka, but they stirred his agitated soul profoundly. All the good that radiated over the world, all the anguish of a soul that yearned for joy, rest, and peace, that yearned for God, this little angel united within itself ; and so it burned with a soft, heavenly light, while its transparent, tiny wings fluttered noiselessly with its longing.

Father and son did not look at each other. Each one suffered and rejoiced in his own way. Their sick hearts wept and trembled with delight, each for itself ; and yet there was something in their emotion that bound them into one and bridged the abysmal chasm that divides one soul from another and makes each one solitary, weak, and unhappy. Unconsciously the father placed his hand on his son's shoulder, and his son's head sank unconsciously on the breast of his poor, consumptive father.

" Did she give it to you ? " whispered the father, without turning his eyes from the little angel.

At another time Sashka would have answered rudely in the negative, but now the reply came from his soul, and his lips unhesitatingly uttered the conscious lie :

" She ? Of course ; who else ? "

The father was silent, and Sashka also. A soft creaking sound came from the next room, followed by a buzzing noise, then a rattle, and raucously the clock struck, one, two, three !

" Sashka, do you ever have dreams ? " asked his father thoughtfully.

" No," Sashka confessed. " Oh yes, once I did. I dreamt I fell down the roof. I wanted to catch some pigeons, and I fell."

" And I always dream," said his father. " Sometimes I have very remarkable dreams. I see everything as it used to be ; I love and suffer just as in reality."

He was silent again, and Sashka felt the trembling of the hand that lay on his shoulder. More and more it trembled and quivered, and suddenly the sensitive stillness of night was interrupted by the faint, piteous sound of a repressed sigh. Sashka knit his eyebrows sternly, raised his head carefully so as not to disturb his father, and stealthily wiped a tear from his eye. It was so strange to see a big, old man weep !

" Ah, Sashka, Sashka," sobbed the father, " why is all this ? "

" Well, what is the matter ? " whispered Sashka sternly. " Why, you are like a baby—just like a baby."

" I won't any more ; I won't," apologised the father, with a sorrowful smile. " Anyway, what does it matter ? "

The mother moved in her bed near by. She heaved a sigh, spat, and mumbled with strange emphasis : " Hold that stick ! Hold that stick ! "

It was time to go to sleep. But first the angel must be accommodated for the night. To put it on the floor was out of the question, and the table also was dirty, so it was attached by a thread to the draught-hole of the stove. It stood out so sharply against the white background of Dutch tiles that both Sashka and the father could see it distinctly.

Having hurriedly thrown together in the corner the heap of rags upon which he was used to sleeping, Sashka quickly took off some of his clothes and lay down on his back in order to regain immediately his view of the little angel.

" Why don't you undress ? " asked his father.

" It isn't worth while ; I will soon get up."

Sashka intended to add that he was not at all sleepy, but he had no time for this, for he fell asleep as quickly as a stone falls to the bottom of a deep, precipitous river. Gentle rest and peace settled at once upon the worn face of the decrepit old man and on the bold countenance of the boy who was just starting out upon life.

But the angel that was hung over the hot stove began to melt. The lamp, which had been left burning at Sashka's request, filled the room with smoke, and through the blackened shade it cast a dismal yellow light upon this picture of gradual dissolution.

The little angel seemed to move. Thick drops of molten wax flowed down its rosy feet and fell heavily on the stove-couch. The odour of kerosene oil mingled with the strong smell of molten wax. The angel trembled as if in an attempt to fly away, and then fell down with a soft thud upon the hot hearthstone.

An inquisitive beetle ran quickly around the heap of wax, burning its feet, and as quickly sped away again. A bluish light filtered through the curtained window and ushered in the new day.

LEONID N. ANDREYEV

VALIA

VALIA was reading a huge, a very huge book, almost half as large as himself, with very black letters and pictures occupying the entire page. To see the top line Valia had to stretch out his neck, lean far over the table, kneeling in his chair, and putting his short chubby finger on the letters for fear they should be lost among the other ones like them, in which case it was a difficult task to find them again. Owing to these circumstances, unforeseen by the publishers, the reading advanced very slowly, notwithstanding the breath-catching interest of the book.

It was a story about a very strong boy whose name was Prince Bova, and who could, by merely grasping the legs or arms of other boys, wrench them away from the body.

But Valia was suddenly interrupted in his reading ; his mother entered with some other woman.

" Here he is," said his mother, her eyes red with weeping. The tears had evidently been shed very recently, as she was still crushing a white lace handkerchief in her hand.

" Valichka, darling ! " exclaimed the other woman ; and putting her arms about his head, she began to kiss his face and eyes, pressing her thin, hard lips to them. She did not fondle him as did his mother, whose kisses were soft and melting ; this one seemed loth to let go of him. Valia accepted her prickly caresses with a frown and silence ; he was very much displeased at being interrupted, and he did not at all like this strange woman, tall, with bony, long fingers upon which there was not even one ring. And she smelled so bad : a damp, mouldy smell, while his mother always exhaled a fresh, exquisite perfume.

At last the woman left him in peace, and while he was wiping his lips she looked him over with that quick sort of glance which seems to photograph one. His short nose with its indication of a future little hump, his thick, unchildish brows over dark eyes, and the general appearance of stern seriousness, recalled some one to her, and she began to cry. Even her weeping was unlike mamma's :

the face remained immovable while the tears quickly rolled down
one after the other—before one had time to fall another was already
chasing after it.. Her tears ceased as suddenly as they had begun,
and she asked : " Valichka, do you know me ? "

" No."

" I called to see you.   Twice I called to see you."

Perhaps she had called upon him, perhaps she had called twice,
but how should Valia know of it ?   With her questions she only
hindered him from reading.

" I am your mamma, Valia ! " said the woman.

Valia looked around in astonishment to find his mamma, but she
was no longer in the room.

" Why, can there be two mammas ? " he asked.   " What nonsense you are telling me."

The woman laughed, but this laugh did not please Valia ; it
was evident that the woman did not need to laugh at all, and
did it purposely to mislead him.   For some moments both were
silent.

" And what book is it you are reading ? "

" About Prince Bova," Valia informed her, with serious self-
esteem and an evident respect for the big book.

" Ah, it must be very interesting !   Tell me, please ! " the woman
asked with an ingratiating smile.

And once more something unnatural and false sounded in this
voice, which tried to be soft and round like the voice of his mother,
but remained sharp and prickly.   The same insincerity appeared
also in all the movements of the woman ; she turned on her chair
and even stretched out her neck with a manner as if preparing for
a long and attentive listening ; and when Valia reluctantly began
the story, she immediately retired within herself, like a dark lantern
on which the cover is suddenly thrown.   Valia felt the discourtesy
toward himself and Prince Bova, but, wishing to be polite, he
quickly finished the story and added : " That is all."

" Well, good-bye, my dear, my dove ! " said the strange woman,
and once more pressed her lips to Valia's face.   " I shall soon call
again. Will you be glad ? "

" Yes, please come," politely replied Valia, and to get rid of her
more quickly he added : " I shall be very glad."

The visitor left him, but hardly had Valia found in the book again
the word at which he had been interrupted, when mamma entered,.
looked at him, and she also began to weep.   He could easily understand why the other woman should have wept ; she must have been
sorry that she was so unpleasant and tiresome ; but why should his
mamma weep ?

" Listen, mamma," he said musingly ; " how that woman bored

me ! She says that she is my mamma. Why, could there be two mammas to one boy ? "

" No, baby, there could not ; but she speaks the truth ; she is your mother."

" And what are you, then ? "

" I am your auntie."

This was a very unexpected discovery, but Valia received it with unshakable indifference ; auntie, well, let it be auntie—was it not just the same ? A word did not, as yet, have the same meaning for him as it would have for a grown person. But his former mother did not understand this, and began to explain why it had so happened that she had been a mother and had become an aunt. Once, very long ago, when Valia was very, very little——

" How little ? So ? " Valia raised his hand about a quarter of a yard from the table. " Like Kiska ? " Valia exclaimed, joyfully surprised, with mouth half opened and brow lifted. He spoke of the white kitten that had been presented to him.

" Yes."

Valia broke into a happy laugh, but immediately resumed his usual earnestness, and with the condescension of a grown person recalling the mistakes of his youth, he remarked : " How funny I must have been ! "

When he was so very little and funny, like Kiska, he had been brought by that woman and given away for ever, also like Kiska. And now, when he had become so big and clever, the woman wanted him.

" Do you wish to go to her ? " asked his former mother, and reddened with joy when Valia resolutely and sternly said : " No, she does not please me ! " and once more took up his book.

Valia considered the affair closed, but he was mistaken. This strange woman, with a face as devoid of life as if all the blood had been drained out of it, who had appeared from no one knew where, and vanished without leaving a trace, seemed to have set the whole house in turmoil and filled it with a dull alarm. Mamma-auntie often cried and repeatedly asked Valia if he wished to leave her ; uncle-papa grumbled, patted his bald pate so that the sparse, grey hair on it stood up, and when auntie-mamma was absent from the room he also asked Valia if he would like to go to that woman. Once, in the evening, when Valia was already in his little bed but was not yet sleeping, he heard his uncle and auntie speaking of him and the woman. The uncle spoke in an angry growl at which the crystal pendants of the chandelier gently trembled and sparkled with bluish and reddish lights.

" You speak nonsense, Nastasia Philippovna. We have no right to give the child away."

"She loves him, Grisha."

"And we! Do we not love him? You are arguing very strangely, Nastasia Philippovna. It seems as if you would be glad to get rid of the child——"

"Are you not ashamed of yourself?"

"Well, well, how quick you are to take offence! Just consider this matter cold-bloodedly and reasonably. Some frivolous thing or other gives birth to children, light-heartedly disposes of them by placing them on your threshold, and afterward says, 'Kindly give me my child, because, on account of my lover having abandoned me, I feel lonesome. For theatres and concerts I have no money, so give me the child to serve as a toy to play with.' No, madam, be easy, we shall see who wins in this case!"

"You are unjust to her, Grisha. You know well how ill and lonely she is——"

"You, Nastasia Philippovna, can make even a saint lose patience, by God! And you seem to have forgotten the child. Is it wholly immaterial whether he is brought up an honest man or a scoundrel? And I could bet my head that he would be brought up by her a scoundrel, rascal, and—scoundrel!"

"Grisha!"

"I ask you, for God's sake, not to irritate me! And where did you get this devilish habit of contradicting? 'She is so lonely.' And are *we* not lonely? The heartless woman that you are, Nastasia Philippovna! And why the devil did I marry you?"

The heartless woman broke into tears, and her husband immediately begged her pardon, declaring that only a born fool could pay any attention to the words of such an old ass as he was. Gradually she became calmer and asked, "What does Talonsky say?"

"And what makes you think that he is such a clever fellow?" Gregory Aristarchovich again flew into a passion. "He says that everything depends on how the court will look at it. . . . Something new, is it not, as if we did not know without his telling that everything depends on how the court will look at it! Of course it matters little to him—what does he care?—he will have his say and then safely go his way. If I had *my* way, it would go ill with all these empty talkers——"

Here Nastasia Philippovna shut the dining-room door and Valia did not hear the end of the conversation. But he lay for a long time with open eyes, trying to understand what sort of woman it was who wished to take him away from his home and ruin him.

On the next day he waited from early morning, expecting his auntie to ask him if he wished to go to his mother; but auntie did not ask. Neither did his uncle. Instead of this, they both gazed at Valia as if he were dangerously ill and would soon die; they caressed him and brought him large books with coloured pictures. The woman did not call any more, but it seemed to Valia that she must be lurking outside the door watching for him, and that as soon as he should pass the threshold she would seize him and carry him out into a black and dismal distance where cruel monsters were wriggling and breathing fire.

In the evenings, while his uncle Gregory Aristarchovich was occupied in his study and Nastasia Philippovna was knitting something, or playing a game of patience, Valia read his books, in which the lines would grow gradually thicker and the letters smaller. Everything in the room was quiet, so quiet that the only thing to be heard was the rustling of the pages he turned, and occasionally the uncle's loud cough from the study, or the falling of the cards.   The lamp, with its blue shade, threw a bright light on the blue plush table-cover, but the corners of the room were full of a quiet, mysterious gloom.   There stood large plants with curious leaves, and roots crawling out upon the surface and looking very much like fighting serpents, and it seemed as if something large and dark was moving amid them.   Valia read, and before his wide-open eyes passed terrible, beautiful, and sad images which awakened in him pity and love, but more often fear.   Valia was sorry for the poor water-nymph who so dearly loved the handsome prince that for him she had given up her sisters and the deep, peaceful ocean ; and the prince knew nothing of this love, because the poor water-nymph was dumb, and so he married a gay princess ; and while great festivities in honour of the wedding were in full swing on board the ship, and music was playing and all were enjoying themselves, the poor water-nymph threw herself into the dark waves to die.   Poor, sweet, little water-nymph, so quiet and sad and modest !   But often terrible, cruel, human monsters appeared before Valia.   In the dark nights they flew somewhere on their prickly wings, and the air whistled over their heads, and their eyes burned like red-hot coals. And afterward, they were surrounded by other monsters like themselves while a mysterious and terrible something was happening there.   Laughter as sharp as a knife, long and pitiful wailing ; strange weird dances in the purplish light of torches, their slant, fiery tongues wrapped in the red clouds of smoke ; and dead men with long, black beards.   All this was the manifestation of a single enigmatic and cruel power, wishing to destroy man.   Angry and mysterious spectres filled the air, hid among the plants, whispered something, and pointed their bony fingers at Valia ; they gazed at him from behind the door of the adjoining unlit room, giggled and waited till he would go to bed, when they would silently dart about over his head ; they peeped at him from out of the garden through the large, dark windows, and wailed sorrowfully with the wind.

In and out among all this vicious and terrible throng appeared the image of that woman who had come for Valia. Many people came and went in the house of Gregory Aristarchovich, and Valia did not remember their faces, but this face lived in his memory. It was such an elongated, thin, yellow face, and smiled with a sly, dissembling smile, from which two deep lines appeared at the two corners of the mouth. If this woman took Valia he would die.

" Listen," Valia once said to his aunt, tearing himself away from his book for a moment. " Listen," he repeated with his usual earnestness, and with a glance that gazed straight into the eyes of the person to whom he spoke : " I shall call you mamma, not auntie. You talk nonsense when you say that the woman—is mamma. You are mamma, not she."

" Why ? " asked Nastasia Philippovna, blushing like a young girl who has just received a compliment. But along with her joy there could also be heard in her voice the sound of fear for Valia. He had become so strange of late, and timid ; feared to sleep alone, as he used to do, raved in his sleep and cried.

" But, Valichka, it is true, she is your mother."

" I really wonder where you get this habit of contradicting ! " Valia said after some musing, imitating the tone of Gregory Aristarchovich.

Nastasia Philippovna laughed, but while preparing for bed that night she spoke for a considerable time with her husband, who boomed like a Turkish drum, abused the empty talkers and frivolous, hare-brained women, and afterward went with his wife to see Valia.

They gazed long and silently into the face of the sleeping child. The flame of the candle swayed in the trembling hand of Gregory Aristarchovich and lent a fantastic, death-like colouring to the face of the boy, which was as white as the pillows on which it rested. It seemed as if a pair of stern, black eyes looked at them from the dark hollows, demanding a reply and threatening them with misfortune and unknown sorrow, and the lips twitched into a strange, ironic smile as if upon his helpless child-head lay a vague reflection of those cruel and mysterious spectre monsters that silently hovered over it.

" Valia ! " whispered the frightened Nastasia. The boy sighed deeply but did not move, as if enchained in the sleep of death.

" Valia ! Valia ! " the deep, trembling voice of her husband was added to that of Nastasia Philippovna.

Valia opened his eyes, shaded by thick eyelashes ; the light of the candle made him blink, and he sprang to his knees, pale and frightened. His uncovered, thin little arms like a pearl necklace encircled his auntie's full, rosy neck, and hiding his little head upon her breast and screwing up his eyes tight as if fearing that they would open of themselves, he whispered : " I am afraid, mamma, I am afraid ! Do not go ! "

That was a bad night for the whole household. When Valia at last fell asleep, Gregory Aristarchovich got an attack of asthma. He choked, and his full, white breast rose and fell spasmodically under the ice compresses. Toward morning he grew more tranquil, and the worn Nastasia fell asleep with the thought that her husband would not survive the loss of the child.

After a family council at which it was decided that Valia ought to read less and to see more of children of his own age, little girls and boys were brought to the house to play with him. But Valia from the first conceived a dislike for these foolish children, who, in his eyes, were too noisy, loud, and indecorous. They pulled flowers, tore books, jumped over chairs, and fought like little monkeys ; and he, serious and thoughtful, looked on at their pranks with amazement and displeasure, and, going up to Nastasia Philippovna, said : " They tire me ! I would rather sit by you."

And in the evenings he once more took up his book, and when Gregory Aristarchovich, grumbling at all the devilry the child read about, and by which he was losing his senses, gently tried to take the book from Valia's hands, the child silently and resolutely pressed it to himself. And the improvised pedagogue beat a confused retreat and angrily scolded his wife :

" Is this what you call bringing up ! No, Nastasia Philippovna, I see you are more fit to take care of kittens than to bring up children. The boy is so spoiled that one cannot even take a book away from him."

One morning, while Valia was sitting at breakfast with Nastasia Philippovna, Gregory Aristarchovich suddenly came rushing into the dining-room. His hat was tilted on the back of his head, his face was covered with perspiration ; while still at the other side of the door he shouted joyfully into the room :

" Refused ! The court has refused ! "

The diamond earrings in Nastasia Philippovna's ears began to sparkle, and the little knife she held in her hand dropped to the plate with a clatter.

" Is it true ? " she asked breathlessly.

Gregory Aristarchovich made a serious face, just to show that he had spoken the truth, but immediately forgetting his intention, his face became covered with a whole network of merry wrinkles. Then once more remembering that he lacked that earnestness of demeanour with which important news is usually imparted, he frowned, pushed a chair up to the table, placed his hat upon it, forgot that it was his hat, and thinking the chair to be already occupied by some one, threw a stern look at Nastasia Philippovna, then on Valia, winked

his eye at Valia ; and only after all these solemn preliminaries did
he declare :

" I always said that Talonsky was a devilish clever fellow ; can't
fool *him* easily, Nastasia Philippovna."

" So it is true ? "

" You are always ready with your eternal doubts. I said the
case of Mme. Akimova is dismissed. Clever, is it not, little brother ? "
he turned to Valia and added in a stern, official tone : " And that
said Akimova is to pay the costs."

" That woman will not take me, then ? "

" I guess she won't, brother mine ! Ah, I have entirely forgotten,
I brought you some books ! "

Gregory Aristarchovich rushed into the corridor, but halted on
hearing Nastasia Philippovna's scream. Valia had fallen back on
his chair in a faint.

A happy time began for the family. It was as if some one who
had lain dangerously ill in the house had suddenly recovered, and
all began to breathe more easily and freely. Valia lost his fear of
the terrible monsters and no longer suffered from nightmares. When
the little monkeys, as he called the children, came to see him again,
he was the most inventive of the lot. But even into the most
fantastic plays he introduced his habitual earnestness and staidness,
and when they played Indians he found it indispensable to divest
himself of almost all his clothing and cover his body with red
paint.

In view of the businesslike manner in which these games were
conducted, Gregory Aristarchovich now found it possible to partici-
pate in them, as far as his abilities allowed. In the role of a bear he
did not appear to great advantage, but he had a great and well-
deserved success in that of an elephant. And when Valia, silent
and earnest as a true son of the Goddess Kali, sat upon his father's
shoulders and gently tapped upon his rosy bald pate with a tiny
toy hammer, he really reminded one of a little Eastern prince who
despotically reigns over people and animals.

The lawyer Talonsky tried to convey a hint to Gregory Aristarchovich that all was not safe yet, but the former could not comprehend
how three judges could reverse the decision of three other judges,
when the laws are the same here and everywhere. And when the
lawyer insisted, Gregory Aristarchovich grew angry, and to prove
that there was nothing to be feared from the higher court, he brought
forward that same Talonsky on whom he now implicitly relied :

" Why, are you not going to be present when the case is brought
before the court ? Well, then, what is there to be talked about ?
I wish you, Nastasia Philippovna, would make him ashamed of
himself."

Talonsky smiled, and Nastasia Philippovna gently chid him for his purposeless doubts. They also spoke of the woman who had caused all the trouble ; but now that she could menace them no more, and the court had decided that she must bear all the costs of the trial, they often dubbed her " poor woman."

Since the day Valia had heard that the woman had no longer any power to take him, she had lost in his eyes the halo of mysterious fear which enveloped her like a mist and distorted the features of her thin face, and Valia began to think of her as he did of all other people. He now often heard that she was unhappy and could not understand why ; but this pale, bloodless face grew more simple, natural, and near to him ; the " poor woman," as they called her, began to interest him, and recalling other poor women of whom he had read, he felt a growing pity and a timid tenderness for her.

He imagined that she must sit alone in some dark room, fearing something and weeping, always weeping, as she had wept then when she had come to see him. And he felt sorry that he had not told her the story of Prince Bova better than he had done at the time.

.   .   .   .

It appeared that three judges could, after all, disagree with the decision of three other judges. The higher court had reversed the decision of the district court ; the child was adjudged to his real mother. And the appeal was not considered by the senate.

When the woman came to take Valia away with her, Gregory Aristarchovich was not at home ; he was at Talonsky's house and was lying in Talonsky's bedroom, and only the bald, rosy pate was visible above the sea of snow-white pillows.

Nastasia Philippovna did not leave her room, and the maid led Valia forth from it already dressed for the road. He wore a fur coat and high overshoes in which he moved his feet with difficulty. From under his fur cap looked out a pale little face with a frank and serious expression in the dark eyes. Under his arm Valia carried a book in which was the story of a poor water-nymph.

The tall, gaunt woman pressed the boy to her shabby coat and sobbed out : " How you have grown, Valichka ! You are un-recognisable," she said, trying to jest ; but Valia adjusted his cap, and, contrary to habit, did not look into the eyes of the one who from this day on was to be his mother, but into her mouth. It was large, but with beautiful, small teeth ; the two wrinkles on the corners of the mouth were still in the same place where Valia had seen them first, only now they were deeper.

" You are not angry with me ? " asked mamma ; but Valia, not replying to her question, said : " Let us be gone."

" Valichka ! " came a pitiful scream from Nastasia Philippovna's room, and she appeared on the threshold with eyes swollen from weeping, and clasping her hands she rushed toward the child, sank on her knees, and put her head on his shoulder. She did not utter a sound, only the diamonds in her ears trembled.

"Come, Valia," sternly said the tall woman, taking his hand. "We must not remain any longer among people who have subjected your mother to such torture—such torture!"

Her dry voice was full of hatred, and she longed to strike the kneeling woman with her foot.

"Ugh! Heartless wretches! You would be glad to take even my only child from me!" she wrathfully whispered, and pulled Valia away by his hand. "Come! Don't be like your father, who abandoned me."

"Take care of him," Nastasia called after them.

The hired sleigh which stood waiting for them flew softly and lightly over the snow, and noiselessly carried Valia away from the quiet house with its wonderful plants and flowers, its mysterious fairy-tale world, immeasurable and deep as the sea, with its windows gently screened by the boughs of the tall trees of the garden. Soon the house was lost in the mass of other houses, as similar to each other as the letters in Valia's book, and vanished for ever from Valia.

It seemed to him as if they were swimming in a river, the banks of which were constituted of rows of lanterns as close to each other as beads on a string; but when they approached nearer, the beads were scattered, forming large, dark spaces and merging behind into just such a line of light. And then Valia thought that they were standing motionless on the very same spot; and everything began to be like a fairy tale—he himself and the tall woman who was pressing him to her with her bony hand, and everything around him.

The hand in which he carried his book was getting stiff with cold, but he would not ask his mother to take the book from him.

The small room into which Valia's mother had taken him was untidy and hot; in a corner near the large bed stood a little curtained bed such as Valia had not slept in for a long, long time.

"You are frozen! Well, wait, we shall soon have some tea! Well, now you are with your mamma. Are you glad?" his mother asked with the hard, unpleasant look of one who has been forced to smile beneath blows all her life long.

"No," Valia replied shyly, frightened at his own frankness.

"No? And I had bought some toys for you. Just look, there they are on the window."

Valia approached the window and examined the toys. They were wretched paper horses with straight, thick legs, Punch with a red cap on, with an idiotically grinning face and a large nose, and little tin soldiers with one foot raised in the air.

Valia had long ago given up playing with toys and did not like them, but from politeness he did not show it to his mother. " Yes, they are nice toys," he said.

She noticed the glance he threw at the window, and said with that unpleasant, ingratiating smile :

" I did not know what you liked, darling, and I bought them for you a long time ago."

Valia was silent, not knowing what to reply.

" You must know that I am all alone, Valia, all alone in the wide world ; I have no one whose advice I could ask ; I thought they would please you." Valia was silent.

Suddenly the muscles of the woman's face relaxed and the tears began to drop from her eyes, quickly, quickly, one after the other ; and she threw herself on the bed, which gave a pitiful squeak under the weight of her body, and with one hand pressed to her breast, the other to her temples, she looked vacantly through the wall with her pale, faded eyes, and whispered :

" He was not pleased !   Not pleased ! "

Valia promptly approached the bed, put his little hand, still red with the cold, on the large head of his mother, and spoke with the same serious staidness which distinguished this boy's speech :

" Do not cry, mamma.   I will love you very much.   I do not care to play with toys, but I will love you ever so much.   If you wish, I will read to you the story of the poor water-nymph."

LEONID N. ANDREYEV

SILENCE

I

On a moonlight night in May, when the nightingales were singing, Father Ignaty's wife entered his study. Her face wore an expression of intense suffering, and the little lamp in her hand trembled. Going up to her husband, and touching his shoulder, she burst into tears, saying :

" Father, let us go to Verotchka ! "

Without turning his head, Father Ignaty looked down at his wife from over his spectacles. He looked long and fixedly, until she motioned with her free hand and sank on to the low sofa.

" How pitiless you both are ! " she said slowly, with a stress on the word pitiless, while her good-natured face twitched with pain and determination, as though by her expression she wished to convey how cruel her husband and daughter were.

Father Ignaty smiled and got up. He shut his book, took off his spectacles, put them into their case, and grew thoughtful. His long black beard, with threads of silver in it, lay in a beautiful mass on his chest, and slowly rose and fell with his breathing.

" Very well, then ; let us go ! " he said.

Olga Stepanovna got up quickly and asked in a timid, wheedling voice :

" You won't scold her, Father, will you ? You know what she is. . . . "

Vera's room was upstairs, and the narrow winding staircase bent and groaned under Father Ignaty's heavy tread. Tall and heavy, he stooped down so as not to hit the ceiling, and frowned squeamishly when his wife's white blouse came in contact with his face. He knew that nothing would come of their talk to Vera.

" Why have you come ? " asked Vera, a bare arm uplifted to her eyes. The other arm lay on the white summer bedcover, and could hardly be distinguished from it, so white and transparent and cold it was.

" Verotchka ! " . . . the mother began, but burst into tears and could not continue.

" Vera ! " the father said, trying to soften his hard, dry voice. " Vera, tell us what is the matter with you."

Vera was silent.

" Vera, have not your mother and I deserved your confidence ? Do we not love you ? Have you any one nearer to you than us ? Tell us about your sorrow, and, believe an old, experienced man, you will feel better afterwards. It will be better for us too. Just look at your old mother, see how she suffers. . . ."

" Verotchka ! "

" And I, too . . ." the hard voice broke and trembled. " And I . . . do you think it is easy for me ? Do you think I do not see that you are consumed by some sorrow . . . and what that sorrow is I, your own father, do not know. Do you think that right ? "

Vera was silent. Father Ignaty stroked his beard gently, as though he feared that involuntarily his fingers would clutch it violently.

" Against my wish you went to St. Petersburg. I did not revile you as an undutiful daughter, did I ? Before your departure I gave you all the money you wanted. Have I not been a good father to you ? Why don't you speak ? This is what has resulted from your St. Petersburg ! "

Father Ignaty ceased. He pictured St. Petersburg to himself as some terrible, monstrous, crushing place, fraught with unknown dangers and full of strange, indifferent people. There his Vera, alone and weak, had been ruined. An intense hatred arose in Father Ignaty's heart towards the terrible town and towards his daughter who was so obstinately silent.

" St. Petersburg has nothing to do with it," Vera said morosely, and closed her eyes. " And there is nothing the matter with me. You had better both go to bed ; it is late."

" Verotchka ! " the mother moaned. " Little one, tell me everything ! "

" Oh, mother ! " Vera interrupted her impatiently.

Father Ignaty sat down and laughed.

" Well, so there is nothing whatever the matter ? " he asked sarcastically.

" Father," Vera said sharply, raising herself in bed, " you know that I love you and mother, but . . . It is nothing. I am merely lonely. It will wear off. You had better go to bed. I want to sleep too ; to-morrow, or some other time, we can talk about it."

Father Ignaty started up so suddenly that his chair fell against the wall, and took his wife's arm.

" Come ! "

" Verotchka ! "

" Come, Verotchka, I tell you ! " Father Ignaty shouted. " If she has forgotten God, then we . . . we do not count."

He led his wife almost forcibly from the room. As they were descending the stairs, Olga Stepanovna, slackening her pace, said in a spiteful whisper :

" Well, that is what you have made of her, priest ! She has copied this manner from you. You will have to answer for it. Poor unfortunate that I am. . . ."

And she burst into tears. She did not see the steps, but put down each foot as if beneath lay an abyss into which she wanted to fall. From that day Father Ignaty refused to speak to his daughter, but she did not seem to notice it. As before, she would lie in her own room or wander about, frequently rubbing her eyes with the palms of her hands, as though she were trying to regain her vision. And oppressed by these two silent people, the priest's wife, who was fond of laughter and fun, became timid and flurried, and did not know what to say or do. Sometimes Vera would go out for a walk. About a week after the evening of their conversation Vera went out one evening as usual. The parents did not see her again alive, for on that evening she threw herself under a train and was cut in two. Father Ignaty himself read the funeral service. His wife was not present at the church, as she had suffered a stroke on hearing the news of Vera's death. She lost the use of her hands, legs and tongue, and lay immovable in the semi-darkened room, while the sound of funeral bells came in from the belfry next door. She heard the people issue from the church and sing the hymn for the dead in front of her house ; she tried to lift a hand to make the sign of the cross, but the hand would not obey ; she wanted to say " Good-bye, Vera," but her tongue lay in her mouth, huge and heavy. Her expression was so calm that one looking at her would have thought her resting or asleep ; only her eyes were open.

Many people were present at the funeral, acquaintances and strangers. Every one there pitied Vera for having suffered such a horrible death ; and tried to detect in Father Ignaty signs of the great sorrow. They did not like him, for he was harsh and proud, hated sinners and did not forgive them, while at the same time he himself was envious and greedy, and lost no occasion of taking more than his due share from the parishioners. Every one wanted to see him suffering and crushed ; to realise that he was twice guilty of his daughter's death, because he had been a cruel father and a bad minister not to have protected his own flesh and blood from sin. All looked at him inquisitively, and he, feeling all eyes on his back, tried to straighten that broad back, while the thought uppermost in his mind was not of his daughter's death but of the effort he must make not to let himself drop.

"Cursed priest!" said Karsenov the joiner, with a shake of his head. Father Ignaty owed him five roubles for frames.

And thus, hard and straight, Father Ignaty walked to the grave-yard and thus he returned. It was only at the door of his wife's room that his back bent somewhat, but that may have been because most doors were not high enough for him. Coming in from the daylight he could not at first distinguish his wife's face, but when he did see it he was amazed at its calmness, and that there were no tears in the eyes. They bore no expression, either of anger or of grief—they were dumb and silent, just as obstinately so as the rest of that heavy helpless body that lay immovable on the feather bed.

"How do you feel?" Father Ignaty asked. But the lips were silent, and silent were the eyes. He laid his hand on his wife's fore-head; it was cold and moist, and Olga Stepanova made no sign that she felt the contact; and when he removed his hand there gazed at him steadily two large grey eyes that the enlarged pupils made almost black, and in them there was no sign of sorrow or anger.

"Well, I will go to my room," Father Ignaty said.

He grew cold, and a feeling of terror seized him. He went into the drawing-room, where everything was as clean and tidy as usual, the tall arm-chairs in their white covers looking like corpses in shrouds. By one of the windows hung a wire cage, but it was empty and the door was open.

"Nastasia!" he shouted, and his voice seemed to him so rough that he felt uncomfortable to be shouting so loudly in these quiet rooms so soon after his daughter's funeral. "Nastasia!" he called, lowering his voice, "where is the canary?"

The cook, who had cried so much that her nose was swollen and red as a beetroot, replied angrily:

"Can't you see it has flown away?"

"Why did you let it out?" He frowned threateningly.

Nastasia burst into tears, and wiping her eyes on her cotton kerchief, said through her sobs:

"Darling . . . young lady. . . . How could you do it?"

It seemed to Father Ignaty that the gay yellow canary, always singing, with head cocked, was in reality Vera's soul, and that had it not flown away, one could not have said that Vera was dead. He grew still angrier with the cook and shouted:

"Get out!" and, when Nastasia did not reach the door as soon as she might have done, added: "You fool!"

II

From the day of the funeral, silence reigned in the little house. It was not quietness, because quietness is the absence of sound; it was silence, for it seemed as though those who were silent would have spoken if they could. Thus thought Father Ignaty when he went into his wife's room and met her steadfast gaze, and he felt as though the whole atmosphere had turned to lead and weighed upon his back. Thus he thought as he looked through his daughter's music, which contained her voice in print, her books, and the large coloured portrait she had brought from St. Petersburg. He would look at the portrait methodically; first he would examine the cheeks, lit up in the portrait, and picture to himself the bruise that he had seen on dead Vera's cheek, and which he could not explain. Every time he puzzled about the cause of it he came to the conclusion that had it been done by the train the whole head would have been crushed, whereas actually it had been quite uninjured. Perhaps some one had kicked it or scratched it accidentally in lifting the corpse.

But to ponder long over the details of Vera's death was terrible, and he took to examining the eyes in the portrait. They were beautiful eyes, black in colour, with long lashes that cast such a deep shadow that the whites through it seemed bright by comparison, and looked as though surrounded by a frame of mourning. The clever, unknown, artist had given them a strange expression—as though between the eyes and what they gazed on there lay a thin transparent veil. They were a little like the black piano-case, on which was a thin imperceptible layer of summer dust that softened the sheen of the polished wood. No matter where he put the portrait, the eyes followed him, did not speak, and were silent; and this silence was so palpable that it seemed to him one could hear it, and gradually he began to believe that he could hear the silence.

Every morning after service Father Ignaty came into the drawing-room, took in at a glance the empty cage and all the other familiar things there, sat down in a chair, closed his eyes, and listened to the silence of the house. There was something strange about it. The silence of the cage was soft and tender, but in this silence one could feel sorrow and tears and distant, dead laughter. His wife's silence, softened by the walls, was steadfast, heavy as lead, and awful; so awful that on the hottest day he would feel cold. Eternal, cold as the grave and incomprehensible as death, was his daughter's silence. It seemed to him that this silence was a torture to itself and wanted to speak, but something strong and ruthless as a machine held it rigid and pulled it taut like a wire. Somewhere at the far end the wire began to vibrate, and emitted a soft, timid, and pitiful note. With joy and terror he caught this new-born sound, and resting his arms on the arms of the chair he stretched out his head and waited for the sound to come towards him, but it broke off and was silent.

"Nonsense!" Father Ignaty said angrily, rising, still tall and straight, from his chair. From the window he saw the sunlit square with its round even cobbles, and, opposite, the long, stone, windowless wall of the shed. At the corner stood a cabman, motionless as a graven image, and it seemed strange that he should stand there; for hours at a time there was not a single passer-by.

III

Out of the house, Father Ignaty had to talk a good deal: to the deacons and parishioners about Church matters; and to acquaintances with whom he played "preference." But when he returned home it seemed to him that he had been silent the whole day. This was because he had not been able to mention to any of the people to whom he had spoken the thing that lay uppermost in his mind: the cause of Vera's death. He did not realise that now he would never get to know this, and still thought it possible. Every night—they were all sleepless nights now—he pictured to himself the moment when, at midnight, he and his wife had stood at the foot of Vera's bed and had implored her: "Tell us!" And when his memory reached these two words, what had happened afterwards came to him not as it had really been. His closed eyes held in their depth the living Vera, not torn by grief as she had been on that night, but raising herself in bed with a smile and saying. . . . What was she saying? And those unuttered words of hers, that would have decided everything, seemed so near that if he strained his ears and held his breath he might hear them—yet at the same time they were so far away. He rose from the bed and, stretching out his hands, said:

"Vera!" The only answer was silence.

One evening he went into Olga Stepanova's room—where he had not been for about a week—and sat down at the head of her bed, and, avoiding her persistent, heavy gaze, said:

"Mother, I want to talk to you about Vera. Do you hear?"

The eyes were silent, and raising his voice he spoke austerely and severely as he did at the confessional.

"I know you think that I was the cause of Vera's death; but just consider, did I love her less than you did? You judge strangely.

It is true I was severe, but did that prevent her from doing just what she wanted ? I waived a father's dignity. I quietly bent my neck when she, not fearing my curses, went away . . . there. And you, did you not implore her with tears in your eyes, until I commanded you to dry them ? Was it my fault that she was born so cruel ? Did I not teach her about God and humility and love ? "

Father Ignaty looked for a moment into his wife's eyes and turned away. " What could I do with her if she did not want to tell us of her sorrow ? Command her ? I did command. Forgive her ? I forgave. Should I have gone down on my knees to her, and cried like an old woman ? How could I know what was in her mind ? Cruel, heartless daughter ? " He laughed silently.

" She loved us ! As a proof, that was the sort of death she chose. A cruel, shameless death ! She died in the dust . . . in the dirt . . . like a dog that had been spurned." His voice sounded soft and hoarse.

" I am ashamed to go out into the street. I am ashamed to leave the altar. I am ashamed before God. Cruel, worthless daughter ! I ought to curse you in your grave ! "

When he looked at his wife he found her unconscious, and she did not recover for several hours. When she opened her eyes it was impossible to tell whether she remembered what Father Ignaty had said to her or not. That same night—it was a July moonlit night, quiet, warm, and still—he crept up the stairs on tiptoe so that his wife and the nurse should not hear him, and went into Vera's room. The windows had not been opened since her death, and the air was hot and stuffy, with a faint smell of burnt iron from the hot roof. There was something dead and neglected about this room from which the inhabitant had been absent so long. The wooden walls, the furniture and other objects emitted a faint mustiness. The moonlight fell in a broad beam through the window, and was reflected from the white, spotless boards ; the half light lit up the corners of the room ; and the clean, white bed, with its small and large pillow, seemed transparent and ethereal. Father Ignaty opened the window and let in a draught of air that smelt of earth, the distant river, the flowering lime ; the cows were heard lowing. People, no doubt rowing on the river, were singing. Moving with noiseless tread, barefooted, looking like some ghost, he went up to the empty bed, knelt down, buried his face in the pillows and kissed the place where Vera's head would have lain. Thus he remained for some time. The singing grew louder and then died away, but he stayed there, his long black hair flowing over his shoulders and on to the bed. It was now dark in the room, the moon had moved round. He raised his head and whispered—putting into his voice the whole strength of his suppressed love and affection, and listening to his own words as though not he, but Vera, were talking :

" Vera, my daughter ! Do you know what that word daughter means ? Little one ! Flesh of my flesh and blood of my blood ! My darling ! Your old father . . . grey and weak. . . ." His shoulders heaved and his body shook convulsively. Giving way to his feelings, he murmured gently as though to a child :

" Your old father . . . forgives you . . . no, Vera, . . . implores you. He is crying . . . he has never cried before. Your sorrow, little one, . . . your sufferings are mine. More than mine ! "

He shook his head.

" More, Verotchka. What is death to an old man like me ? But you . . . if only you knew how weak and gentle and timid you are ! Do you remember when you pricked your finger and the blood came and you cried ? My little one, I know you love me. You love me very much. Every morning you kiss me. Tell me ! Tell me what tortures your poor soul, and I . . . with both these hands . . . I will smother your sorrow. These hands are still strong, Vera."

He shook back his hair. " Tell me ! " he said, looking up and stretching out his hands. " Tell me ! "

It was still in the room ; from the dim distance the prolonged whistle of a river steamer could be heard. Father Ignaty looked round with wide-open eyes as though before him stood the terrible ghost of that mangled body. He slowly rose to his feet and, with an uncertain movement, raised his hand, with its strained outspread fingers, to his head. Going towards the door he whispered brokenly :

" Tell me ! "

But his answer was silence.

IV

On the following day, after an early and solitary lunch, Father Ignaty went to the cemetery—for the first time since his daughter's death. Outside it was hot, deserted, and quiet, as though it were night turned day ; but, by force of habit, he straightened his back and glanced austerely from side to side, thinking that he was all he used to be. He did not notice that his legs were weak and that his long beard was quite white, as though a cruel frost had withered it. The way to the cemetery was through a long, narrow, rising street, and at the end shone the arch of the cemetery gate, that looked like a black, eternally gaping mouth with glistening teeth.

Vera's grave was at the back of the cemetery, where the gravel paths ended, and Father Ignaty wandered long among the narrow paths which ran in broken lines through the green mounds, forgotten and neglected by all. The old heavy gravestones, green with age, and the broken railings seemed to press viciously into the earth.

Vera's grave also was oppressed by a stone. It was covered with new yellow turf, but all around was green. A mountain ash and a maple mingled together near by, and a broad-spreading clump of hazel trees, with its leafy rustling branches, threw a deep shade over the grave. Sitting down near it, on a neighbouring grave, he glanced around and looked up at the clear cloudless sky where hung the sun, immovable, like a huge flat disc. He felt here that peculiar stillness that reigns only in cemeteries when there is no wind and the dying leaves make no sound ; and again there occurred to him the thought that this was not stillness but silence. It penetrated the brick walls of the cemetery, and settled over the town, and the end of it was there in the grey, steadfast, silent eyes. He was cold, but bracing himself he looked down on Vera's grave. Long he gazed on that short yellow grass—grass taken from the open fields over which played the wind, and not yet accustomed to this new soil. He could not imagine that there under the grass, only two yards away from him, lay Vera. And this nearness seemed unattainable to him and filled his soul with agitation and unrest. The thing he had been accustomed to think had disappeared for ever into the dark depths of eternity was here beside him . . . and it was difficult to realise that she was not and never would be. It seemed to him that if he but uttered the words that were on his lips, or made a single gesture, Vera would come out of her grave and stand before him, tall and beautiful as ever. And not only Vera would arise, but all the dead with her : the dead that were so terribly expressive in their triumphant, cold silence.

He took off his hat, passed his hand through his hair, and whispered : " Vera ! "

He felt apprehensive lest any stranger should overhear him, and standing on the grave he looked over the tops of the crosses. There was nobody in sight, and he repeated loudly : " Vera ! "

It was Father Ignaty's old voice, dry and commanding, and it was strange that a command uttered with such force should receive no response.

" Vera ! " Loud and insistent sounded the voice, and when he was silent it seemed to him that from somewhere down below there sounded a faint reply. Once more he looked round, shook back the hair from about his ears, and laid his head against the cruel, prickly turf.

" Vera, tell me ! "

With terror he felt that into his ear there flowed something like the coldness of the grave that benumbed his brain, and Vera spoke ; but she spoke with the same prolonged silence.   It became still more terrible and agitating, and when with difficulty—pale as a corpse—he lifted his head from the ground, it seemed to him that the air vibrated with a resounding silence, as if a w"'d storm had arisen on this awful sea.   The silence was suffocating him ; its icy waves rolled over his head and ruffled his hair ; it beat against his breast, moaning under the blows.   Trembling in every limb, he glanced round sharply and, rising slowly, made a great effort to straighten his back and to give a proud carriage to his shaking body ; and he succeeded in this.   Deliberately he shook the dust from his knees, put on his hat, made the sign of the cross three times over the grave, and with a firm step walked away ; but he did not recognise the familiar paths of the cemetery.   " I have lost myself," he thought, and smiled bitterly as he stopped at the crossways.   He remained still only for a second and, without considering, turned to the left, because to stand still and wait was intolerable.   The silence was pursuing him.   It rose from the green graves ; the gloomy grey crosses exhaled it ; it rose in thick suffocating streams from every corner of that earth filled with dead.   Father Ignaty quickened his pace.   Dizzily he wound his way about the same paths, jumping over graves, climbing over railings, and tearing flesh and clothes on the metal wreaths.   One thought only possessed him : to get away from the cemetery.   He wandered from side to side, and at last began to run softly, with his hair floating in the wind, and tall and strange in his flowing robe.   Any one meeting this wild figure, running, jumping, waving its arms, with a mad look on its face and the hoarse sound that came from its open mouth, would have been more frightened than if they had seen an actual ghost.   Finally, Father Ignaty got out into the little square at the end of which glimmered the small cemetery church.   An old man was dozing on a bench by the porch—from the look of him a pilgrim from a distant part—and near by two old beggars gesticulated, quarrelling and abusing each other.

When Father Ignaty got to the house it was already dark, and in Olga Stepanovna's room a lamp was burning.   Without taking off his torn and dusty hat and robe, he went up to his wife quickly, and fell down on his knees by the bed.

" Mother . . . Olga . . . . Have pity on me ! " he sobbed.   " I am going mad ! "   And he beat his head against the bed-rail tempestuously, agonising like a man who had never cried before. He raised his head, prepared to see a miracle, thinking that his wife would speak words of pity.

" My dear ! "   His huge body bent towards his wife and met the look of the grey eyes.   In them there was neither pity nor anger. Perhaps his wife had forgiven him, and pitied him, but in her eyes there was neither pity nor forgiveness.   They were dumb and silent.

．　　　．　　　．　　　．　　　．　　　．　　　．

And silent was the dark, empty house.

LEONID N. ANDREYEV

THE GRAND SLAM

THEY played vint[1] three times a week : on Tuesdays, Thursdays, and Saturdays. Sunday was a most suitable day for card play but had to be set apart for other duties, such as visits and the theatre, wherefore it was considered the dullest day in the week. However, in the country, in the summer, they played on Sundays as well.

They played as follows : the corpulent and hot-tempered Maslenikov played with Jacob Ivanovitch, and Evpraksia Vassileona partnered her brother, the morose Prokopi Vassilevitch. This arrangement was of long standing, six years or more, and was due to Evpraksia Vassileona. The reason was that to play against her brother gave no sort of interest, for if one lost, the other won, and although the stakes were insignificant, and Evpraksia and her brother were comfortably off, yet she never could understand the use of playing a game for the game's sake, and was always pleased when she won. Her winnings were always placed apart, and appeared far more important and precious to her than the large sums she disbursed on house-keeping or on the rent of their expensive flat.

The players always assembled in Prokopi Vassilevitch's flat, for it was large, and he lived there alone with his sister—there was also a large white cat, but he always slept in an arm-chair—and the necessary silence reigned in the rooms. Prokopi Vassilevitch was a widower : he lost his wife in the second year of their marriage, and for two months after lay sick in a hospital for mental affections. Evpraksia was unmarried, though she had once had a romance with a student. No one knew, and she, it appears, had forgotten, why she never married her student ; but each year when the appeal for needy students appeared she sent a hundred-rouble note " From an unknown Friend." In age she was the youngest of the party : forty-three years old.

---

[1] A kind of auction bridge in which the declarer only scores his contract even if he makes more tricks. After the original deal, players are allowed to exchange some cards (as in nap) with a view to improving the hands.

When the original arrangement of partners was made, Maslenikov, the eldest of the four, was especially displeased with it. He was annoyed at always having to play with Jacob Ivanovitch, that is, in other words, to lose all hope of ever making a grand slam in no trumps. In every way he and his partner were entirely unsuited. Jacob Ivanovitch was a dried-up little old man, dressed summer and winter in dark coat and trousers, and was silent and severe. He always appeared punctually at eight o'clock, not a moment before or after, and straightway took the pack in his dried-up fingers, on one of which was a large diamond ring. But what annoyed Maslenikov most in his partner was that he refused to make a higher contract than four tricks, even if his hand was certainly worth more.

Once it happened that Jacob Ivanovitch started with the two of a suit and led right through the suit up to the ace, taking all thirteen tricks. Maslenikov threw his cards angrily on the table, his partner picked them up quietly and wrote down his winnings for making a contract of four tricks.

" But why didn't you declare grand slam ? " shouted Nicholas Dimitrievitch (that was Maslenikov's name).

" I never bid more than four," returned his partner drily ; " you never can tell what will happen."

So Maslenikov could never convince him. He himself always took risks, and as he was a bad card holder, always lost, but he never lost heart, invariably hoping to win next time. At last he got reconciled to his partner and they played happily enough together. Nicholas Dimitrievitch took risks, and his partner quietly wrote down his losses and bid up to four tricks.

In this way they played, summer and winter, spring and autumn. Outside the doddering old world pursued its varied career, now red with blood, now drenched with tears, leaving in its track the groans of the sick, naked, and wronged. Some faint suggestion of all this was brought by Nicholas Dimitrievitch. Sometimes he was late and came in when the others were already seated at table, the pink cards laid fanwise on the green cloth.

Nicholas Dimitrievitch, red cheeked, and carrying an atmosphere of fresh air with him, hurriedly occupied his place opposite Jacob Ivanovitch, excused himself, and said :

" What a crowd there is on the Boulevard. Just a constant stream. . . ." Evpraksia Vassileona considered it her duty as hostess not to notice the idiosyncrasies of her guests. Thus she alone answered, while Jacob Ivanovitch shuffled the pack in grim silence, and her brother saw about tea.

" Yes, probably,—the weather's lovely. But hadn't we better start ? " And they began. The lofty room, destroying all sound by its soft upholstery and door-hangings, became silent as the tomb.

The maid moved silently about on the soft carpet, carrying glasses full of strong tea, and nothing was heard but the *frou-frou* of her starched apron, the scrape of the scoring chalk, and Nicholas Dimitrievitch's sigh as he paid a large fine. Very weak tea was poured out for him and placed on a special table, as he liked to drink out of a saucer, with long sips.

In the winter he would inform them that there had been ten degrees of frost in the morning and that now there were twenty, and in summer would say :

" A large party has just gone off into the forest with hampers." Evpraksia Vassileona would look politely at the sky—in the summer they played on the terrace—and though the sky was clear, and the tops of the fir trees glistened in the sun, would remark : " I hope it won't rain." And Jacob Ivanovitch solemnly shuffled the cards, and dropping the two of hearts, reflected that Nicholas Dimitrievitch was flighty and incorrigible. At one time, especially, Maslenikov used to upset his partner. Every time he came he would make one or two remarks about Dreyfus. With a lugubrious expression he would inform them :

" Dreyfus's case is going badly." Or, on the other hand, he would tell them smiling that the sentence was unjust and would doubtless be changed. Then he would bring out the paper and start reading certain passages about Dreyfus.

" Read it already," Jacob Ivanovitch would remark drily, but his partner, paying no attention, would read out what he thought interesting and important. Once he roused the others to argument and almost to strife, as Evpraksia Vassileona refused to acknowledge the legality of the proceedings and demanded his immediate release, while Jacob Ivanovitch and her brother insisted that certain formalities must be observed first. Jacob Ivanovitch was the first to remember himself, and, pointing at the table, said : " Isn't it time ? "

So they started to play, and thereafter, however much Nicholas Dimitrievitch talked of Dreyfus, he was answered by complete silence.

So they played, summer, winter, spring, autumn. There were incidents, but chiefly of an amusing character. Sometimes Prokopi Vassilevitch would forget altogether what his partner had said, and once having contracted for five tricks failed to make one. Then Nicholas Dimitrievitch laughed loudly and magnified his loss, while Jacob Ivanovitch remarked drily : " If you'd only gone four you'd have been nearer getting it."

Intense excitement was always displayed when Evpraksia Vassileona contracted for slam. She grew red, trembled, not knowing which card to play, and looked piteously at her taciturn brother,

while her two opponents, with knightly courtesy for her womanhood
and helplessness, encouraged her with condescending smiles and
waited patiently.   Generally speaking, however, they took the game
very seriously.   To them the cards had long ceased to be mere
inanimate objects.   Each hand, and every card in that hand, had its
own particular individuality and lived its own life.   Hands were
liked and disliked, lucky and unlucky.   The cards always combined
differently, and these combinations were subject to no analysis or
laws, but at the same time strictly fair ; and in that fairness existed
the individuality of the cards as opposed to the individuality of the
players.   The players used them for their own ends, and the cards
did their share, as if animated by their own wishes, tastes,
sympathies and caprices.   Hearts usually went to Jacob Ivanovitch,
and Evpraksia Vassileona's hand was usually full of spades, though
she didn't like them at all.   Somtimes the cards were capricious and
Jacob Ivanovitch couldn't get away from spades, while Evpraksia
Vassileona rejoiced in hearts, made high contracts and lost.
Nicholas Dimitrievitch always held bad hands, and was ready to
exchange any of his cards, which, like visitors in a hotel, were quite
indifferent as to where they made a short stay.   At times, for
several evenings in succession, he could hold nothing but twos and
threes, for which reason he was firmly convinced he could never
make a grand slam, as the cards knew of his wish and thwarted him
on purpose ; so he pretended it was a matter of complete indifference
to him and tried to cut short the preliminary exchanges of cards,
usually drawing sixes and sevens with a solitary picture card to
tantalise him.

Evpraksia Vassileona concealed her feelings best, and Jacob
Ivanovitch had long ago learnt to assume a philosophical indifference
whatever his hand was, having a sovereign remedy in never going
more than four.   Nicholas Dimitrievitch alone had never learnt to
conceal his annoyance at the capriciousness of the cards.   As he
fell asleep he would dream of winning a grand slam in no trumps :
how on picking up his hand he found first ace, then king, then
another ace.   But when he sat down to play again his hand was full
of small cards, in all of which he felt the sinister designs of fate.   By
degrees, sleeping and waking, he dreamed of making grand slam,
till it became the strongest wish of his life.

Other incidents happened, not immediately connected with cards.
Evpraksia Vassileona's white cat died, and by decision of his owner
was buried in the garden underneath the lime trees.   Then Nicholas
Dimitrievitch disappeared for two whole weeks, and his partners did
not know what to do, as three-handed vint was contrary to their habit
and turned out to be boring.   The cards themselves proved that
by their unaccustomed groupings.   When Nicholas Dimitrievitch

appeared again his red face, which had shown up so against his scanty white locks, had grown pale, and he seemed to have shrunk. He informed them that his son had been arrested for some offence and sent off to St. Petersburg. All were astonished, for they never knew he had a son : perhaps he had mentioned it some time or other, but they had forgotten all about it. Soon afterwards he again failed to appear, and on a Saturday, which day they were accustomed to play longer than usual,—and all learnt with astonishment that he had suffered from angina for a long time and had had a severe attack that day. But afterwards all went on as before, and the game became even more serious and interesting as Nicholas Dimitrievitch regaled them less with outside topics.

On the Thursday, however, there was a startling change. As soon as the game began Nicholas Dimitrievitch made a contract of five, and won not only his contract but a small slam, as Jacob Ivanovitch had an ace he'd kept quiet about. For some time after he held his usual cards, but then started a series of good cards in suits, as if the cards wished to see how pleased he would be. He bid to play for the game, and all were astonished, even the phlegmatic Jacob Ivanovitch. The excitement of Nicholas Dimitrievitch, whose fat fingers were trembling, infected the other players.

"What's up with you to-day ?" said the gloomy Prokopi Vassilevitch, who feared good luck as the precursor of misfortune. Evpraksia Vassileona was delighted to think that Nicholas Dimitrievitch at length held good cards, and on hearing her brother spit on the floor three times to avert misfortune, cried : "Fi, fi ! there's nothing exceptional in it, the cards must give every one a turn."

For a moment during the deal fortune seemed to have deserted Nicholas Dimitrievitch, and a few twos turned up, but then followed aces, kings, and queens with great rapidity. He hardly had time to pick up the cards and begin the game, misdealing twice in his agitation, so that they had to have a fresh deal. All his bids were successful, though Jacob Ivanovitch kept obstinate silence about his aces : astonishment had given place to doubt in his partner's change of fortune, and he remained constant to his role,— not to contract more than four. He no longer thought of his leads, but boldly bid grand slam, certain that the exchanges would give him the cards he wanted.

After Prokopi Vassilevitch had dealt, Maslenikov picked up his cards. His heart almost stopped beating and a mist rose before his eyes—he held twelve certain tricks in his hand : the clubs and hearts from ace to ten, the ace and king of diamonds. If only he could pick up the ace of spades in the exchange he had the grand slam in no trumps.

" Two no trumps," he began, controlling his voice with difficulty.

" Three spades," said Evpraksia Vassileona, who was almost as excited, having nearly all the spades from the king downwards.

" Four hearts," retorted Jacob Ivanovitch drily. Nicholas Dimitrievitch promptly declared small slam, but Evpraksia Vassileona, carried away by excitement, bid grand slam in spades, though she saw she could not make it. Nicholas Dimitrievitch reflected for a moment, and affecting an air of triumph to conceal his agitation, declared " Grand slam no trumps."

Nicholas Dimitrievitch declaring grand slam no trumps! All were astonished, and the hostess's brother exclaimed :

" Oho ! "

Nicholas Dimitrievitch stretched out his hand to draw a card, but swayed and knocked over a candle. Evpraksia Vassileona picked it up, and Nicholas Dimitrievitch sat motionless one second, placed his cards on the table, and fell slowly to the left. Falling, he knocked over the table on which the tea was standing and lay across it on the floor.

When the doctor arrived he found that Nicholas Dimitrievitch had died from heart failure, and, by way of comforting the living, added a few words on the painlessness of his death. They placed the dead man on a sofa in the card-room, and covered by a sheet he looked large and fearful. One leg was not covered by the sheet and looked as if it belonged to another man : a large piece of paper stuck to the sole of the black boot. The card-table had not been cleared and the cards lay face down on it, those of Nicholas Dimitrievitch in a neat pile as he had laid them down.

Jacob Ivanovitch walked about the room with small uncertain steps, trying not to look at the corpse or go off the carpet on to the polished parquet, where his heels made a nerve-racking noise. After passing the table several times he stopped and picked up Nicholas Dimitrievitch's cards, looked at them, and put them down in a neat pile as before. Then he looked at the card Nicholas Dimitrievitch would have drawn : it was the ace of spades, which would have given him the grand slam. Walking up and down a few times more, Jacob Ivanovitch went into the next room, sat down and wept because the dead man's fate appeared to him so pitiable. Shutting his eyes, he tried to picture Nicholas Dimitrievitch's face as it was in life when he won and was happy. Especially sorry was he when he remembered the dead man's longing to win grand slam in no trumps. The events of the evening passed in review before him, beginning with the five diamonds which the deceased had won and ending with this series of good cards, so exceptional as to be ominous. And here Nicholas Dimitrievitch lay dead when he might have made grand slam.

But what appeared to him most pitiable was that Nicholas Dimitrievitch would never know that the ace of spades was waiting to be drawn and that he held grand slam in his hand. Never! It seemed to him he had never before realised what death was, but now he saw how irrational, terrible, and unavoidable it was. Would never know! Even if Jacob Ivanovitch was to shout in his ear, weep, and show him the cards he would never know because he existed no more on the earth. Just one moment more of life and he would have seen the ace of spades, but he was dead without knowing it.

" Ne—ver," said Jacob Ivanovitch, pronouncing the word slowly, syllable by syllable, to convince himself of its reality and meaning. The word existed and had meaning, and was so horrible and bitter that Jacob Ivanovitch again fell back in his chair and wept. He played the hand for Nicholas Dimitrievitch, picking up the tricks one by one till he had all thirteen, and thought how large the score would have been and that the dead would never know it. It was the first and last time that Jacob Ivanovitch went more than his contract of four, and won the grand slam in the name of friendship.

" You here, Jacob Ivanovitch ? " said Evpraksia Vassileona as she entered the room, and sitting at the table, burst into tears— " how horrible, how horrible."

They looked at each other and wept in silence, feeling that on the sofa in the next room lay the deceased, cold, heavy, and dumb.

" Have you sent the news ? " asked Jacob Ivanovitch.

" Yes, my brother went with the maid, but I don't know how they will find the flat—we don't know the address."

" But doesn't he live in the same flat as last year ? " asked Jacob Ivanovitch in consternation.

" No, he moved. The maid says he used to hire an isvoshchip (small carriage) on the Boulevard."

" You'll find the address through the police," said Jacob Ivanovitch soothingly. " He has a wife, hasn't he ? "

Evpraksia Vassileona looked pensively at Jacob Ivanovitch without answering. He thought the same idea was in her mind as in his. He sniffed once more, put his handkerchief in his pocket, and raising his eyebrows interrogatively over his swollen eyes, asked : " And where shall we find a fourth now ? "

But Evpraksia Vassileona did not hear him. Her practical mind was at work, and after a moment's silence she asked, " And do you live in the same place, Jacob Ivanovitch ? "

LEONID N. ANDREYEV

LAUGHTER

I

At half-past six I felt sure that she would come, and I was anxiously cheerful. My overcoat, secured by the upper button only, flapped in the cold wind, but I did not feel the cold. I carried my head proudly erect with my student's cap pushed right back. My eyes glanced with a sort of patronage and bravado upon the men I met, while at the women I looked appealingly and endearingly in spite of the fact that I had loved her only four days. I was so young and my heart was so rich that I could not remain altogether indifferent to other women. And I walked rapidly, boldly, and lightly.

At a quarter to seven my overcoat was fastened by two buttons, and I looked at the women only—no longer endearingly, but rather with aversion. I wanted to see but one woman, the rest might go to the deuce—they were only in the way. Their resemblance to her seemed to lessen my confidence in myself and touched me to the wavering point.

At five minutes to seven I began to feel warm.

At two minutes to seven I was growing cold.

At the stroke of seven I felt convinced that she would not come.

At half-past eight I was the picture of despair. My overcoat was all buttoned, the collar was up, and my cap pulled down over my nose, now blue with cold. My hair, moustache, and eyelashes were white with frost, and my teeth were chattering. From my shuffling gait and bent back I might be taken for a rather strong old man going back to the poorhouse from a visit to his friends.

It was she who had made this change! Oh, the devil! No, I must not say that. Perhaps she was not allowed to come ; perhaps she was sick, or perhaps she was dead. Dead! And I swearing at her !

II

" Eugenia too will be there to-night," said a fellow-student to me. He could have had no malice, since he could not have known that I had been waiting for Eugenia in the cold from seven until half-past eight.

" Is that so ? " I replied. But to myself I burst out : " Oh, the devil ! "

She would be there, at the evening party given by the Polozovs. I had never visited the Polozovs ; but I then and there made up my mind to be at their house that night.

" Gentlemen ! " I shouted gleefully, " this is Christmas Eve ! Everybody is merry to-night—let us be merry, too."

" But how ? " asked a fellow-student sadly.

" But where ? " queried another.

" Let's dress up and go to all the parties given in town to-night," I suggested.

Joyous cries of assent immediately arose. They shouted and jumped and sang, and even thanked me for the idea. We collected all the ready money we had about us, and within half an hour ten of us students of the town were gathered together—regular dancing merry imps—making for the costumier's, whose shop we finally filled with laughter and the chill night air.

I wished for something dark, beautiful, with a shade of fine melancholy in it, and I asked the wig-maker for the costume of a Spanish nobleman.

The costume I received must have belonged to a very tall noble-man indeed, for I was completely lost in it, and I felt as if all alone in a vast empty parlour. I got out of it as quickly as I could and asked for another.

" Would you not like a clown's, parti-coloured, with bells ? "

" A clown's ! " I exclaimed contemptuously.

" Well, a bandit's, then, with a hat and a dagger."

A dagger ! That suited my present state of mind. To my regret, however, the bandit whose clothes they gave me could scarcely have been of age. In all probability he must have been a spoilt child about eight years old. His hat hardly covered my head, and I had to be peeled out of his velvet trousers as from tights. The costume of a page was worthless—it was all stained, and a friar's was full of holes.

" What are you fussing about ? Hurry up ! It's getting late ! " cried the other fellows, who were already dressed. There was only one costume left—that of a Chinese nobleman.

" Give me the Chinaman ! " I cried, with a wave of my hand,

and they gave me the costume.   I won't dwell on the idiotic coloured
slippers, which were so small that only half my feet got into them,
nor need I speak of the piece of pink silk which covered my head
like a wig and fastened to my ears by strings, making them stand
out like a bat's.

Then came the mask.   Oh, that mask !

It had a nose, eyes, and a mouth, all in their proper places—but
there was nothing human about it.   It was a sort of physiognomy
in the abstract.   A human being could never look so calm as this
looked, even in the grave.   It expressed neither sadness nor merriment nor surprise—actually it expressed nothing.   It looked at
you straight and calmly, and as you looked at it irrepressible
laughter took hold of you.   When I put it on my comrades rolled
on the couches for laughter, they fell on the chairs waving their
hands.   "That'll be the most original mask," they shouted.   I
was almost crying, but when I looked into the mirror I was seized
with laughter myself.   Yes, it would indeed be the most original
mask.

" We must promise not to remove our masks under any circumstances," said one as we stepped out.   " Upon our word of honour ! "

" Upon our word of honour !   Upon our word of honour ! " we
cried in chorus.

III

It was certainly a unique mask.   Crowds followed me, turned
me on all sides, jostled me, pinched me—and when, exhausted, I
turned round angrily I was greeted with irrepressible laughter.
All the way I was surrounded and oppressed by a roaring cloud of
laughter ;   it moved with me, and I could not tear myself out of
this ring of mad cachinnation.   At times it caught me.   I shouted,
sang, and skipped, while the whole world whirled before my eyes
as though I were drunk.   And yet, how far off it all was from me !
How lonely I was beneath that mask of mine !

At last they let me alone.   We met at Polozov's.   I looked
at her ; emotions of anger and fear, resentment and tenderness
filled me.

" It is I," I whispered.

Her heavy eyelashes were raised slowly, she looked at me in
amazement, a whole sheaf of black rays burst upon me—and then,
suddenly, she burst into laughter, ringing, merry, bright like the
sun in spring.

" It is I !   It is I ! " I repeated, and I smiled.   " Why did you
not come this evening ? "

But she was laughing—laughing uncontrollably.

"I am so tired. My heart is filled with pain." I implored her to answer me.

But she kept on laughing. The black flash of her eyes grew dim, and her smile grew clearer and clearer. It was the sun—but a burning, merciless, harsh sun.

"What's the matter with you?" I said.

"Is it you?" she said, restraining herself. "How funny you look!" My shoulders were lowered and my head bent down. There was deep despair in my pose. She had turned to look at the young, joyous couples fleeting past us, the dying dawn of a smile on her face.

"It is a shame to laugh," I said. "Do you know that beneath my mask is a live, suffering face? It was but for the sake of seeing you that I put it on. You have given me hope for your love, and now you take it away so soon, so cruelly! Why did you not come?"

She turned to me quickly as if with a reply upon her sweet, smiling lips, but the sight of me set her off again into a fit of that cruel laughter. Hardly breathing, almost crying, she covered her face with her perfumed lace handkerchief. With difficulty she uttered her answer:

"Just look at yourself. Turn round to the mirror and look. Oh, what a face!"

I knit my brows and gritted my teeth together in pain. I felt that my face had frozen, and a deathly pallor seemed to creep over it. I glanced into the mirror—an idiotically calm, a stolidly indifferent, inhuman, immobile physiognomy stared at me. And I —I burst into laughter. And before the laughter had quite died away, but with a quiver of rising anger at the same time, I said, almost shrieking with the madness of despair:

"Why are you laughing?"

She became silent. I began to speak to her in a whisper of my love. I had never before pleaded so well, because I had never loved so deeply. I spoke of the torture of waiting, of the poisonous tears of mad jealously and of grief, of my soul which was all love. I saw how her eyelashes, lowering, had cast a heavy shadow on her cheeks, now grown pale. I saw how the fire from within her had cast a red reflection through this dull whiteness, and how her whole flexible body inclined involuntarily toward me. She was dressed as Queen of Night, and, all enigmatic, in black lace, as though clothed in darkness, glittering through the brilliancy of the stars, she was beautiful, like a forgotten dream of childhood. Still I spoke, and tears began to well into my eyes and my heart to beat with joy. And I noticed at last—I noticed that a gentle, pitiful smile parted her lips, while her eyelashes were lifted with a quiver. Slowly, timidly, as if with infinite faith, she turned her little face towards me, and—I had never before heard such laughter as came from her.

" No, no, I can't ! " she uttered, almost moaning, again bursting into a ringing cascade.

Oh, if only I could have a human face for a minute ! I bit my lips, the tears were rolling down my burning cheeks, and this idiotic physiognomy of mine, in which everything—the nose, the eyes, and the lips,—so placid and calm, looked with unshaken indifference— it was terrible in its absurdity. I limped from her in my coloured slippers and heard her ringing laughter following me. It sounded as if a silver stream of water were falling from an immense height and dashing itself against a rock.

Scattered over the sleepy street, waking the silence of the night with our strong, excited voices, we were returning home. One of my comrades said to me : " You have made an enormous success. I have never in my life seen people laugh so. Hold on ! What are you doing ? Why are you tearing the mask ? Say boys, he has gone mad ! Look, he is tearing his costume ! . . . He is crying ! "

LEONID N. ANDREYEV

THE "MARSEILLAISE"

HE was a nonentity : the spirit of a hare and the shameless patience of an ox. When fate, jestingly and maliciously, threw him into our black ranks we laughed like madmen : some mistakes are so laughable, so absurd. And he—he of course wept. I never in my life met another man with such a supply of tears, or which flowed so readily—from his eyes, his nose, his mouth. He was just like a sponge, dipped in water and squeezed in your hand. I have seen men weep even in our ranks, but their tears were—fire, from which ran savage beasts. These manly tears aged the face but gave youth to the eyes : like lava, stirred up from the boiling heart of the earth, they burnt ineradicable traces and buried whole towns of insignificant wishes and petty cares in their career. But the only results of this man's tears were a red nose and wet handkerchief. Probably he dried them afterwards on the line, otherwise whence could he have procured a sufficiency of handkerchiefs ?

During all his days of banishment he dogged the authorities, all authorities, those who existed and those whom his imagination created, bowed to them, wept, swore he was innocent, begged them to pity his youth, promised never more to open his mouth except for petitions or singing in praise ; and they, like us, laughed at him, called him " the unhappy little swine," and shouted at him : " Ah, you little swine ! "

He ran obediently to every call : every time he expected to hear tidings of his speedy return to his native land, and they were only jesting. They knew, as we did, that he was innocent, but they thought by torturing him to frighten other little swine—as if they were not already sufficiently cowardly !

He even came to us, driven by animal fear of loneliness ; but our faces were hard and flintlike, and secretly he sought the key. Quaking he called us dear comrades and friends, and we, nodding our heads, said : " Take care ! They are listening to you."

And he would get up and look furtively through the door, that poor little swine. Well, could we keep serious then ? And we

248

laughed with voices long unused to laughter, but he took heart again, and sitting closer to us told us through his tears of his beloved books at home, of his mamma and brothers, of whom he knew nothing, whether they were alive or dead through grief and fear.

Eventually we would send him away.

When famine started, terror seized him, inexpressibly comic terror. You see the poor swine was very fond of eating, and was also very frightened of his dear comrades and the authorities : he wandered distractedly amongst us and frequently wiped his forehead with his handkerchief—either tears or perspiration, and asked me irresolutely :

" You are going to starve long ? "

" A long time," I answered sternly.

" And you won't eat anything in secret ? "

" Perhaps our mammas will send us cakes," I agreed seriously. He looked doubtfully at me, shook his head, and, sighing, went away. The next day, green with terror like a parrot, he announced :

" Dear comrades ! I also will starve with you."

And there was a general answer :

" Starve alone."

And he starved ! We did not believe it, we thought he ate something in secret, as the warders also thought. And when near the end he fell ill with hunger typhus we merely shrugged our shoulders :

" Poor little swine ! "

But one of us, the one who never laughed, said gloriously :

" He's our comrade. Let's go to him."

He was delirious, and his disconnected raving was pitiable as his life. He talked of his beloved books, of his mamma and brothers ; he asked for cakes, swore he was innocent and begged for pardon. He called for his native country, called for dear France—oh, a curse on the feeble heart of man ! He tore his soul with that cry :

" Dear France ! "

We were all in the hut when he died. Consciousness returned to him before death, and he lay there quietly, so small and feeble, and we, his comrades, stood round him. And all of us heard how he said :

" When I die, sing the *Marseillaise* over me."

" What are you saying ? " we shouted, trembling partly with joy, partly with boiling anger. And he repeated :

" When I die, sing the *Marseillaise* over me."

And for the first time it happened that he was dry-eyed, and we—we wept down to the very last man, and our tears burnt like the fire from which run savage beasts.

He died, and we sang the *Marseillaise* over him. Strong, young voices sang the great song of freedom, and the mighty ocean seconded us, carrying it on on its crested waves to dear France, telling of present horror and crushed hope. And his memory ever remained famous to us,—that nonentity, with the body of a hare and the great soul of a man. On your knees before the hero, comrades and friends !

We sang. Rifles look down at us, their triggers glinting evilly and their sharp bayonets pointing at our hearts, and ever louder, ever happier rose the mighty song ; the black coffin was gently lowered by tender hands.

We sang the *Marseillaise*.

(1903.)

MICHAIL P. ARTSIBASHEV
1878-1926

FROM A BASEMENT

I

ANTON the shoemaker stood bent, his long arms, gnarled and knotted like roots, hanging down by his side, while his customer, a young merchant's clerk, also stood in the middle of the basement— among scraps of leather, blocks and old boots, shaking his fist and screaming in exasperation at Anton :

" The devil only knows what they are ! The left boot pinches and the right creases ! Do you call these boots ? The devil knows what they are, they are not boots ! "

He thrust the boots, soles upward, almost into Anton's face, and in his unnaturally strained voice could clearly be distinguished a desire to bully and command.

" Wait until you come to me for the money ! . . . You . . . " the customer shouted, and irresolutely, but with spiteful pleasure, added : " beast ! "

And from pleasure and apprehension the blood rushed to his face, so that his thick, short neck could not be distinguished from his red tie.

Anton, without a word, passed his awl from his right hand to his left and sighed deeply.

It was quite dark in the basement, and the air, thick and heavy, hung like a blue curtain. Beneath the ceiling and in the corners, mingling with the smell of leather, oil and wax, was a dense vapour. Only Anton's figure, a black, ragged silhouette, stood out against the faint light of the square window.

" Now I've told you what I think of you ! " the customer shouted, and, panting, went out of the basement, bending his head so as not to dent the crown of his new bowler hat.

Anton accompanied him to the door and held it open while the customer went up the slippery winding stairs. Then he sighed still more deeply and went in again.

Though it was still light outside, the basement was clothed in a dark blue half-light, so that all that could be seen was an empty pot containing a dry and withered onion stalk planted by some former tenant.   Anton often looked at the poor sorry plant that was dying a slow death for want of sun and air, but somehow he did not like to throw it away.

He trimmed the little lamp with some thin matches, sighing deeply meanwhile.

He was not sighing because he had just been abused and had had the boots thrust in his face.   He was so accustomed to such incidents that he scarcely remembered it.   All his customers abused him in one way or another, threw their boots at him, struck him sometimes, and, what was more frequent, did not pay his money.   They were all such little people, so dependent, so crushed and miserable, that they felt a vital necessity to shout at some one else in their turn, to bully and feel themselves above some one else.   And Anton would have done exactly the same had any one depended on him as he depended on all.   For this reason Anton unconsciously felt that it could not be otherwise, and that all must quarrel, swagger and bully, so that the petty animal spite in their cowardly, withered little souls should not suffocate them.   But Anton never felt that he was to blame—he did what he could—as he could.   He sewed boots no better and no worse than any one else, not so much by measurement as by rule of thumb. He did not even wonder whether he could have become a master of his trade because it was a dirty, hungry, monotonous, dull trade.

He sighed because living always in the damp, low basement amidst the smell of leather and wax, in hunger and without love, light, or joy, had crushed his whole being, and whenever he tried to straighten his back that ached from his bent position, it seemed to him that he raised some terrible, irresistible weight that would not let him breathe." O—oh," he would say at such times.

For a whole hour after his angry customer went he sat bent, mending the heels of the neighbouring dvornik's heavy boots by the light of the smoky lamp, which flickered gently at the blows of his hammer.   Then he got up, left his tools wherever they happened to fall, turned down the lamp, and went out to sit on the stairs, taking his concertina with him.

By now it was already dark even out of doors—blue and transparent above, black and dark below.   The walls of the house, which stood like a well in which Anton lived, seemed pale and blue, as though dead ; above them, somewhere higher up, was seen the darkening sky in which two or three stars twinkled faintly.

" Thus it is," Anton thought, scarcely knowing why he did so, and shaking his head, he pulled out his concertina, bending his right ear towards it.

It gave out a faint squeaky sound, but to Anton it seemed so loud that he looked round apprehensively. Then he took the concertina and played on the lower notes. He always began like that because he was not allowed to play out of doors, and with these cautious sounds he tried to ascertain whether the elder dvornik was at home.

And, as usual, at the open window of the dvornik's quarters a form appeared, seen dimly in the darkness, and a furious voice called out : "Again ! . . . You ! "

Anton trembled, quickly put down the concertina, and picked up his cap guiltily. But the dvornik did not see him, and grumbling a little longer as a big dog growls, he disappeared from the window.

Anton let his hands hang between his legs and, picking at the holes in his boots, began to think. He wanted to play, and was thinking how nice it would be to go out of the town for the whole day one Sunday, sit down on a green bank by the railway line, and play to his heart's content, play so that his ears rang with the sound. He enjoyed the thought, though he knew perfectly well that he would never go out of town, because he would never have enough spare time. On holidays he spent his mornings buying leather, his afternoons in delivering his work to the customers, and in the evenings he was always drunk.

He sat on the stairs until it was quite dark and above, between the walls, the stars shone clearly and freely, while the walls were lit up from below with a yellow light from the windows. When he raised his head everything above seemed bright and gay and when he looked down it seemed darker and gloomier than ever. Anton gazed at the sky and the stars with a strange despairing yet joyful feeling, but the habit of sitting bent drew him down to fix his eyes on the blue darkness of the yard. From boredom and a burning desire for drink he tried to remember his past life, but it appeared dim and uninteresting. How he had got to this town he could hardly remember. The only things he remembered clearly of his childhood were blows from the shoemaker's lasts, running for vodka, the streets, and the police. Later, when he had grown up, he had run away from his master and had begun to live in corners and work for himself, pasting in his window the cutting of a lady's boot from an old magazine. Thus he had lived, year in, year out, drinking heavily, spending his nights in dens and police stations and being terribly beaten by the police. Then he had fallen in love with a neighbouring seamstress, though she laughed at him and called him a fool, saying that his shoemaker's last must have damaged his wits. Nevertheless, he gave up drinking, made himself a new shirt, and went to the baths. He was most persistent in his attentions to the seamstress without being able to express in words his feelings that were as sweet as music. One day he made a new pair of boots and presented them to her.   Then she began to call him Anton Vasilevitch and invited him to take tea with her.   When she got to know how much he earned she began to sigh, weep, and worry over something, and told the dvornik's wife that she had no objection to Anton, and, on the contrary, was well disposed towards him.   Anton's soul was filled with joy.   He went to church, bought her nuts and chocolates, put on a new shirt, and was just about to go to the seamstress feeling that his grey life had been lit up with a soft caressing light, when the dvornik and a policeman came and took him to the police station. There he was questioned about a certain bundle and one Vanka Svistunov, and whether he had drunk beer on a certain day at eight o'clock in the evening at the Ivanov public-house on the St. Petersburg side and for which he had paid fifty kopeks.   Then there were questions about his appearance.

Anton had seen no sort of bundle, knew no Vanka Svistunov, but had been to the public-house.   As for the fifty kopeks, he looked like a donkey at the water, not understanding what it was all about.

In the end he found himself in prison, and, though innocent, remained there for six months, torn by a desire for freedom, light, and his seamstress, and oppressed by a sense of cruel injustice.   When he came out, the light in his soul was so crushed by the prison dirt that he did not go to his seamstress, and only heard indirectly that she had " gone wrong " with a " nice gentleman."

Dull grief and despair took possession of his soul, the more difficult to bear because he did not understand it and did not know where to go—where it was better and where worse.   Life became even more dull and monotonous than before, varied only by dull, mechanical drunkenness in which there was no pleasure and no gaiety.

He recalled all this as indifferently as though it had happened not to him but to some one else ; nevertheless he felt depressed and seemed to regret something—he wanted to get drunk on vodka.

A window was opened on the second floor and a shaft of yellow light fell on the dark yard.   The elegant muslin curtains were seen clearly, there was a sound of animated voices, then some one played quickly and loudly, laughed gaily, and banged the lid of the piano.

Anton listened intently to these strange, clear sounds until the window was shut and all grew quiet, then he mechanically touched his concertina, turning it over in his hand, and trying not to miss a single sound.   It seemed to him that he would feel better if he could play.   It was late ; Anton sighed as usual and went to bed.   He lay in bed with eyes open, thinking that he must pay for the leather, and how, the week before, the leather-seller, without any reason, had struck him on the mouth.   His lips had swollen and the blood had appeared on his blue gums.

The heavy air penetrated through him, and grew thicker and colder. He dreamt that he was drunk and that a cab had run over him, the heavy wheels crushing him to the hard bridge.

II

The following day was Sunday and towards the evening Anton was already sitting in the public-house.

The mechanical organ was playing some tune, loud but not gay. The room was full of smoke ; the waiters darted to and fro ; people were shouting and laughing, though not with joy ; the click of the balls could be heard from the billiard-room. Anton went in there. He could not play, but he liked the game—the cloth was so green, the balls so pure and white and clicked against each other so merrily.

Two clerks were playing, and one of them, a tall young fellow, hit the balls so cleverly that Anton smiled with pleasure.

" Clever fellow ! " he thought, looking with respect and envy at the clerk, who was perspiring with the effort.

" Why shouldn't I play too. . . . I am good at these things."
He felt quite affectionate towards the clerk.

But the clerk caught his cue against Anton's chest, missed his aim, and turned upon Anton fiercely :

" What the devil do you want here ? Isn't there room enough for you ? "

Anton grew timid and went away, a feeling of pain and insult in his heart.

" Poking his nose in here ! " the clerk went on, chalking his cue.

" Go away, please, don't you see you are in the way," the marker considered it his duty to add, looking Anton up and down quickly with beady eyes.

" A beggar ! " he mumbled, handing the cue to the player. Anton sniffed and grew red, moving further and further away until the back of his neck hit against the billiard-ball box, and then his confusion made him stand still, blinking nervously.

The others soon forgot about him. The players hit the balls, two boys of gloomy countenance were quarrelling about a certain twenty kopeks, the lamp over the billiard-table smoked darkly, and from the saloon was heard a boisterous melody by Heish. Anton grew calmer, began to look about him, and even asked the marker for a light. The marker scratched himself, thought for a moment, and then said :

" There are always matches on the table for that purpose."

But Anton very much wanted to talk. Since the night before he had felt sad for some reason or other, and the vodka he had drunk. far from banishing this sadness, seemed to oppress him.

" It is dull without company," he said in an ingratiating voice as
he lit a cigarette, and by his face the marker could see that he wanted
to offer him one but was afraid.   And for this very reason the marker
looked at him with unfeigned contempt, smiled, and went away.

Anton blinked still more quickly and walked into the saloon.
There he asked for another half-bottle of vodka, drank it all, and
then sat for a long time hanging his head and gazing bitterly at a
green cucumber that lay before him on a plate.   By the well-known
din in his ears and the fact that sounds about him seemed to come
from afar, Anton understood that he was drunk, and this
annoyed him as though some one else was to blame, some one
who was constantly annoying and insulting him.

" I am a working man ! " he thought, " and I want to cry and
complain to some one."   The musical box made him sadder and
sadder, and Anton, shaking his head and pressing his cheeks firmly
against his hands, began to sing incoherently without words or tune.
The song seemed very nice and touching to him ; tears appeared in
his eyes.

" You mustn't sing or make yourself a nuisance here ! " a waiter
said, slipping over to Anton in his soft shoes.

" Why not ? " Anton asked in aggrieved amazement, raising his
dim tearful eyes.

" Because ! " the waiter replied, adding, " Will you go out,
please ? "

" But why ? " Anton repeated with greater amazement and a
rising irritation.

" You are making yourself a nuisance.   Will you go, please ? "
the waiter continued, obstinately.

Anton grew timid and rose.

" Very well . . . I'll go.   A workman can't sit anywhere.   H'm.
. . . Very strange . . . " he muttered, trying to find his cap that
had fallen down near his chair.

" It's all right, it's all right," the waiter said.

Anton staggered out of the saloon, and the feeling of insult grew
greater and greater, causing his drunken brain almost physical
suffering.   The waiter followed him, but staggering between the
tables, Anton turned and flew into the billiard-room.   By then he
was so drunk that he could scarcely see or understand anything ;
before his eyes there was a kind of orange mirage in which floated
faces, sounds, voices and balls quickly flying over a green cloth.   The
waiter stood watching by the door, but some one called him and he
vanished.   Anton, with legs wide apart and head dropped, stood
staring dully at the billiard-table, trying to understand what it all
meant, not only the billiard-table but also the things happening
within him.   The very same clerk who had knocked against and

abused Anton appeared before his eyes, and Anton stared at him mechanically.

" A cannon at the top of the table ! " the clerk shouted, and at the same moment Anton remembered his face and the aimless sense of injury that tortured him suddenly found an outlet.

" Allow me," he said suddenly, going up to the billiard-table and leaning right over it.

" What ? " the clerk asked mechanically, and without waiting for a reply pushed Anton away with his shoulder and shouted, " the fifteenth in the right corner ! "

" What is in the . . . right ? " Anton asked with a senseless viciousness.

" Go away, go away, please ! " the marker interposed, putting a cue between them. But Anton pushed the cue away with his hand and without removing his swollen eyes from the clerk, continued :

" No, this is . . . I also want to play. I also want to . . . that . . . to the right ! Why shouldn't a workman . . . if he likes ? "

The marker took him by the elbows.

" Let go . . . why are you holding me ? He pushed me . . . a working man ! My hands are black," Anton said tearfully, showing his black, gnarled fingers. " A working man . . . he pushed. . . . I want to know why a working man can't go to the right ! "

" Ugh, the drunken beast ? " the clerk laughed. " Marker, what are you looking at ? "

" Get out ! " the marker said angrily, seizing Anton by the shoulder.

And suddenly the sense of insult in Anton reached a tremendous intensity.

" Let go ! " he cried in an oppressed voice between clenched teeth, and tore himself away forcibly so that his coat was rent. " He pushed me and I am being seized ! " he shouted in a firm, sober voice, and swept the balls off the billiard-table with his hand.

The balls flew over the edge, but Anton had already been grabbed by the arm, knocked down, and dragged along the half-dark corridor.

" Let go ! . . . You devils ! " he cried.

Some one struck him a heavy blow on the jaw and the salt blood instantly filled his mouth, and a voice, the clerk's, as it seemed to Anton, cried :

" That's right. Splendid ! "

And at the same moment Anton saw before him the open door leading to the street and the fresh damp air blew on his face.

" You liar ! " Anton said hoarsely, clutching the doorpost with his bent fingers.

But his hands were thrust aside, and receiving a blow on the back of his neck that made the whole world spin round, he flew out into the darkness and emptiness, rolled over the pavement, hit his knees on the curb-stones, and rolled heavily down the bridge.

"Take care, you devil!" a frightened cabman cried in a thin voice, and Anton heard somewhere near him the frightened snorting and soft warm odour of a horse. He staggered up, spitting blood. There was a ringing in his ears, stars danced before his eyes, and his jaw trembled with the pain. Mechanically he touched his damp knees and could not make out whether it was blood or water.

"So," he said aloud bitterly; was silent a moment, and added, "So, it seems. . . ."

And now he saw clearly and consciously that life—his unhappy bitter life—abused him always and unceasingly. He shed tears and shook his clenched fist at the shut door.

"A working man!" he said through his tears as he walked down the street, and he felt himself infinitely unfortunate and insulted. He turned the corner into the main street and again reached the front entrance of the public-house, where the porter stood in his shining cap and a bright lamp was burning, and the cabmen were quarrelling amongst themselves. At this moment the two clerks came out, having finished their game, and, smoking cigarettes, walked down the street. Anton caught sight of them and grew dazed at the terrible, still unconscious impulse that seized him, and then, fumbling for his shoemaker's knife in his pocket, and staggering on feeble legs, he ran after them.

There were many people about—laughing women—an officer who pushed Anton aside—two workmen who made way for him, but Anton saw nothing. With a terrible clearness there danced before his eyes the bowler hat that receded along the street. At one moment he nearly lost sight of it; his way was barred, but running in the road he caught them up after passing two or three groups.

They were laughing, and one of them, not the one who had pushed Anton, said:

"There she is, Mashka!"

And they stopped near a woman in a large red hat, which shook fantastically in the uncertain light of the lantern.

"Where are you going?" she asked in a hoarse contralto, and at this moment Anton caught them up, and thrust his knife into the clerk's back with all his strength, with all the weight of his body.

He had time to feel how for a moment the knife cut through the thick cloth, and with a creak reaching to the blade it penetrated through something elastic and firm that instantly turned soft and damp. He dropped the knife, and without knowing why or wherefore, ran away. He did not know whether the clerk had cried out or not, but he saw in the lamplight a dark formless mass on the spot where a man had been a moment before. Then it seemed that the whole world, with hue and cry, set out to run after him.

Covered with a cold sweat, with wildly rolling eyes and in greatest animal terror, Anton rushed down a dark lane, flew down the length of the street without seeing what was happening behind him, but hearing the desperate shouting of many voices behind him.

Stamping and panting there came after him dvorniks, a policeman, and three workmen in shabby boots.

" Stop him ! " resounded terribly from one end of the street to the other.

Panting and choking with the saliva that filled his throat, he turned down one street after another, lurched heavily against some one in the road, and with protruding eyes and bathed in sweat, dashed down the tow-path of a dark dirty canal, the black water of which smelt cold and damp. The policeman who met him at the turning caught hold of him by the sleeve, but slipped and hit his sword against the damp paving-stones of the bridge.

Anton flew on, jumping over obstacles, squeezing through holes, roaring and panting like a wild, hunted animal. His terror imbued him with such strength that the cries of his pursuers and the piercing blasts of the whistle receded into the gloomy darkness that was scarcely dispersed by the faint yellow light of the street lamps.

Anton ran over a bridge, jumped to the other side of a ditch, frightening a stray dog, fell on his hands, jumped up and ran on to some dark desert place overgrown with dank grass, which swayed monotonously in the wind. Here it was dark and desolate, the lamps twinkled far away in front and behind him, while to one side was a dark mass that looked like a wood, whence issued the persistent mournful rustling of trees.

III

He lay in a ditch full of leaves the whole night ; around him was only the soft rustling grass and above him the cold black sky drizzling with an unseen rain. Anton lay huddled up with cold, the cold water soaking through and through him, while hasty disconnected thoughts floated through his brain. One thing only was clear to him —his former life was finished—he could never go back to his basement again and resume his work. At first this idea was strange and terrible to him, but sooner than he himself realised it, a vague feeling of gladness arose in his soul.

" Is it all over ? " he asked himself, and at the thought he even sat up.

" Fugh ! . . . enough ! " he said with a soft triumph, as though bragging before some one who had long oppressed him, and his feeling of joy grew stronger and his sense of freedom drowned the fear and vague apprehension of the future.

The field was cold and deserted, but it was pleasant and the air was good.

In the morning, wet and dishevelled, he walked across the fields and wound his way through a long lane, to the other end of the town, where he had never been before.   Because the place was unknown to him, it seemed lighter and more free.   He walked along the sunny streets afraid, yet glad that he was not working at an hour when he usually worked ; that he could do what he liked and not have to worry about paying for his basement, leather, and lasts.   At first he was nervous and made way for every one, but, torn and dirty, he was a strange and terrible sight, and all willingly stepped away from him. He noticed this, and realising that he was terrifying, walked straight at people, enjoying a sensation unknown to him till then.   The whole day he wandered about the streets, got some food at an eating-house, and in the afternoon went out to the fields, where he lay on on the dry grass thinking in the sun.

At the bottom of the fields and over the whole horizon were slender, red factory chimneys, and the smoke from them hung over the town like a thick curtain.   In the field it was light and still. The dark mass that he had taken to be a wood at night was a cemetery.   He could see, from where he lay, the tiny toy-like crosses and memorials gleaming white against the golden leaves of the birches.   Anton lay face downwards in the ditch, and raising his head, looked out on the cemetery.

He tried to imagine terrible things, but simply felt tranquil, free and at ease.   He had no fear of the police, because the prison life that he knew was better than the life of cold, hunger, boredom and injustice that he had experienced in freedom.   Of the fact that he had killed a man he thought little and vaguely.   He was too dull and blind to understand the scene of the previous night in all its horror.   He had no feeling of remorse or pity ; on the contrary, he was possessed by a vague triumphant feeling of being unusually bold and desperate.   It was as though he had said to some one :

" So that is what you . . . Then there you are ! "

It was only towards evening, when deep, pensive shadows crept over the field, when the golden cemetery grew dark and the white crosses merged into the brown mass, that Anton grew sad.   He began to breathe heavily and turned from side to side in the ditch.   He regretted something, something good and pure.   He turned over on his back and looked up into the distant fathomless sky, in which the cold transparent sunset was melting away.   It was thence, from the eternally pure space, that the sadness came.   Then he got up in the ditch, black and dishevelled, and climbed out on to the banks ; the field was dark and desolate.

" If . . . then . . ." he said aloud, waving his hand with a feeling of despair and an ache in his heart.

Then he made his way to the town, staggering as he walked, and looking round obstinately and heavily, with a deep frown, as though he were looking for some one's throat to fly at.

Over the broad fields, the strong, free wind blew evenly and sadly.

MME. ESTAFIEVA

VANIA

WITH her pretty, rosy little face buried deep in the sofa pillow, Milochka cried bitterly. Fate had cruelly and unexpectedly brought the first grievous disappointment of her young life. She had impatiently awaited the day when she was to become sixteen years of age and would change from a little girl into a young lady ; would put on for the first time a long white muslin dress and go to her first ball.

She had been dreaming of this event for a long time ; but that morning, suddenly, her mother told her that she would not get the dress, and that the ball was not even to be thought of, as their means would not permit such an expenditure.

This was a terrible blow for poor Milochka. From her early childhood the pet of the whole family, she did not know what it was to be refused anything. Up to a very short time before, she had been surrounded with luxury, and somehow she could not become used to the thought that, with her father's death, the means for the life of opulence were at an end ; and that in the year and a half that had passed since he had been so suddenly taken from them, the few thousands he had left had been spent, and they were now compelled to start a new and very different mode of living.

She had come home from boarding-school for the Christmas holiday, full of joyous anticipation of her first ball, and now all her dreams were cruelly shattered. It was terrible.

Preparations for Christmas were going on in the house, but Milochka, who was wholly engrossed in her own sorrow, did not pay any attention to them. At times she lifted her tear-stained, charming little face from the pillow and addressed her brother Vania, a youth of nineteen, dressed in the uniform of a high-school boy, and repeated with a voice full of despair.

"You understand, Vania, that this had been my dream, my sweetest dream ! " and forgetting her sorrow for a moment, she continued : "I and Tania. You remember Tania ? A cunning little red-haired thing ! "

Vania nodded his head.

" I and Tania always talked about our first ball, and decided that she would get a pink dress and I a white one, but mother told me to-day that if I even got the dress she could not take me to the ball, as she hasn't anything decent to wear, having sold all her nice gowns. I shall not be able to go to my first ball, my beautiful first ball," she added tearfully, and burying her head once more in the pillow she broke into weeping anew.

Vania stood thoughtfully looking at his sister, then he turned and went into the corridor with a nervous, ungainly gait. In passing Anna's (his step-mother's) room he anxiously looked at the door as if trying to assure himself that he would be able to slip out unnoticed, and hastily began to put on his coat.

" Oh, leave me alone ! " he heard Anna's angry voice. " I have told you again and again that we shall not have any Christmas tree this year, and if you do not stop crying I shall drive you out of the room."

But this energetic warning evidently did no good, because a moment later he heard his step-mother exclaim in a sharper tone :

" So that is how you listen to what your mother tells you ! Go into the nursery ! " On the threshold Anna appeared, pushing angrily before her a little girl of five, who was crying as if her heart would break.

" And where are you off to now ? " Anna turned to Vania in a displeased tone, seeing him dressed for the street in his coat and with cap in hand.

" I shall—I shall soon come back," replied Vania in a shaking voice, trying to avoid her eyes and awkwardly pulling at his cap.

" I do not like your continual absences," said Anna, gazing with cold, almost hostile eyes at her step-son. " I cannot understand where you are going all the time. For two months now you have been at home only during meals ; you do not even find it necessary to tell me where you go. And you know well that the whole responsibility for your behaviour falls upon me. People will say that I am a bad mother to you."

" But I assure you that I am not doing any wrong, mother, I am simply going to my lessons."

" To-day you could have stayed at home just as well ; you know that there is a great deal of work in the house just before the holidays. You could be of some help to me. By the way, why do you always lock your door lately ? "

Vania became very confused and blushed.

" I have in there—I am afraid that Sonia and Mitia will tear my books and papers——"

" How thoughtful you are ! Since when have you become so careful of your books ? " she asked ironically, and turning abruptly she entered the nursery with the whimpering child.

Vania looked after the retreating figure of his step-mother for a moment, and pulling his cap down over his head he quickly left the house.

In the dining-room Milochka was still crying. In the nursery the two smaller children, Mitia and Sonia, were vying with each other in telling the nurse about the lovely big Christmas tree they had had a long, long time ago. They complained bitterly and sadly that the dear Lord had taken their papa away, and mother said that they would never again have a Christmas tree.

The old nurse tried to comfort the children as well as she could, gently stroked their pretty, curly heads and told them of the wonderful Child who had been born many centuries ago in the manger, of the great Star which had appeared in the sky and had led the shepherds and the Wise Men to that place where rested the Redeemer. She spoke to them of the Wonderful Infant long and earnestly, and the children pressed close to her, forgetting their own sorrow and listening to the simple narrative of their old nurse with delight and curiosity.

In the meanwhile Anna was sitting with sadly bowed head upon her still unmade bed. A long string of memories flooded her mind. She recollected her free, joyous childhood in her father's house, her girlhood, the years she had spent at college surrounded by loving friends. At last she had reached her long-wished-for sixteenth year ; she was now a young lady in long skirts. How bright and enticing seemed to her the future ! Her heart beat joyously, longing for the unknown but very sweet future. She was only seventeen when she married a young widower with a year-old child by his first wife.

She had loved her husband passionately and was very happy in her married life. If they quarrelled at times, it was only on account of Vania ; she could not reconcile herself to the idea that another woman had loved him and was loved by him only such a short time ago, and that this other woman had left him a pledge of their love, a little boy whom the father adored. This boy, a capricious, homely, obstinate child, Vania, who always looked at her distrustfully with his large grey eyes, and who bore a passionate love for his father and received his caresses with transports of joy, was taking away a part of her husband's heart from her, so it seemed to her, and he was the cause of all the friction in their otherwise happy life. She disliked him, and could only with difficulty suppress this feeling, and now, sitting on the bed, sunk in the recollections and memories of her past life, she did not for a moment reproach herself for her unkindness and injustice towards her step-son. She thought only of her own children, of the terrible poverty which was threatening them. She also thought that fate had dealt very unjustly with her, too.

She recollected how many years before, she, a beautiful young woman surrounded by luxury, the tender care of a loving husband, with a host of admirers, began to preach the idea of equality. She had become passionately attached to this idea, and declared in a tone of firm conviction that the despotic times had passed long ago, when a wife depended on her husband ; that now a wife had just as many rights in the family as the husband, and that, so far as she knew, a wife and mother was even of more consequence in the family than the husband.

Anna smiled bitterly.

" Yes," she whispered : " I have retained my independence and equal rights ; all the rest is in the grave ! "

She, who was only thirty-five years of age and still looking young and beautiful, considered herself, since the death of her husband, an old woman and devoted herself wholly to the bringing up of her children, protecting them as far as possible from want and privation. She had almost entirely forgotten self !

Only the deep sorrow for the man she had loved so dearly, and the eternal fear for the children's future, never left her for a moment. The feeling of loneliness and helplessness grew within her stronger and stronger. She recollected how they used to spend Yuletide in her dear husband's lifetime, the splendid suppers, the crowds of richly-dressed, joyous guests, and her heart contracted with pain. Sighing deeply and brushing away a tear, she rose slowly from the bed.

It was time to set the table. Night was already descending. In the darkened sky, solitary stars were appearing, shedding a soft, silvery light.

" And where is Vania ? Again away ? " asked Anna, sitting down to the table, around which were already seated Mitia and Sonia dressed in their holiday best, and Milochka, who was still very sad, and whose eyes were red with weeping.

" He is always away ! " she added severely, serving the soup to the children.

Seeing that their mother was angry, the children grew quiet and ate their meal in silence.

In the cosy little dining-room the quiet was only broken by the clatter of the spoons in the plates. At last even that noise ceased. Every one was sitting motionless, sunk in his own thoughts. Only pink-cheeked little Mitia looked around as if he were seeking something. At last he turned to his old nurse, who stood behind his little chair, and asked her in a whisper:

" Niania, have the little angels come already ? "

" They have, they have, my sweet. Be good, as I have taught you, because otherwise they might fly away and carry back the nice little Christmas story of the dear Lord ! "

At these words Anna made a gesture of impatience and sharply remarked:

" I would ask you, Niania, to tell the children these fairy tales some other time, not when they are at the table."

" But these are not fairy tales, madame ! I simply told them to conduct themselves properly or they might not get their Christmas tree."

" It is my affair if they receive one or not. But what have the angels to do with it ? "

" How is that ? " asked the old woman, greatly offended. " Of course the angels have to do with it. Everybody knows that on Christmas Eve the angels fly among good people and distribute presents."

" Mother, mother, Vania has come ! " joyfully cried Sonia, who had seen her elder brother pass through the corridor.

" Well, and if he has, then he has ! What are you shouting for ? " Anna said in an irritated tone. Turning towards her step-son, who had just at that moment crossed the threshold, she sternly asked:

" Where have you been ? " and not waiting for his reply, she added: " You ought, at least, to have dressed a little nicer in honour of the holiday. True, we have no guests, but nevertheless it does no harm to make a proper appearance. Just see what you look like ! " and she critically pointed to his short coat covered with stains.

The boy reddened.

" I have nothing better to put on. My clothes are all worn out," he replied, looking down into his plate.

" And your lessons ? Why, you are earning more than twenty roubles a month."

" But I am giving you almost the whole of it," Vania said in a very low voice, looking reproachfully at his step-mother.

This reply deeply mortified Anna. Without saying another word she turned her whole attention to the children.

" I saw a nice, large picture in Vania's room," Sonia said, suddenly interrupting the painful silence. " It was lying on the floor and Vania drew something on it with coloured pencils ; such a large picture ! " drawled out the little girl, and pouting her rosy lips she added : " Vania always locks the door on me and would not let me into his room, but I saw everything."

" What is this I hear, Vania ? You are playing at painting ? I congratulate you ; this is a fine pastime for a pupil of the sixth form at school whose final examinations are close at hand ! " Anna said sarcastically.

Vania did not reply, he only bent his head lower over his plate.

He was already accustomed to the unkind treatment of his step-mother, but he suffered at her stinging words ; the joyful mood in which he had come home vanished at once. His heart contracted painfully as before his eyes rose one after another the sad pictures of his childhood and early youth. Vania, who had never known the caresses of a mother, lived in his father's house like a stranger. His father had loved him dearly, but his work, that of a civil engineer, had left him but little time for his family. Energetic, active, and always taken up with some very responsible work, he did not spoil his children with excessive tenderness, and treated Vania exactly as he did his other children, calmly and collectedly. How Vania's heart used to beat with joy when his father, noticing some injustice done by his step-mother, used to try to comfort and soothe him with gentle words and caresses ! But this did not often happen ; time passed, and from the unsociable, ill-treated child, Vania became a youth who perfectly understood his position in the family. His relations with his step-mother did not improve, though he tried his best not to displease her in anything. Always respectful and polite, he bore her ill-will with a calmness which exasperated her.

But suddenly his father died and the conditions of Vania's life as well as those of the whole family underwent a radical change. The luxurious surroundings, large circle of acquaintances, the merry, free existence, all vanished as if by magic. The father, notwith-standing the enormous sums of money he made yearly from his work, had left the family almost penniless, with only a small pension to fall back upon which hardly sufficed to keep the wolf from the door.

From the large, richly-appointed house the family was forced to move into five little rooms, and here began for them all a life of care and privation. Vania was fully eighteen years of age at that time.

Seeing the sad plight of the family, he secured some work which enabled him to pay for his schooling and for the room he occupied.

At first Anna would not hear of his paying, but afterwards she very unwillingly agreed to accept this help from her unloved step-son.

Vania, who adored his little brother and sisters, was very diligent in his studies and awaited with the greatest impatience the time when he should enter the technical school. He dreamed of following in the footsteps of his father, choosing the same vocation. His aim in life was to restore the material well-being of the family destroyed by his father's untimely death, and gaining a moral victory over the step-mother who hated him, to make an end of the hostile treatment to which he had been subjected for so many years.

It pained him very much to hear from her lips now the unjust rebuke ; but he did not show how deeply he was hurt and offended, he respectfully kissed his step-mother's hand as usual on rising from the table and went into his room.

Anna looked after Vania's retreating form, and shrugging her shoulders, rose silently from the table.

Milochka sighed deeply and went back to her sofa, while the old nurse whispered something to the children and led them away to the nursery.

An oppressive feeling of sadness took possession of Anna. She paced the room for a long time, evidently not noticing either the servant who cleared the things from the table or Milochka who sat motionless upon the sofa.

Her thoughts had once more strayed to the past, and against her will, pictures of her free, happy life with her husband rose before her.

Good-natured and gay, notwithstanding the enormous amount of work he had to do, he imbued every one around him with the joy of life.

" What striking dissimilarity between the characters of father and son ! " thought Anna, picturing to herself the quiet, unsociable Vania. " He must resemble his mother ! " and once more the feeling of jealousy which had tortured her so much in the past, awakened in her heart. She sharply turned, intending to go to her room, when she suddenly heard Vania's quick voice :

" Mother, Milochka, please come into my room. I have prepared a little surprise for the children. Please call Sonia and Mitia, and tell them to hurry," and suddenly reddening with confusion, he hastily added : " I have prepared a little Christmas tree for them, and have already lit the candles."

" You ? For the children—a Christmas tree ? " asked Anna, looking at him with astonishment, as if distrusting her own ears.

He lifted his eyes to her face, and smiling with a guilty smile, he said in a low voice :

" Yes, I have only hidden it from you because I wanted to surprise the little ones."

Anna could only with difficulty force herself to believe that this ungainly, serious youth, indifferent, as it seemed to her, to the family, could have thought of giving them such a surprise.

And Vania ran into the nursery shouting :

"Sonia, Mitia, the good God has sent you a Christmas tree ! Hurry up to my room ! " and again he ran for his step-mother and sister, whom he already found at the door of his room.

Vania's little room was neatly tidied up by himself for the event ; the table and chairs were pushed to the wall, and in the centre of the room, sparkling with light, stood a lovely little tree.

The children looked at it with delight, and clapping their hands, repeated :

"The dear Lord has sent us a Christmas tree ! The good Lord ! "

Milochka, who had entirely forgotten her own personal sorrow, joyously rushed toward her brother and asked him with a voice full of curiosity :

"Vaniusha, you sly, bad boy, how did you manage to buy and prepare everything in time ? "

"I have even something ready for you and mother," he said, visibly confused. "Sonia, this is for you, darling," putting into the little girl's arms a large, beautifully-dressed doll with long, flaxen curls, which filled Sonia with the most tumultuous joy. "And this is for you," he said, giving Mitia a high horse on wheels, which the boy immediately mounted and, throwing upon his sister the glances of a victorious rider, began to whip up his horse.

"Look out, Sonia, do not come too near the horse or it will run you over ! " shouted Vania, pressing close to the wall and making believe that he was afraid of the horse.

Anna looked smilingly at the awkward youth, and involuntarily rested upon him a deeply-touched, tender glance. She gazed at the face of Vania, reddened with joyful excitement, at his eyes that were now sparkling with merriment from under his thick eyelashes, and noted with surprise the striking resemblance of the boy to her dead husband.

"Why have I never before noticed it ? " she reproached herself in thought, and looked with still greater tenderness at the face of the transformed youth.

How unlike his present joyful glance was to that stern, morose look his face generally wore, and to which they were all so accustomed !

A ray of bright spring sun melted the crust of ice which had for so many years covered Anna Nickolaievna's heart, and called up from the depth of her soul a tender, motherly feeling toward the, until now, unloved step-son.

"Mother, this is what I have for you," said Vania, and timidly handed her a small velvet case.

She opened it with growing curiosity and her heart began to throb joyously.

In the case, on a bed of dark-red velvet, lay a long and ardently-desired gold brooch, in which was set a beautifully-executed miniature of her husband.

Anna, for the first time in all the eighteen years, imprinted a loving kiss on the bent head of the youth.

He replied to her caress impetuously, pressing her hand to his lips. Then he hastily walked over to the table and opened a package.

" Ah ! " screamed Milochka and rushed to the table.   Vania held before her a roll of the finest white muslin.

Milochka could hardly believe her own eyes.   The present was too unexpected !

" And here is material also for mother's dress," spoke Vania, untying another package and taking out of it a grey shimmering silk.

" Now you can go with mother to your first ball on New Year's Eve."   He smiled a sweet, bright smile, and seeing his sister's face alight with happiness, he added :

" Now you won't cry any more, will you ? "

" Vaniusha, darling, dearest ! " excitedly exclaimed Milochka, throwing her arms around her brother's neck.   " You are such a good, noble boy, and I love you so much, so very much ! "

The stuff fell to the floor, but the young girl paid no attention to it, but continued to press her brother closely in her arms and repeat :

" I love you, love you, Vaniusha——"

Anna also approached Vania.

" But you must not forget that I have also something to thank him for, you selfish little thing," she said to her daughter jestingly. " I also want to kiss Vania, and to thank him for the merry Christmas he has given us."   And pushing Milochka aside, she tenderly drew the youth to herself and, gazing lovingly into his eyes, she said in a low voice : " Vania, you have given us all this day a great joy.   I thank you, my dearest boy, from all my heart."

She called him for the first time in his life " dearest," and spoke to him with a tenderness in her voice with which he had never before been addressed by her.   Under the motherly, caressing glance of Anna's large black eyes the youth forgot his solitary, joyless childhood, forgot the bitterness of the many years of unjust treatment. His heart, which had so longed for love and sympathy, responded at once, and he, forgiving and happy, trustfully met his step-mother's gaze, which was now alight with unfeigned love and tenderness.

They stood for a long time closely pressed to each other, and it seemed as if this woman, whose whole life had been so cruelly broken by the untimely death of a passionately-loved husband, looked to this strong, energetic young man for help.

Mitia and Sonia joyfully danced round the Christmas tree, looking

at the many sweets with sparkling, expectant eyes. Milochka gazed
smilingly at her present, singing softly to herself, and the old nurse
stood on the threshold, and watching with good-natured smiles the
exulting children, whispered :

" Thanks be to God, glory to the Creator ! We have a merry
Christmas, as it should be ! "

" But tell me, tell me frankly," said Anna, a short time after,
forcing Vania to sit by her side, " how it came into your head to
get a Christmas tree for the children, and where did you get the
money for it ? "

" Oh, I thought of it a long time," Vania said with a deep sigh.
" In fact, I thought of it during the whole year. Seeing how hard it
was for you to make ends meet, and that it was becoming harder
and harder with every month, I began to look for something to do
aside from my lessons. A friend of my father, the Government
architect, gave me some plans to draw——"

" That must have been what Sonia called pictures ? " impetuously
asked Anna.

" The same," replied Vania. " I have spent almost whole nights
over them during the past three months. I wanted to earn enough
money to get the children a tree, so they would not be disappointed.
I thought you would also like the children to be happy on this day.
Afterwards I could give you all my extra earnings and make it a
little easier. To-day," continued the boy hastily, as if fearing that
he would not have time to tell all, " to-day, when I saw Milochka's
tears I could not stand it any longer, and going over to the
architect I borrowed the money for the dresses from him. I shall
pay him back afterwards with my work," concluded the boy,
reddening with excitement and joy.

" But, Vania, this work is more than your strength will allow,"
broke out Anna with a sob. " It is too much. I cannot permit you
to do it. I——"

" It is nothing—really nothing, mother," he hastily interrupted.
" You must not worry on my account. I am very strong and can
do a lot of work. I am like papa—I only hope that you and the
children will somehow pull through till I graduate, and then we
will live as comfortably as we did when papa was alive," he added
gaily, and tossed his thick hair. " Is that not so, Milochka ? " and
not waiting for a reply, he sprang from his chair and rushed to his
youngest sister.

A moment later Sonia, choking with laughter, sat on Vania's
shoulders and he ran around the tree with her, making believe that
he wanted to catch Mitia, who ran before him, neighing and
imitating a horse.

" The picture of his father ! " thought Anna Nickolaievna, gazing at the face of her step-son, which was alight with infinite joy and excitement. And through the noisy merriment which filled the room Vania's confident voice came back to her : " I can do a lot of work. I am like papa ! "

A sweet, joyful feeling took possession of her. Of her former anger and dissatisfaction with life, not a vestige remained. The oppressive sadness and the fear for the unknown future of her children vanished like a mist at sunrise.

She saw before her the powerful form of Vania, who boldly followed in the steps of his father ; she saw a strong hand stretched out to her, and once more heard the words : " I am strong, I am like papa."

PRINCESS METCHERSKY

A RACE ON THE NEVA

I

IT was the morning of Epiphany. The intense cold of the preceding night had moderated, but the thermometer still marked fifteen degrees below zero. The sun shone brilliantly in a sky of cloudless blue ; the air was like a revivifying elixir. All sounds were vibrant, distinct, penetrating, and every object seemed sharply outlined in the transparent light. The bells of the innumerable churches in St. Petersburg were ringing the chimes at full swing.

In a drawing-room where the sunshine, subdued by green shades, filtered through curtains of yellow silk, filling the great apartment with a golden atmosphere, a young woman was walking rapidly to and fro. She was above the average height, but slender and graceful. She wore a long robe of white cashmere whose severe cut brought into sculptural relief the outlines of her superb figure. Her hair of reddish gold rippled in close waves around her temples and forehead, and was gathered in a loose knot at the top of her head. A kind of sweet severity, singularly suggestive of repressed strength, characterised her whole personality. At times she paused in her rapid walk up and down the room, as if thinking deeply, then suddenly resumed her interrupted promenade.

A servant in livery covered with gold braid opened the door and announced : "Captain Répnine."

He had scarcely finished speaking when Alexander Répnine entered, out of breath, exclaiming : " Pardon, my dear Elisaveta, have I kept you waiting ? " And the new arrival, a handsome young man with keen, dark eyes and a silky brown moustache which shaded a smiling mouth, looked at Elisaveta Petrovna, who was taller than he, with an air of anxiety.

She shook her head.

" Ah, so much the better, so much the better, for I had begun to think that I would never get here in time to escort you to the races. Until the last moment I was detained—interrupted and delayed. I scarcely knew where I was. Oh, but the races are going to be superb, extraordinary. Never in the memory of man has the track been so perfect—so hard and smooth ; not a flake of snow on the ice, which is blue and polished like steel. You know how seldom it is so, with that infernal wind that sends drifts of snow blowing from Lake Ladoga. But during the night more than five hundred men have been working on it steadily ; for the most famous horses in Russia are engaged. The Imperial stud furnishes several, but the most brilliant, the most miraculous of all will be the three-horse race. Never, never were such superb teams. If you saw them you would compare them to nothing but the coursers of Phaeton. I am really becoming lyrical. But you have not changed your dress."

" Oh, as to that," replied Elisaveta, " I need only my long fur coat, my toque and my gloves. But there is no need to hurry, dear Alexander. Let us sit down and talk a while. It is only twelve o'clock ; we have just finished breakfast—and you too, I hope. The races begin at one. It is but a ten minutes' drive from here to the Neva ; we will surely arrive, as you always do, among the first. And besides, I want to ask you something. Some occult influence must have been at work with me, for I don't know why I should think of it now—do you remember Jean Hotzko ? "

" How could I forget him ? Didn't he disappear in a most mysterious manner—though not more mysterious than his personality ? Was there ever a being more absolutely original, and who has left more ineffaceable traces in the memory of all who knew him ? But as for knowing him—who ever really knew him ? "

" Oh, that most abused word ' original,' " said Veta sadly, as if interrogating her own thoughts. " What has become of this man ? " she continued, without listening to the jealous exclamations of her betrothed. " Two years ago he appeared in our world, young, of unknown parentage. Fabulously rich, for a whole season he astonished St. Petersburg by his generous and eccentric prodigalities, or, as some called them, his follies. And his manner, at once so gentle and so haughty—sometimes frozen by impenetrable reserve, then exuberant, emotional, in striking contrast to the conventional correctness of those triflers who only tolerated Hotzko because he was rich. What has become of him ? "

" I do not know, though there were a thousand rumours. He was engaged and compromised in certain political and financial complications, not so much on his own account as to oblige some of his friends, who proved unscrupulous and ungrateful. Hotzko dis-

appeared one day, as you know. His creditors were all paid in full,
and he discharged all the immense obligations that had accumulated
through his inexperience. His house and all it contained, its
numberless objects of art and luxury, were sold. But what dis-
tressed him more than all the rest was the sale of his horses. Almost
all of his famous racers were bought at shamefully low prices by
horse dealers. That is really all I know."

II

The Neva, its broad surface frozen and glittering, becomes for
seven long months the passive and powerful slave of man, like a
Titan enchained by some magic charm. During that time it is
really a broad carriage-way between the two superb quays of rose-
coloured granite which enclose it. Between the quays, on the
snowy plain of the benumbed Neva, is laid out a broad ribbon of
steel blue, forming an ellipse several versts in circumference. This
is the race-track, hollowed out and swept clean in the solid ice.
Washed with warm water, by dint of unremitting labour, it resembles
a mirror of polished steel. More than a hundred thousand spectators
surround the arena. Light wooden galleries are built around a
third of the enclosure. These are crowded with officers, with rich
merchants, with landed proprietors from every zone in Russia,
accompanied by their wives. It is a dazzling sea of vivid colours
which are somewhat softened by their own variety ; the richest
silks and velvets are mingled with the glittering uniforms and waving
plumes of the officers. In the centre rises a great pavilion, hung
with crimson, where are assembled the highest nobility, dignitaries
of state and the vassal princes of tributary countries, grand dukes
and grand duchesses surrounded by their respective courts.
Innumerable equipages are massed behind the crowd. From this
human hive rises and swells an increasing murmur—cries, laughter,
oaths, calls to the vendors of kvass, quarrels, songs, the clinking of
sabres of the mounted guard, and the echo of hoofs striking the ice ;
all are confounded in this vast uproar. One by one the light sleighs
bring more spectators, and in the weighing stand are placed the
horses booked for the races. There are superb animals from
princely stables, the noblest mares of the Orloff breed, covered with
Persian carpets or priceless cashmeres, waiting their turn to enter
the arena. At the head of each is a groom wearing a shirt of white
or red silk, with a close-fitting caftan of black velvet. The coachmen, in long coats of fine cloth bordered with castor or zibeline and
wearing oddly-shaped hats that resemble mitres, sit motionless like

painted figures of terra-cotta, holding their reins of closely twisted silk.

A rosewood sleigh lined with crimson velvet pauses before the peristyle of the principal gallery already crowded with spectators. The president of the races makes his way through a crowd of officers of the guard, judges of the races and the principal owners of horses. He offers his arm to a beautiful woman wearing a long coat of blue fox fur, with a toque of the same pressed down on her red-gold hair. She descends from the sleigh and advances very calmly.   Her tall figure and queenly bearing reveal Elisaveta Petrovna.   Répnine follows close behind her.   Together they ascend the steps covered with velvet moquette carpet.   Then the president, after conducting Elisaveta to her place, bows profoundly and retires.   Veta's face, under the toque drawn down to her eyebrows, is serious, full of a sweet impenetrability.

Suddenly a profound silence falls on the crowd.   The president hurries to the seat reserved for him and the bell sounds.   The gates of the weighing stand are thrown open, and two horses, each harnessed to a tiny sleigh of gilded osier, appear, led by their grooms. They advance, stepping high with proudly arching necks.   Their long manes float in the wind, their tails, crimped and waved like a woman's hair, sweep like trains, and are cut squarely across just to clear the ground.   At each movement the silky hair undulates and gives to their carefully balanced steps an air of majesty.   Their harness, of lightest leather, and almost imperceptible, is caught together with delicate silver chains.   A light arch of some precious wood rises above the little heads of the racers.   They advance with measured steps, these horses of the Orient, looking from right to left and neighing as if in acknowledgment of the admiration they excite. One is black, a blue-black, without a single white spot, of slight build, with a full, round chest, small, nervous feet, short, straight back—a magnificent scion of the famous trotters reared in the East. The other is a stallion bred in the Imperial stables, a pure Orloff, a dapple grey with a white mane that sparkles like spun glass.   His nobly moulded flanks and slender legs indicate that his origin is more Arabian than Flemish—the two strains which Prince Orloff crossed so successfully after his campaign in Turkey.   A network of veins runs over his supple body, and from the pointed tips of his little ears to his small, round hoofs, that might be carved in polished agate, he quivers with suppressed eagerness.

By the side of the black horse, inscribed on the programme as " L'Aigle," ambles a little fawn-coloured Cossack runner, slim as a greyhound, with high haunches, slender legs and coarse, bristling mane.   His ears are laid back, his eye full of fire ; all nerve and muscle, he is a perfect type of ugliness, but one of those animals that will make two hundred versts in twenty-four hours, without failing on the road ; those animals which, massed together, have created the finest cavalry in the world, the Cossack legions which were a terror even to Napoleon himself ; absolutely incomparable in attack and on forced marches. A young Tartar, about fifteen years old, perched on a high saddle, is mounted on this wild specimen of the savage races of the Ukraine. He pulls with all his might at the reins of untanned leather, which are ornamented with plaques of wrought silver and two enormous turquoise talismans. This wild-looking rider carries a short ivory whip with several thongs, the classic Russian knout. This enables him while galloping near the black horse to excite and encourage him in the race.

There is a sudden stir ; a bell strikes one brief note, and the horses start simultaneously. At first, swaying from side to side, and measuring their strength, they seem only to observe. The spectators can even hear the quick breath that escapes from their nostrils in jets of hot vapour, visible in the icy air. The little Tartar, bent forward to his horse's ears, seems to have every sense fixed on the sleigh of L'Aigle, just half a head in front of him. His wild face, yellow with frenzy, breathes the most intense and unconscious ferocity. The horse under him has the exact motion of a hound following a hare. By his easy, restrained gallop it is clear that he is not putting forth a quarter of his strength.

L'Aigle, without precipitating his pace, moves with a certain precision, throwing his hoofs with such force that each time they cleave the air one expects to see them break. At each stride he insensibly covers a longer space on the track. But the grey Orloff, Lovki, with a perfectly measured trot, as if merely playing with his superb and supple body, gains by degrees on his adversary. Then the betting begins. A confused noise, gradually growing louder, excites the crowd. It is like the roll of approaching thunder.

The Tartar utters a hoarse cry. He lightly touches his horse, which bounds in the air, and L'Aigle, going with the regularity of a machine and a solid power of muscle, reveals to the connoisseurs that the longer the distance, the more favourable are his chances of winning the race. Without raising his head, his sombre eye shaded by his long forelock, he appears perfectly sure of his strength and endurance. In a few minutes he reaches the Orloff, and they run side by side. Then suddenly he rears his ebony head, passes the grey stallion with a bound, and is some paces ahead.

Cries rend the air : " L'Aigle—L'Aigle gains ! One hundred— two hundred—three hundred roubles on L'Aigle ! " But the coachman of the grey horse shakes his reins, gives a sharp click of his tongue, and is off like an arrow shot from a bow, and Lovki rears his head like an angry swan. His hoofs scarcely touch the ice ; he swims, he seems to fly, to float ; he reaches his rival, and after some seconds of palpitating struggle, passes him and is in front.   The little Tartar becomes not only yellow, but green with rage.   He utters cries that are unlike anything human—inarticulate interjections like the bay of a jackal.   Nevertheless, L'Aigle, always impassive, pursues his rhythmic course, and follows close behind his rival. Suddenly, at the last minute, only two hundred metres from the end, as if the consciousness of his peril had just struck him, he breaks into a full trot.   There is something miraculous in this sudden and unexpected increase of velocity in an animal so calm and imperturbable.   At ten metres from the end they are running neck to neck. At five metres L'Aigle is a length in advance.   The Tartar is howling like an orchestra of demons.   But in the end Lovki wins by a half-length.

The tumult that ensues is indescribable.   The entire crowd to a man rush to the track, and surround the conqueror.   They kiss his forehead, his eyes, his hoofs ; they embrace the coachman, who remains impassive during the interminable hurrahs.   Finally his groom, with a Persian carpet under his arm, arrives to clear the way for Lovki ; and covered with this magnificent housing, which sweeps the ground, and in which he resembles a palfrey of the Middle Ages, draped in gorgeous stuffs, Lovki is slowly led away amid the general delirium.

During the race, insensible to all the clamour around her, Veta had remained in her seat, her elbows resting on the railing in front of her.   She clasped her lorgnette with both hands, and followed the movements of the horses without giving a sign of the passionate interest that she felt.   Only at the moment when, in spite of the vociferations of the Tartar, the Orloff had affirmed his superiority, she rose in her seat.   Her beautiful, frigid mask never softened. Her closely compressed lips restrained the cry of triumph which filled her breast while she seconded with all her heart the victorious efforts of her favourite.   But when all was over, she resumed her seat and said very calmly to Répnine :

" I knew it all the time—the noblest blood is always sure of victory."

Several other races succeeded.   Then came the turn of the horses driven in pairs, and the interest increased.   One would have thought that each man and each woman pressing around the enclosure felt themselves in some way proprietors of those beautiful animals, champions of the favourite sport of the Slavs.

Finally the programme announced the last and most eagerly expected of the races—that of three horses driven abreast to the Russian vehicle *par excellence*, the troïka.   This was really the grand feature of the day.   As the bell sounds, three sleighs, each drawn by three horses, approach and draw up at the starting-post. Every one seated in the galleries rises, and in the profound silence that suddenly prevails can be felt the intense strain of expectation throughout the multitude.

The distance to be covered is twenty versts. Very melodious in the rare and icy air is the tinkling of the innumerable little bells attached to each harness. The first vehicle is drawn by three fine horses of golden chestnut colour, with manes of a lighter shade. Their harness is of fawn-coloured leather, skilfully twisted with strands of emerald-green silk ; their reins are of the same colour.

The second team is composed of three Finnish horses—brown bays, with thick, crinkly hair and long, sweeping manes. Their harness is of black leather with plaques of copper. The third troïka follows, drawn by three snow-white stallions. Their coats shine like satin ; silvery reflections seem to play about their silky manes and slender, elegant necks. Their noses only are black as charcoal, with immense, quivering red nostrils. Their eyes, slightly prominent, are soft yet full of fire, with circles of bistre like those of Asiatic women. Their harness of brown leather is wonderfully woven of tiny strips like ribbons caught together by small gold crowns. Their coachman is a youth with a brown face and bright dark eyes, a genuine type of the peasants of Bessarabia. The owner of this equipage, beautiful as some fairy chariot, is no other than the Polish Prince Sangoushko, who is the fortunate possessor of the only pure Arabian horses in Europe. The other two coachmen are tall, bearded men with Calmuck faces and narrow, sparkling eyes.

They stand there, these nine horses, immovable before the Imperial tribune, so marvellously trained that not one steps over the imaginary line which seems drawn by the starter. The minutes are passing ; the signal for departure is not given—the horses seem petrified ! The bell fails to sound the eagerly expected stroke. Veta herself, standing, leans forward, mechanically seizes Répnine's arm, and presses it with all her strength. From the furthest extremity of the track people crowd close to the barriers. The wait endures about fifteen minutes.

So intense is the strain that the spectators seem scarcely able to bear it, when suddenly the gates of the weighing stand open and the most startling and unexpected spectacle is presented to the breathless and bewildered multitude. Three wretched, red sorrel horses appear, with thin flanks and melancholy air, covered with patches of muddy snow, with old, worn-out harness, half rope and half leather, attached to a dilapidated sleigh of birch bark, such as is used by the Laplanders to carry dried fish and frozen meat. The horses advance with hanging heads and dragging feet to take their place by the side of their aristocratic predecessors, who toss their heads with an air of disdain, and look with scornful eyes on the miserable intruders. A groan of horror and surprise escapes the breasts of the multitude, like a hoarse cry from one monstrous throat. Veta trembles and bites her lip till it bleeds.

The bell sounds three strokes, which resound with thrilling intensity in the midst of the general astonishment. The numerous hoofs beat in unison on the resounding ice ; this is a sound whose echo strikes gratefully on the ears of the crowd, wearied by long waiting. The chestnut horses detach themselves from the group, and suddenly find themselves several paces ahead. The middle horse, called by the picturesque name of " The Kicker," an old racer famous for his past exploits, throws his feet about with the grace of a former star in the Imperial hippodrome. His age not permitting him to run alone, and the competition of the troïkas exacting more strength than speed, he steps lightly and disdains the aid of the other two horses, lean and fiery coursers of the Don, who gallop with their noses to the ground, bent in a half-circle. After them come the Finns, straining the reins until they seem in danger of breaking ; already the eye of the wheel horse darts fire, and connoisseurs predict that they will give trouble to their competitors. Quite in the rear come the white stallions, marvels of beauty and breed, incomparably matched, and so perfectly trained that their supple and graceful bodies, their fine heads and silvery manes present the strange aspect of a single heraldic animal, so complete is the harmony of their movements. With their red nostrils quivering, light, elastic in their movements, they bound along like horses quite free from rein or harness.

Finally, following mournfully behind these proud coursers, come the poor emaciated sorrel horses, scarcely raising their feet. The faint tinkle of their little copper bells is inexpressibly melancholy. The thinness of these poor creatures makes them appear deformed ; they seem to be there only as the result of some ridiculous wager. Their coachman is a peasant with his back bowed, dressed in a ragged overcoat. Is he drunk, or mad ? No one can guess ; as he drives around the track, rude jests and bursts of laughter accompany the strange apparition. No one has ever beheld such a spectacle on the aristocratic stretch of the Neva.

In this order the troïkas pass before the tribune. Halfway in the second round the little brown bay horses, flinging their feet with such velocity that one can hardly distinguish them from the spokes of the wheels, pass the chestnuts easily enough. In vain the latter struggle and quicken their pace. The Finns are some distance ahead, below the tribune of the starter.

During a greater part of the third round the same distances are maintained, but as they again draw near the starting-post the

Sangoushkos, restrained until now by the cunning little Russian coachman, bound suddenly with spirit, and without perceptible effort overtake the chestnuts, pass the Finns, and leave them irrevocably behind.

The crowd start to their feet, shouting : " The whites are gaining ! Hurrah for the Sangoushkos ! " and the horses, excited by the clamour, as if they quite understood the applause, quicken their pace in a frenzy of ardour. They neigh proudly, as if filled with the fire of combat, and at the end of the third round are still far in advance.

Then comes the last round. During the various exploits of its rivals, the sleigh with the peasant driver, while always behind the others, has lost no ground in spite of the indifferent, fatigued gallop of its horses.

Suddenly the peasant sits erect in his sleigh, pushes back the fur cap from his forehead, gathers up the reins, and utters a shrill, piercing, prolonged whistle. Then a most astonishing metamorphosis fairly stupefies the spectators ! The horses, as if responding to some supernatural voice, raise their heads and gather up their strength. Their bony silhouettes take on lines of actual beauty, which seem the outcome of their moral transformation. Their chests expand, their poor heads, lately hanging and dejected, are proudly flung high, their nostrils quiver, their eyes dart fire, their legs recover the powerful grace of an almost forgotten force, their tails, outspread like standards, lash their meagre flanks ! They are like the steeds of some spectral vision, bent with decrepitude, in whom a sudden regenerating breath is instilled, a heroic reminiscence that re-echoes like the clarion of victory. As an old war-horse with bent knees, deaf and half blind, toiling wearily beneath the weight of some heavy vehicle, suddenly catching the sound of the trumpet from the regiment with whom his early years were passed, pricks up his ears, shakes the harness, beats time with his hoofs, bounds forward, dragging the heavy vehicle, his daily martyrdom, as if he scarcely feels its weight ; thus the sorrels, roused from their stupor by the strident whistle, cleave the air with a prodigious bound for which no one was prepared. The transfigured horses responding to the appeal to their blood, carried forward by some unknown secret power, suddenly awakened, rush on like the wind. Soon they are between the bays and the chestnuts, pass them both, and, keeping up their frenzied gallop, gain on the Sangoushkos. Then by one supreme effort, no longer meagre, wretched, broken, but with all the proud exultation of coming victory, straining their limbs of steel, filling the air with their loud breathing, they reach the white stallions. Side by side the teams run for a few minutes, then like a whirlwind the sorrels leave their competitors behind, and stand still for an instant beneath the princely tribune, victors by ten lengths.

For one long moment the crowd remains mute with astonishment. It was literally impossible to shout or applaud. They gazed stupefied at those wretched horses who had beaten the noblest blood of the empire and then, still and calm, seemed to have resumed their mournful attitudes and former ugliness, like Cinderella in the fairy tale, when she suddenly found herself in the midst of the dance in her poor grey dress and wooden shoes. Never did a magic charm act more speedily or more completely.

And then suddenly from a hundred thousand throats broke prolonged cheers, saluting the victory of those unknown horses over their princely and aristocratic rivals. The fashionable world and the peasants crowded together around the track. All the occupants of the tribunes rose to their feet. They clapped their hands ; the cheers redoubled. It was an apotheosis. Everybody wished to find out the name of the peasant, the pedigree of his horses. But without paying the slightest attention to the clamour or to the ovation that surrounded him, he turned his bridle, drew his fur cap low on his forehead, and as piteously as they had entered the arena, with drooping heads and meagre flanks, the poor sorrels resumed their weary road. The light birch bark sleigh seemed to have become an insupportable burden. Nothing could stay their obstinate and obscure retreat. Soon they disappeared behind the gates of the weighing stand.

Elisaveta Petrovna had risen ; with trembling hands she thrust her lorgnette into her muff, and buttoning her long fur coat, she took Répnine's arm, and drew him toward the entrance. " Quick, quick ! " she murmured. " I must see him, I must see them ! "

Without replying Répnine guided her through the excited group who were discussing the events of the day.

" Quick ! " repeated Veta, drawing him to the weighing stand. Her glance was full of disquiet, her lips were trembling with suppressed emotion. At this moment the red sorrels, drawing the victorious sleigh, passed so close to them that Répnine drew her back quickly ; but she, disengaging herself from his hold, advanced rapidly in front of the horses.

" How I should love to speak to him—how proud I should be to have those noble horses," she said, in a clear, distinct voice.

The peasant trembled and turned his head in the direction from which the voice came. With a trembling hand he raised his fur cap, and their eyes met—his, dark, melancholy, despairing ; hers, imploring and filled with tears. She grew very pale ; that was all. Not a word escaped her lips. The muddy sleigh, almost dropping to pieces, was driven over the frozen snow by the peasant, who had sunk back in his seat in his former attitude, while the poor horses seemed ready to drop on their knees.

III

Some months had passed—the astounding event which excited the curiosity of all St. Petersburg was almost forgotten.   No one had ever learned the name of the peasant who with his wretched team had won the most astonishing victory inscribed on the records of the races.   Some declared that he was a sorcerer, others said that a mysterious doctor had given his horses a powerful draught, potent enough to galvanise the muscles of the poor animals.   But then other things occurred which made people forget this unaccountable victory.

Répnine was married to Elisaveta Petrovna.   It was the event of the day.   On the afternoon of the ceremony, returning from the church where all the court and the aristocracy had witnessed the marriage of one of the most celebrated beauties of the season, an elegant coupé bearing the initials of the newly wedded pair drove them to the door of their new home.   At the threshold Répnine opened the door, sprang out and offered his hand to his bride.   She descended in her turn very slowly, and paused a moment to admire the silvery splendour of the boreal twilight.   Répnine had dismissed the servants with a gesture.

Suddenly Veta turned as if drawn by some mysterious influence ; then she saw attached to the railing of the park at some distance from the courtyard, a sleigh and three horses.   Their forms cast monstrous shadows, giving the equipage a supernatural aspect, and the silence and immobility of these animals added to the spectral impression of their appearance.   Veta went swiftly down the marble step and walked rapidly toward the mysterious vision.   She approached the sleigh without the slightest hesitation, but a suppressed excitement made her heart beat wildly.   She recognised the three victorious horses of the great race on the Neva.

The sleigh was empty, but on the faded, tattered cushion of the seat was pinned a slip of paper.   She opened it and read : " Jean Hotzko to Elisaveta Petrovna Répnine."

Veta trembled ; with an involuntary movement she pressed her lips to the scrap of paper, then let it fall with a frightened air.   She approached the horses, which, at the sound of her sweet, caressing voice, whinnied softly.   She caressed the noble heads that hunger and privation had blighted, but which still preserved their perfect form, and she recognised the famous racers that had been Hotzko's pride in the days of his prosperity.   Then she passed a trembling hand over their beautiful eyes, and gently detaching the cord that bound them to the railing, she led them herself to the stables, where she installed them with all possible care in the safe, warm, luxurious shelter which they were never again to quit.

J. MITROPOLSKY

WATER

IT happened in the Russo-Turkish war in Transcaucasia.

After a doubtful battle, in which the chances were often against us, we had finally become masters of the famous Red Mountain, had just taken it for the second time, and were getting ready to clear it from the enemy. Our regiment had been pushed forward to reinforce the exhausted troops, and we found ourselves suddenly in the first line.

It was night when we marched out. A southern sky, luminous with stars, looked down upon the earth. A mystical silence lay over the landscape ; far ahead in the dusky twilight could be seen the flickering line of shining dots. We all knew that over there were the camps of the Turks whom at daybreak we were to face in battle.

The soldiers marched on in silence. Noise and smoking were strictly forbidden. Careless clashing of the bayonets brought upon the guilty ones furiously whispered reprimands from their superior officers, or a silent nudging in the back from their comrades.

Our cavalcade wound its way along the serpentine mountain road, and the scraping of the eight thousand marching feet in the sand was like the noise of a rushing brook. After the nervous tension we had gone through we had a vague feeling of depression, which we could not get rid of, much as we struggled against it.

With my rifle on my shoulder and straps fastened securely to avoid all noise, I moved in the throng of men, trying to ease each step, in order to save my strength as much as possible.

Beside me walked a volunteer of the same company. His name was Vassiljev and he seemed almost a boy. I could not see his face very well, but, somehow, I had a vague feeling that it showed traces of terror and exhaustion. Suddenly he put his hand on my arm and said in almost a whisper :

" Do you suppose that we shall have to fight during the night ? "

" And what if we do ? " said I. " Are you afraid ? "

His only answer was a sigh. Around us was a dead silence ;

285

with measured steps and in pensive mood the soldiers marched on.

At last we arrived at the position. The camp fires of the Turks were yet visible. The stillness of death reigned on the side of the enemy. Our battalion halted and we were able to lie down. We seemed to breathe more freely near the enemy than when marching on the road ; though the darkness of night rose like an impenetrable wall between ourselves and him, we knew well what that wall hid from our sight. A gentle wind blew from the direction of the Turks, exhaling a misty vapour.

" There is a river over there," whispered Vassiljev, who was lying beside me. " Do you think, Petrov, that it will be hot to-morrow ? "

" The sky is brilliant with stars ; we shall surely have a hot day."

" If the Turks attack us, it will be hot enough without the sun," murmured Kudinov, my second neighbour. " We have orders to keep this position and to defend this mountain until the Second Brigade comes to join us."

" Why do we not dig trenches ? " asked Vassiljev.

" They are digging them where the outposts are," answered Kudinov carelessly ; " but you had better go to sleep, for a hard day's work is before you."

However, this kind advice, which had in it something of a father's tenderness, was not followed by Vassiljev. The whole company loved this boy, who, with his head resting on his hands, was gazing pensively toward the distant fires in the enemy's camp.

" Vassiljev, what made you go to war ? " I asked.

" Oh, I was a poor student at college. In Greek I always got the worst marks of all. I have an uncle in the army, and the thought came to me that I might as well become a lieutenant, and perhaps rise to something. That is how I came to enlist. And now the war has come ! Do you suppose that I was anxious to go to war ? "

I did not reply. To look at the delicate, beardless, almost girlish face, which even the sun had not burned, was enough to know that he did not wish to go to war. It was, perhaps, for this reason that all the soldiers were so fond of him.

" However," he continued, as though to excuse himself, " I do not repent of my action, except sometimes when I think of home. We have a large family and my mother did not want me to be a soldier. We live in the country, where living is a joy ; there is a fine river and I am so fond of fishing."

" Oh, what a paradise ! " said some one with a sigh, evidently stirred by old memories.

Vassiljev and I talked in low tones throughout the long night, until gradually the darkness vanished and a new day was born. The stars went out one by one ; the fires of the Turks were extinguished. From behind the mountain-tops rose in wondrous beauty the glowing ball of the sun. Gradually it rose, as though dipped in blood, and made one think of the glowing Moloch, who is ready to burn to ashes all things alive.

The captain of the company passed along the ranks and said to the soldiers :

" If you have any water left in your flasks, be very careful with it, as there is no water left. All the barrels have been sent away and will not be back before evening."

" But, Nikolai Ivanovich," said Lieutenant Lastochkin, a young subaltern, pointing in the direction of the Turks, " there is water enough—a whole river ! "

" We are forbidden to send even a single soldier over there, so as not to provoke the Turks to an attack," replied the captain. " The Second Brigade cannot be here before evening, and until that time we must remain where we are."

" No water ! " With lightning speed these words passed down the line.

" How long can one live without water ? " said a young light-bearded fellow not far from me. " Without bread one can live on ; without water—never ! "

" Do not talk foolishly, Blinov," said Kudinov severely. " Is it not said that a soldier should be able to stand cold, hunger, and every want ? "

" But thirst is not mentioned, Uncle Kudinov. Hunger, cold, want, yes, but not thirst."

" You stupid ! " replied Kudinov in a superior tone. " Can't you understand ? ' Every want '—does not that include thirst, also ? "

The soldiers laughed and the embarrassed Blinov became silent.

" How can we save water," said another, " when there is none to be saved—when every drop has been used on the road ? "

A sadness came over all. " No water ! " Would the barrels travel the distance fast enough in a mountainous country to bring relief in time ?

Vassiljev's childlike eyes looked at me half in terror, half in surprise.

" How can we get along without water ? " he asked ; " I should like a drink even now ! "

The sun rose higher and higher and began to send out heat. The day promised to be sultry. I believe every one of us felt himself a victim of Moloch, lying on his knees before him, while the funeral pyre was being prepared.

The Turks still kept quiet. Not even isolated horsemen were to be seen on our flank. The Turks were well off. They had water.

With the whole river before them, they could—such is Oriental cunning—well afford to wait and see what the scorching sun would accomplish without their help. The stone hills, behind which we were hiding, were like a burning oven.

Thus hours passed ; the heat became intense ; no breath of air was visible. The dry lips, trying to drink in the least breath of air, felt only the oppressive sultriness. Everywhere was heard the word " water," nothing but water ; all else had lost interest. And the sun was burning, burning with such an intensity that one could not put his hand on a rifle-barrel.

" Oh, what a beautiful river we have ! " said Vassiljev in his fancies. " Such a bright, clear, deep river ! The water flows along its banks on beautifully coloured stones like pearls, or like silver with shining brilliants. And there rises a bubble, a large, trans-parent bubble, and swims with the stream, until it bursts on the sharp stones. Small fishes are swimming around, and if you stretch out your hand, they fly away like arrows in all directions. And if you want to drink, you bend your knees and take the water in the hollow of your hand——"

" Stop, you devil of a fellow ! " cried out some one furiously. " Here we are dying of thirst and he sings of water ! "

Vassiljev started in confusion and became silent.

The sun's scorching rays became more fierce and more pitiless.

" Brothers, the barrels will surely be here soon," said the captain in an encouraging tone. If the barrels had been filled with gold we could not have waited for them with more impatience. It was to be real water. Can there be anything better in this world than water ?

Water !—Water !

And over there in the Turks' camp everything was quiet. Only faintly we heard the neighing of the horses. Surely the Turks are taking them to the horse-pond. They were watering the horses, while we had not a drop to moisten our throats.

Water !

" What is the use of lying here ? " said Kudinov gloomily. " If they would only let us go against the Turks, then we should have water ! Hurrah ! How bravely we would fight ! No need of reinforcement then ! "

I looked upon the soldiers. Some were sitting, others were lying down ; with their heads resting on their arms, they gazed, motionless, towards the enemy's camp. Their dim eyes had a vacant look.

The murderous sun soon reached the zenith. Rising higher and higher his scorching rays were bent on destruction. And we thirsted for water like fish thrown upon a shore.

Two hours passed thus. The sun was still above our heads.

Many soldiers became ill with sunstroke. Their unconscious bodies were carried to a field-hospital and a few drops of water were forced down their throats.

I was lying down, hiding my face from the sun, while an ever-increasing thirst tormented me. I know of no greater torture than thirst. My tongue stuck to my throat, my head began to swim, and the pitiless sun shone on.

Water! At times I seemed to be dreaming, though I was always conscious of the noise around me. I saw water. I heard it ripple, I heard it murmur. I seemed to feel its cooling influence. But as soon as I lifted my head, the illusion vanished, and instead of water I saw only the hot and dusty sand.

Vassiljev was sitting beside me with his hands clasped around his knees. In his dim eyes was a look that startled me.

" Do you feel very badly ? " I asked.

" I am going to die soon," he said between his compressed teeth. " I cannot bear it any longer—everything swims before me." And slowly the tears trickled down his cheeks.

Something stirred within my heart, but those tears—how my eyes hung upon them! Why, there was real water, water enough to drink!

Gazing at Vassiljev, I reflected that these tears would probably only half fill the field-flask. Suddenly I saw Vassiljev put his hand to his head and sink slowly to the ground. I understood— it was sunstroke.

" Field-surgeon ! " cried some one hoarsely. " Take him to the ambulance ! "

" Take him yourself ! " replied some angry voices. " It is just the same where he lies—there is no more water, here or there."

Kudinov, who had just come from that place, confirmed their words ; there was really no more water.

" A whole company over there is unconscious with sunstroke," he said. " I fear that, unless the barrels come soon, many will perish. This one, too," pointing to Vassiljev, " will die," and his face twitched.

The soldiers fell like flies. Had the Turks thought of an attack then, they would have met with little resistance, but it was likely that they, too, had lost all energy in this scorching sun, in spite of the water.

I was lying beside the unconscious Vassiljev, when some one suddenly grasped me roughly by the shoulder, and a voice yelled into my ears :

" Water ! The barrels have come ! "

I jumped up—no, I seemed to be lifted, to be carried along on wings—and after a few minutes found myself with a large crowd at the place whither the barrels had been brought. Kudinov was with me. Only those struck down with heat had remained behind. Among them was Vassiljev.

The throng and confusion round the barrels defied all description. It was in vain that the officers tried to restore order, or threatened with revolvers ; thirst was stronger than discipline. Everything became like an entangled ball, and there was a yelling and screaming and gasping, as though every one had gone mad. I had been pushed back from Kudinov and found myself suddenly behind them all, cut off from the life-giving water. I remember that I screamed in despair, that I punched my fists into the backs of those who were pushing me, but they abused me and kicked me with their feet.

At last I saw Kudinov again. He seemed to have risen from the ground. His face was red and perspiring and his hat was gone. With both his hands he pressed the field-flask to his breast. I heard it gurgle. Water ! How had he been able to get through the throng with water in his field-flask ?

I rushed toward him.

" Kudinov ! " I gasped. " Give me a drink ! I will give you anything you want ! "

" Did you not get some yourself ? " he said. " Now it is all gone ; the barrels have been emptied."

" I have had nothing ! " I answered. " Give me only one mouthful and I will give you anything you like ! "

" Well, I do not know," said Kudinov irresolutely. " I have only enough for myself and Vassiljev. It would be too bad to let him die."

Then all self in me was aroused. Vassiljev, I thought, will die anyway, or there will be some one else to give him water. I shall be tormented by thirst and die like Vassiljev. Suddenly there flashed across my mind an idea. I must try cunning, I must convince Kudinov that Vassiljev is dead and thus take possession of his portion.

" Vassiljev," I lied, " is dead. I saw with my own eyes how he stretched himself. He had no more need of water. Would you bring water to the dead ? But I am dying with thirst. There, take two roubles for half of the bottle. For God's sake, give it to me, give it to me ! "

I imagine that I looked miserable enough to excite compassion, but Kudinov was still wavering. " Well," he said at last, " if he is dead—God have mercy upon his soul ! He was a good fellow— but such is a soldier's life—— Now give me your bottle and I will pour in a little water, but the roubles you may keep for yourself."

I understood that he wanted my field-flask, because he feared that I would drink all, my portion and his ; and he was right.

After some seconds I eagerly swallowed warm and dirty water that smelled of clay, but never in my life did a drink taste so good. After Kudinov had swallowed a few drops, he patted his flask fondly and said : " This I will keep for emergencies. But how long will you be able to stand it without water ? "

I did not reply. I wanted to drink more water, but yet, the terrible thirst, the torture which had let me forget everything else in the world, was gone. And at this moment I was overcome with shame and grief at my selfish action. I thought of Vassiljev, of his water-fancies—and his swoon.

Near us the excited crowd pushed one another and turned the empty barrels to all sides in the vain hope of finding one drop of water.

" Now let us go to the company," said Kudinov ; " there is no more to be had."

We went.

" Kudinov," I said, turning my face away, " I have lied to you. Vassiljev is not dead. He only fainted."

I had not yet finished, when Kudinov stopped suddenly. Involuntarily I, also, stopped and lifted my head. For one moment our eyes met, then mine fell before the contemptuous glance of Kudinov.

" You scoundrel ! " he said and spat at me. " You are stronger than he ; you could have waited until evening when the dew appears. And he will die now ! Oh, what a shameful act ! And to think that I also have been led to commit this sin ! "

He turned around and, without taking further notice of me, rushed toward Vassiljev. I saw how he ran, saw how he bent over him and moistened his head with the rest of his water, never thinking of himself.

I saw all this, and in a sort of fear I remained at a distance. I could not bear to hear his well-deserved abuse. A feeling of terror came over me—a feeling of such intense anguish as Cain must have felt after murdering his brother.

ALEXEY REMISOV

B. 1877

THE OPERA

It was a cold, dusty morning.

The policeman on duty turned over the leaves of the register with a yawn—he was sleepy and felt bilious.

The telephone buzzed unceasingly. The sergeant standing by it sat down and said :

" Where are the papers about the fire ? . . . reward of medals ? . yes, medals. . . . Eh ? "

The heavily-laden postman came in, and the grey, closely cropped old clerk examined the mail.

" This parcel is not for us," he mumbled through his nose, " not for us. . . ."

" Your highness," came a voice from the back entrance, " this is the third month that I've been here about it ; show a little human kindness."

" Are you Snegerov ? " the sergeant asked as though talking into the telephone. " Then go into the council chamber and wait there ; it will do you no harm to wait a bit."

Somewhere in the back-yard a barrel-organ was playing.

There was a rumbling and stamping of cart-horses.

The grey clouds slowly moved over the sun, turned golden awhile, and then floated away again, as grey as before.

A pen squeaked.

" Wait a moment ; he'll soon be here," the policeman said, showing a petitioner into the inspector's office.

The church bells rang for late service, and their monotonous sound was depressing.

" It must be a funeral," Slankin thought ; " otherwise they would have stopped long ago " ; and removing his gaze from the dirty barred window of his " noble lodgings " to the wall, let it wander over all until it came to the inscription, " Kuskov, Conjurer," and once more he re-read the scrap of the pink play-bill announcing a touring opera company.

Stretching himself nervously, and at a loss what to do, he yawned like a dog.

The battered, rickety stool groaned and rocked to and fro.

.   .   .   .

Slankin brought everything to mind, from the very beginning ;
not only yesterday's unfortunate evening that had ended in this
ignoble fashion, but the whole of his life from the early years in
St. Petersburg to the time he had spent in this miserable hole of
a town to which the devil had brought him.   Thus he passed the
endless period of waiting until the inspector should come and
decide whether he was to go on sitting on that wretched stool, in
gaol, or to walk freely along the miserable streets.

Everybody knew Slankin ; he had the reputation of being a
good teacher, and had the respect of all the mothers, for the children
whom he taught went up to the next form without losing time.
There were few who did not know his past, but they all looked upon
his misfortunes if not with approval yet with a certain amount of
pity ; with the same feeling as they would have had if his only
overcoat had chanced to get stolen during the bad weather ; it
seemed as if he always went about without an overcoat, his soaking
trousers clinging to him ; that even in fine weather the rain was
sure to get at him.

He was inoffensive—would hurt nobody ; and then this wretched
opera had come along, seeming to drop from the very skies.   To
miss an opera in a town where there was not even a string band
was like keeping bees without tasting the honey.   Seeking out some
friends who were fond of music—and there were many such—
Slankin arranged with them to take a box together, which they
did, in good time ; they agreed to behave themselves properly, not
to join in the singing, not to talk and, most important of all, not
to be late.   When would such another chance of an opera come
along !   But obviously some evil angel must have had a hand in
the unfortunate business, for, otherwise, how could one explain
those events from which it would have been a blessing to have
escaped.   An unfortunate incident had happened to Slankin—he
had arrived late at the opera—and all that followed, the fact that
he was sitting there waiting for the inspector, arose in consequence.

He got to the theatre before the curtain rose, but in the time he
took to remove his overcoat and find the box, the opera had begun,
and he found the door of the box locked.   It was impossible to
remain outside, it was not his fault, a pupil had detained him, and
his watch was a little slow—it was not his fault.   Slankin knocked
at the door but got no reply—and there was no reply because he
had originally suggested that course.

The opera was in full swing.   Gods !   How they sang !   As they
sing in no foreign theatre ; a tenor brought out a trill so beautifully

that it seemed there was no one greater in the world and that there was nothing more desirable than to listen to his singing forever, or to be the tenor and sing trills through all eternity.

Slankin caught a few trills that merely irritated him, and losing all patience, and forgetting their agreement, he knocked at the door with all his might, demanding an instantaneous admittance.

It was not his fault—he had come in time—it was not his fault the attendant had been so long taking his overcoat and that, owing to his short sight, it had taken him some time to find the box. For fourteen years he had had to wear glasses ; it was five years since he had seen an opera, since the time when he had unwillingly been shoved into that town—he had been long enough in that hole—he demanded that they should open the door—he had a right to demand it.

" Let me in, do you hear ? Open the door. It is so mean ! Don't you understand ? " he urged with voice, hands, and feet until even from the other side of the theatre could be heard his obstinate and increasingly insistent cries for admission.

Meanwhile the police inspector had arrived, and two gendarmes, holding up their sabres and sniffing the air, set out for the scene of disorder, and finding the cause, in one voice and with the same words both requested Slankin to stop making himself a nuisance. They spoke quietly but determinedly :

" Listen . . . the Chief of Police . . . don't behave in this disgraceful way. . . ."

Slankin heard nothing, and, frowning, went on thumping at the door. Suddenly there was a stamping of feet and shouting, no doubt the act had finished, then something hit against his chest with a swing. He felt himself thrust in somewhere, and then found himself flying in the air ; then some one grabbed his leg and he ceased to fly. The door opened and he was dragged out. He would see to-morrow—the tenor held him—the Chief of Police . . . disorder. . . .

Then the same hand under the guise of applause caught him as a hook catches a fish, threw him up high, whispered something resolutely, and, as in a dream, the carriage jerked forward.

Slankin was taken to the police station and locked up for the night in the " gentry's quarters."

He rocked himself on the rickety chair and could hardly notice the flight of time that dragged as slowly as though it did not want to get to the fateful hour when the superintendent should come. " Perhaps he will not come at all ! And supposing he doesn't ? " Slankin clutched his knees, closed his eyes, and made a tremendous effort to get back there to St. Petersburg, to those days when he had walked about so proudly, where he had been listened to, and had listened to operas—operas in which Chaliapin took part. . . . And he too had a voice. He too could sing. . . .

Suddenly everything grew quiet on the other side of the door and outside; the church bells had stopped ringing, the clouds were no longer moving, and only the sound of a carriage approaching could be heard. . . .

Slankin rose quickly, and wiping his clammy hands on his trousers, murmured in a hoarse voice:

" Sir, Mr. Superintendent. . . ."

And " Kuskov, the conjurer," the happy conjurer, slipped from the wall, and the pink play-bill flew out of the window into the street.

The doors were opened and Slankin was released.

There was an opera for you !

NICOLAI TELESHOV

THE DUEL

It was early morning.

Vladimir Kladunov, a tall, graceful young man, twenty-two years of age, almost boyish in appearance, with a handsome face and thick, fair curls, dressed in the uniform of an officer and in long riding-boots, minus overcoat and cap, stood upon a meadow covered with new-fallen snow, and gazed at another officer, a tall, red-faced, moustached man, who faced him at a distance of thirty paces, and was slowly lifting his hand in which he held a revolver, and aimed it straight at Vladimir.

With his arms crossed over his breast and also holding in one hand a revolver, Kladunov, almost with indifference, awaited the shot of his opponent. His handsome young face, though a little paler than usual, was alight with courage, and wore a scornful smile. His dangerous position, and the merciless determination of his adversary, the strenuous attention of the seconds who silently stood at one side, and the imminence of death, made the moment one of terrible intensity, mysterious, solemn. A question of honour was to be decided. Every one felt the importance of the question ; the less they understood what they were doing, the deeper seemed the solemnity of the moment.

A shot was fired ; a shiver ran through all. Vladimir threw his hands about, bent his knees, and fell. He lay upon the snow, shot through the head, his hands apart, his hair, face, and even the snow around his head covered with blood. The seconds ran toward him and lifted him ; the doctor certified his death, and the question of honour was solved. It only remained to announce the news to the regiment and to inform, as tenderly and carefully as possible, the mother, who was now left alone in the world ; for the boy who had been killed was her only son. Before the duel no one had given her even a thought ; but now they all became very thoughtful. All knew and loved her, and recognised the fact that she must be prepared by degrees for the terrible news. At last Ivan Golubenko was chosen as most fit to tell the mother, and smooth out matters as much as possible.

.   .   .   .

Pelageia Petrovna had just risen, and was preparing her morning tea when Ivan Golubenko, gloomy and confused, entered the room.

" Just in time for tea, Ivan Ivanovitch ! " amiably exclaimed the old lady, rising to meet her guest. " You have surely called to see Vladimir ! "

" No, I—in passing by——" Golubenko stammered, abashed.

" You will have to excuse him, he is still asleep. He walked up and down his room the whole of last night, and I told the servant not to wake him, as it is a festival. But probably you come on urgent business ? "

" No, I only stepped in for a moment in passing——"

" If you wish to see him, I will give the order to wake him up."

" No, no, do not trouble yourself ! "

But Pelageia Petrovna, believing that he had called to see her son on some business or other, left the room, murmuring to herself.

Golubenko walked excitedly to and fro, wringing his hands, not knowing how to tell her the terrible news. The decisive moment was quickly approaching ; but he lost control of himself, was frightened, and cursed the fate that had so mixed him up with the whole business.

" Now ! How can a body trust you young people ! " good-naturedly exclaimed Pelageia Petrovna to her visitor, entering the room. " Here I have been taking care not to make the least noise with the cups and saucers, and asking you not to wake my boy, and he has long ago departed without leaving a trace ! But why do you not take a seat, Ivan Ivanovitch, and have a cup of tea ? You have been neglecting us terribly lately ! "

She smiled as with a secret joy, and added in a low voice :

" And we have had so much news during that time ! Vladimir surely could not keep it secret. He must have told you all about it by now ; for he is very straightforward and open-hearted, my Vladimir. I was thinking last night, in my sinful thoughts : " Well, when my Vladimir paces the room the whole night, that means that he is dreaming of Lenochka ! ' That is always the case with him : if he paces the room the whole night, he will surely leave to-morrow. Ah, Ivan Ivanovitch, I only ask the Lord to send me this joy in my old age. What more does an old woman need ? I have but one desire, one joy ; and it seems to me I shall have nothing more to pray for after Vladimir and Lenochka are married. So joyful and happy it would make me ! I do not need anything besides Vladimir ; there is nothing dearer to me than his happiness."

The old lady became so affected that she had to wipe away the tears which came to her eyes.

"Do you remember ? " she continued ; " things did not go well in the beginning—either between the two or on account of the money. You young officers are not even allowed to marry without investments. Well, now everything has been arranged : I have obtained the necessary five thousand roubles for Vladimir, and they could go to the altar even to-morrow ! Yes, and Lenochka has written such a lovely letter to me. My heart is rejoicing ! "

Continuing to speak, Pelageia Petrovna took a letter out of her pocket, which she showed to Golubenko, and then put back again.

"She is such a dear girl ! And so good ! "

Ivan Golubenko, listening to her talk, sat as if on red-hot coals. He wanted to interrupt her flow of words, to tell her everything was at an end, that her Vladimir was dead, and that in one short hour nothing would remain to her of all her bright hopes ; but he listened to her and kept silent. Looking upon her good, gentle face, he felt a convulsive movement in his throat.

"But why are you looking so gloomy to-day ? " the old lady at last asked. "Why, your face looks as black as night ! "

Ivan wanted to say "Yes ! And yours will be the same when I tell you ! " but instead of telling her anything, he turned his head away, and began to twirl his moustaches.

Pelageia Petrovna did not notice it, and wholly absorbed in her own thoughts, continued :

"I have a greeting for you. Lenochka writes that I must give Ivan Ivanovitch her kind regards, and ask him to come with Vladimir and pay her a visit. You know yourself how she likes you, Ivan Ivanovitch ! No, it seems I cannot keep it to myself. I must show you the letter. Just see for yourself how loving and sweet it is."

And Pelageia Petrovna again fetched the packet of letters from her pocket, took from it a thin sheet, closely written, and unfolded it before Ivan Golubenko, whose face had become still gloomier. He tried to push away the extended note, but Pelageia Petrovna had already begun reading—

"DEAR PELAGEIA PETROVNA—When will the time arrive when I will be able to address you, not thus, but as my dear, sweet mother ! I am anxiously awaiting the time, and hope so much that it will soon come that even now I do not want to call you otherwise than mother——"

Pelageia Petrovna lifted her head, and ceasing to read, looked at Golubenko with eyes suffused with tears.

" You see, Ivan Ivanovitch ! " she added ; but seeing that Golubenko was biting his moustaches, and that his eyes too were moist, she rose, placed a trembling hand up on his hair, and quietly kissed him on the forehead. " Thank you, Ivan Ivanovitch," she whispered, greatly moved. " I always thought that you and Vladimir were more like brothers than like ordinary friends. Forgive me. I am so very happy, God be thanked ! "

Tears streamed down her cheeks, and Ivan Golubenko was so disturbed and confused that he could only catch in his own her cold, bony hand and cover it with kisses ; tears were suffocating him, and he could not utter a word ; but in this outburst of motherly love he felt such a terrible reproach to himself that he would have preferred to be lying himself upon the field, shot through the head, than to hear himself praised for his friendship by this woman who would in half an hour find out the whole truth. What would she then think of him ? Did not he, the friend, the almost brother, stand quietly by when a revolver was aimed at Vladimir ? Did not this brother himself measure the space between the two antagonists and load the revolvers ? All this he did himself, did consciously ; and now this friend and brother silently sat there without even having the courage to fulfil his duty.

He was afraid. At this moment he despised himself, yet could not prevail upon himself to say even one word. His soul was oppressed by a strange lack of harmony ; he felt sick at heart and stifling. And in the meanwhile time flew. He knew it ; and the more he knew it the less had he the courage to deprive Pelageia Petrovna of her few last happy moments. What should he say to her ? How should he prepare her ? Ivan Golubenko lost his head entirely.

He had already had time enough to curse in his thoughts all duels, all quarrels, every kind of heroism, and all kinds of so-called questions of honour, and he at last rose from his seat ready to confess or to run away. Silently and quickly he caught the hand of Pelageia Petrovna, and stooping over it to touch it with his lips, thus hid his face, over which a torrent of tears suddenly streamed down ; impetuously, without another thought, he ran out into the corridor, seized his great-coat, and then went out of the house without a word.

Pelageia Petrovna looked after him with astonishment, and thought :

" He also must be in love, poor fellow. Well, that is their young sorrow—before happiness ! " . . .

And she soon forgot him, absorbed in her dreams of the happiness which seemed to her so inviolable and entire.